"WHATEVER GAVE YOU THE IDEA OF A SLED RIDE?"

"I saw how you looked at Miss Quinlan when Farley took her for a ride," Adam answered.

"How was that?" Gypsy was glad the darkness hid her face; she did not want him to see her amazement.

He chuckled. "I've seen envy before. I figured you weren't envious of her silly hat or the fact she was with Farley."

"Certainly not." Gypsy peered along the road. "Where are we going?"

"I told you. For a spin about town."

This time she laughed. "That would be possible only if we had a town to spin about." When she leaned back against the seat, she flinched as his hand curved around her shoulder.

"You can trust me," he murmured.

"Can I?"

"Sure." He grinned before looking back at the road. "If I rile you, Gypsy, you can send me walking."

When his fingers drifted along her arm with the warmth of spring, she remained silent. Soft snowflakes floated around them in a silent waltz, and she wanted to enjoy the rare chance escape from the demands of the cook shack. It was easier to admit that than to imagine how wonderful it would feel to lean her head against his shoulder.

Books by Jo Ann Ferguson

An Unexpected Husband
Her Only Hero
Mistletoe Kittens
An Offer of Marriage
Lord Radcliffe's Season
No Price Too High
The Jewel Palace
O'Neal's Daughter
The Convenient Arrangement
Just Her Type
Destiny's Kiss
Raven Quest
A Model Marriage
Rhyme and Reason
Spellbound Hearts
The Counterfeit Count
A Winter Case
A Phantom Affair
Miss Charity's Kiss
Valentine Love
The Wolfe Wager
An Undomesticated Wife
A Mother's Joy
The Smithfield Bargain
The Fortune Hunter

And writing as Rebecca North

A June Betrothal

Published by Zebra Books

ANYTHING FOR YOU

JO ANN FERGUSON

Zebra Books
Kensington Publishing Corp.

http://www.zebrabooks.com

ZEBRA BOOKS are published by

Kensington Publishing Corp.
850 Third Avenue
New York, NY 10022

First Printing: April, 2000
10 9 8 7 6 5 4 3 2 1

Printed in the United States of America

For Debbie Brigham—
you have inspired me in so many ways.
This one is especially for you.

CHAPTER ONE

"What in the blazes am I supposed to do with a lame man?"

"Ain't got no idea, Gypsy." The burly lumberjack, dressed in a dirty flannel shirt and denims, rubbed the back of his hand under his reddened nose. "Instructions came from Farley. Didn't tell me nothing 'cept this guy's supposed to work for you."

Gypsy Elliott muttered a phrase that once would have made her blush. She glanced around her cramped kitchen. That her crew scurried back to work as soon as her gaze settled on them did not surprise her. The flunkeys working in her kitchen understood there was only one boss, and her name was Gypsy Elliott. She wiped her hands on her stained apron.

"Look, Benson," she said quietly, "I don't have time to mollycoddle a banged-up lumberjack."

"But Farley said—"

"Farley says too much about nothing!" She untied her apron and whipped it over her head and threw it on the table by the huge cast-iron stove, then tucked her white blouse back into her dark skirt.

"You've got that right," said a young man sitting on a tall stool while he peeled onions. The gangly lad, barely old enough to scrape a straight-edged razor along his chin, grinned. She hated giving Oscar the job of chopping ten pounds of onions by himself, but the rest of her crew was busy fixing the supper the jacks would expect as soon as they were done with their day's work in the woods.

Benson backed away as she reached for her coat, which hung from a peg by the door. He said uneasily, "Farley was sure 'bout this. Wants this man working in the kitchen."

"I'll deal with Farley." Putting her hand on his sleeve, which was stained with smoke from the forge in the blacksmith's shop where he worked, she added, "Thanks for bringing the message, Benson, but if Farley thought he was going to avoid dealing with me on this, he was wrong."

Gypsy pulled on her black wool coat, but paused when her name was called. Glancing over her shoulder, she saw a tall man hurrying toward her. His brown hair was in dire need of a cut, and, like most of the men in the camp, his face was hidden behind a dark, bushy beard. Grease and flour spotted his plaid shirt.

"What is it, Bert?" she asked impatiently. "I've got to convince Farley to see sense on this."

As always, Bert's broad Cockney accent colored every word he spoke. "Why don't you just knock some sense into 'is 'ead?"

She laughed. Buttoning her coat, she said, "It might be the only way to get him to listen." She opened the door to the dining room. "Keep an eye on that venison. After they dragged it out of the woods, Peabody's men won't want it burned."

"I'll 'ave it cooked just right."

"Good! I'll be back as soon as I can."

Benson stepped aside as she bustled into the dining room at the front of the cookhouse. She paused and ran her fingers along one of the primitive tables where the jacks would be eating in two hours. Calling back an order to wash the soiled oilcloth, she threw open the door.

Gypsy no longer recoiled each time the frigid air struck her. She had become accustomed to having her breath stripped away by the cold. Cautiously, she stepped down, because the cookhouse was built high off the ground. Boards topping the logs around the foundation prevented cold from seeping under the cookhouse during the long Michigan winter.

Wind burned her face, peppering her with specks of snow. Past a clump of pine trees, the river slumbered beneath a thick, silvery blanket of ice. Winter held the north woods in its thrall.

Gypsy's dark skirts twisted around her legs, threatening to trip her into the nearest snowbank, but she did not slow as she walked toward the camp manager's office. She was no greenhorn, unacquainted with a rough north woods winter. Her third winter at Glenmark Timber Company, north of Saginaw, was almost over. Hunching into her turned-up collar, she wished she had not been in such a hurry to deal with Farley's unreasonable demand. She had left her scarf in the kitchen.

Her black, high-topped shoes sank into the snow because her strides were not as long as those of the men who had cut a trail through the drifts. She winced as chilly flakes drifted down past her ankles, but waved to the men by the blacksmith's shop.

The two log bunkhouses were deserted. With snow piled halfway up their walls, the long buildings awaited the return of the weary men who would eat a huge meal and fall into their bunks to sleep until called back to work before dawn. Six days a week, the routine was the same. Only on Sundays did the men have some time to themselves. No one complained. The wages would feed the jacks' families for a year.

The camp manager's office was set on the opposite side of the camp. Beyond it, in the shadows of the trees, Farley's house glowed with warmth. Gypsy's room at the back of the kitchen was much more modest. She ignored the tantalizing idea of living in a house with rugs on the floor and curtains at the windows. Instead, she stamped her feet on the rickety porch of the office and entered without knocking.

The man sitting at a desk in the middle of the cramped room looked more suited to an office in Lansing or Detroit than to a rough logging camp. His slicked-back hair was gray at the temples. Near his eyes, lines from past laughter were etched into his skin. A gigantic brown mustache was his only concession to the hairy faces favored by the jacks. He rose, smiling, and smoothed the wrinkles from the black coat he wore over a simple vest and trousers.

Motioning for her to sit on the bench in front of his desk, Calvin Farley said in his precise voice, "What a pleasant surprise, Gypsy."

"Surprise?" Her eyebrows arched in cool amusement. She shook off beads of water as heat from the potbellied stove melted the snow clinging to her wool coat. "You sent Benson with the order that I'm supposed to find work for some jack who's broken his ankle. I came to check whether you'd gone completely out of your mind."

He leaned on his paper-strewn desk. "You complained last week you were shorthanded after we hired new men to cut that stand out west of the main group. This jack just hired on. I figured you might as well have him, instead of shipping him back to Saginaw."

"Farley, be reasonable. If you want someone to mother him, let Rose look after him."

Walking around his desk, he shook his head. "Gypsy, *you* be reasonable. You know Rose has enough to do."

"And I don't?" She laughed as coldly as the wind clawing at the logs. "While your mistress works at prettying herself up for an evening with you, I have to make meals for a hundred jacks."

"I wouldn't ask if I thought you couldn't handle this."

Her lips twitched as he smiled with an innocence he had left behind in Maine when he followed the loggers west. Shaking her finger, she laughed. "If you weren't too old for me, Calvin Farley, I swear I'd let you woo me into taking Rose's place. You know your way around a woman."

"If I knew my way around you," he said, chuckling, "I'd find things a lot easier here. And, Gypsy, I'm not too old for you."

"Maybe I'm too old for you. After all, Rose must be right out of the schoolroom."

His lips tightened, but she did not apologize. She did not have to worry about Farley's firing her. A skillful cook enticed men to sign on for long hours and long months of work. A bad cook meant losing good workers. She was reputed to be the best head cook in the north woods. It was a standing she worked hard to keep.

As if there had been no flaring of anger in Farley's dark eyes, she added, "Whether or not Rose is busy is irrelevant. *I'm* too busy to come up with things for a lame man to do."

"He can't work in the blacksmith's shop or out on the hill."

"Farley, be fair! Bert Sayre has finally learned what he needs to do, so I don't have to watch him every minute, as I have for the past couple of months. I've got too much to do with all these new jacks. Normally I'd be glad to do you a favor, but I don't have the time now."

He folded his arms over his perfectly pressed vest. "Gypsy, don't force me to make this an order."

"What is so important about this man?"

A knock brought a deep sigh of relief from Farley. "Come in!"

She heard the irregular clunk of a crutch and a heavy boot. She had thought Farley understood how busy the cookhouse was. Clenching her hands at her sides, she took a deep breath. She had not wanted to have this argument in front of the injured logger, but she was not going to let Farley run roughshod over her.

"Come in, Lassiter, and close the door," Farley called, as if greeting his best friend.

"Farley—"

"Gypsy, give the man a chance to get in first. It's nasty out there."

She was about to remind him she had fought the wind just minutes ago. Her retort vanished as she stared at a tall, dark-haired man who bent his head to come through the low door. A roughly trimmed mustache hid his upper lip and drooped over his patchy beard. Although she wondered why he had started growing his beard so late into the logging season, she said nothing. The jacks were eccentric, and she had learned to accept their idiosyncrasies as they tolerated hers.

She saw amazement in his blue eyes and pulled her gaze away from his. Except for the crutch, he was dressed identically to every jack in the camp. His denim trousers were held up by suspenders cutting across a brightly printed mackinaw shirt. On his right foot, he wore a boot laced to his knee. The other foot was balanced off the floor. A thick plaster of paris cast was visible above a loosely tied moccasin.

Yet he was not like the other jacks. She sensed that instantly, although she was not sure why. His shoulders were as broad as any of the other men's. The sculptured planes of his face were tanned from hours of sun splashing off the snow. Even the astonishment in his eyes as he looked her up and down like a crew chief appraising a stand of trees was not new. None of the jacks expected to see a woman working in the camp.

His hands—she tried to keep from staring at his hands, but she could not help herself. His fingers were long and tapering and totally unlike the blunt, weathered hands of a jack. She could not imagine them holding an ax. Instead, they should be caressing the strings of a violin or the body of a woman.

Gypsy shook the thought from her head. If Farley discovered she was having moony thoughts about some lame jack, he would roar with laughter and repeat the tale to everyone within hearing. She would never hear the end of it. She frowned at both men.

Farley said, with almost childlike eagerness, "Gypsy Elliott, this is Adam Lassiter. He'll be working for you until he's healed."

Lassiter held out his hand to her. She gasped when he clasped her fingers in a warm grip and lifted her hand to his lips. The brush of his mustache tickled her skin, sending a ripple of indescribable heat along her arm. She jerked her hand back, then tensed at his low chuckle.

Blast Lassiter! If he thought he was going to unsettle her with his highfalutin ways, she would show him right away who was in charge of the cookhouse.

"What talents do you have beside wrecking your ankle?" Gypsy asked.

Farley laughed. "I warned you, Lassiter."

"So you did. You told me the kingbee cook here was irascible, but you didn't tell me Gypsy Elliott is a woman." Limping past her, he leaned on the back of the bench. He faced her, and his smile broadened. "To answer your question, Miss Elliott, I've had some experience in the kitchen."

"Cooking?"

"What else?"

"How long have you been in the north woods?" she asked, crossing her arms in front of her. "Any lumberjack worth his pay can tell you tales about the so-called saloon down the road where the back rooms double as kitchen and cribs for the jacks' entertainment."

"Haven't heard about the place yet," he answered, but his gaze avoided hers. He was hiding something. That did not surprise her. Most people in the north woods were. "Just got here. I've been working for Tellison Timber south of here."

"You sure picked the worst time to cuddle up to a log." Shaking her head, she looked back at the camp manager and smiled as she met Farley's broad grin. "This is going to cost you."

He sat on the edge of his desk and clasped his hands around the knee of his immaculate trousers. "I'd rather you considered it a favor."

"Favors get repaid."

"I'm sure you'll remind me."

Glancing at the man who was fitting his crutch under his arm again, she sighed. "You're right about that! If I'd wanted to play nursemaid, I could have stayed home in Mississippi."

"Just give me a list the next time I go to Saginaw."

"It'll be long."

"I don't doubt that."

"And costly."

"I don't doubt that, either."

She swallowed her shock. Calvin Farley was usually as stingy with a penny as a miser, except when it came to his mistress. Just the threat of separating him from some of his money should have been enough to change his mind about Lassiter. She looked back at the tall man, who was leaning on his crutch. Something was wrong here.

"You don't look like much of a jack to me," she said, deciding one of them had to be honest. "Were you told to walk at Tellison Timber?"

Lassiter smiled, but his eyes grew as cold as the blue lips of a dead man. "I left of my own accord, Miss Elliott."

"Gypsy," she corrected. "We don't stand on formalities here."

"I heard Glenmark Timber was offering a bonus to anyone hiring on now."

"Bonus?" she gasped. Farley was trying to hide his sheepish expression. "Is that why you want me to put him to work in my kitchen? You paid him the bonus already? Before he'd done a single day's work? Are you mad? Mr. Glenmark will have your hide!"

"Gypsy, as your boss, I'm asking——"

"My only boss at Glenmark Timber Company is Daniel Glenmark. You know that as well as I do!" Stamping to the door, she jerked it open. Wind scattered snow about the floor, but she paid no attention, except to brush her hair away from her face. "I have to get back to the cookhouse, but we'll discuss this again."

"There's nothing to discuss. Lassiter is working for you. I don't have anything else to say on this."

"Good! Because I have plenty to say, and you can just sit and listen."

"Gypsy——"

"Later! I've got to make sure supper is ready, or we'll all be walking." She glowered at the injured man. "Well, Lassiter, come along. I guess you're about to learn first-hand about my being irascible."

Again Farley began, "Gypsy, I didn't mean that as an insult. I——"

"Don't bother apologizing when you know it's true." Walking out, she tossed over her shoulder, "C'mon, Lassiter. We can't jaw all afternoon."

Adam Lassiter jammed his crutch under his arm and limped toward the door. Glancing back, he saw Farley's chagrined frown. That a slender woman with a temper as fiery as her auburn hair could cow the manager of the logging camp told him a lot.

When he closed the door behind them, Gypsy asked, with a compassion he had not expected, "Can you manage?"

"I'm learning. The snow's tough." He offered her a smile, but she continued toward the cookhouse. Charm was not going to work on Gypsy Elliott. He needed another way to deal with her.

"If you want to eat," she called back, "you'll have to do a full day's work. I don't have time to pamper a crippled jack."

He allowed himself a moment to enjoy the view of her black skirt swaying through the snow. This woman did not mince words. He realized her frustration was not focused on him, but on Farley. Adam Lassiter was no more than an irritation to her.

Softly, he chuckled. He suspected he would irritate her more before he found a way to get out of her kitchen and back to the work he preferred. Somehow, he always irritated his bosses. He doubted it would be any different with Gypsy Elliott.

His eyes were caught by the sight of a slender ankle as she raised her skirt to edge around a drift. She certainly was better to look at than his last boss. Curiosity taunted him to figure out what a lovely woman with startlingly green eyes and the absurd name of Gypsy was doing in this logging camp so far from anywhere.

He glanced around the camp. Every tree wore a film of snow on the windward side. When he had decided to come north, he had not considered how barbaric the living conditions would be. He thought fondly of a hearth in Lansing and a glass of something glowing golden in his hand. Silently he reminded himself he had chosen this job.

He reached the door to the cook shack, which Gypsy was holding open. Smiling at her, he asked, ''How long have you been the kingbee cook here?''

''Three years,'' Gypsy answered as she stepped up into the cookhouse. Holding out her hand, she asked, ''Can you get up here?''

''It's steep.'' He swore, then smiled an apology. ''Pardon me, Gypsy.''

''Don't worry. You'll hear far worse from everyone in the cookhouse, including me. Do you want help?'' Impatience returned to her voice. ''Make up your mind before my fingers freeze off.''

With a chuckle, he held up the crutch.

Gypsy frowned as she took it, wondering how he could cope without it. When he leaped up, his arms windmilled. She dropped the crutch and wrapped her arms around his waist. They teetered. He grabbed a table. A yelp burst from her when her hip crashed into it.

His arm curved around her, and her breath snagged at the very spot where her breasts brushed his firm chest. Raising her eyes, she stared up at the mysteries in his. A slow smile inched beneath his mustache.

Was she completely witless? She had let every jack know that she was here only to cook for them. Adam Lassiter had better learn that, too, or . . . she was not sure what she would do if he did not, because his touch was as intriguing as his eyes.

Gypsy Elliott, are you crazy? How can you forget what can happen if you get too close to anyone?

A shiver coursed through her. When she started to take a step back, he wobbled. She gripped his arms, and he pulled her back against him. Her breath exploded from her.

"You don't want me to fall and break my other ankle, do you?" he asked, grinning.

She grabbed the crude crutch. Shoving it into his hands, she said, "If you're done with your clowning, Lassiter, the kitchen is this way."

"It's Adam," he called as she walked toward the kitchen door.

Gypsy looked back. "Excuse me?"

"My name's Adam." He lurched toward her as the crutch threatened to trip him. Halting, he cursed vividly, then tried again. "I thought you said informality was the hallmark of your kitchen."

"*Hallmark?* You speak pretty fancy for a jack."

He chuckled and shrugged. "Blame my parents. They believed a classical education was more important than teaching a boy how to survive in this world."

"You learned a lesson in that today." Again she smiled in spite of herself. "You should leave the rough work to folks who can handle it."

"Like you?"

"Like me." She motioned toward the kitchen. "Come

along. The bread should be ready, and there are potatoes to peel and gravy to make before the men come back for supper.''

''That's only an hour or so from now.''

''Exactly.'' Her smile became as cold as the snow glittering beyond the single window. ''Welcome to the cookhouse, Mr. Lassiter. I wouldn't be surprised if, in a few days, you'll be begging that ankle to heal at top speed so you can return to the soft life of a jack.''

Adam almost laughed, but saw she meant her words. As she went into the kitchen, he grimaced. This job was going to take more time than he had thought. He had been a fool to think he was prepared for the worst the north woods could hand out. No doubt Gypsy Elliott intended to teach him what the worst could be.

CHAPTER TWO

If her crew was amazed that Gypsy had returned with a new flunkey, they were wise enough to keep their opinions to themselves. Adam said nothing when the four men stared at him. He could not keep from smiling as he took a deep breath. Roast venison. His stomach grumbled, reminding him he had not eaten since breakfast, when he had washed down a slice of dried bread with a mouthful of melted snow.

He whistled under his breath. How did Gypsy and her crew work here? The kitchen was no bigger than the dining room. Like all the buildings in the camp, the cookhouse had been built of pine logs. The sole window was nearly hidden behind a massive cast-iron stove. With barrels edging the walls, there was barely enough room for the table in the middle of the floor. Bowls and cooking utensils were set on crooked shelves over the barrels, and huge cooking pots were stacked beside the stove. Overhead, each rafter supported boxes of salt and sugar. Two doors were set on the wall to his left, and he wondered where they went. He would check as soon as he had a chance.

Adam forced a smile when Gypsy rattled off the other men's names before she asked, "Bert, did you get that barrel from the storage room?"

"Not yet, Gypsy."

"Don't let us delay you."

Bert nodded.

Fascinated, Adam listened as she asked each man what he had been doing. She was not reluctant to give praise, but she was just as ready to reprimand. Farley had been right. She would be a demanding boss.

"Gypsy," he began when she paused to take a breath.

"Wait here." She pointed to a bench by the table.

Adam smiled when she hurried to talk to the wide man standing by the open oven door. Hank Johnson, if he recalled correctly. That Gypsy had not waited to see if he obeyed was further warning she was not used to having her orders questioned. Not that he should be surprised. She was the "kingbee."

He silenced his chuckle as he lowered himself gingerly to the bench. His leg ached worse than he had guessed it would.

He had not guessed he would end up in the cookhouse. He tried to convince Farley to let him work in the camp manager's office as a clerk or an inkslinger, as the jacks would say. Instead, he had been sent to the kitchen to slave under a red-haired taskmaster.

Adam winced as he adjusted his left leg and tried to make himself more comfortable on the narrow bench. The cast must weigh as much as the stove. He had not worn it more than two hours, and already his skin burned along the plaster edges and itched beneath it.

"Problem?" asked a young voice.

"Nothing a few weeks won't cure," he answered as he grinned at the light-haired boy Gypsy had called Oscar.

Wiping his sleeve against his eyes, Oscar gave him a weak smile and bent to pick up another onion from the pile next to his stool. With quick, efficient strokes, the boy stripped off the skin, which fell into a basket by his feet. A powerful reek surrounded him.

"How many of those do you have to do?" Adam asked, looking toward where Gypsy was talking with another of her flunkeys. Flunkey! What a ridiculous term! Not a single man wore livery as a proper flunkey should, unless their aprons were their uniform.

Oscar interrupted his thoughts. "Just a dozen more. Gypsy doesn't need more than ten pounds of onions tonight."

"What did you do to rate this punishment?"

"Nothing." His knife did not falter as he sliced through the red-gold skin to leave the white glistening like moonlight on an icy river. "I'm the quickest, so I do this. Bert chops meat from the beef out in the locker. Per does—"

Adam interrupted, "You *like* doing this?"

"Not really. It's just . . ." He shrugged his thin shoulders. "Gypsy depends on me." A smile pulled at his narrow cheeks. "I guess that's why I don't mind."

If Gypsy inspired this loyalty, Adam decided, she must be pretty remarkable.

"Get me a knife," he said to Oscar, "and I'll help you."

Oscar hesitated, then mumbled, "No, thanks. Gypsy'll tell you what she wants you to do."

"So she really is in charge here?"

"Yes. Do you have a problem with that?"

Astounded by Oscar's abrupt fury, Adam answered before the lad's raised voice caught Gypsy's attention. "No problem. None at all."

Adam glanced across the crowded kitchen. For a moment, he thought Gypsy had left. Then he saw her leaning over an open oven door.

He rested his chin on the heel of his palm and smiled. Without her shapeless black coat, her slender curves were a pleasure to behold. Her pert nose advised him to watch out for the cantankerous nature that contrasted with the honeyed smoothness of her Southern drawl. Her face was flushed with heat as she stood and pushed back her hair, drawing his eyes along her throat. Hank said something to her, and she laughed, her eyes sparkling like dew-washed grass.

What was a captivating woman like Gypsy Elliott doing in the north woods? He could not think of a single reason why she might be here—unless she was trying to hide from someone. Maybe she had left a lover—or a husband—behind. He knew he would find out eventually. Secrets had a way of not staying secret when he put his mind to them.

She turned, and her gaze locked with his. Her smile evaporated as she hastily looked away. She *was* hiding something! He chuckled to himself. This might be more interesting than he had guessed.

Gypsy tried to ignore Adam Lassiter's gaze on her. Other jacks had been stupid enough to think she needed someone to fill her leisure hours. First, she had no leisure time. Even if she did, she was not likely to get involved with a jack.

A tingle coursed through her. Adam was still watching her. Bending to check the biscuits in the second oven, she was glad when Bert came to stand between her and Adam. She was silly, she knew. What she did not know was how to halt the quivers each time his eyes captured hers.

"It's a bad idea to bring 'im 'ere," Bert muttered as he pulled biscuits out of the oven. "Is Farley crazy? You don't 'ave time to take care of a bumped-up jack."

She smiled wryly as she stirred the chicken soup, raising its rich scent. "I tried to convince Farley to let Rose take care of Adam."

Instead of laughing as she had expected, Bert glared across the room.

Hank grumbled, "She'd probably like having him about. He looks like her type. Cheap and flashy."

"All the more reason for Farley to want him here instead of at his house," she answered. She called to

Per. The older man hurried to her. Beneath the perpetual shadow of silvery whiskers, he did not wear his usual smile.

"What do you want, Gypsy?" he asked as he glanced at the newcomer.

"Just keep an eye on the soup." When she saw his dismay, she knew he had hoped she would ask him to throw Adam out. She almost laughed at the idea of Per, who was old enough to be her father, tossing Adam through the cookhouse door.

Going to the back of the room, she paused and scooped up a huge bowl. She took it to the table and placed it in front of Adam. "If you're going to sit and stare at us, you might as well do something useful. These peas need to be shucked."

"I wasn't staring at all of you."

She raised her chin. "Get started on these. The jacks want to eat as soon as they get back to camp. Unlike you, they've worked a full day."

Low chuckles rumbled from the other flunkeys as she went to the larder. She kept her smile hidden until she was out of view. Greenhorns were fair game. Although they had little time for pranks in the cookhouse, she was sure that, over the next few days, all the most horrible jobs would be heaped on Adam.

Which suited her. He needed to see that working in her kitchen was no holiday.

Edging around barrels of molasses and sacks of potatoes, she wished she had brought a lantern. She did not want to trip over some small box which had been left on the floor. She picked her way through the maze cautiously.

In spite of herself, her thoughts fled back to Adam Lassiter. She could not accept Hank's opinion. Adam was not cheap and flashy. She was not sure what he was . . . or who.

"Hallmark," she mumbled to herself. That word was too fancy even for Farley.

A smile tugged at her lips. Rose Quinlan would have

been interested in Adam. Gypsy could not imagine a man who would not catch Farley's mistress's eye, nor a man who would not be pleased to be caught, because Rose was a beautiful blonde. Farley was a fool to bring her to the camp. A woman in the north woods was sure to cause trouble.

As she pulled down a box of crackers, she laughed softly. The old-timers had probably said the same about a cook named Gypsy Elliott when she first arrived in Glenmark Timber Company's cookhouse. She had proven them wrong. Soon they had forgotten she was a woman and respected her ability to match their work hour by hour.

She concentrated on having supper ready on time. When she heard deep voices filling the camp, she ordered her flunkeys to a more frantic pace. The loggers would go to the bunkhouses only long enough to change out of their calked boots so the spikes would not cut into the floors. They would expect their meal as soon as they reached the cookhouse.

Leaving Per to take the mounds of biscuits and potatoes covered with gravy into the dining room, Gypsy worked with Bert to get the meat sliced. Oscar and Hank carried in enormous bowls of squash and peas. Aware of Adam watching, she ignored him. Supper was not the time to look after a new flunkey. Explaining to him would take too many of the precious minutes they had to get the food on the table.

Gypsy sliced the dozens of pies she had put on the shelf by the door. Dumping cookies into a dishpan, she placed them in the center of the table. She laughed and slapped Oscar's hand as he reached for a chocolate one.

"After they eat," she chided, although he was well aware of the rules.

"Let him have one or two. At the speed you work these poor fellows, they deserve something to eat."

Gypsy gasped as she heard amusement in Adam's warm voice from behind her. Exasperation filled her. Looking over her shoulder, she met a chin covered with black whiskers. She took a deep breath as she raised her gaze to meet the laughter in Adam's blue eyes. His hand rose toward her cheek, and she held her breath as she thought of those long fingers touching her again.

Oscar's retort freed her from her silly fantasies. "Gypsy's rules are good ones. Don't give her lip when you don't know what we do here."

"Oscar, take the cookies into the dining room," she said.

"I can—"

"Take them in the other room, Oscar." Her voice remained calm. When he nodded and left, she added, "I assume I won't have to remind you again that you aren't in charge here, Adam. I have very good reasons for the rules in my cookhouse."

"Letting the kid take a single cookie won't hurt any of those jacks out there."

She recoiled as he motioned broadly toward the dining room door. He wobbled on his crutch. Again she reached to steady him. He cursed under his breath as he leaned heavily on her. She fought to keep her knees from foundering.

"Are you all right?" she choked as she tried to keep him on his feet. *On his foot.* She forced the silly thought from her head.

"I am now."

"Good. Then you can . . ." Her voice disappeared into another gasp as his fingers tightened around her shoulder.

His hand cupped her chin to tilt it back so she could not avoid his compelling gaze. Slowly, lightly, his thumb grazed her jaw, sending heated shivers through her. That warmth became exasperation when she saw his challenging grin. She tried to pull away, but his arm held her against him.

"If you don't take your hands off me," she snapped, "I'll break your other leg."

He chuckled. "You? I doubt you can break anything but a man's heart."

"You'll find out if you don't let me go." Gypsy hid her surprise when, with another laugh, he drew away. She pointed toward the bench. "Finish the job I gave you. If I hear a peep from you, you may learn I'm more resourceful than you suspect, Mr. Lassiter."

"I thought it was going to be Adam."

She reached for the earthenware bowls which had been set behind the pies on the shelf. As she placed them on the table and sprinkled cinnamon on the rice pudding in them, she said, "I don't need troublemakers in my kitchen."

"I'm not—" He halted as the dining room door opened.

"Ah, Hank, Per, just in time for the pudding," Gypsy said, not wanting them to guess anything was amiss. She preferred to handle problems herself, but if Adam continued to question her authority, she needed only to mention that to the flunkeys. Her crew would help her deal with him. They were a team, like the loggers on the hill. "Take this pudding out, and make sure Chauncey gets his share. You know how fond he is of rice pudding."

Per hefted two of the heavy bowls and laughed. "Maybe I should just give the inkslinger these and a spoon."

She smiled. To be angry around Per was impossible. Only Per had been working here longer than she had, and she appreciated how he had accepted her as the kingbee cook.

Gypsy did not look at Adam as she rubbed one tired hand against the other before she reached for the almost empty flour bag under the shelf. With a sigh, she swung it onto the table. A white cloud billowed outward, but she waved it aside while she took down a bucket as large as the water bucket by the door.

"What are you doing?" asked Adam.

"If you want doughnuts for breakfast, I have to mix up the batter now. That way, they can rise while we clean up. I'll put them in the larder overnight to slow the yeast.

By morning, they're ready." She smiled coolly. "You'll learn, if you're around here for any time, that there's as much precision to running a cookhouse as felling a tree."

"More, apparently." He grimaced as he moved his left leg, but his voice remained cheerful. "You do this every night?"

"Every night and every morning and every afternoon. Three meals a day six days a week, and two meals on Sunday." Sprinkling flour on the stained oilcloth, she poured more into the bucket. "Welcome to the cookhouse."

He dropped the last pea pod into his bucket. Folding his arms on the table, he said, "I'm impressed."

"You should be. Our Gypsy's the best kingbee in the north woods."

In surprise, Gypsy turned to see Farley standing in the larder door. Slapping her hands against her apron, she asked, "What are you doing here at this time of night?"

"On my way home." He glanced uneasily at Adam. "I just thought I'd see how . . ." Clearing his throat, he gave Gypsy a smile she knew was false. "Just wanted to see how you were doing."

Why did Adam upset the camp manager so much? Farley could freeze up as tight as the river when he wanted to, so she knew it was useless to ask him. She stirred the dough and said, "Everything's fine."

"Is that so?"

"Take her word for it, Farley," Adam said before she could answer. "If the rest of the camp ran as smoothly as this cookhouse, you wouldn't have anything to do but sit in your office and enjoy a cheroot."

Farley tensed at Adam's easy grin. "Gypsy, can I talk with you?"

"I'm listening," she said, ladling sugar into the thick dough.

"I need to talk with you privately."

Seeing his uneasiness, she pushed the heavy bucket toward Adam. "Stir this. Don't stop until I tell you to."

"Now there's something I like to hear a lady say." His fingers closed over the edge of the bucket, capturing hers beneath them.

Again the warm pulse careened through her. Hastily she pulled her hands out from under his. Aware of Farley's presence, she was not sure if she was more furious at Adam for his provocative words or at herself for reacting to them. Adam Lassiter's smooth-talking ways would only cause trouble.

"Do you like hearing a lady say," she asked when she was sure her voice was under control, "that you'll be sorry if you let the dough sit too long before you add the other flour?" She did not give him a chance to reply before she added to Farley, "It's got to be quick. I've got too much to do to chatter the evening away."

The camp manager put his hand on her elbow and led her toward the larder door. With the stove and a rack of shelves between them and Adam, he lowered his voice and said, "Gypsy, I don't like the looks of this."

"Looks of what?" she asked, although she already knew.

"Lassiter's attitude. He's going to cause you trouble."

"Then why did you send him to my cookhouse?"

"What else could I do with him?"

"You could have—never mind." Having this argument over again would just be a waste of time. Time she did not have. "Don't pay any attention to him. I don't." She flinched as she lied.

"If you have any trouble with him, let me know."

"I don't expect any I can't deal with." That much was the truth. She smiled and patted Farley's arm. "Go home. Rose will be worried if you're late."

He nodded as he pulled up his coat collar. His relieved smile told her he was willing to leave his problem in her hands.

Hands. She fought not to turn and stare at Adam's. More than any other part of him, they spoke the truth. The men who worked out here in the north woods had hands that were chapped, cracked, and scarred. His were not.

"Gypsy," Farley said, drawing her attention back to him, "Lassiter is right about one thing. I wish I had a dozen more like you."

"If you find another me, send her here. I could use a vacation."

Taking his laughter out into the night where the snow had slowed to a few lazy flakes wafting on the night breeze, he closed the back door. Gypsy wrapped her arms around herself as she edged toward the stove. The cold was so deep even the kitchen would be freezing tonight.

When she saw the flunkeys were back, she set Bert to finishing the doughnuts while the others hurried to do the jobs they did each evening. She wiped her hands on her apron as she walked to the dining room door.

"How about me, Gypsy?"

At Adam's question, she called over her shoulder, "Wash the dishes. If you need anything, ask Per. He has the stove watch tonight."

"Yes, ma'am!"

She turned to see him snapping a salute. Memory sliced through her, sharp and painful. She had seen too many salutes during the horrible war nearly a decade ago. A shudder of horror threatened to smother her in those memories.

Adam was shocked when Gypsy's face blanched to the color of moon-swept snow. Gripping the table, he started to rise. The clunk of the cast halted him, and she vanished into the dining room before he could ask what was wrong.

"Look out!" snapped Hank.

Adam leaned back as a large galvanized tub was set on the floor in front of him. Buckets of steaming water were poured into it.

With a wink, Oscar shoved soap and a rag into his hand. "Now you'll learn that peeling onions ain't the worst job in the cookhouse. A hundred jacks make quite a pile of dirty dishes."

"A hundred?" He grinned, then groaned as Bert and Per brought in armloads of plates and boxes of flatware and mugs. "I'm going to have a broken back to go along with my ankle."

Hank patted him on the shoulder. "Gypsy breaks us all in to the hard work straightaway. You might as well get used to it, or you won't last a week here."

"Maybe not the night." With a deep sigh, which brought more laughs from the other flunkeys, he set the nearest pile of plates in the water. "If I don't get started, I'll be here all night."

"Naw, shouldn't take you more than a couple of hours," Oscar replied, before going to help Hank clean the stove.

Adam's thought that the kid was jesting vanished when Bert returned with more dishes, and Hank began to stack the cooking pots on the table. Gypsy was out to pay him back for intruding on her little kingdom here. He rubbed at stubborn bits of gravy and frowned. Washing dishes all night was not how he planned to spend his time in the north woods.

His stomach rumbled as he worked, and he wondered when the kitchen crew got to eat. He forgot his discomfort as he listened to the flunkeys gossiping. Nothing caught his attention, because they spoke only of work and the other loggers. To think he would be successful his first night was foolish. He should know better.

When Per brought more warm water, Adam said, "Gypsy mentioned you had the stove watch. What's that?"

The old man chuckled as he picked up a towel and began to dry plates. "Gypsy has her own terms for everything. The stove watch is just what it sounds like. One of us has to stay awake in the kitchen all night to make sure the fire doesn't go out in the cookstove."

"Why not just bank the embers and let it burn low?"

"Do you want to wake up an hour earlier to get the fire hot enough to cook breakfast?" Stretching to place a stack of plates on the middle shelf, he smiled. "Gypsy used to watch it herself, but that was too much on top of everything else she does. Now we rotate the chore, and we lose a night's sleep only once every five nights. Now that you're here, it'll be only once every six nights."

Adam set more filthy plates in the tub. "Once a week, in other words."

Per glanced at him oddly. "The cookhouse doesn't close on Sunday. Gypsy serves only two meals that day, but one of them is breakfast. At least the flunkeys have every other Sunday off."

"But she works every Sunday." He saw no reason to make it a question.

"She's a stickler for everything being right the first time."

Adam laughed. "I've noticed that. She warned me I'd be working hard here."

"You can't say she asks anything of us she wouldn't ask of herself. A young gal like Gypsy should be kicking up her heels with some dandy of stuck out here with us old jacks, but she's the best there is."

"So everyone says."

"You don't believe it?"

"I didn't say that."

"But you were thinking it." Per chuckled. "You'll see, my boy. Trust me, you will."

Adam let the gray-haired man chatter on about the camp. He stored away any pertinent facts and any questions he wanted to get answers to tomorrow. He yawned. He would check around tomorrow, if he could catch up on sleep tonight.

Finally the last dish was clean. He was grateful when Oscar volunteered to dump the dishpan out the back door. Rising, Adam stretched. His cast banged into the bench, ringing hollowly through the kitchen.

He winced. "I'll get used to this eventually . . . I think."

Per pointed to a plate on the opposite end of the table. "Why don't you eat instead of jawing?"

"Eat?"

He chuckled. "It's about time. The rest of us ate hours ago."

"That's right," seconded Hank, his round belly making him look as wide as he was tall. "We don't want to overwork you your first night here."

"Not overwork?" He bit back his retort when he saw their grins. "I hope you saved me something decent." His eyes widened in surprise when Hank pointed to a steaming slab of roasted venison and heaping servings of potatoes and vegetables. A flaky biscuit held a pat of melting butter.

Next to it, Gypsy placed a large cup of coffee and a generous portion of apple pie. "Eat up. We don't like our cooking to get cold, Adam."

"The rest of you ate?" he asked, surprised he had not noticed her come back into the kitchen.

She laughed. "I'm not as gullible as Farley. I wanted to be sure you could earn your keep before I fed you."

He did not need a second invitation. Dropping back onto the bench, he began to eat. On his first bite, he paused and looked over to where Gypsy was bidding the other flunkeys good night.

"What is it?" she asked when she faced him. She closed the door after Per, who was going out to bring in more logs for the woodbox behind the stove.

"This is good."

"Why are you surprised? The jacks want good food. Cooking here isn't that different from cooking for a family."

He stabbed a piece of squash. "Is that what you did before you came here? Cook for a family?"

"I've done all kinds of interesting things."

"Like what?"

Gypsy opened the door again to let in a puffing Per. The old man grinned as he dropped the wood into the box and dashed back out.

"Do you think you can get back to the bunkhouse by

yourself?'' She hung her apron on a nail by the larder door. Brushing at a spot on her dark skirt, she added, ''I'm sure Per would be glad to help you.''

''If you want to wait until I'm done,'' he said, reaching for the pie, ''I can walk you to where you're going. No one should be out alone on a night like tonight.''

''Me?'' She laughed. ''If you're trying to be a gentleman, Adam, it isn't necessary. I live here.'' She pointed to the door behind her.

''You live in the cookhouse?''

''Where did you think I lived? In one of the bunkhouses with the jacks? I don't think they'd appreciate my bumbling around when I have to get up to start breakfast.''

He took a bite of the delicious pie as he watched her pour a cup of tea, then set the pot on the warming shelf over the stove. Shaking his head when she offered to refill his cup, he said, ''I can't imagine any man would be angry if you woke him up in the middle of the night.''

Gypsy's face burned like the coals at the bottom of the firebox. She had worked hard to gain the respect of these brawny men, and she would not have that respect undermined by Adam Lassiter.

''I won't tell you this again. Like you, like every man here, I'm a valued employee of Glenmark Timber Company.'' She kept her chin high. That astonishment glowed in his eyes added to her outrage. ''Not a man sleeping in those bunkhouses cares whether I'm male or female.''

''Then they've been out in the north woods too long.''

''They've been here long enough to know how important it is that I can make three good meals a day for them. Listen to them. They might fantasize about Farley's mistress Rose, they might brag about which gal they like best at Nissa's Porcelain Feather Saloon down the road, but to them and to you, I'm the kingbee cook here. No more and certainly no less.''

When she paused to take a breath, he jumped in. ''I didn't mean to insult you.''

''No?''

"No."

She shrugged, although her shoulders were heavy with fatigue. "Out here, we depend on each other, no matter who we are."

"Obviously I stand corrected."

A satisfied smile tilted her lips. "Obviously." Taking a sip of her tea, she said, "You're beginning to learn."

"I assume I still have a lot to learn."

She watched him take another bite of pie. When he smiled at the lightly spiced flavor none of the flunkeys had been able to copy, she nodded. "You have a lot to learn, and you'd better learn it fast if you want to stay in my kitchen."

"I'm not sure I do."

"That's what makes us different. I wouldn't trade this life for any other."

"That's insane. You'd rather work twenty-hour days every day for months on end?"

She rinsed her mug in the bucket by the stove. "If you give it a chance, in a few weeks you may see I'm right."

"Maybe."

She laughed. "Get a good night's sleep."

"I've been looking forward to a good night's sleep all day."

"Just as long as you're back here by four."

He choked on the last bite of pie. "In the morning?"

"Welcome to the north woods, Adam." She rested one hand on the table. "Don't worry. You'll be working so hard here you'll be asleep in no time at all."

"On one of those bunks topped with pine boughs and a single blanket?"

"You'll be able to sleep anywhere after a full day's work."

"That sounds like an invitation."

"It is."

His ebony brows rose as he smiled. "I know I'll be sorry to ask this, but I have to. An invitation to what?"

"To work hard all day long." She chuckled.

"I was afraid you'd say that."

"I'll see you at four." She straightened and yawned. "Don't be late."

"Or there will be all kinds of trouble?"

"I won't have trouble in my cookhouse. Don't forget that."

"That sounds like a threat."

"It is." She met his gaze evenly, all amusement gone from her voice. "Cause trouble, and I'll see you on the hay trail out of here so fast the speed of your boots will melt the snow."

CHAPTER THREE

Through the winter darkness, Gypsy heard the muffled sound of the bull cook blowing the bugle that signaled the beginning of another day for the jacks—but not for her crew. Their day had started more than an hour before, when the winter stars had shown feebly through the kitchen window.

She urged her flunkeys to a faster pace as the bull cook, who was also the camp's handyman, shouted into the two bunkhouses. His voice carried on the crisp air, which would not be warmed by the sunrise for another hour.

"Where do you want this, Gypsy?"

She whirled to see Adam struggling to balance himself and a tall pot of coffee. That he was trying to do his best impressed her. He was getting about the cookhouse better than she had anticipated. He gave her a lopsided grin as he wobbled. His smile had a boyish charm, but she did not trust it for a moment. She had not been surprised when he had come to work clean shaven except for his mustache. It was too warm in the kitchen for a fuzzy face. Only Bert insisted on wearing a beard.

"Give me that before you drop it!" she ordered. Taking

the pot in both hands, she pointed with her elbow toward the stove. "Help Per with the flapjacks. For the love of heaven, don't do something which will end up causing us more work."

"More work?"

She heard his annoyance, but ignored it. "I don't have time to clean up a mess. Go and help Per."

Gypsy set the pot in the middle of the closest table in the dining room and called for the flunkeys to finish pouring coffee for the men, who would need it to warm their guts. Outside, snow fell steadily. The day would not be as frigid as last week, when she had been sure the men's breaths would freeze into a solid wall.

Going back to the kitchen, she smiled when she noted Adam stood by the stove and held a washtub to collect the flapjacks Per cooked.

"Bert," she called with sudden concern, "check that oatmeal. It's scorching!"

He pulled the lid off the pot. He yelped as he dropped it, letting it clatter on the stove.

Shaking her head, Gypsy turned to check the gingerbread Oscar was slicing. Bert worked hard, but he was careless about grabbing a hot pot without a cloth to protect his hands. No amount of warnings seemed to help.

"Is the maple syrup poured?" she asked.

"Hank is taking it in." Oscar scooped up a handful of crumbs and sprinkled them into her hand. "Try it, Gypsy. Tell me what you think."

She heard his anxiety and recalled this gingerbread was Oscar's first attempt at baking for the loggers. He was the only flunkey with the skill and ambition to become a kingbee cook. She tasted the crumbs and grinned. "That's the best gingerbread I've ever tasted."

"My granny's recipe." Pride puffed out his narrow chest.

"If you know more of your granny's recipes, let me know. We'll try them."

With the ease of so many mornings of working together

in the cramped kitchen, Per moved aside while Gypsy pulled flaky biscuits from the oven. Her call for more wood to keep the stove hot sent Hank rushing toward the woodbox.

As she straightened, a steady stare cut into her. She looked over her shoulder. The surprise on Adam's face was familiar. No one who had not spent time in her kitchen could believe how well it ran.

She tried to look away, but his gaze held hers. The plop of flapjacks into the bucket vanished beneath the rush of her heartbeat in her ears. A smile which began beneath his mustache climbed to sparkle in his eyes. She brushed her hands against her skirt, her fingers curling into the thick wool. A question glowed in his eyes, but she could not guess what it was.

"Gypsy, move aside!"

She scurried back at Hank's muttered order. As a flush seared her cheeks, she berated herself. She was no young miss to be overwhelmed by a man's admiration. If she wanted that, she could have as much as she wanted any day. Checking on the flunkeys' work, she hoped no one had noticed her idiotic reaction to Adam's scintillating eyes.

But Adam had.

Shaking the thought from her head, Gypsy told Bert to take the last trays from the oven. She heard footsteps coming toward the cookhouse. The loggers were about to arrive. As tradition dictated, she tried to be there to greet them if she could steal time from the kitchen.

The loggers poured into the dining room. Each man was as strong as the trees he wrestled to the ground. Nodding a good morning, she checked the tables to be sure sugar and salt were set next to the plates. The jacks had no time to wait. A day's labor on the hill awaited them, and they must not waste a moment.

She smiled at a young man standing to one side. His gaunt shoulders seemed too narrow, and he pulled at his coat as if trying to get his suspenders back into place.

While the other men found their seats as they had for weeks, he hung back, knowing he could not be seated for the first time in her cookhouse without her permission. Here, she reigned supreme.

Going to him, she said, "I'm Gypsy Elliott, the kingbee cook, Mr.—?"

"Worth," he said in a shockingly deep voice. "Bobby Worth, Miss Elliott."

"Gypsy will do."

He blushed. "Yes, Miss Elliott. I mean, yes, Miss Gypsy."

"Why don't you go over there and sit by Old Vic? He's the one with no hair. Third table on the left."

"Thank you." His boots thumped on the floor. Lifting his long legs over the bench, he nodded to the other men, but said nothing. The lad must not be a greenhorn. Occasionally a new man had not learned the rule that no one spoke during meals. Conversation slowed eating and led to rowdiness. Neither could be tolerated when acres of timber waited to fall.

She went into the kitchen. Like the jacks, she had no time to dawdle. While the other flunkeys served the men in the dining room, Oscar and Adam began the preparations for the midday meal. Bread and meat had to be sliced for sandwiches, and more doughnuts must be fried for dessert. Coffee would be brewed just before the flunkeys took the sled out to where the loggers were working.

She kept an eye on Adam. This morning, she could not complain about his willingness to work. He had not spoken a word of complaint or questioned her orders.

Gypsy timed her return to the dining hall exactly. She needed to talk to the short, muscular man who sat on the bench closest to the kitchen. He had taken that privileged place on the first day camp opened so he could have the warmest food. As the crew chief, Waldo Peabody had the respected title of bull of the woods.

As the other jacks left in a steady parade, she picked up the empty plates and stacked them on the tables. When

Peabody drained his coffee mug, she put her hand on the shoulder of his wool coat.

"Morning, Gypsy. Fine breakfast." He winked at her from beneath his shock of black hair. "Just like always."

"Can you spare a moment?"

"Sure thing. Always have a moment for the best kingbee cook in the north woods." To his men, who were rising from the table, he added, "Get started. I'll be with you directly." He smiled, revealing the gold tooth of which he was so proud. Standing, he settled his wool stocking cap on his head and glanced at the plate she held. With a laugh, he picked up another pancake and took a big bite. "What is it?"

"You know Adam Lassiter is working for me, don't you?"

He nodded, his smile vanishing. "Heard Farley sent him here."

"Was he on your crew yesterday?"

"Sure was. You know I keep an eye on the greenhorns." Taking another bite, he said nothing more.

"And how did he do?"

"Is he giving you trouble, Gypsy?" His eyes narrowed.

"I just want to know what happened." She must not give Peabody any clue why she was asking. She could have asked Adam, but he answered every question too smoothly.

"Strangest thing, Gypsy," he mused as he grabbed another flapjack from the plate. Grinning, he bit off more than half of it. "Lassiter was supposed to be helping Swede and Edvard skid a log to where the sky-loaders were heaping them onto a sled to take them down to the river. Nothing any jack can't do with his eyes closed and half a bottle of whiskey burning in his gut."

"Was the skid path freshly frozen?"

He nodded. "Boys laid it down the night before. My road monkeys know how to do it right—tree wide, no more. We can't afford to have a log taking off on us and upsetting a sled."

"I know that," she said, wishing he would get to the point. "So what happened?"

"All of the sudden, Lassiter lets out a shout loud enough to wake Satan. Swede and Edvard were as surprised as any jack out there. They told me everything was going just as it should. I don't know what happened."

"Adam says he slipped and twisted his ankle."

"Slipped?" He snorted before smiling and stealing the final pancake. "He's no more cut out to be a jack than you are, Gypsy. Naw, you'd do a lot better."

She laughed as she put the empty plate onto the stack beside her. "I'll accept that as a compliment."

"I meant it as one. I wasn't sure that he'd broken it, but better to be safe than sorry, you know." With a grin, he said, "Gotta go, Gypsy. My saw is itching to find the tallest timber in the woods today." He paused, concern darkening his eyes. "Look, if Lassiter is a problem, I can find him something to do out on the hill."

"What?"

He shrugged. "Set him as a lookout for axhandle hounds, so the blasted varmints don't come and eat all the handles off the branding mallets and axes."

"Axhandle hounds?" She shook her head and shooed him toward the door. "Get out of here. I have enough to do without listening to idiotic tall tales. If you jacks would take better care of your tools, you wouldn't have to invent stupid excuses."

Gypsy's smile left with Peabody. With a sigh, she lifted the stack of plates and went into the kitchen. She was unsure what she had hoped to hear, but his story corroborated what Adam had told Farley. Everything confirmed that her new flunkey was telling the truth—everything but her own instincts, which warned her Adam Lassiter was not what he wanted them to believe.

She let her work banish her uneasy thoughts. She had Adam wash the dishes again. Although he grumbled, she ignored him. It was a chore he could handle.

She frowned when she saw Hank chatting with Oscar

by the woodbox. Clapping her hands, she asked, "What's so important that you have to talk about it now?"

Oscar colored as Hank said, "Just making plans for Saturday night."

"Nissa and her girls won't be too interested in seeing you if you don't have a job."

Hank chuckled and slapped Oscar on the back. "C'mon, boy. She's right. The hay trail doesn't lead to the Porcelain Feather."

Gypsy hid her sympathy for Oscar when his blush brightened another shade. "Oscar, you and Bert can take the grub out to the men on the west hill at noon."

"Ah, Gypsy, we did it yesterday."

"You were also half an hour late yesterday. I convinced Farley not to send both of you packing by telling him you'd make up for your tardiness today." Although she expected none, she asked, "Any questions?"

She went to check the larder. There should be plenty of food until the camp was broken down at the spring thaw, but she did not want to be forced to use salt pork at both meals during the final weeks. Scanning the shelves, she rubbed her lower back. Cherry pies might make a pleasant change, or she might try an apple crisp. She could serve it warm with a bit of syrup for those who had a sweet tooth.

She tapped her chin as she thought about the meat in the locker. The cold winter kept it from going bad. A beef roast would make a good supper. If Bert cut off a big chunk with an ax, there would be enough for sandwiches tomorrow at lunch.

An uneven thump interrupted her planning. She turned to see Adam in the doorway.

She grinned when she noticed the dark stain of water climbing nearly to the elbow of each sleeve and across the front of his shirt. Even the suspenders that stretched across his lean chest were splattered.

When he rested his shoulder against the doorframe, he

said, "The dishes are done. What do you want me to do now?"

"From the looks of you, I'd say you washed the whole cookhouse."

He plucked at his wet shirt. "It's not easy working with this cast and half a night's sleep."

She chuckled. "It'll get worse."

"I thought you'd tell me it would get better."

"You've got eyes. You can see how hard we all work. But isn't it worth it?"

"Worth it?"

"How else could we enjoy the glorious weather up here?"

His smile returned as his gaze slipped along her with slow appreciation. "You don't look the worse for wear, if you don't mind my saying so."

"I do."

"Look worse or mind that I say so?"

"Adam, I've got too many things to do to stand here and jaw with you."

He shifted so his broad shoulders nearly filled the door. "That's an easy excuse, Gypsy."

"It's no excuse. It's the truth."

"All right, so what do you want me to do next?"

Gypsy folded her arms in front of her as his gaze brushed her again. "I'm not sure how much you can do while you're on that crutch."

"Oscar was weeping over the onions yesterday. I could spell the poor lad."

"Yes, you could." She hid her surprise that he would volunteer for the horrible job.

"How many do you need for supper?"

"These." She pointed to a burlap bag beside a barrel of sugar.

He grimaced. "That whole bag? It must weigh—"

"Twenty-five pounds."

"Twenty-five? Can I take back my offer?"

"Too late." She laughed. "If you need help carrying them, just call Per."

When she started to walk past him, he blocked the doorway with his crutch. "I see you aren't going to waste sympathy on this poor jack," he said in a hushed voice which would not carry to where the other men were toting the canisters for the loggers' midday meal out to the sled.

"Why should I? You tried to ride a log and it bucked you off. Maybe you should be a cowboy instead."

"And miss this chance to work in your kitchen, Gypsy? I think I'm going to like working here." His fingers lightly caressed her shoulder. "I think there are quite a few things I can do to help you."

She stepped away. "You're pretty useless while you're wearing that cast."

"Are you sure there's nothing I can do for you?" He cupped her elbow and drew her closer.

"There are the onions . . ."

"That's doing something for the jacks," he said softly, as her voice trailed off. "Is there something I can do for *you?*"

"Adam, I think—"

"About all the wrong things," he grumbled, pulling her against him.

She gasped as his arm curved around her. He silenced the sound when his lips brushed hers with sweet fire.

"What do you think you're doing?" She jerked away and bumped into a cask of flour. Wincing, she rubbed her hip. Her fingers fled from her skirt when she saw his grin as he watched her.

"I thought I was kissing you."

"I don't want you kissing me."

The mirth vanished from his eyes. "Thanks for the compliment, boss."

"That's right. I *am* your boss."

"A friendly kiss won't cause trouble in the kitchen."

"Friendly?" She jammed her fists against her waist. "Friendship doesn't require your hands all over me."

Holding up his right hand, he corrected, "Hand. If you haven't noticed, I need one hand to keep myself on my feet."

"Just don't get any ideas about you and me."

"No ideas except about onions and cookies and a hundred ravenous jacks?"

"Exactly."

"You're smart, Gypsy, to be just the boss." He sighed. "Never get too close to anyone. It's much safer that way, isn't it?"

She flinched. How had a single kiss revealed so much to him? When his eyes slitted, she feared he was trying to discover more. She pushed past him. She heard him wobble on his crutch, but at the moment, she did not care if he landed on his butt on the rough boards.

The other flunkeys looked up as she strode past them to get the beans she had set to soak earlier. She saw the startled glances they exchanged. Her cheeks heated as she wondered what they might have witnessed.

Somehow she must keep Adam away before his charming smile and enticing lips convinced her to pay more attention to him than to her work.

"Howdy, Farley!"

At Per's greeting, Gypsy turned, shocked. The camp manager was coming to the kitchen for the second time in as many days. She could not recall the last time that had happened. Usually he left his mistress only long enough to work in his office.

Farley motioned for her to join him in the dining room. She wondered what was bothering him now. Wishing he had chosen another time for a chat, she sighed. She must give him an ear if he needed to talk.

"Hank, stir the soup for me, will you?" she asked.

"Sure thing," he said, but he glanced uneasily toward Farley.

The thick pea soup's smoky scent followed her across the kitchen. "Don't let it burn."

A smile tightened her lips as she walked past Adam. He was cutting onions with a fervor that suggested the job was his lifework, but she knew he was not oblivious to a single thing in the kitchen.

Farley closed the door behind her, pressing on it to be sure the latch had caught.

"Do you want to seal the edges so you can be sure no one eavesdrops?" she asked with more than a touch of sarcasm.

"I don't have to worry about your crew. You keep them too busy to listen at keyholes."

"Easy when there are no keyholes in the cook shack."

His chuckle sounded forced as he sat. Gypsy was astounded. Farley's manners were usually impeccable. That he would sit while she still stood warned there might be more trouble brewing.

"What's wrong?" she asked as she pulled out the bench across from him.

"That's what I wanted to find out from you."

"Pardon me?"

He pointed toward the kitchen door before folding his arms on the table. "It's Lassiter. I wondered how he was doing."

"Why should he be doing any differently than last night?" She was astonished when her laugh was as strained as his. "He's only been here a day. What do you expect?"

Rubbing his eyes, Farley sighed. "I'm not sure, but I heard you threatened to send him on the hay trail last night."

"Who told you that?"

"Just heard it."

Her fingers clasped in her lap. She did not need someone running to Farley and repeating every word she spoke. "Don't worry. I know proper procedures. I'll let you know before I fire anyone."

"Gypsy . . ." He rubbed his eyes again. "Look, I'm sorry. I know you know how things work. It's just with Lassiter . . ."

"What do you know about him that you're not telling me?"

"Know? Gypsy, I don't know anything." He reached inside his coat and pulled out a slip of paper. "Here. I should have shown you this right away."

Gypsy scanned the letter. Even if it had not borne the ornate letterhead of Glenmark Timber Company, she would have recognized the carefully crafted handwriting. It belonged to Daniel Glenmark. The very simplicity of the request that Adam Lassiter be hired on for the rest of the winter astounded her.

Why would a jack arrive with a letter from the owner of the company? Work was always available for men who were unafraid of hard labor.

Glancing toward the door, Farley muttered, "Maybe he caught Glenmark with his fingers in the cookie jar."

"Mr. Glenmark wouldn't let anyone blackmail him." She folded the letter and handed it back to him. "After all, if he wanted to skim the profits from the company, who's to gainsay him? It's his company, after all."

"Then why did he write this letter? Glenmark wants Lassiter to work here for the rest of the winter. Why?"

"I don't have any idea."

"None?"

Her brow furrowed in a scowl. "Why should I know anything more than you do?"

With a sigh, he stood. "I was hoping you had discovered something I didn't when I talked to Lassiter. I admit I was surprised when I heard you might be firing him."

"Just trying to get him to toe the line."

"He acts so friendly," he continued, as if he had not heard her, "but I think he's hiding something."

Gypsy resisted agreeing. Looking for trouble where there might not be any was sure to create problems. "Farley, you're becoming too suspicious in your old age."

"Maybe."

"I promise if I have any problem with him, he'll walk."

A reluctant smile lessened the lines across his forehead. "All right. I'll leave the matter in your hands."

"Which means that I have to explain it to Mr. Glenmark if I want him fired?"

He nodded. "I'd better get back to the office. I have to check Peabody's schedule for work on the west hill." He put on his hat and grinned. "With Lassiter ending up in your kitchen, Glenmark did him no favor."

Hours later, as she banked the fire in the dining room stove and blew out the lantern, Gypsy could not stop thinking about Farley's words. Adam might have come to the camp under unusual circumstances, but he had done his share of work today. He spent more time with the other flunkeys than with her. Oscar was already seeking out Adam to chat with while they worked. If she dismissed what had happened in the larder, Adam was settling in well.

She walked to the window. On moonlit nights, she could see the glitter of the river's ice through the pine branches, but tonight a fury of snowflakes hid everything.

Folding her arms on the sill, she shivered with the cold prying past the windowpanes. Even a blizzard would not halt work, but the fresh snow would add to the peril the jacks faced every day. When the windows rattled with the music of the wind, she stepped back. It was senseless to stay here when her stove warmed her bedroom.

Gypsy smiled as she entered the kitchen and saw Bert pushing logs into the cookstove. "Your turn tonight?"

The tall man offered his ready grin. " 'Fraid so. It's been one lousy day. First, 'aving to cart lunch up to the 'ill, then stoking the fire tonight. At least, I won't 'ave to listen to all the snoring in the bunkhouse."

"Just have the stove ready early tomorrow."

"If you'll 'ave your swamp water ready first thing."

With a laugh, she patted his arm. "You know my coffee is as legendary as Paul Bunyan himself." She walked toward her bedroom, but paused as he called her name. "What is it, Bert?"

"This was brought over for you." He held out a simple white envelope. "I guess they forgot to deliver it with the mail earlier."

She smiled her thanks, but wondered why Daniel had written to her. It had to be from the company's owner. No one else would write to her here. Had he guessed Adam might end up in her kitchen?

Bidding Bert good night, she went into her bedroom. She lit the lantern by the door and set it on a brad hooked to a rafter. Light spread to reveal the plain room she called home. A simple rag rug between the potbellied stove and the bed was the only bright spot on the rough floorboards. By the room's one window, her plain iron bed waited to enfold her in sleep. The worn counterpane was one of her few connections with the place which had been home before she came to the north woods. This was home now. After nearly three years, she had set aside her dreams of living anywhere else.

Gypsy tossed the envelope on the bed. She would read it after she had slipped under the covers. Slowly she unbuttoned the pearl buttons along the back of her blouse. She yawned as she hung it on one of the pegs behind the door. Undoing her skirt, she let it fall to the floor. Her petticoats dropped on top of the black wool.

Only when she had pulled on her flannel nightgown and buttoned it into place did she reach for the envelope. Daniel owed both her and Farley an explanation of why he had sent Adam to the camp under such strange circumstances. With a laugh, she thought about not telling Farley for a few days and watching him squirm with curiosity. That would repay him for his high-handed insistence that Adam work in her kitchen.

When she opened the letter, her smile vanished and

her breath caught in her throat. She slid to sit on the mattress as she read:

Gypsy Elliott,

I know who you are. I know what you did. I know you should pay. Death is about to overtake you, just as it has the ones you love.
Sleep well by your icy river before I send you to burn in hell.

"No," she whispered as her trembling fingers turned the envelope so she could see the postmark. Saginaw!

Who in Saginaw wanted her dead? Why? She knew no one in Saginaw. She had spent less than an hour there on her way to the logging camp.

She looked back at the letter. It was written in large square letters. The childish handwriting added to the insanity of such a threat.

I know who you are. I know what you did.

"What did I do?" she cried. She searched her memories. She had teased the other children she had grown up with and been teased back. Once, when she was six, she had stolen half a sweet potato pie from Mrs. Mulligan next door. Papa made sure she paid for that. Just childish crimes. What had she done to deserve this?

Nothing!

Then why was someone sending her this? Hadn't she suffered enough already? Her parents dead, her brother dead, her sister far from her. She had left everything that was familiar to come here and build a new life. She had put that grief behind her.

Cursing, she leaped to her feet, grabbed a thick cloth, and opened the small door of the woodstove. The stove's hot breath reddened her face as she crushed the page and threw it in. Her breath burned in her chest as she watched

the letter disappear in the fire. Whirling, she scooped up
the envelope and sent it to the same end.

She dropped to her knees and hid her face in her hands.
She had thought the terror was over . . . dead and buried
along with those she loved.

She had been wrong.

CHAPTER FOUR

Gypsy fought not to shift on the hard bench in the dining room. Reverend Frisch had brought an endless supply of parables with him this afternoon. With a sigh, she folded her hands in her lap. She should be grateful he had come after midday. She and her crew had had time to serve breakfast and clean up before the dining room was altered into a makeshift church by the sky pilot.

A smile teased her lips. The loggers had a vocabulary of their own. Not a man in the camp would think of calling the blacksmith anything but an iron burner. The clerk was an inkslinger. The itinerant preacher who made his way here every other week was a sky pilot. She liked that term. It fit Reverend Frisch.

The silver-haired minister wore his backward collar beneath a mackinaw shirt. He never acted as if it was unusual to use a dining room table for an altar while he offered communion out of a cracker box. With his cheeks above his thick beard rosy with the cold, his strong hands emphasized every word coming from his generous heart.

"Is he always this long-winded?"

Glancing at Adam, who sat beside her, she almost

laughed. He had to sit sideways so his left foot did not stick between the legs of the man in front of him, and he could not move.

She whispered, "He's almost done."

"I hope so." His grin lessened the edge on his complaint.

Gypsy tried to listen to Reverend Frisch, but could not keep her thoughts from straying. In the past few days, Adam had relented in their battle of words. She could not relax, though. She feared she was becoming too obvious in her attempts to avoid any motion that might graze her fingers against his.

Her hands clenched in her lap. She might have been able to handle her own silliness, except for Farley's suspicions. They were more trouble than Adam. She looked at Farley, who was sitting alone on the opposite side of the room. Some residual conscience kept him from bringing his mistress to church. She found that hypocrisy ludicrous, because Reverend Frisch knew all about Rose Quinlan.

When she put her hand up to hide a yawn, Gypsy heard Adam's muffled laughter. The sky pilot glanced in their direction. Meeting Reverend Frisch's dark eyes, she hoped he would not guess she was thinking of anything but his sermon.

The service came to a quick close when his words were interrupted by a loud snore. The sleepy logger was routed awake to laughter and a hurried benediction. As the men rose, the makeshift church dissolved back into the dining room.

"Fool should have come back from the Porcelain Feather earlier," mumbled Adam as he reached for his crutch.

"Maybe he didn't have your self-restraint."

He grinned when he stood to look down at her from his height, which was impressive even when he leaned on his crutch. "As you may recall, Miss Elliott, I had no chance to go gallivanting off for a few drinks and a pleasant armful. I had the stove watch last night."

"It was your turn."

"True." He chuckled. "I'm not complaining, although I had hoped for some company last evening."

"There will be other Saturday nights when you can go to the Porcelain—"

"Your company, Gypsy." When his fingers slipped over hers on the table top, a flame erupted up her arm. He caressed her hand gently as his sapphire gaze enticed her. "How about sharing a cup of coffee with me tonight after the kitchen's clean?"

"I do have the stove watch tonight." She blinked and drew away, startled by the longing in her voice.

He caught her elbow to keep her near. "Is that a yes or a no?"

"I—" She wished someone would interrupt. How could the room be so crowded and yet no one intruded?

"If you don't want my company, you need only say so." His grin became self-deprecatory. "I don't make it a practice to force myself on pretty redheads. I can be reasonable."

"Can you?"

"When necessary. So do you want me to stay for that cup of coffee tonight?"

No words formed on her lips when he stroked her sleeve, the crisp muslin heating beneath his touch. Each touch lured her closer. As she stared up at the invitation in his eyes, a rush of unfamiliar sensations flooded her with pleasure.

"Good afternoon, Gypsy."

Farley's voice released her from the sweet tangle of dreams which had no place in her life. Turning away, she smiled weakly at the camp manager. "Good afternoon. How are you?"

Farley glanced at Adam, making no effort to hide his disquiet. She risked a peek over her shoulder. Adam's face was tranquil, as if they had been discussing nothing important.

Listening to the camp manager greet Adam, she reminded herself a cup of coffee at the end of the day was nothing. Only her reaction to his beguiling touch made it more.

Adam asked, "Do you want us to get some coffee for the jacks, Gypsy?"

"Coffee?" She ignored Farley's baffled expression at the squeaked word. Taking a deep breath as Adam grinned, she shook off the cloying delight. "That's a good idea. Farley, do you want a cup?"

He shook his head. "Sorry, I can't. Rose's expecting me. I told her I'd take her for a sled ride this afternoon." Tapping his hat into place, he tipped it toward her. "Thanks anyhow, Gypsy."

Hearing another smothered chuckle as Farley elbowed his way to the door, Gypsy glared at Adam.

"I think," he said with a grin, "your friend Farley is sorry he transplanted his sweet Rose here in the north woods."

"That's none of your concern."

"True, but that doesn't stop any of the jacks from talking about Farley and his light lady. And I'm a jack, aren't I?"

She did not lower her gaze from the challenge in his eyes. He wanted her to answer so he could learn what she suspected. Almost laughing, she wondered what he would think if she were honest. She was certain he was no jack.

Motioning toward the kitchen, Gypsy said, "Get Bert and make up coffee for the jacks. I want to talk to Reverend Frisch."

"All right. Gypsy, how about tonight?"

"I'll let you know later."

His gaze followed her as she went to where the sky pilot was passing out recent magazines to the men clustered around a table. She could not escape Adam's eyes even when she slipped past a tableful of jacks who were writing home under the minister's supervision. Only when she heard the muted thump of his crutch vanish into the kitchen did her heart slow its frantic beating.

She released the breath that had been burning in her chest and smiled at Reverend Frisch. "Excellent sermon."

"I saw your yawn," he answered, laughing. His face bore the scars of years of riding in the north woods cold. The wind had sucked his skin dry, leaving it as rutted as a dead riverbed.

"Now, Reverend, you know I need Sunday to catch up on sleep."

He chuckled. "You need to convince Farley to hire you an assistant."

"I've told him more than once I could use a cookee."

"I'm sure you have." He put his boot on the end of a bench and leaned his elbow on his knee. In a voice that did not match the boom of his sermons, he asked, "Is there a problem, Gypsy? You keep glancing at the kitchen as if you expect something to catch on fire."

"Not really. I'm just waiting for the word that the flunkeys have the swamp water ready." Another prick of guilt stabbed her as she lied to the minister. "Would you like a cup of coffee before you leave?"

He pulled his pipe from a pocket of his denims. Putting it into his mouth, he spoke around the stem. "I could use a bit of your swamp water to char these old bones." He reached into his pocket again, then grimaced like a guilty lad. "And I'll remember not to smoke. You don't have to remind me about your rules."

"If I didn't have rules, I'd have Bert and Hank bringing their cheroots into the kitchen. I don't think the jacks would appreciate ashes in their soup."

Gypsy wove through the crowded room. She smiled when she heard the jacks complaining about aching heads after a long night at the Porcelain Feather Saloon. Listening to their outrageous descriptions of how badly they hurt, she suspected they exaggerated their hangovers as they did everything else. Each logger wanted to be the biggest, strongest, fastest. She wondered what prestige there was in having the worst headache.

The kitchen was quiet. Faint scents of fried eggs and toast were overpowered by the aroma of fresh coffee. Mounds of rising bread sat on the table, but the hectic pace had slowed to Adam reaching for two cups. He grinned at Reverend Frisch and took down another.

"Oscar volunteered to take the big pot in after he reminded me I shouldn't be toting it around," Adam said as he poured coffee from a smaller pot.

"It's good *he* has sense." Gypsy stirred sugar into her coffee. "Reverend, I don't think you've met Adam Lassiter. He's new in my kitchen."

The minister took the cup of coffee Adam held out. "What happened to you?"

"A log and I had an argument." Adam tapped the crutch against his cast. "The log won, and I ended up here working for Gypsy."

"Is she working you hard?"

"Gypsy believes idle hands are the devil's tool."

"Nonsense." The minister grinned. "She refuses to give the devil his due, but she makes sure Glenmark gets a fair day's work for his dollar."

"I'd say she gets more than a fair day's work out of us. I've been trying to figure out how Hank can stay so fat when she's been working my fingers to the bone."

"Gentlemen," Gypsy interjected, "if you're finished talking about me, I have some pie."

Reverend Frisch took a deep drink and put his cup on the table. "Sorry, Gypsy. I've got to leave. There's a funeral I have to speak at up the river."

"Funeral?"

"Not an accident," he said hastily. "The inkslinger at Bradbury Lumber died two days ago. They want me to say a few words over him before they send him home for a decent burial." He laughed as he pulled on his coat. "What's wrong, Gypsy? You have less color in your face than the corpse will. It isn't like you to be spooked like one of these superstitious lumberjacks.''

She shrugged, but her shoulders were heavy. She had told no one about the note she had received almost a week ago. Forgetting it would be the best thing. No one was going to traipse all the way through these woods to find her. A letter was one thing. Risking freezing to death was another.

Yet she could not put it out of her mind unless . . . she bit back the curse she should not speak in the minister's hearing. Adam's touch had banished every thought of that letter from her head. That only proved she was as stupid as whoever had written the note.

"Gypsy?"

She blinked at Adam's question. Raising her gaze to his blue eyes, she saw his confusion. Not that she blamed him. No one could understand her fear. No one must, or . . . she did not want to think of that.

She forced her voice to be calm as she said, "I'm just tired."

"You should let your flunkeys do more of your jobs," Reverend Frisch chided. "You do too much for a—"

"A woman?"

"I was going to say a kingbee cook." The sky pilot tapped his pipe against his empty cup, then put it in his pocket. He wrapped a brightly colored muffler around his neck and pulled on a garish stocking cap. "But you're right, Gypsy. No woman—no man, either—should work as hard as you do."

"Who else is going to do it?"

"That's the problem, isn't it? Why don't you let Adam help you? He looks like he can carry his weight."

"He can barely tote himself!"

Reverend Frisch chuckled and patted her shoulder. "Take care of yourself, Gypsy. Don't let one of these lads convince you to run off with him without giving me a chance to propose."

"You, Reverend?" Her eyes widened. "Now, what would your wife say?"

"She probably wouldn't be pleased, but I have to admit I have a hankering for more of your swamp water and pie."

After the minister left with half a pie wrapped for the trip, Gypsy sat at the kitchen table and stared at her coffee. While he refilled his cup, Adam remained silent. The mumbled voices from the dining room drifted over them as he sat across from her. He pushed the rising loaves of bread aside.

"Be careful," she warned.

"You worry too much."

"I don't want to have to remake those loaves because of your clumsiness."

Leaning his elbows on the table, he asked, "When's the last time you took a break from the work here?"

"You've seen how much time it takes. If I want to keep my job, I have to do what's necessary."

"But you love it?"

"There's no need to make that a question." Swirling the coffee in her cup, she smiled.

Adam grimaced as he stood and walked to where another pie waited by the window. Cutting a slice, he took a bite before saying, "Maybe for you, but I'm looking forward to the end of winter. Then I can see Saginaw and civilization again."

"It's hard to imagine being in a city with real streets and trees that are for sitting under instead of chopping down."

"You've never been to Saginaw?"

Gypsy gave him what she hoped was a withering glower. "Don't be ridiculous! Of course I've been there."

"When's the last time you took a day off?"

"A whole day?"

He rested his shoulder against the wall and put his elbow on his crutch. "Twenty-four hours, Gypsy. One day. Three meals for these ravenous lumbermen. When's the last time you took a whole day off?''

"It's been a while," she hedged.

"How long is a while?"

Putting her spoon on the table, she rose and went to the flour barrel. ''You know how many hours are in a day. Why don't you figure out how many hours are in *a while* while you peel potatoes for stew?''

"You're just as bad as Farley warned you'd be."

She faced him. Until she saw his frown, she had been unsure if he were joking or not. ''You didn't have to take this job!''

"No? I like the feel of that bonus in my pocket. I sure wasn't about to give it back because I had to work for an unreasonable dictator.''

"I'm not unreasonable."

Despite his determination not to let her best him with her honed words, Adam smiled. She stood with her hands planted firmly on her slender waistband. Her apron could not hide the feminine lace of her blouse, which accented the pleasing curves of her body. They drew his eyes too often for a man who should be thinking of other things. Her mouth was as warm as her hair, and her jade eyes challenged him to discover which was softer. Not just a hint of a kiss, but a deep, lingering kiss as he tasted every luscious corner of her mouth.

He started toward her, but remembered his crutch in time. Placing it under his arm, which no longer throbbed from hours of having the wood jammed beneath him, he hobbled to where she stood in the larder doorway. ''I hope we can be less cynical than we were the last time we spoke here.''

"That depends on how you handle yourself."

"Or how I don't handle you."

Gypsy did not smile. ''I'd prefer you didn't remind me about that.''

"You remind me of it all the time."

"*I* do? You're crazy!"

Shaking his head, he leaned his shoulder against the door. His body ached from long days of working in the kitchen and being near this woman who would have enticed him even if there had been dozens of other women around. After sitting on the bench all night while he kept the fire stoked, he was ready for bed. He would gladly take her with him.

He almost laughed at that thought. One thing he had learned about Gypsy Elliott this week: She thought about one thing and one thing only—making meals for the jacks working for Glenmark. Too bad he could not be so single-minded. It would help him sleep instead of tossing on that uncomfortable bunk.

"I'm not crazy." He swallowed a yawn. "Just honest when I say I think about you in my arms when I see you flitting about like a bee."

"Which I can't do if you don't move aside. Adam, I have to—"

He caught her hand in his. When her wide eyes rose from his red plaid shirt to his smile, he shook his head. "No, you don't have anything to do right now. It's Sunday, Gypsy. Let's take a walk and enjoy the sunshine. It's the first time we've seen the sun in a week."

"I'd love to, but I have to start supper."

"Let Oscar and Per start it."

"It's not fair that—"

"Gypsy, they'll be glad to get away from Hank's belly-aching about his headache." He rubbed her fingers slowly. When they quivered in his, he bent toward her to whisper, "And I deserve some time off after sitting up all night to tend to the stove and listen to you pace in your room."

She drew back. "You must have heard the snow shifting on the roof. I slept well last night."

His fingers under her chin tipped her face back toward him. "Why are you lying to me? Even if I hadn't heard you with my own two ears, those sooty circles under your eyes tell me the truth."

As her lips parted, he knew he did not want to hear

her excuses. He wanted to kiss her. His hands framed her face, sifting up through her hair as he brought her mouth beneath his.

Shock stiffened her, but she softened as he delved deep into her mouth, wanting to sample every sweet secret. When his tongue touched hers, she shivered in his arms.

His hands slipped down her back to draw her even closer as his mouth trailed along her throat, pausing when her pulse leaped like the flames in the stove. Hungrily, his mouth found her lips again. They were even more delicious than he had remembered.

"No," Gypsy moaned, pulling away. She could not keep her fingers from trembling as she patted her hair back into its bun.

"Gypsy—"

"No. I told you this was impossible."

He smiled and ran a single finger along her arm, renewing the swirls of enchantment dancing through her. "I think we both know this is quite possible."

She took a deep, steadying breath. "I need to get supper started."

"After we go for a walk."

"Adam, I—"

"You need to get out of here." He grinned. "For a while."

She hesitated. "Just a walk?"

"Just a walk."

"Nothing else?"

"Do you want a promise written in blood?" He laughed shortly. "You can ask your buddy Farley along if you'd like a chaperon."

A smile eased the tension across her lips. "I think he's probably pretty busy with Rose right now."

"Is that a yes, then?"

"If we don't talk about this."

"This?" He pointed to the stove. "Or this?" His finger traced the curve of her lips.

Fighting the yearning to melt beneath his touch, she whispered, "None of it."

"All right."

"Just like that?"

"I can be reasonable. Once in a while."

She laughed. The idea of escaping from the kitchen for even an hour was intoxicating. "I have to get my bonnet and coat."

He smiled, then gave her a roguish wink. "Allow me, Gypsy. After all, I know you consider me less than a gentleman."

"Do you think you should?"

"Get your coat?" His forehead creased in bafflement.

"No. Take a walk." She touched the crutch. "You don't want to hurt your ankle more."

His fingers slid over hers. When she did not pull her hand away, he stroked it. The sweet warmth burst forth again, but not where he touched her. Deep inside.

Not wanting it to end, she feared what might happen if she let it continue. She swallowed her gasp of surprise as he drew away. His smile warned her he had guessed what she was thinking.

"I'll be able to manage in the snow." His low voice resonated through her with the power of a falling tree striking the frozen ground. "If you're looking for an excuse not to go with me, just say so."

"I want to go with you. I mean . . ." She laughed at her girlish shyness. She often spent a rare free hour gossiping with one of the flunkeys or a jack. This would be just the same.

Wouldn't it?

CHAPTER FIVE

Gypsy tried to tell herself she had not made a mistake. When Adam hobbled across the room to get her coat and her simple straw bonnet with its black grosgrain ribbons, she drew her apron over her head and hung it on the peg by her bedroom door. This walk might give her the chance to learn more about Adam Lassiter and why he was at this camp.

She reached for her coat, but he smiled and held it up. "Be careful," she warned when she saw how precariously he was balanced on the crutch.

"I'm not planning on throwing myself at your feet."

"I didn't think you were." She slid her arms into the cool wool. As she buttoned her coat, she watched him shrug on his. "You're doing much better than I thought you would. You've never complained."

"I've complained."

Gypsy laughed as he dropped her bonnet on her hair. Adjusting it, she tied the ribbons beneath her chin. "Not about your leg. You've only griped about your cast."

"The blasted thing crashes against everything until I

feel like a clown.'' He wagged a finger at her. ''Don't
say it.''

Gypsy smiled as they walked out through the dining
room. It was nearly deserted except for a few jacks still
reading the magazines Reverend Frisch had brought. She
jumped down past the slick spot where the eaves dripped.
Turning, she held out her hand to steady Adam.

''Back away, Gypsy,'' he ordered. ''If I slip, I'll send
you flying into that snowbank over there.''

With a laugh, she obeyed. She tensed, but he managed
with no trouble. Letting him draw her hand within his
arm, she matched his uneven steps. She yearned to put
aside her worries and delight in the sunshine, which glittered like glorious diamonds in the snow.

Shouts sounded from across the camp. When Gypsy
waved to the jacks, she heard Adam laugh. ''What's
funny?'' she asked.

''You are well loved here.''

''My cooking is.''

''No, it's more than the cooking. They like *you*.''

''I like them.''

''All of them?''

She smiled as her black boots swept aside the newly
fallen snow. They were walking toward the river that
slept beneath the ice. ''Of course I don't like all of them.
I wish Peabody would order some of them to walk. I
avoid anyone I don't like.''

''Nice and simple?''

Gypsy's smile faltered as they emerged from beneath
the trees to stand on the low riverbank. She listened to
the thin song of the winter birds, then bent to look at tiny
footprints interspersed by a tail print. A muskrat. Standing,
she said, ''I try to keep peace in my home.''

''You consider this home?''

''Why do you question everything I say?''

''How else can I learn anything?'' He grinned and held
up his hands when she frowned. ''Sorry. I'm just trying
to be friendly, Gypsy.''

"I've noticed. But I thought we weren't going to talk about that."

He caught her elbow in his hand and the humor vanished from his eyes. "It's not as if we did anything criminal."

"Let's not start arguing again." Slowly she pulled away. "I'd like to spend an hour *not* arguing with you."

"Impossible."

"If you think that, why—" She paused as she saw his smile. She never could guess when he was teasing her. "If you want to avoid quarreling, you should find something to talk about that won't cause an argument."

He drew even with her as she slowly strolled along the river. "All right. What can we talk about? How about home?"

"What about home?"

"Your home, my home, whatever."

"I told you. My home is right here."

"And mine is here, too."

"Really? You live around here?"

He grinned. "Not exactly right here. I grew up near Ann Arbor. I've been to places where the buildings are fancier or the mountains are higher, but Michigan is home."

"I know. It's home for me, too."

He paused, curiosity on his face. "That amazes me."

"Why?"

"Every time you open your mouth, you remind everyone you're from the South. Why do you stay here?"

She stuffed her hands into her pockets, smiling. "This is home for me now. I like it better than the hot, sticky summers in Mississippi."

"Where do you spend your summers now?"

Flinging out a hand in a pose she had seen in *Harper's Bazar,* she said, "Why, Mr. Lassiter, I summer in Saratoga."

"And rub elbows with the rich?"

"Why not?"

"If you don't want to tell me the truth, I guess it's none of my business."

"I didn't mean it that way." Uneasily she looked at the frozen river. A tight band encased her chest, centering around her heart. Other people had asked the same questions, and she had managed to laugh the answers aside. She should have guessed Adam would not be distracted as easily.

"How did you mean it?"

"As a joke."

He took her hand and brought her to face him. A wry grin was visible beneath his frosted mustache. "That I knew. I just wondered why you never answer a question about anything beyond the cookhouse."

"Maybe because there's nothing exciting about my life beyond the cookhouse."

"No flirtations? No lovers?"

She laughed. "Can you imagine an adoring swain who would allow his lady fair to disappear into the north woods for months with a hundred brawny lumberjacks?"

"How about your folks? What do they think of your job?"

Gypsy fought to keep her face from revealing her grief. She knew she had failed when he drew her down to sit on a fallen tree.

"I'm sorry," he said quietly as he slanted his crutch across another tree. "That was the wrong question, wasn't it?"

"No, it's all right," she whispered. "My parents died a few years ago. It still hurts to think about that."

"A few years ago? About the time you came here?"

"I had no reason not to come here when Mr. Glenmark offered me a job."

"No brothers or sisters?"

"One sister." She stared down at her skirt and brushed flakes of snow from it. "She's happily married, and I didn't want to be the spinster who's just in everyone's way." This was not going at all as she had hoped. Instead of satisfying her curiosity about him, she was answering his questions. Raising her chin, she said, ''I have a respectable position. Undoubtedly it would be different if I worked at the Porcelain Feather Saloon.''

''Undoubtedly.''

Before he could continue, Gypsy asked, ''And where do you go when you're away from Michigan?''

''Besides Saratoga?'' He sent a stone skidding across the ice. When it slid to a stop near the middle of the frozen river, he said, ''Different places. Wherever my work takes me. I like to see different parts of the country.''

''What place did you like best?'' She had to keep the conversation going. Maybe he would divulge more about himself.

He leaned his arm behind her. Even though the waning sunlight added to the chill, the mere brush of his sleeve against the back of her coat sent fiery delight along her. She did not move as he raised his other hand and swept it across the sky as if building a scene from his imagination.

''San Francisco,'' he answered. ''I loved the hills and the sea and the bay and all the excitement of a city coming to life.'' His fingertip brushed her cheek, bringing her face toward his. ''You'd love it there, too, Gypsy. Instead of staying up day and night to cook for these jacks, you could be dancing and gambling and playing host to the city's rich.''

''Not my idea of fun.'' She wanted to lower her eyes, but she could not keep from staring at his lips as he spoke.

''But it's a lot like Saratoga.'' His hand glided up her back, and his mustache brushed her mouth when he leaned toward her to whisper, ''We could have fun there together.''

With a soft groan, she turned away before he could tempt her with another soul-sapping kiss. She was finding out nothing but how much she wanted to be in his arms. She clasped her hands in her lap and fought to keep her voice even as she asked, ''Which place did you like least?''

His smile faded. "South to fight in the war."

She bit back her gasp as pain tightened his face. Pressing her hand over her stomach, which twisted like a branch in a high wind, she realized if she had met Adam Lassiter then, he would have been one of the enemy. She easily could imagine him in a kepi cap only a few shades darker than his deep blue eyes. Whether he had worn the shoulder straps of an officer or the stripes of an enlisted man, he had been a Yankee.

"I don't want to talk about it," he continued.

She nodded, for once eager to agree with him. She did not want to talk about that horrible time when hunger and death had stalked the street in front of her house.

She whispered, "Now it's my turn to apologize."

"Nothing to apologize for." He pushed himself to his feet. Draping one arm over the crutch, he jammed his hands into his pockets. "You weren't shooting at us." A sudden smile tore the anguish from his face. "After working for you this week, I know you'd never let a man die so quickly and easily."

She shivered and lowered her eyes. At his laugh, she looked up to discover his grin.

He tapped her nose as he asked, "Cold?"

"Not very."

"You're shivering. Someone step on your grave?"

With a gasp of horror, she stood. He caught her arm, holding her easily even though he was balanced on his crutch.

"Let me go!" she cried.

"Whoa! What's wrong with you?"

"How could you say something like that?"

"Something like what?" His raven brows dipped toward each other. "What's wrong with you? All I said was—"

"Don't say it again!"

He swayed as she tried to pull away, but refused to release her. "It's just a saying my grandmother used to use. I didn't mean to upset you."

"I know. It's just all this talk of the war and dying and . . . I'm sorry, Adam."

"Me, too." He gave her a lopsided grin. "At least we aren't arguing."

"I think I'd rather argue with you."

"Are those our only choices?" His fingers stroked hers as his sapphire eyes glowed.

She frowned. "What do you mean?"

Chuckling, he said, "You may be satisfied with just those two choices, but I'm not."

She could have walked away before his lips brushed her cheek. As slow as he was with the crutch, he would be unable to catch her. But she did not pull away. She wanted a moment more of his bewitching gaze holding her in an invisible embrace.

When a smile tilted one corner of his ragged mustache, her pulse throbbed through her at the speed of her rapid breath. She gasped when his hand settled on her waist. The slightest pressure from his fingers leaned her toward him.

As she touched the firm breadth of his shoulder, she was sure lightning had riveted her. Fire raced along her skin, setting every inch of her ablaze. He tugged her more tightly to him. His mustache was cold against her face, but his lips scorched her mouth. Like his words, his kiss teased her. As his tongue savored the shadowed secrets of her mouth, her arms slipped around his neck. She let the strength of his arm cradle her.

A soft moan escaped her lips as his mouth pressed against the pulse on her neck. When he spoke, the caress of his words sent a tremor to her very toes.

"Can you be satisfied with less than this, honey?"

Her fingers curled on his strong back as she whispered, "This is crazy."

"Yes, it is." He etched her skin with the sparks of his kisses, following the ribbons of her bonnet to the very center of her throat. Decorating her chin with the same luscious flame, he murmured against her lips, "It's crazy to think *I* could be satisfied with just this."

He silenced her question with his mouth over hers. Demanding, his lips pressed into hers as he leaned her back against his arm, his fingers tangling in her hair and loosening it. The strands drifted across his hand.

With a frayed gasp, she pulled away. She jabbed her hair back under her bonnet and stared up at him in dismay. "We can't—I mean, we shouldn't—"

He smiled as he brushed her cheek with a crooked finger. "Probably not."

"I don't know you very well."

"You could know me very, very well."

She shook her head, trying to free herself from the web of his silken voice and his touch as dangerous as a spider's venom. "I told you, I don't—"

"Sleep with any of the jacks." Adam chuckled when that appealing blush slapped her cheeks again. She could speak so plainly about anything but her own passions. "I heard you the first time you said that."

"I never said *that.*"

"No, you were much more ladylike."

"One of us has to have good manners." She gathered her coat more closely to her as she stepped back.

He wanted to tell her that was a mistake, because the black wool was pulled tautly across her breasts. He bit back the words, choosing ones that were almost the truth. "I was just checking something out."

"And what would that be?"

"To find out if my kiss is what's made you so skittish all week."

"Don't flatter yourself."

He closed the distance between them in a single step, seizing her hand before she could flee. As the setting sun splashed scarlet across her face, he saw fury in her eyes—fury and something else that was most certainly not pleasure. He hoped it was not fear. What could be frightening

Gypsy here, so far from anywhere? The answer might be the very one he needed.

"I'm not flattering myself." When her eyes grew wide at his suddenly somber tone, he added, "You like kissing me."

Her hand striking his cheek shocked him as much as it did her, if he were to judge by how all color fled from her face. He let her hand slip out of his and watched as she took another step back.

"Adam, I—I'm sorry. I've never slapped anyone in my whole life."

"Don't apologize." He rubbed his cheek and arched a brow. "I suspect I deserved that and more." With his finger, he tipped up her chin. "What's got you as nervous as a cat in a kennel? If it's not me, then what?"

"I have no idea what you're talking about."

"You don't lie very well." Laughing, he sat back on the log again. Somewhere in the distance, the sound of tinny bells rang through the afternoon. "Don't get all huffy, Gypsy. If you want to be treated like one of the jacks, then stop acting like the wounded heroine out of a dime novel."

She smiled. "And you should stop acting like a burlesque villain."

"I thought I was doing a good job as the hero."

"I don't need a hero."

"You do if you're in trouble."

She started to speak, but said nothing as she walked closer to the river. Prying a small stone from the snow, she tossed it at the one he had thrown onto the ice. It hit the first stone easily, sending them both toward the far shore. She faced him and said, "I can do things for myself. I don't need a—"

Adam leaped from where he was sitting as the sound of bells exploded through the clearing. Hoofbeats and a man's shout rang in his ears.

He wrapped his arms around Gypsy's waist and propelled them both onto the frozen river. Her startled cry drowned out another feminine screech.

As they hit the ice, her breath burst from her in a painful gasp.

He sat before they had stopped sliding and gathered her up in his arms. "Gypsy, are you all right?"

"I'm not sure." She blinked as if she could not bring his face into focus. Suddenly her lips became a straight line. "You're crazy! Why did you knock me off my feet?"

He was tempted to tell her she would not let him *sweep* her off her feet, but he looked over his shoulder. "No matter what you say, honey, you do need a hero once in a while."

Gypsy clenched the front of Adam's coat as she followed his gaze to where a sled was stopping farther along the riverbank. The tracks of the runners ran over where she had been standing. If he had not pushed her aside, she might have been hit.

"Who's driving like a madman?" she gasped, scrambling to her feet. The jacks knew the rules. No racing near the camp. Farley would send this fool down the hay trail for being so witless. If—

She groaned when she heard a familiar voice call, "Gypsy? Are you there?"

"Farley!" Adam muttered as he tried to stand. He fell back to the ice, his cast clunking hollowly on it.

Crossing the ice and jumping up onto the bank, Gypsy demanded, "What in hell did you think you were doing driving like that?"

Farley looked back at the sled. "Gypsy, watch your language."

She wanted to groan again. His warning meant only one thing, the very thing she should have guessed. Rose Quinlan must be in the sled, and Farley must have been showing off for his mistress.

Picking up the crutch, she tossed it to Adam. "Are you out of your mind, Farley?"

He held out a hand to assist Adam back up onto the bank.

Adam disdained it and clambered up to stand beside Gypsy. Putting his hand on her shoulder, he asked, "Are you sure you aren't hurt?"

"I'm fine. You?"

Instead of answering her, he turned to Farley. The camp manager almost cowered when Adam demanded, "What would you have done if you had run her down, Farley? How would you have explained to Glenmark that you'd killed his kingbee cook?"

"Kill?" she gasped. She looked from Adam's anger to Farley's dismay. Had this been more than just an accident? The threatening letter had said death would overtake her and someone she loved by an icy river. Hadn't it? She could not remember the exact words. No! She would not be terrified by someone's idea of a bad joke.

"Look, Lassiter, you keep your nose out of this!" Farley jutted his chin out. "If—"

"Calvin dearest," murmured a squeaky voice, "do remember your manners."

Gypsy grimaced when Rose Quinlan slipped her arm possessively through Farley's. Beneath her fur-lined cape, her fashionable gown of a green the color of pine needles had a short coat that clung to her while the slender skirt followed the lines of her trim body. Each step revealed a hint of the lacy petticoat she wore below her tightly corseted waist. With the small hat set at a rakish angle on her upswept blond curls, Rose displayed the wealth showered on her by her besotted paramour.

"How do you do, Mr.—" She giggled childishly. "Is it Mr. Lassiter?" She held out her hand to Adam.

"Yes, miss." Taking her hand, he bowed over it with a grace Gypsy was surprised he could manage while on his crutch.

"I saw what you did to save Gypsy." Her nose wrinkled as if speaking Gypsy's name sullied her in some way. A brilliant smile tilted her lips again. "You are so very brave."

"I was fortunate to be able to help."

"Think what would have happened if you had not been here." A fragile shudder barely moved her shoulders. "I quiver at the thought." Fluttering her eyelashes, she asked, "Are you new here, Mr. Lassiter? I'm sure I haven't seen you before."

Gypsy watched Farley's eyes become dark slits when Adam continued to hold Rose's hand. She was torn between wanting to laugh at the camp manager's obvious jealousy and her own irritation that Adam would kiss her one minute and flirt with Rose the next.

Her elbow was scraped, and her head ached from where she had hit it on the ice. That must be why she was having such silly thoughts about the threatening note and being bothered that Adam *still* held Rose's hand.

Farley plucked Rose's fingers out of Adam's. Gruffly he said, "If no one is hurt, we'll be on our way. It'll be dark soon."

"I'll see Gypsy gets home safely," Adam called as Farley lifted his mistress back into the sled. "No need for you to bother."

The camp manager's back stiffened. His mouth worked angrily as Rose waved and said, "How kind of you, Mr. Lassiter. I'm certain I shall see you again about the camp."

"Not if I have any choice in the matter," Adam murmured, stepping back as Farley turned the sled toward the logging road. Even before it was out of sight, he asked, "Can you walk back to the cookhouse, Gypsy?"

"Are you going to carry me if I can't?"

"I could try."

"And we'd end up in a snowbank." When he frowned, she hurried to add, "Thanks for saving me from Farley's driving."

"Now you owe me a favor." He brushed snow and ice off his denims. Raising his gaze to lock with hers, he said, "And I intend to collect right away."

"Adam . . ." She wanted to tell him they should not compound one mistake of nearly losing themselves in a feverish kiss by falling victim to pleasure once more. She liked Adam. He was brash, a bit arrogant, and his kisses drained her of every thought but desire.

But she had learned what happened to those she cared about. Too many had died, leaving her with little but grief and this life far from home. She would not let someone else get hurt.

Her sister had called her a fool, telling her not to let coincidence ruin her life. Gypsy had been ready to agree, until the threatening note resurrected all her fears. If she even considered falling in love with Adam, she would be doubly foolish—first for letting herself be seduced by his quick wit and quicksilver touch; second for putting him in what might be deadly danger.

Adam grinned, warning her that, for once, he had not gauged the course of her thoughts. "Don't worry, Gypsy. You'll be happy to repay this favor. I saved you. Now I need you to save me."

"From what?"

He hooked a thumb toward the logging road. "From that woman. I have a feeling once Rose Quinlan gets her fangs into a man, he doesn't get away until she sucks him dry."

"What a horrible thing to say!"

"But true."

Gypsy laughed as they began to walk back toward the cookhouse through the lengthening shadows. "Most definitely true. All right, Adam. I'll protect you from Rose Quinlan with my very life if necessary."

He grasped her arm and twisted her to face him. Again his mouth was taut. "I hope, Gypsy, it will never come to that."

"What do you mean?"

"With luck, you'll never have to know."

CHAPTER SIX

A week later, shivering in the stinging cold, Gypsy wrapped her arms around her thick coat and listened to the strange silence.

On Saturday nights, the camp was quieter than when the jacks were on the hill. No hammer struck the anvil at the iron burner's shop. The shouts from the carpenter's shop had vanished. She could hear nothing but the wind in the trees.

She made sure the lids were tightly closed on the garbage barrels. She did not want scavengers rifling through the trash. Raccoons and deer were bad enough, but open barrels would lure wolves and bears. When the camp closed in spring, one of the flunkeys would crack the barrels open, and the foragers would have all the rotten food cleared up before autumn.

Not that it mattered. She sighed as she walked from the trash dump to look at the somnolent camp, which glittered in the fresh snow drifting from the sky. This would be their last winter here. Next year, they would rebuild Glenmark Timber Company's camp on land surveyed by the timber cruisers last summer. North along the river, it eventually would become home.

For the jacks, but not for her. The letter warned her it was time to move on, to leave friendships behind. No one else must suffer because of her.

"Gypsy? Gypsy, are you about?"

Rounding the end of the cookhouse, she gasped at the sight of Adam sitting on the sled the flunkeys used to take lunch to the loggers. He wore his hat low over his ears, and the collar of his coat was turned up to protect him from the insidious wind. She waded through the knee-deep snow to where the horse whooshed and stamped its feet.

"What's this?" she asked.

He laughed and held out his gloved hand. When she placed hers on it, he brought her up to sit next to him. He patted the uncushioned seat. "This is a sled. That, in front of us, is a horse. Together they're the way for a too dedicated lady to take a spin about town with the most charming gentleman in the cookhouse of Glenmark Timber Company."

When he raised the reins, she asked, "Aren't we going to wait for him?"

"Him? Who?"

She flashed him a smile as she smoothed her dark skirt over her knees and cooed, "Why, the most charming man in my kitchen, Mr. Lassiter. I'm looking forward to meeting this paragon."

He captured her hand in his, and his gaze held hers as he lifted her fingers to his mouth. The brush of his mustache caressed her through her gloves.

"What are you doing?" she gasped.

"You don't know? You really do need a night off, Gypsy, if you can't recognize when a man's kissing your hand. Or do you allow that only when you summer in Saratoga?"

When she drew her fingers away, he let them slip slowly through his. "I know quite well what you're doing. I just wonder if you remember I'm your boss—in the cookhouse or out of it.''

"And what does that mean?"

"It means I'd like to be invited before you assume I want to go with you."

Instead of answering, he slapped the reins on the horse. The sled's runners whistled an excited tune against the icy road. "That has nothing to do with your being my boss. That has to do with your being Gypsy.'' He grinned. "However, once again, you are correct.''

"It's about time you admitted it."

"So I guess I should ask if you want to go out for an evening on the town.''

Laughing, she relaxed. She could not stay vexed at him, even though she should. "Hank has the stove watch, so I suppose I should agree."

"It would be a good idea at this point."

"Whatever gave you the idea of a sled ride tonight?"

"I saw how you looked at Miss Quinlan when Farley took her for a ride.''

"How was that?" She was glad the darkness hid her face; she did not want him to see her amazement. She had thought Adam was the one staring at Rose Quinlan.

He chuckled. "I've seen envy before. I figured you weren't envious of her silly hat or the fact she was with Farley.''

"Certainly not."

"So it had to be the sled. I thought you wanted to go for a ride.'' He rested back against the wooden seat and balanced his heavy cast on the low dash. "At least, I hope that was it. I had to promise Seger that I'd take good care of the sled and the horse. I was sure he'd want a cup of blood in exchange.''

"Not a pound of flesh?"

He cocked a single eyebrow at her. "Shakespeare? Who else wasted their youth on a classical education?"

"I don't consider it a waste." She peered along the road. "Where are we going?"

"I told you. For a spin about town."

Again she laughed. "That would be possible only if we had a town to spin about." When she leaned back against the seat, she flinched as his hand curved around her shoulder.

"You can trust me," he murmured. The icy road glistened in the sparse light.

"Can I?"

"Sure." He grinned before looking back at the road again. "If I rile you, Gypsy, you can send me walking."

When his fingers drifted along her arm with the warmth of spring, she remained silent. Soft snowflakes floated around them in a silent waltz, and she wanted to enjoy the rare chance to escape from the demands of the cook shack. It was easier to admit that than to imagine how wonderful it would be to lean her head against his shoulder.

When lights appeared ahead of them, Gypsy was not surprised. There was only one road out of camp and only one building along it. She had passed it a few times in daylight, when the building looked deserted. That had all changed with sunset on a Saturday night.

Lanterns glowed on a sign proclaiming this the Porcelain Feather Saloon. Tinny music and the low rumble of voices oozed through every chink in the walls. The snow had been trampled by heavy boots. Men congregated near the door, talking and tipping back bottles.

Gypsy stiffened when Adam pulled back on the reins. She gasped, "We're stopping here?"

"Why not?" He reached to kick the brake and scowled when he had to stretch to push it with his right foot. "If you don't want to go in, we don't have to. I thought we'd have a drink."

"A drink?" she repeated in a choked voice.

"Why not?" he asked again. A smile inched across his lips as his arm slipped around her waist. "Unless you'd rather . . ."

She squared her shoulders. She was no innocent child

frightened by the raw side of life. She had heard all kinds of tales about what went on here. Some of the stories might be true, although the lumberjacks could be trusted to exaggerate everything.

"A drink would be fine, as long as it's not rotgut," she answered.

"Rotgut?" He slid off the seat and reached up to help her. "Where did a fine lady like you learn words like that? Certainly not in Saratoga."

She grimaced. "I'm sorry I ever mentioned that place."

"Let's go inside."

His broad hands easily lifted her from the seat. When her feet settled into the snow, she was aware of the men watching them. Soon, every logger would know Gypsy Elliott had arrived at the Porcelain Feather Saloon in the company of her newest flunkey.

She should jump back onto the sled and head home to the cook shack. Her feet refused to listen to good sense. Her hands were just as rebellious as they remained on Adam's shoulders while she gazed up into his eyes. When his fingers glided around her waist, hers explored the breadth of his shoulders. He pulled her to him, and she gasped at the pressure of his strong legs against her skirt.

"Let's go inside," he repeated in a low whisper. "You're going to freeze if you stay out here. You're shivering as if you're ready to come apart."

"Yes, let's go in," she answered, although she could not imagine freezing when she stood in his arms.

As she walked with him toward the saloon, she nodded to the men by the flamboyantly lit door and pretended not to see their astonishment.

" 'Evening, boys," Adam said.

The jacks just stared.

When Adam opened the door, cigar smoke smothered Gypsy. Blinking, she brushed it aside. Her eyes widened.

A woman sat on a counter near the entrance, her freckled skin bared by the scandalous neckline of her gown. Her chubby knees, dimpled above rolled down stockings, were visible beneath her kilted dress. Gypsy had never seen the owner of the Porcelain Feather Saloon, but she knew the black-haired woman in the outrageous emerald green dress must be Nissa Jensen. The flunkeys had talked many times about Nissa's wide cigar.

Not that Nissa was homely. Her round face was apple cheeked as she smiled brazenly and winked at Adam. Her mouth became as round as her eyes when she stared at Gypsy. Gypsy looked past her to see tables scattered in front of the long bar that took up the whole back wall.

Nissa jumped down. Tugging her gown over her full hips, she grinned. "I'll be, Adam. You convinced her to come. I should have guessed a looker like you would be able to twist any gal's heart, even Gypsy Elliott's." Without giving him a chance to reply, she went on. "It's about time you stopped by, Gypsy."

"It's nice to meet you," Gypsy replied, not sure what else to say.

"You're lying, and we both know it, but it's nice to meet you, too." Nissa's infectious grin broadened to reveal a pair of gold teeth. "That ain't a lie. Whatever else my life offers, I don't have to hide behind propriety."

Gypsy smiled. "You don't seem to be hiding much here."

"Not on the floor," she said as she yanked on the shoulder of her dress to let it fall farther down her pudgy arm. Again she winked at Adam. "In the cribs, the gals get used to lying in a man's ear while they're lying in his arms. Right, laddie?"

Heat warned Gypsy she was blushing. Before Adam had burst into her life, she had not blushed in years. Coming to the Porcelain Feather had been a mistake. She should leave right away.

She gasped as Nissa linked arms with her. "C'mon, Gypsy. Let me show you around the place."

"I don't think that's a good idea."

"Scared we'll ruffle your sensibilities?"

Gypsy was about to reply when her eyes were caught

by Adam's amusement. He must have set this up. Nissa had not been surprised Gypsy was here, only that Adam had persuaded her to come.

"What few sensibilities I have left after my years in the north woods don't ruffle easily." Gypsy arched a brow in Adam's direction.

"Good girl," Nissa crowed. "C'mon." Over her shoulder, she added, "Come along, Adam. Let's see what entertainment we can find for your Gypsy. We ain't used to the jacks bringing their own gals with them. This should be fun."

Fun was the last word Gypsy would have chosen. As she stepped beneath the ring of lanterns, she understood a beast's fear when it was caught in one of the traps set by the jacks. As Nissa chattered, she led Gypsy on a sinuous path between the tables, which were cramped with men.

A pain-filled screech froze Gypsy in midstep. She scanned the room, sure someone was strangling a woman.

"Don't look like that, Gypsy." Pointing toward the end of the bar, Nissa said, "That's just Lolly. Lolly Yerkes. Fortunately the loggers like looking at her enough to put up with her singing."

Gypsy stared at the blonde, who wore a short wrapper. The singer stood with her foot on a bottle so the men had a view of her silk stockings topped by a lacy garter. Waving her hands like an opera diva, she continued to make that horrid sound. Cheers met every trill.

Laughter came from behind Gypsy. When she glanced back, she gasped. Where was Adam? Blast him for bringing her here and leaving her with Nissa!

Her flush of fury vanished. It must be almost impossible to maneuver through the crowd with his crutch.

But where was he? She searched the room. Every male face was familiar. She was astonished to see Chauncey Lewis, the camp's inkslinger, with the young blond singer perched on his knee.

He was not the only man with a woman draped over

him. Peabody should know better than to cavort with some whore while his wife was at his farm raising his six children alone.

Where was Adam? Once she found him, she would leave. This was no place for her. The jacks were going to be embarrassed to see her here. Farley would be furious if this upset the men. Not that she was worried about his sending her on the hay trail, but if Daniel heard about this . . .

"Nissa, I think—"

"Lost Adam, haven't we?" gushed Nissa. "Go on over to the bar, Gypsy, and I'll round up your gentleman. Have yourself a drink on the house."

"Thank you."

Nissa grinned. "Don't thank me, dearie. This should make for an interesting evening." She vanished into the crowd.

Knowing it was useless to try to find Adam in the packed room, Gypsy turned to the rough bar. It was crowded, but her elbow in the back of a logger gained her enough room to fold her hands on the scarred top. Posters of half-dressed women were nailed to the wall behind a vast collection of whiskey bottles. A keg of beer sat to one side, a damp spot on the floor where the foam had spilled over the rims of the tin mugs.

"Gypsy!"

She glanced over her shoulder, not surprised to see Oscar when she heard his voice break. Smiling, she asked, "Is it always this crowded?"

"Yes, ma'am." He blushed to his roots and fled.

"Ma'am?" she repeated. He always called her Gypsy. This *was* going to cause all kinds of trouble.

"What'll you have?" The burly bartender must have noticed she had no drink.

Glancing at the whiskey the men were downing as if it tasted as good as her apple pie, she said, "Nothing, thank you."

"Then move away." His tiny eyes nearly popped from

his head. "What are you doing here? Ain't no place for a woman who don't work here."

Wanting to agree, Gypsy pushed through the crowd. There was scarcely room for twenty people in the room, and more than three times that number must be packed into it. Every breath she took was flavored with sweat and whiskey. Finding Adam among this press of flesh wrapped in stinking wool might be impossible, even for Nissa.

An arm slithered around her, and she tried to pull away. It clamped tightly to her, tugging her against a hard body. Bold fingers settled on her waist.

"Well, well, little lady, don't think I've seen you about afore. What do you say to finding a place to get better acquainted? I—" The man choked as if he had swallowed his drink the wrong way. "Gypsy!"

She pulled away and said coldly, "Good evening, Benson."

His face became as red as the coals in the blacksmith's shop. Shocked that she had seen two jacks blush tonight, she left him stuttering. She had to get out of here. Now!

She elbowed through the crowd. The men let her pass, but their amazed gazes pierced her. She had learned a lesson tonight. Listening to Adam was a sure way to find herself neck-deep in trouble.

Another hand grabbed her arm. Trying to shake it off, she snapped, "I've got nothing for sale tonight."

"For free then?"

"Adam!"

He grinned as he folded his arms on top of his crutch. "Where did you go?"

"Where I went isn't as important as where I'm going."

"At least let's have a drink, Gypsy. It's a long, cold ride to camp. I'd like something to warm my belly for the trip back."

"That's not a good idea. I'm making the jacks uncomfortable."

"Gypsy—"

"Let her go," answered a high-pitched voice.

Gypsy stared at the woman who slunk around Adam and leaned one bare arm on his crutch. It was Lolly, the woman who had been screeching on stage. Beneath her short wrapper, her bright garter rubbed against Adam's leg in an open invitation.

Lolly ran her fingers along his arm and whispered, "Let your kingbee cook go. I'll show you some real heat in the kitchen."

Adam brushed her fingers off and looked at Gypsy. When he saw her trying to hide a smile, he wondered if he would ever understand her. One minute, she was fleeing from the saloon as if the devil were on her tail. The next, she was ready to laugh at Lolly.

"You warned me about kitchen skills, Gypsy," he said with a chuckle. To Lolly, he added, "Not tonight, darling." As he reached for Gypsy's hand, the blonde stepped between them. He frowned. "Lolly, I said I'm not interested."

"Maybe you're no man after all. She'll never do anything for you. Cold as a Michigan winter, she is."

Gypsy said quietly, "Mr. Lassiter said he wasn't interested. Why don't you crawl away and bother someone else?"

"Why don't you get out of here?" Lolly's voice rose to a screech. "We don't want your type here."

"And what type is that? Decent? Hardworking?"

"Watch it, Gypsy," Adam warned as he drew her back from Lolly. "Let's go."

"And I was beginning to have fun," she said with a chuckle.

"Just be care—"

He swore as Gypsy was spun away. She screamed when Lolly clawed at her. Shouts erupted all over the room. He reached out to keep Lolly from hurting Gypsy, and ducked when a fist came at him.

No, not at him. Lolly rocked back and collapsed into

a pile at his feet. Looking past her, he saw Gypsy shaking her hand and rubbing her knuckles.

"Nice hit," he said.

"Couldn't have done better myself," Nissa said, shoving her way through the clump of men.

Gypsy blinked, glancing from Lolly to Adam's grin to the astonishment on the jacks' faces. What was she doing? She had never been in a saloon brawl. This was insane!

Embarrassment flooded through her when she saw how fury tightened Peabody's lips. Chauncey grumbled something to Bert.

Nissa flung her arm around Gypsy's shoulders. "You all right, dearie?" Her chuckle rumbled around the stub of her cigar. Tapping ashes onto the floor next to Lolly, she waved the cigar at the men. "Show's over, boys. Drink up a round on me."

Cheers met her words, and the men surged almost as one toward the bar. Nissa signaled to two of her women. They came to wake Lolly.

Peabody did not go to the bar. "Gypsy, are you crazy? You shouldn't be here."

"I did—"

Stepping between her and the irate bull of the woods, Adam said, "I brought her. If you've got a problem, talk to me."

"You both should have known better."

Wagging her finger, Nissa chided, "Simmer down. Gypsy did just fine without you butting in like two old goats." She patted Gypsy's arm. "C'mon. You need a drink. Might put some color back into your cheeks."

Gypsy shook her head. "No, thank you. I'm going home."

"Just when the fun's begun?"

Pushing her hair back under her bonnet, she retied the ribbons. "For me, the fun's over."

Laughter twinkled in Adam's eyes as he offered his arm. Too low for anyone else to hear, he said, "I didn't think when I asked you to go for a spin that you'd leave Lolly with a spinning head."

She groaned. "I can't believe I hit her."

"Looks as if you had experience."

"My brother taught me to defend myself." She opened the door, but faltered as the wind buffeted her. She usually did not go out after dark in order to avoid this bone-numbing cold. When Adam pulled her collar up around her ears, she smiled.

"The Porcelain Feather Saloon isn't quite what you expected, is it?" he asked.

"It's everything I expected. This was one time the jacks didn't have to exaggerate."

Entwining his gloved fingers with hers, he said nothing. She raised her gaze to meet the honesty in his blue eyes, which were as warm and bottomless as a summer pond. The noise from the saloon muted to a whisper as he lifted her hand to his lips. The soft caress of his mustache sent a mesmerizing stream of fire through her as his lips teased her fingers with a brief, questioning kiss.

"Adam," she whispered.

"Yes?"

"This isn't the place."

He smiled. "My dear Gypsy, this is indeed the place. A quick word to Nissa and a coin, and we could have any crib for a delightful tryst."

She jerked her hand away and stamped toward the sled. His laughter added to her fury, but she was angry at herself. When was she going to learn?

"Are you planning on charging all the way back to camp?" He laughed.

"There's no need for your evening to end. I can walk back."

"Alone?"

At his amazement, she faced him. His mustache was already white with his frozen breath, but his eyes burned as hotly as the stove.

"Who would hurt me here?" she asked. "Other than Lolly."

He did not laugh.

"What are you suggesting?" His silence unnerved her. "None of the jacks would hurt me."

"No?"

"No! Don't try to scare me just so you can . . ."

Adam shoved his crutch under his arm and followed her through the softly falling snow. "Scaring you just so I could take you back to camp was not my primary intention. Didn't you want honesty?"

"Yes, but why are you trying to frighten me?"

"So you'll know that just because these men work with you doesn't mean you can trust them."

Gypsy pressed her hand over her heart, which she feared had forgotten how to beat. If Adam even had a suspicion of the truth . . . no, he could not. She had burned the letter.

"Don't be silly," she chided, hoping he did not hear the tremor in her voice. "No one wants to hurt me."

His gaze, now as cold as the wind, raked along her, and she longed to pull back into the shadows. "These men might respect you, Gypsy, but they can't ignore that you're an incredibly lovely woman. Glenmark was an idiot to send you up here to be a temptation to his men."

"I'm tired of listening to this nonsense. Why don't you go back to the saloon and give all the boys a good laugh?"

His crutch whipped in front of her. Using it like a shepherd's crook, he herded her to him. He did not touch her as he bent to whisper in her ear, "Don't be blind to the darker side of a man's soul, Gypsy. I can't be the only man who looks at your soft lips and hungers to taste them."

An involuntary shiver coursed through her. His fingers settled on her shoulder, stroking her arm in a sinuous invitation. She put her hand over his and closed her eyes as his finger grazed her cheek and swept along her lips.

"So soft your lips are." His velvety tone whipped her

heart to a frantic beat. "Even when they snap at me, I want them on me."

The cold scoured the heat from her face, but did not lessen the fever within her. Snow caught on her eyelashes and whitened her coat as he stepped away to climb onto the sled. He brushed snow off the seat and held out his hand to her. Silent, she watched her fingers rise to touch his.

He drew her up beside him. Slipping her arm through his, he reached for the reins and turned the sled into the night.

The voices and music from the tavern followed them only a short distance into the forest. The metallic song of the runners was nearly lost beneath the clump of the horse's hoofs on the packed snow. With snow whitening the tired drifts, the night closed around them.

Adam said quietly, "You might not have enjoyed the evening, but Nissa did."

"More than Lolly."

"Do I owe you a thank-you for defending my honor?"

With a laugh, she retorted, "I suspect I'm too late to save your honor, Adam."

"Undoubtedly."

She did not move away when his arm curved around her shoulders. The gentle pressure against her sleeve teased her to lean against him as she stared at the spiral of snowflakes. Even his thick coat could not soften the hard muscles of his shoulder.

Her muted heartbeat and the puff of their breaths in a soft, gray fog could not disturb the night's peace. It was as if nobody existed beyond the sled.

Adam pulled back on the reins and steered the sled up onto a shallow embankment.

Sitting straighter, Gypsy looked about in bafflement. "Why are you stopping? We're still half a mile from camp."

"Exactly." He wrapped the reins around the dash and propped his cast on the curved board. Facing her, he said,

"No one can hear us there. No one can hear us at Nissa's place. Maybe now you'll explain why you turned as gray as the snow when I said something about someone hurting you."

"You were threatening me."

"*I* wasn't threatening you." He took her hand and slowly closed it into a fist. "I've seen you take care of yourself. What are you afraid of?"

Reaching for the reins, she said, "You're making something out of nothing."

He caught her wrists in his wide hands. With a hushed laugh, he drew her fingers back. "Now, now, Gypsy, that's no attitude to take when I want to help you."

"By scaring me? You think that's helping me?"

"Helping you isn't the only thing I want," he whispered huskily. He pulled on her arms to tilt her toward him. His arm encircled her waist and drew her along the seat. When her leg touched his, she gasped. He laughed again. "See, Gypsy, it isn't the only thing you want, either."

"I'm glad you've become such an expert on my feelings tonight."

"I have no idea how you feel tonight," he whispered as his fingers tipped her face back so her gaze met his shadowed eyes, "but I sure would enjoy finding out."

His lips touched hers in a fleeting caress, then drew back. She moaned a protest. Her breath burst outward in a pleasured gasp as he recaptured her lips. Eagerly he explored each soft texture, warming the skin scraped by the cold. He cradled her against his arm to surround her with desire. As he tantalized the corners of her lips with his tongue, his gloved hand splayed along her back. Her fingers sought upward to twist through the sable strands drifting over his collar.

Fire burned on his lips as he boldly drew aside her scarf which closed her coat beneath her chin. She melted against him, wanting his skin against hers, relishing the warmth of his hair sifting over her hands. She wanted . . .

Gypsy groaned again as she tugged away. She snatched

the reins from the dash and slapped them on the back of the horse. The startled horse whinnied before dragging the sled onto the road. Without speaking, she shoved the reins into Adam's hands.

"I guess this means you don't appreciate my attempts to seduce you." He laughed with an iciness that matched the night air.

"It's too cold here."

Watching the rough road, which was crisscrossed with sled marks, he put his arm around her shoulders and drew her to him. "Do you mind if I insult you?"

"Do I have any choice?"

"None." His fingers brought her head onto his shoulder as he relaxed against the back of the seat. Laughter remained in his voice as he said, "When I first saw you, I was sure that, despite your assertions, you satisfied the jacks' hunger for things other than apple pie."

"That *is* insulting."

"You should consider it a compliment. I couldn't imagine why else you would be in this rough camp." His finger against her cheek steered her mouth toward his. Slowing the horse to a walk, he held the reins against the dash with his uninjured foot. The scratchy texture of his gloves grazed her face as he sampled her lips.

She whispered against his mouth, "Did you ever consider I might like this life?"

"Not then, but you're persuading me." Framing her face, he smiled, his eyes sparkling like freshly fallen snow. "You're persuading me there's a lot to like here."

His words gave her no warning of his lips' fervor when they found hers again. The light, teasing touch vanished. Demanding, insistent, titillating, his tongue traced her lips with molten honey. When she gasped, overwhelmed by swiftly blossoming desire, he sought deep in her mouth. She quivered in his arms, lost amid the uncontrollable yearning.

Her breath mingled with his, growing more swift. Boldly his fingers moved along her, leaving a trail of scintillating sparks in their wake. As his mouth delighted her neck, his hand stroked her leg through her thick skirts. Yearning to touch him, aching to be touched, she ran her fingers across the strength of his chest.

He raised his mouth from hers, and she stared at his lips, which she wanted against her again. Combing her fingers up through his hair, she guided his mouth to hers.

The sled bounced. Adam pulled away with a curse as he groped with one hand for the reins. Rocking against her, he shouted when the horse neighed with fright.

The sled tilted. Adam's arm tightened around her, and he shouted a warning. Gripping his coat, she tried to stay on the seat, but she was flung away, her shriek hanging frozen in the sky.

Snow billowed around Gypsy when she struck a surprisingly hard snow drift. A weight imprisoned her in the smothering flakes. Choking, she cried out when something heavy glanced off her leg. As pain careened through her, she wiggled her toes. She could not afford a broken leg, too.

She opened her eyes to see Adam intriguingly close to her. Her arms curved around him when she realized he was holding her down into the snow.

When he smiled, she whispered, "Is this what you meant when you offered to take me for a spin?"

"I just wanted to give you a night you wouldn't forget."

"You have."

"Tell me, Gypsy." He pushed her bonnet back. "Tell me you'll dream tonight of these kisses. Tell me you long for my mouth against you. Tell me, honey."

"I'd rather show you."

His laugh had a wicked tinge to it. Slowly, making each second a torment, his lips descended toward hers. She feared time had come to a halt as she waited for his kiss.

Suddenly he sat and waved. Gypsy struggled to hear past the pulse pounding in her ears. Anxious voices warned that some jacks on their way back to camp must have seen the sled tip over.

She smiled as she was helped to her feet. Assuring the men she was fine, she listened while they teased Adam about his poor driving. The men continued to joke while they righted the sled. She clasped her hands behind her back and made sure her smile remained in place.

Adam murmured with regret, ''We have to offer them a ride back to camp.''

''Of course.''

''How about another spin next Saturday night?''

''Adam . . .''

A shout from one of the jacks kept her from having to come up with a lie. While she had been in his arms, alone in the snowy night, she had been able to forget the horror lurking just beyond the trees. Or maybe even closer.

Tonight was precious, because she could not let it be repeated. She had to push Adam away. She knew too well what happened to everyone she cared about.

They died.

CHAPTER SEVEN

"Farley wants to speak with me," Adam said as Gypsy stepped aside to let Per lower the trapdoor to the root cellar beneath the kitchen.

Gypsy nodded. Concentrating as she counted the cups of sugar into the cookie dough, she asked no questions. When she did not hear the clatter of his crutch as he left, she glanced up to see he still stood behind her.

"Go ahead," she replied.

"Just wanted you to know where I was going to be."

"And you've told me. Go." She turned back to her work.

She knew Adam had expected things would be different after their visit to Nissa's Porcelain Feather Saloon. Things were different. She made sure she never was alone with him in the cramped cookhouse. Only that way could she maintain her control over her cook shack and herself.

The flunkeys exchanged uneasy glances whenever she cut short a conversation with Adam. She resisted explaining, for she could not forget the precarious position she had put herself in by listening to the longings of her heart.

Not only was she endangering herself, but Adam. Too many she cared for were now dead. Others had said it was just coincidence. She had tried to believe that, but it was better to put an end to it this way, she told herself over and over as she struggled to sleep.

But she couldn't sleep. She was afraid to dream of Adam holding her again. One magical night had altered her in ways she would have been unable to imagine before he drew her into his arms and against his lips.

"I'll be back soon, Gypsy."

She glanced away before her eyes could betray her yearning. "Hurry back so you can help us load the sled for lunch."

Adam swore under his breath. He reached for her, but paused. Embarrassing Gypsy in front of her crew would drive her farther from his arms.

Tossing his apron onto the bench, he went to the door. He should take his cue from her. He was here to do a job, not to enjoy a flirtation. If he had any sense, he would keep those few kisses as a pleasant memory, find himself a pretty girl down at Nissa's, and keep everything simple. That had been his style, and it had served him well.

His cast crashed against a barrel in front of the pegs where their coats hung. With a grumbled curse, he pulled his jacket on and went to see what problem Farley was going to add to his day. Only the truth would get Farley off his back, and he could not reveal that.

The wind coursed viciously around him as he opened the door. Leaping down into the latest storm, he smiled. Dealing with a suspicious Farley was easier than trying to break through the barrier Gypsy had raised.

He tucked his hands in his pockets and hobbled through the thick snow, which blew at him with the speed and ferocity of a minié ball. Hunching into his coat, he peered through the storm toward Farley's office. He could barely see it—not that it mattered. Farley had sent for him to come up to the house.

He did not like that at all. In the time he had been here,

Adam had not seen Farley do any business at his house, nor had he seen him do much in the office. It had not taken long to realize Peabody and Gypsy had their men so well trained that Farley was superfluous.

That was about the only thing he had found out. The jacks were glad to talk his ear off night and day, but they seldom said anything worth listening to. They bragged; they talked about work; they were wistful about their families waiting beyond the north woods.

None of that helped him. He had hoped he might find something out at the Porcelain Feather Saloon.

He smiled through the stinging snow. If Gypsy discovered he had had an ulterior motive for asking her to join him on that sled ride, she would be even more furious at him. He had not guessed when he took her there, hoping she would create a diversion, that she would knock Lolly off her feet in his defense.

Maybe he had been the one distracted. He had been too anxious to get Gypsy out of there and off somewhere secluded. He was not sure how much time he had to get this job completed, but every minute he spent thinking about Gypsy kept him from doing what he was supposed to and getting out of this icy misery.

The trees barely slowed the wind, and he was half frozen by the time he reached the house, set a quarter mile from the camp. Stamping the snow off his boot and more cautiously from the moccasin over his cast, he crossed the narrow porch to the front door. His eyes widened when he saw the etched glass oval set in it. A fancy door was an affectation here in the north woods where no one ever called on neighbors. There were no neighbors.

At Adam's knock, the door opened. The swish of rose silk and lavender perfume swept over him as Miss Quinlan said, "Mr. Lassiter, do come in before we both catch our deaths of cold."

"Thank you." He stepped inside, wondering why he

had not considered Farley might not answer the door himself.

"May I take your coat, Mr. Lassiter?"

"Thank you." Shrugging out of it, he added, "Let me hang it up. It's cold and not too clean."

Her laugh was as sharp as icicles breaking off the roof. "How wondrous to find a gentleman in this barbaric place! You aren't like the others who come here."

"Others?"

"The jacks my dear Calvin has come in to help maintain the house. You didn't think I cleaned this myself, did you?" She gave him no chance to answer as she swayed to a door on the right. "Do come and sit, Mr. Lassiter."

"I can wait for Mr. Farley here."

"Nonsense." She grabbed his sleeve. "He's shaving."

"At this hour?" he asked before he thought.

Miss Quinlan gave him a knowing smile before leading him into the parlor. Again his eyes grew wide.

The black maple parlor set with its matching marble-topped tables was complemented by a piano, which sat in one corner. He could not imagine how much it had cost to tote that piano all the way from Saginaw.

As his boot sank into the thick rug, he thought about the spartan quarters where the jacks slept on pine boughs. Gypsy's room was not much fancier, but here Rose Quinlan lived as well as if she were in Chicago or . . . he smiled. Or Saratoga.

Sitting gracefully on the settee, which was covered with pink brocade, Miss Quinlan purred, "Please join me, Mr. Lassiter."

He considered arguing his clothes were not meant for such delicate fabric, but he could tell by her narrowed eyes she would not accept no for an answer. Going to the sturdier-looking chair, he started to sit.

"No," Miss Quinlan chided, "I said please join me." She patted the cushion next to her. "Right here, Mr. Lassiter."

Adam almost laughed at his hesitation. He had not been

worried about a wrestling match on a parlor settee since before he left home for the first—and last—time. Then he had thought only of stealing a kiss instead of acting like a frightened virgin about to be set upon by a lascivious rogue.

He wiped his hands on his denims and held them up. Ashes and grease clung to his skin. ''I don't think you'll want me soiling your pretty furniture, Miss Quinlan.''

She rose with that hushed whisper of silk. Laughing, she said, ''You wear the badges of your work with pride.''

''I'm not sure *pride* is the proper word.''

''I see you're serving the jacks chocolate cake today.''

''How do you know that?''

''You have chocolate on your shirt.'' She reached out. When he stepped back, she smiled. ''I was just going to show you where.''

Adam returned her smile, but coolly. This woman was as subtle as the blades of a jack's saw. ''Really?''

''Yes, it's right here on your shirt.'' She slowly ran her hands over her right breast. ''Right here,'' she whispered.

He brushed his hand against his shirt, trying to ignore her candid invitation. No wonder Farley kept her up here away from the camp. If she toyed with every jack as she was with him, she would create all kinds of trouble.

''Thanks.''

Miss Quinlan's eyes widened at his gruff tone, but they narrowed again as she murmured, ''And I can see you've been making bread.'' She stepped closer and gazed up at him. ''I can just imagine your strong hands kneading that bread, massaging and shaping it—the softness beneath your palms as you hold it under you.''

This woman knew every trick to entice a man into her arms. He clasped his hands behind his back and smiled. ''To be honest, Miss Quinlan, the closest I've come to kneading bread is to watch Gypsy do it. Her hands—''

''Gypsy!'' Her voice became sharp.

''Gypsy is here?'' The question came from the hallway. Miss Quinlan's face altered again into a simpering smile as she rushed to Farley's side. Linking her fingers with his, she murmured, "Did you send for her, Calvin dear?"

"I sent for—" He straightened his false collar. "Oh, Lassiter, you're here. Don't just stand there. Come with me."

For once, Adam was glad to do as Farley ordered. He did not look back as he followed the camp manager to a small office behind the parlor. No need—Rose Quinlan's fury billowed around him like a cold wind.

Her animosity toward Gypsy was a surprise. Rose Quinlan was living in luxury here, doted upon by her lover, while Gypsy slaved day after day to keep the jacks fed and then retired each night to spartan quarters. As he closed the door to Farley's small office, he wondered if he finally had stumbled upon the clue he needed.

Cold burst into the kitchen, and Gypsy glanced up in surprise as the door struck the wall.

"Gypsy!" Bert's shout reverberated through the cook shack, freezing the flunkeys. The door slammed shut. He reeled to where she was spooning cookie dough onto long sheets. Panting, he leaned on the table.

"What is it?"

"Accident on the 'ill! It's—it's—"

Gypsy clutched her hand to her chest, wondering if she could force her breath to escape. It burst out in a spurt of coughs. She waved aside Bert's offer of assistance as she grabbed a cup of tea and downed a mouthful.

"I'm fine." That was a lie, but it did not matter. "Who?"

"Green'orn. Worth." Through his beard, he choked out, "Tree toppled on 'im. Peabody's all adither up there. 'E sent a message. 'E needs 'elp. What can we do?"

Gypsy snapped out of her horror to order, "Pack what food is ready for lunch. Bert, get the sled." She did not wait to see if the flunkeys would obey. She knew they would.

She pulled out the large canisters for the coffee and poured what was ready into them, then filled the rest with tea.

Her crew worked in silent perfection. She wondered why she had let Farley insist that Adam work in the kitchen. Things ran more smoothly without his cast clunking about. Later she should demand Adam be given a different job.

She should, but she would not.

Adam was not the problem. Her reaction to him was. If she could treat him like the other men, the situation would right itself in no time. A stolen kiss or two or even more in the midst of a gentle snowfall should not make her falter in her job.

Pushing the troubling thought aside, she fished a key out of a buttoned pocket in her skirt and unlocked the cupboard behind her bedroom door. She lifted out three bottles and relatched the cabinet. Although she had put the bottles in there at the beginning of the logging season, she had hoped no emergency would require her to get them out. No one spoke as she came back into the kitchen. She poured the whiskey into the canisters holding coffee and twisted on the lids.

She frowned when she saw the small amount of food on the table. They had finished washing the breakfast dishes less than an hour before. No one had guessed they would need food so quickly and under such horrible circumstances.

Pulling her coat over her shoulders, she rammed her hands into the sleeves even as she was lifting a canister. Per did not bother to put on his jacket as he picked up the box of sandwiches. As he followed her, he was silent.

Like a parade of ants, they carried the food to the sled. The men listened to her instructions and obeyed without comment. Wishing she could let someone else think in the midst of the numbing pain, she tried to concentrate on what must be done to help Peabody and his crew.

A shadow draped over Gypsy as she adjusted the boxes

so they would not tip off. She did not need to turn around. With a sense she could not name, she knew Adam stood behind her. She longed to throw herself in his arms and forget all this in his kisses.

She could not. She could not give in to her grief now, not when Peabody and his men were depending on her.

"Gypsy . . ."

The tenderness Adam put into her name nearly undid her. Blinking back tears, she used irritation to conceal her despair. "Either step aside or help me."

"What's happened?" When she explained, he said, "Coffee won't do much good."

She walked back toward the kitchen. "It'll help when it's laced with whiskey."

"Gypsy, you know Farley's rule about alcohol in camp."

"Don't quote regulations to me." She lifted two more of the canisters from the table. Stamping past him, she shouted, "I reckon a little whiskey for medicinal purposes won't break any rule."

Adam cursed as he tried to keep pace with her, hating the cast that slowed him down. "Have you sent for Farley?"

"Why? What could he do?" She faltered and readjusted the heavy canisters in her hands. "Bert will let him know."

"He should be here."

She stopped in front of him. "Look," she said, her lips taut, "if you want an excuse to pay another call on him and Rose, go. Just get out of my way. The jacks need me."

He stepped aside. She was right. Farley would be useless here. His ears still rang with Farley's harangue, fueled by the camp manager's frustration that Adam would not explain why Glenmark had written that letter. Adam had warned Glenmark it would create all kinds of questions, but Glenmark had insisted, not wanting anything to prevent Adam from doing his job.

And Rose Quinlan? He swallowed his laugh. She seemed interested only in causing trouble.

When Gypsy coughed as she put the last of the containers on the sled, he frowned. She might have caught cold during their visit to Nissa's saloon. Vowing to keep an eye on her, for she would push herself too hard, he shoved the boxes more securely into place.

"Thanks, Chauncey," she said as a litter was placed on the boxes in the back of the sled.

The gawky inkslinger tipped his cap. "Sure you don't want me to come with you?"

"No. I'm taking Adam with me."

"Adam? Who—Lassiter, right?"

"My reputation precedes me," Adam answered with a smile.

"Naw, just curiosity about how a man could wreck his ankle so bad on the first day of work. These jacks don't like anyone who stinks of bad fortune." Chauncey's aged lips twisted in his full beard. "Your accident. Now this one. Bad, bad sign."

When Adam looked at Gypsy, she said, "Adam, this is the camp's inkslinger, Chauncey Lewis. He runs the wanigan."

"Wanigan?" Adam asked cautiously.

"Over there."

He glanced at the simple log building that served as a combination company store, supply hut, and occasionally as a church when Reverend Frisch arrived before the dining room was clean. He forced a smile as he climbed into the sled, where Gypsy competently held the reins. He needed to be careful. He could not afford to make many mistakes if he hoped to stay at Glenmark Timber Company's camp.

"How long did you work at Tellison Timber?" Gypsy asked, and he knew her keen ears had caught his mistake.

"Not long."

"Obviously, but you've been here long enough to know what the wanigan is."

"I know what. I just didn't know where." He laughed at her astonishment. "I guess I've been spending too much time worrying about this ankle to learn what I should have."

"Most jacks look for it first, so they can buy tobacco for their pipes or to chew."

He scratched at his leg. Curse this itch! "I guess that's the cost of never having taken up that habit."

"I guess it is." Gypsy steered the sled toward where the jacks were cutting a hillside of white pine. The vast amount of lumber from that stand would add to the bonus paid at the end of the season.

She watched the road, which could be slick where the loggers were sliding logs down to stack by the river— not that she expected anyone to be working. With a silent sigh, she wondered what else could bring bad luck to Glenmark Timber Company and its owner.

"How come you didn't tend to me when I was hurt?" Adam asked.

"Peabody can handle something simple like binding up a broken limb." She shivered, but kept the sled moving along the rutted road. "I hope the whiskey helps them before they get themselves into a dither over this."

He nodded. "Your buddy Chauncey was right. This accident is going to put a scare into these superstitious jacks."

"That's why I wanted you to come along. They'll be saying things happen in threes. First you, now today. They'll be looking over their shoulders for an accident until they cause one."

"Tell them to count our sled tipping over on the road as an accident. One, two, three. All done."

She answered carefully, "They don't consider that much of an accident."

"They were worried about you."

"They're my friends."

"And me?"

Glad the rough road required all her attention, she admonished, "This isn't the time for such a discussion."

Leaning his elbows on his knees, he asked, "When is? You've been avoiding me. We need to talk."

"Not now."

Adam nodded as he heard her desperation. More fragile than the piecrust she made day after day, she would crumble if he pushed too hard. He sat back and watched as she competently steered the sled. Short of chopping down trees, he wondered if there were anything she could not do in the logging camp.

He had no time to ask more questions, because they drove into a clearing marked by fresh stumps and logs that were longer than the cook shack. Men clustered in silence. As Gypsy drew the sled to a stop, no shouts welcomed them.

Adam jumped down off the seat and held up his hands to Gypsy. She nodded her thanks as he assisted her to the ground. Motioning for him to follow, she opened a box of cups and began to pour out the whiskey and coffee mixture. The men crowded around, eager to soothe their icy fear.

Peabody's normally ruddy face was gray. Waiting until his crew had been served, he took the cup Gypsy handed him and drained it in one gulp. She refilled it without comment.

"Thanks," he said in a near whisper. "You'd think after all this time, I could get used to something like this."

Gypsy put her fingers on his arm. "No one can become accustomed to this."

"Gypsy, he was just a boy."

"About your brother's age, right?"

Adam watched as the crew chief nodded. Weeks ago, even days ago, he would not have realized how important Gypsy was in the camp. Now he understood she was the men's mother, sister, and trusted confidante.

Taking a deep drink, Peabody wiped the back of his

hand against his mustache before the coffee could freeze in it. "This is worse than when your buddy Adam here got himself hit."

"My injury was minor," he reminded the distressed man.

"We didn't know that. Not at first." He held his cup out for another serving. Although Adam thought Gypsy might refuse, she served him. Peabody thanked her before adding, "Maybe it's time for me to quit. Glenmark was hinting he had a place for me in the mill downriver. Good work and decent wages. I could spend the winter with my family."

"You'd hate it, Peabody," she said as she offered another jack a cup. "You'll be working on these hills as long as there are trees to cut."

He smiled wryly. "I suppose you're right, but this shakes a man clear to his bones."

"Clear to your heart," Gypsy whispered. She forced fear from her face as she handed another logger a refill. By keeping busy, she could avoid looking at the hill where what remained of Bobby Worth might still be lying under a log.

She took the top off the box of sandwiches and put them on the seat, doubtful that the men had much appetite. As she looked at their haunted eyes, she wondered if anyone would send for Reverend Frisch.

Adam's hand on her shoulder brought her to face him. "I'm fine," she said before he could ask.

"I doubt that, but can you get by without me? Peabody could use an ear at the moment."

"Go ahead." She sighed. "Poor Peabody. He trains his men so well. This shouldn't have happened here."

"You're right."

"What's that supposed to mean?"

His lips were taut as he answered quietly, "You know as well as I do what that means." A hint of a smile lessened the lines etched into his cheeks. "Don't worry,

Gypsy. You should realize I don't know a thing about what goes on up here. Just talking through my hat.''

She watched as he walked toward the crew chief, clenching her hands on the sled as she wondered how much of his unfamiliarity with life in the logging camp was feigned. A jack's quavering question brought her back to her work.

Adam jabbed the crutch at the snowbanks, but nothing lessened his frustration. If this were the beginning of a rash of trouble, as the loggers thought, he needed to be prepared. He had to convince Peabody to confide in him. That way, he might discover something that could help.

He hesitated when he saw the short, stocky jack swipe his sleeve across his eyes. Every instinct told him to turn and get out of here. He did not want any part of this grief. He had had his share and had vowed he would not suffer any more. Yet this might be his best chance to get Peabody to open up to him. The jack would do anything to keep this from happening again.

Stopping in front of the bull of the woods, Adam asked, ''What happened?''

A guilty expression crossed Peabody's face. ''My report should be for Farley first.''

''Half the men know by now. Before you can get back to camp, the rest will know.'' He glanced back at the sled as he added, ''Gypsy's mighty upset.''

''She worries too much about us.'' He tilted his wool hat back and rubbed his wide nape. ''To be honest, I don't know what happened. Everything was fine. The crown had been chopped back several days ago, so there were no big branches to catch. But somehow it fell wrong.''

''Then it *was* an accident.''

Peabody shook his head vehemently. ''My boys take down hundreds of trees a winter, and they fall where we want them to fall.''

''Then it wasn't an accident?''

Gray pallor drained the logger's face. "No, no, that's not what I meant either."

"What was it? An accident or not?"

Stuffing his hands into his pockets, Peabody swayed as he clambered up a bank. A drift caught at his legs and threatened to trip him. When Adam dug his crutch into the snow to climb beside him, the crew chief pointed along the ridge.

"We were working right over there. It's half as steep as the hillside we were clearing when you were with us. There's no reason for anything to go wrong." He shuffled his feet in the snow like an oversized child. "Worth was a quiet kid. The boys liked him well enough. This is going to make every man jumpy!"

"That's what Gypsy said."

"She's right." He burped loudly and grinned. "With that concoction she's serving, I'll have to send the men back to camp. I'll keep a few out here to help me bring Worth back."

"We have the sled."

He shook his head. "I wouldn't do that to Gypsy. Take her to the cookhouse, then send the sled back out."

Again Adam looked at where Gypsy's hair was sunrise bright against the gray snow. "She's not squeamish. Why don't you send—"

"Have you ever seen what a tree can do when it comes crashing down on a man?" Peabody's mouth twisted. "It's enough to turn a man's gut. Gypsy's a lot softer than she wants anyone to think. She's comforting us, but who'll pay attention to her pain when the rest of us are comfortably drunk?"

Adam did not answer. Stumbling down the hill, he went to help Gypsy give out the last of the drink. He lifted her onto the seat and was not surprised when she took the reins as he hoisted his worthless cast aboard. When she remained silent as they drove away, he noted the tight line of her lips.

Quietly, he asked, "How are you?"

"I'm fine."

"How are you?"

"Didn't I just tell you that?"

"I would like the truth."

"The truth?" Gypsy glared at him. "How do you think I am? A kid was killed up here today."

Her eyes widened as his hand settled over hers. She watched in fascination as he drew her gloved fingers off the reins. When he took them and put one arm around her, she leaned against him.

"I'm trying to keep my breakfast where it should be," he murmured. "It's all right to let other folks know you're upset."

"I don't think anyone doubts that."

"I do."

She pulled away, baffled. "If you think anyone thinks I'm thrilled because—"

His finger against her lips silenced her. "They don't think that. Once their minds are clear of your coffee, they'll be sure you're so strong that you dealt with this easily."

"I can deal with it." Her voice shook. "Just not easily."

"Peabody's worried about you."

She turned on the seat. "Peabody?"

Adam smiled sadly. "He asked me to keep an eye on you while he watches out for his drunken crew."

"I don't need you looking after me."

"Then you look after me."

She scowled. "Adam, I know you want to talk about what happened last weekend, but this is neither the time nor the place."

"Gypsy, don't fight me and yourself."

"You're making no sense."

"No?" He put his arm around her. "I know this is ripping you apart."

His sympathetic kiss against her bonnet released gut-wrenching pain to wash over her. Tears bubbled from her eyes as she clung to him, needing his strength as her own evaporated in the heat of anguish.

He held her and stroked her back. She gripped the front of his coat, letting the dark wool blot her tears. For the love of heaven, she had come here to leave her grief behind. So many had died. So many had suffered. She did not want to mourn anymore, but she could not stop crying. The sobs she had silenced for years burst out.

"Adam," she whispered, "forgive me."

"Why? You shouldn't be ashamed of—" His arm tightened around her as the sled bounced. His cast hit the side of the seat with a dull thump. Wiping her eyes, she gasped when she saw a crack in it.

"Don't move!" she warned.

"What's wrong?" He pulled back on the reins.

"Your cast is cracked."

Her outstretched hand was caught in a manacle of flesh. He bent, his broad shoulders blocking her view. He turned and smiled, but a hard glitter remained in his eyes.

"I'm sorry, Gypsy, if I hurt you," he said as he released her hand.

"When I saw the crack in it—"

"What crack?"

She frowned as she glanced at the stained cast. "What a surprise! There's no crack in it, is there?"

"None that I saw." He reached for the reins. "Maybe your tears fooled you."

"I was fooled by something."

When he did not answer, she wondered what he was trying to hide. There *had* been a crack in the cast. She was sure of it. Even if her eyes had played her false, he had no reason to act like a cornered criminal.

None that she could imagine.

CHAPTER EIGHT

Arguing voices greeted Gypsy as she came into the kitchen. Oscar and Bert stood stiff in anger. She stepped between them just as Bert raised his fist.

"I hope you have a good explanation for this behavior," she said.

Bert pointed an accusing finger. " 'E can't say those things!"

"What things?" Since the accident on the hill three days before, she had tried to keep things tranquil in the cookhouse.

" 'E said—"

"Let Oscar speak for himself!"

Oscar flushed and jabbed his toe against the trapdoor. Not meeting her eyes, he mumbled, "I just told him what I thought of a man who says Lolly is lying to me."

"Lolly? Lolly Yerkes? What's she got to do with this?"

Oscar cleared his throat several times.

" 'E don't want to tell you 'e's sweet on Lolly." Bert snickered. "The idiot thinks she cares about 'im. She'll lift 'er skirts for any that's got the money."

"Take that back!" shouted Oscar. "Take it back, or—"

"Or what? You can't beat a flea!"

"I'll show you!"

Gypsy raised her hands. "Stop this! You—" Her order ended in a scream when an arm around her waist dragged her out of the way just as Oscar swung his fist. Bert crouched beneath it and laughed. She tried to escape the arm around her.

"Stay out of it," warned Adam's voice close to her ear.

"Release me! I won't have fighting in my kitchen. Not over some whore."

"Stay out of it."

Oscar toppled into the cooking pots by the larder. The metal containers erupted into a shower which set everyone scattering. Ripping herself away from Adam, Gypsy raced across the room. She seized Bert's arm just as he was about to hit Oscar again.

He shook her off viciously. His face was distorted with a malicious glee. When she began to cough, he blinked and lowered his hand.

Gypsy straightened and pointed to where Oscar was trying to extract himself from the battered pots. "Help him up. Now! The rest of you, back to work. Now!"

She clenched her hands on her skirt. "I'll speak with you, Bert, and you, Oscar, after supper. Get this mess cleaned up. I don't want supper delayed because you two are fighting over some doxy."

"Gypsy, she isn't—"

"Not now, Oscar!" she snapped.

Oscar grumbled something, but turned to restack the pots. Her glare at Bert sent him to complete his chores.

Gypsy struggled to breathe. Congestion clogged her chest. She stood in silence while she fought to keep from coughing. She could not get sick. She must stay healthy until the spring thaw.

Going back to the stove, where she had been cutting

carrots into the merrily bubbling stew, she heard a clunk. She stepped aside as Adam dumped the onions he had been chopping into the pot.

"You'd better be more careful," he murmured.

"I can watch over my kitchen and flunkeys." She reached for the pepper.

His broad hand stopped her. When she looked up into his distressed eyes, he asked, "Can you?"

Her breath caught in her throat, but not from the cold cramping in her chest. She must not blurt out how much she needed someone to watch over her, someone who would stand between her and grief, someone who would thrill her with his touch and tempt her with passion. She fought to keep her fingers from rising to his face.

She wanted the tender Adam who had delighted her with his soft laugh and fiery kisses. Too many lies echoed through her heart to remind her how easily he twisted the truth, to remind her how easily he could twist her into believing his beguiling smile.

"I can oversee my kitchen." She stepped away from him. "I managed quite well before you got here."

"Yes, you did." A twinkle vanquished the gloom in his eyes. "And you did quite well today."

"A compliment?"

She regretted the flip answer when his half smile disappeared, and he hobbled away.

Gypsy found it simple to stay away from Adam during the rest of the afternoon, perhaps because he avoided any opportunity which might allow them to speak of anything other than how many slices to cut from each pie. Work prevented them from revealing the truth.

She almost laughed. The truth! She doubted if she ever would discover the truth. Farley had not forgotten his suspicions of Adam. Neither should she, for she feared Adam's kisses had been a ploy to woo her distrust from her.

The flunkeys were silent as they ate their supper and cleaned the kitchen. Gypsy did not hum as she mixed doughnut dough and set it in the coolest corner of the larder. When she returned to the kitchen, she paused in the doorway to watch Adam put a few more sticks into the stove. It seemed the ultimate insult that he had the stove watch on a night when she wanted to be alone.

He straightened and rubbed his lower back. His eyes remained dark with strong emotions.

As she started to speak, she coughed instead. Pain speared her right through to her back.

Worry entered his voice. "I don't like the sound of that cough."

"It's no worse."

"Gypsy, that cough's been bothering you for quite a while." He pulled on his coat and set his hat on his head. Reaching for the door, he said, "You should be resting."

She laughed. "That's a wonderful fantasy, and I think I'm going to enjoy it."

He stepped in front of her and took her arm as she was about to walk to her bedroom door. When she glared at him with an iciness that always cowed the other flunkeys, he asked, "Why run off? We can do something about your fantasies right here."

She yanked her arm away.

"Don't go, Gypsy."

When he teetered on his crutch, she started to reach out to him. She drew back as his hand tried to capture hers. "This is my kitchen, Mr. Lassiter. Don't give orders. That's my job. Why don't you do yours?"

"It'll wait. You look as if you could use a friend at the moment."

Gypsy fought the temptation to agree. The door to the past must not be opened. Somehow she almost had convinced herself that her pain was only memory.

"I don't need anyone," she said.

"No?" His mouth covered hers. When she pulled away with a laugh, he frowned. "What's funny?"

"This. It's bumped me twice." She tipped up the brim of his hat. It sailed off his head and rolled across the floor. She was amazed she could laugh as he chased it awkwardly.

When he turned, she saw his mischievous smile, and she knew he had been acting like a buffoon to get her to laugh.

"You're going to have to pay for that, Gypsy." His arm snaked around her waist, and he tickled her side.

"N-n-no," she gasped, trying to pull away.

"Oh, yes. First we'll get rid of this." He tossed his hat toward the peg.

She did not see where it fell; she could not escape the probing fire in his eyes. When he touched the buttons closing the front of her blouse, she shivered. His fingers spread across her breast, and she gripped his coat.

"No, Adam," she murmured. "This is far too public a place. One of the flunkeys could . . .could . . ." Her words faded into a sigh as his tongue brushed her ear.

The heat of his breath became a cyclone twisting through her. She was caught by the cobalt yearning glowing in his eyes. He did not have to tell her how much he wanted her. His craving showed on his face.

His mouth scalded her lips. She gasped as she was engulfed by sensations which stripped her of all thought. Her fingers slipped beneath his coat to delight in the muscular expanse of his back as his tongue explored her mouth. Each rapid breath brushed her body against his.

He raised his mouth, and his lips tilted as his fingers moved along her breast. With a slow, tender caress, he encircled it, seducing every bit of its pleasure into his possession. Even through her clothes, his caress against its tip made her writhe with a need which refused to be fettered.

"No!" she gasped. "Please, Adam, no!"

Regret drooped his mustache. "If you want me to stop, honey . . ."

"No, I don't want that." She pushed him aside. "I don't want you to stop, but you must. There are some things I can't compromise, Adam, and one of them is myself.''

He lifted her hair and kissed the back of her neck. "Compromising you was not what I intended. Making love with you was."

"Being tumbled like one of Nissa's girls isn't for me."

"I know."

Glancing over her shoulder, she repeated, "You know? Then why—"

"Because I intend to keep asking, Gypsy, until you say yes. I'm going to ask you here in the cook shack and in the stable and in the wanigan and in Farley's office, if necessary." His eyes twinkled with devilment as, his fingers curving along her breast, he whispered, "Again and again until you know what I know."

Fighting the enchantment threatening to send her on an endless spiral of wanton delight, she managed to murmur, "What do you know?"

"That I've wanted you since I first saw you glaring at me in Farley's office. You looked like an angel that day, but I've discovered you aren't an angel. You're the most desirable woman ever put on earth to tempt a man."

"Adam, I—"

He put his finger over her lips, which were soft from his eager kisses. "No, honey, just let me enjoy having you alone and in my arms. Who knows when we'll have a time like this again?" He bent to tease her neck.

The sound of paper crackling halted him. Reaching into his shirt pocket, he said, "Oh, I forgot to give you this before supper. Chauncey asked me to bring your mail over."

"Thank you."

"A love poem from my competition?"

She laughed. "Not likely. Maybe Mr. Glenmark has sent a list of things for me to do."

"That's not from Glenmark."

"Are you reading my mail?"

"Just the postmark. See?" His finger jabbed at the envelope. "It's not from Lansing. It's from Saginaw."

"Saginaw? I—" In horror, she stared at the childlike handwriting.

"Gypsy, what's wrong?"

Somehow she managed to say, "Adam, put those loaves in the oven and watch them. Good night."

"Gypsy, what's wrong?"

She did not answer. Whirling, she ran to her room. Adam called her name, but, without taking off her apron, she slammed the door. His rapping lasted only a few moments before he cursed and stamped away, his cast pounding the floor.

She stared at the letter, afraid to open it. How could she have forgotten this? Adam's kisses had drained her mind of everything but ecstasy.

She considered throwing the letter into the stove unread, but she could not. Ignoring it would not make the threat vanish, and maybe the writer had left a clue to betray his identity. Her fingers quaked as she pulled out the letter. As she unfolded the single page, her breath clogged in her throat.

Just a reminder that I know where you are. Did you think I wouldn't find you in the frozen northlands?

You may have thought you had found the coldest place on this earth. Maybe so, but you'll soon be in the coldest place in the earth. Don't look for me. I shall find you when the time is right, just as I found your family one by one.

She tore the page into tiny pieces and stuffed it into the fire.

She glanced at the door. If she went to Adam and urged him to put his arms around her, his kisses would sweep aside the fear. She sighed. No one else must be drawn into the tightening web of torment. That painful lesson she would not forget again.

Gypsy wandered about her room, too taut to lie down. Since she had received the second note from Saginaw last week, she had found it impossible to sleep. The flunkeys must have noticed—she had been short-tempered and spent half the time yawning.

Each motion was a strain, for her body was as stiff as the logs around her. As she passed the window and glanced out at another of the seemingly endless snowstorms, she froze. Enough light seeped from the back door to silhouette a man who was skulking across the snow.

The tall man turned toward the window, and she pressed back against the wall. Adam! If he discovered her spying on him, she was unsure what he would do, especially when it was clear by his furtive but smooth steps that his broken ankle had been only a trick.

Cautiously she peered around the logs edging the window and wished her lantern was turned down. She wanted to be wrong, but she could not mistake the profile her fingers knew as well as her eyes.

When Adam sneaked toward Farley's office, she did not hesitate. Her dark wrapper over her shirt would protect her from being seen. If she went no farther than the garbage dump, where broken crates were scattered around the barrels, obscuring the ground, she could not be accused of anything but not sleeping.

Opening the door, she tiptoed across the empty kitchen. Warmth glowed from the stove, lighting that side of the room, but the back door was gaping open. Cold clawed into the cookhouse. She went to close it, then hesitated. Adam must intend to return.

The cold tightened around her chest. Clamping her lips together, she refused to cough. Any sound would alert

Adam. She inched out the door and around the garbage heap.

She gripped the splintered edge of a log. Adam was coming out of Farley's office. No cast widened his shin. Now she understood his reaction when she had seen a crack in the cast. She might have discovered the cast was a fake.

When he disappeared into the trees, she leaned against the wall. Her breath exploded from her, and she wondered if she had been holding it since he emerged from the camp manager's office. Light-headed, she closed her eyes.

She could not imagine a single reason why Adam should have been in Farley's office tonight. She swore. Adam had entered the office easily. Farley would not leave it unlocked.

"Gypsy?"

With a gasp, she whirled to see Oscar in the doorway, bafflement on his young face. She pushed past him.

"What were you doing out there?" he asked as she took off her wrapper and shook snow from the hem.

"Just checking stuff."

"You don't have the stove watch tonight. Adam does."

She wanted to thank him for his quick defense, although he reminded her that six nights had passed without her finding an escape in her dreams.

The sensation of being cared about was pleasant, but she had no time to enjoy it. The tightness in her chest threatened to suffocate her.

Without looking at him, she said, "He's busy, so I thought I'd make sure Hank tightened the lid on the barrel." She coughed and choked out, "I don't want any critters knocking on my door."

"You shouldn't be out there." He scowled, then ran to the stove, poured a cup of the strong coffee, and shoved the mug into her hand.

She dropped her wrapper and raised the cup to her lips, but did not drink. Letting the steam stroke her face, she fought to breathe past the iron chains around her chest. Pain pierced her.

"Gypsy, if you get sick, the jacks'll close the cookhouse until we can get another kingbee cook."

"You'd get by." Her voice was a toad's croak.

Plucking the cup from her weak fingers, he poured sugar into it. "My granny used to give us tea with honey. Maybe coffee with sugar will help."

"Thank you." She sipped and grimaced. All she could taste was sugar.

He scowled. "Be more careful!"

"Oscar—"

"You'd say the same thing to me."

"I would." She sat gingerly on a bench. Glancing past him, she saw he had closed the door, but had not dropped the bar into place. "What are you doing here?"

He grinned sheepishly. "I needed some time to think, so I took a walk."

"At this time of night?"

Shrugging his thin shoulders, he said, "I can't think when everyone's snoring. I saw the lights on here and thought I'd jaw with Adam for a while."

"As you can see, he isn't here."

"Are you sure everything's all right?"

"Of course." She ignored his astonishment at her sharp retort. The problems of a lovesick flunkey would have to wait. She needed to figure out what Adam's scheme was.

Oscar mumbled something before saying good night. When the door closed behind him, she sighed for what seemed the hundredth time that night. She would apologize to Oscar in the morning for not having compassion for his young heart.

Rising, she went to the back door. She peeked out, but saw only the snow, which was dirtied by the night. When she realized she feared something would happen to Adam, she wanted to laugh. He must be involved in something wrong. Why else was he creeping about in the middle of the night?

Cold air struck Gypsy's nape, and she looked over her shoulder. "Bert!"

"Where's Adam?" He kicked the other door closed as he walked toward her with his hands clasped behind his back. His eyes glittered oddly. " 'E didn't sneak out and leave you with the stove watch, did 'e?"

"What's wrong?"

He smiled. "Nothing, Gypsy. Nothing at all."

She stepped backward as he continued toward her. There was something different about him. Since he came to work in her kitchen, she never had been uncomfortable with him . . . until now.

When she bumped into the wall and winced, he smiled. Not his friendly grin, but a satisfied smile. Pleasure sifted into his voice. "What's wrong with you, Gypsy? Something spooked you?"

"Nothing's wrong. If you'll excuse me—" Her words ended in a gasp as he grabbed her arm.

"We 'ave a few things to talk about."

"Things?" No liquor fumes tainted his breath. He could not be drunk. Then what? Trying to keep her voice even, she said, "If you're still angry because I stopped your fight with Oscar, I can tell you that—"

"Don't worry about Oscar and 'is whore. I 'aven't thought of 'im since I popped 'im as 'e should be popped."

"Then what do you want?"

He laughed softly as he took another step toward her. "Let me tell you—"

Stamping feet interrupted. As one, they looked toward the back door. When Adam stepped into the kitchen, Gypsy choked as she saw the crutch under his arm and the filthy cast on his leg. Looking from Bert's grin to Adam's surprise, she wanted to shout that the whole world had gone insane in the middle of a heartbeat.

"Didn't expect to see you here so late." Adam dropped the bar on the back door. "Having a problem, Bert?"

"Not any longer." Sticking his hands in the large pockets of his coat, he nodded toward Gypsy. "Saw the light and thought I'd come over and see what was 'appening. Everything seems to be fine, so I'll go back to bed.''

"But . . ." She silenced her own question. When Bert looked at her, obviously expecting her to continue, his brown eyes were friendly.

As soon as the door closed behind Bert, Adam shrugged off his coat and asked, "Is there some problem?"

"Other than the fact you're supposed to be on the stove watch, and you've been . . ."

His hands settled on her shoulders, and she closed her eyes. Betrayal swelled through her even as the unmistakable warmth rose in a sweet wave.

When he spoke, she leaned her head against his chest to hear his words resonating by her ear. "Is that why you're all jittery? Because you thought I'd abandoned the stove? I heard noises out there. I went to check. When I saw some footprints in the snow, I followed them."

"To Farley's office?"

His hands slid along her arms to lift her hands to his lips. "I assume you saw me."

"Yes."

"Did you see him?"

She faced him. Her forehead furrowed with puzzlement. "What him?"

"The man I was following," he said with impatience. "I thought I caught sight of him just as he was coming out of Farley's office."

"I thought that was you!"

He laughed and limped to the stove to pour himself a cup of coffee. "How did you think I'd get into Farley's office?"

"That was what I planned to ask you."

Taking a sip, he smiled as the frost melted in his mustache. "You'll have to ask that slippery cur. He got away from me. Of course, I didn't expect to catch him when I'm as useless as a three-legged dog."

Although his eyes were carefully blank, Gypsy knew he was lying. Only one set of footprints led to Farley's office, and she was sure they were not accompanied by the mark from a crutch.

Putting her cup on the table, she whispered, "Good night, Adam. I trust you'll remain by the stove the rest of the night."

"I'd planned on that from the beginning."

Stop lying, she begged silently.

His fingers curved along her cheek. As he tilted her lips beneath his, she whispered, "Good night."

"It could be, if you stay here with me instead of hiding in your room. You haven't said two words to me since the last time I had the stove watch, honey."

"Don't call me that."

"Why not?" His mouth grazed hers and he whispered, "You taste as sweet as honey."

"Adam, I . . ."

When her voice vanished into his kiss, he pressed her back against the table. A soft white cloud of flour billowed around her and a slow smile branded itself on his lips as his eyes swept along her with unfettered craving.

His husky tone seeped through her. "I want to be with you all night."

"Adam, please don't say such things!" She tried to wiggle away, but his legs pinned hers against the table as he bent over her. With every breath, she touched his hard body.

Her hands reached to push him away. He grasped her wrists and held them over her head. At the same time, his mouth seized hers. He kissed her until the raw breath of passion exploded from her. His other hand wove a pattern of heat through the thin linen of her blouse. The firm muscles of his legs rubbed against her thighs.

Her resistance dissolved into the emptiness swelling within her. He could make her whole once more with a love that would fill her with ecstasy. As his fingers traced her breast, teasing her with light, butterfly shimmers of rapture, all thought drifted away.

"Say yes, honey," he whispered between placing searing kisses along her neck. "Be mine now."

His arm cradled her shoulders, pressing her ever closer to him. His other hand reached beneath her skirt, climbing her legs. He held her against the table as his fingers grew more bold, curving along the sensitive skin behind her knee.

She moaned and tugged his shirt from his trousers. Stroking the smooth skin of his back, she delighted in the ripple of the muscles beneath her fingers. Her breath strained against his mouth as she quivered.

He reached for the back of her shirt. Something pinged against her back.

"Ouch!" she cried. "What was that?"

He smiled. "Don't worry, honey. Just a button."

"A button?" Gypsy shook her head and stared up at him. What was she doing? Was she mad? If she had any sense at all, she would take him off the stove watch for good. She had not known what temptation was until she discovered his touch.

Pushing him away, she sat up to stare down at his fingerprints in flour along her skirt. She brushed her skirt down over her legs, not wanting to see the marks from his touch along her skin.

He tilted her face up toward him. "Gypsy?"

"I can't." She shoved his hand away and jumped down from the table. Heat scored her face as she imagined what would have happened if someone had come in and seen her and Adam on the kitchen table. She beat at her skirt with her hands, trying to knock the flour off the black wool. When Adam bent to help her, she pulled back. "Please stop."

"I was just trying—"

"I know what you were trying to do."

He put his hands on her shoulders. When she tried to shrug them off, he whispered against her ear, "And do you know how splendid it would be to toss aside caution and surrender to passion?"

She closed her eyes. "I know."

"Do you?" He spun her to face him. "Do you?"

Gypsy backed away from the naked longing in his eyes. If she faltered, if she let him closer, if she forgot her pledge not to let anyone near her and her battered heart, she would be lost in that desire.

Moaning, she raced to her room. His heated gaze followed, tempting her to turn around and give herself to her craving. She closed the door and leaned against it. From the other side, she could hear his uneven steps as he settled himself on the bench.

She slid down to sit on the floor. Resting her head on her folded arms, she tried to catch her breath. How many more times could she tell Adam no? It must be every time, or she would put him in peril.

It's just a coincidence. You're seeing a pattern of murder where there isn't one.

How many people had told her that? How many of those people were now dead? She did not want to count.

Not hearing any other sounds from the kitchen, she guessed Adam's nocturnal wanderings were over . . . for tonight. She could go to him and have him hold her in his arms all night.

No. She must not think of that. She must think about what he was up to.

Her breath caught painfully. The threatening notes had begun to arrive just when Adam came to the camp.

No, she could not believe he had sent them. Not because he held her so sweetly, but because he had Daniel's recommendation.

Adam was involved in something that had nothing to do with the threatening letters. She hoped he found what he was looking for soon. Very soon, because she was unsure how long she could resist the craving to surrender to passion . . . no matter what the cost.

CHAPTER NINE

Gypsy grabbed her coat off the peg. With a quick glance to be sure the firebox door was secure, she hurried out into the windswept day. She trudged through the well-packed snow, keeping her head down and her hands clenched in her coat pockets. She stamped her feet on the narrow porch of the wanigan. A bell clanged as she opened the door.

The small building was as crowded as her larder. Boxes were stacked on every flat surface and along the shelves on the back wall. A cast-iron stove overheated the space, and she unbuttoned her coat as she walked to where the inkslinger was working. His thinning hair draped over his collar. He smiled, his eyes bloodshot from long hours of work.

"Howdy, Gypsy." Chauncey leaned his elbows on the counter. "Didn't expect to see you in the middle of the day."

"The flunkeys are delivering lunch to the jacks. Supper's started, but it can wait a minute or two while I get some thread to sew on a button." She looked past him, as if interested in something on the cluttered shelves. She did not want him to guess how the button had come off.

Had she been crazy? To let Adam hold her that way was an invitation to heartbreak. She wanted him, but it could not be.

"What color?" asked Chauncey.

"I doubt if you have white," she said with a weak grin.

"When's the last time you saw a jack in a white shirt?"

"What's the palest shade you have?"

Rummaging in a box, he shook his head. "Seems all of 'em are black, Gypsy." With his finger, he pushed the wooden spools about. "Say, here's a pale one."

"Pink?" She took the spool. "How in heaven's name did that get in here?"

"Fool clerk in Saginaw must have made a mistake." He pulled a ledger sheet from under the counter. "Shall I put you down for it?"

Peering at the account sheet, which showed the number of days she had worked as well as what she had purchased at the wanigan, she asked quietly, "Can I see the ledgers for my flunkeys?"

He frowned. "Those ledgers aren't supposed to be passed around."

"Chauncey, I'm not about to send a letter to a flunkey's family and tell them he's wasting his money on tobacco or playing cards."

He hesitated, then nodded. Reaching beneath the counter, he pulled out a box. He searched and plucked out a handful of papers. "All here but Per's card. Maybe that's out back 'cause he was in the other day for some tobacco."

"Don't worry about that one. Just let me see the others."

He glanced at the door. "Make it quick, Gypsy. If Farley came in here, he'd have my hide."

She pretended to look at each page, but she was interested only in one. As she had suspected, Adam's was different. She wanted to believe his sheet was not like the others because he had come so late in the season, but Bert Sayre's matched the rest, although she could not read his illegible signature. Yet this confirmed what she had already guessed. Adam was not a jack. So what was he doing here?

"Problem with Lassiter's ledger?"

Raising her gaze from the page, she asked, "No, should there be?"

He put the box of spools on the shelf. "You look displeased."

"I have a white blouse to repair with pink thread, and I should be happy?" She congratulated herself for her frivolous tone. "Oh, you took my sheet. I need to sign for the thread."

With a lighthearted wave, he urged, "Take it. Wasn't supposed to be in the box anyhow. Let the clerk in Saginaw explain it to *his* boss."

"Thanks, Chauncey."

"Any time. I like to do things for my friends."

She wagged a finger at him. "Is this going to cost me?"

"If I can convince you to make more cherry pies, then it is."

When she started to reply, the bell over the door rang. Her eyes widened as she saw who was entering. Only one other woman lived in the logging camp, but Rose Quinlan was seldom seen beyond Farley's house. She was dressed in a scarlet gown bedecked with silk flowers along its wide skirt. The crisp lace of her petticoats rustled as she swept up to the counter.

Gypsy fought her irritation. There was no reason to be vexed because Farley's private whore snubbed her. Rose Quinlan was a fool to think she was better than Gypsy Elliott. She was no better than Nissa's working girls.

Looking past the blonde in her crimson bonnet, Gypsy's

eyes narrowed as she saw Chauncey regarding Rose with loathing. His hands fisted on the counter, and he had lost his bright smile.

She understood when Rose demanded, "I want the material Mr. Farley ordered for me."

"As soon as I finish helping Gypsy."

"Gypsy?" She gave a delicate shiver, making it clear she found being in the same room with the camp's cook distasteful. She drew off her leather gloves one finger at a time and glowered.

Wondering how Rose could not sense the inkslinger's fury, Gypsy took the spool of thread and pushed the ledgers toward Chauncey. At the beginning of the winter, she had felt sorry for the woman who fit into the camp as well as the loggers would have fit into a palace, but all her attempts at friendship had been repulsed.

Quietly, Gypsy said, "Chauncey, I've got to get back to work. Thank you."

"Any time. I'm always glad to help my friends."

Rose's back stiffened and Gypsy decided to leave before things got worse. She hurried back to the cook-house and put the thread in her room.

Checking that everything was cooking as it should, Gypsy sighed as she sat and put her feet up on the wood-box. She was too tired too much lately. With her skirt dropping away to reveal her black cotton stockings and midcalf-high shoes, she leaned against the table and closed her eyes. Getting food out to the hillside was wearing out her and her crew. Farley had promised her only a week or two more before he moved the jacks closer. Then they could serve lunch at the cook shack.

Rubbing her forehead, which was damp with sweat, she tapped her toes to a song rumbling through her mind. She smiled when she realized it was the raucous melody the jacks had been singing about Paul Bunyan this morn-ing. The tales of the gigantic lumberjack were becoming even more outrageous. She needed to have someone explain exactly how a blue ox named Babe fit into the silly story.

As she gazed at the logs, her chuckles became an indulgent smile. Perhaps it was not so silly. The men were lonesome for the wives and families they had left behind. Each of those "babes" was as precious as the huge ox was to Paul Bunyan.

She rose to get a cup of the strong coffee waiting on the stove's warming shelf. The aroma knit her memories together, binding before and now. The fragrance meant mornings, whether in the camp or far to the south.

Coughs abruptly overpowered her. Nearly retching, she leaned on the table. The coughing sapped her, but she had no time to be sick.

Taking a sip, she let the coffee drip along her ravaged throat. She sighed when it washed away the pain. In only a few weeks, the camp would close. If she could stay healthy, she would see a doctor in Lansing and endure his horrible powders.

At a furtive knock on the back door, Gypsy frowned. No one knocked on doors in a logging camp. She opened it, and her eyes widened in surprise.

"Nissa!"

Dressed in a flamboyant gown of royal blue, Nissa Jensen did not smile. "Can I come in?"

"Nissa, I—" Farley had rigid rules that the jacks were not to have visitors from the Porcelain Feather Saloon, and she was unsure if that edict extended to the kingbee cook and the brothel's madam.

"Gypsy, we've got to talk. Just you and me. Heard you've been sending your flunkeys out at midday, so I decided this was the time."

She stepped back to allow Nissa in. When Nissa glanced over her shoulder, Gypsy realized she still held the door open. She closed it and motioned for Nissa to sit on a narrow bench.

"Don't stare, Gypsy," she chided with a throaty laugh as she brushed the modest coat that closed at her throat. "I'm different away from work just as you're different when you take off that apron."

"I don't get to do that often." She smiled.

"You should. Glenmark will work you into an early grave if you let him." Reaching into her bag, she pulled out a cigar and lit it.

"No smoking in the cookhouse," Gypsy said as she put a cup of coffee on the table for Nissa.

"Those rules are for the jacks. What's Farley going to do? Tell me to pack my turkey sack and walk?" Her amusement vanished as a haunted expression filled her faded eyes. "Gypsy, I need this cheroot now. After what happened last night . . ."

"What happened last night?"

"Do you have something stronger than swamp water?" She pushed the cup aside. "I need whiskey."

"Farley allows no liquor in the camp."

She snorted and picked up the cup. "How can you live with all these stupid rules?"

"You have your own rules at the saloon." Folding her hands on the flour-coated oilcloth, Gypsy asked, "What happened last night?"

Nissa took a deep puff on the noxious cigar and followed that with a long swig of the coffee. Sighing, she balanced the cup in one hand and the cheroot in the other. "One of my girls was murdered."

"Murdered?" Gypsy choked on the word. When a cool hand patted her clasped fingers, she raised her gaze to meet Nissa's eyes.

"Should've told you better," Nissa said, her smile sad.

"How?"

"Got no idea. There's no way to ease such news."

Gypsy shook her head. Fighting the coughs tickling the back of her throat, she choked out, "No, I mean how was she murdered?"

"Smothered by a pillow. Right in her crib. That's why we didn't realize Lolly was dead until this morning."

"Lolly? Lolly Yerkes?"

"Why—oh, that's right. You had a run-in with her at the Porcelain Feather." She took another draw on her cigar. The gray-blue smoke surrounded her, but could not hide the pain pulling her lips into a straight line. "Yesterday was Wednesday. The men aren't supposed to be out in the middle of the week."

"But there's no one else within a dozen miles."

"That's why I came to speak to you, Gypsy. Your crew sleeps in the bunkhouse, don't they?"

"All except the one who has to keep the fire up in the stove."

"Who was that last night?"

Her fingers tightened around her cup. Not to speak the truth was insane, especially when it might lead to the identification of a murderer. "Adam Lassiter watched the kitchen last night," she whispered.

Nissa cursed through the malodorous smoke. "I had hoped I could point to the man here as the murderer, but it can't be him."

"Why not?"

"That's a strange question to hear from a woman who was cozying up with Adam a few weeks ago." A flash of a wicked grin lit her eyes. "Lovers' quarrel, Gypsy? Think twice before you get rid of him. He may be limping around now, but Adam Lassiter is just what you need."

"Adam and I haven't had an argument."

She tapped ashes into her cup. "No matter. It couldn't be Lassiter. It's a good two miles between here and the saloon. With that cast, he would have had to start before you finished up here and wouldn't be back yet."

Gypsy pretended to listen as Nissa continued. What the madam said was true. Adam could not have managed the long walk through the heavy snow with his cast. She clenched her hands in her lap until her whitened knuckles protested.

Adam was lying about his ankle, but she did not believe he had killed Lolly. Murder was the act of a madman. Whatever else Adam might be, he was sane.

When Gypsy coughed, knife-sharp pains cutting through her chest, Nissa demanded, "How long have you been sounding like that?"

"A while. It'll go away."

"Sounds bad."

Although she wanted to retort that the cough's sound was not as horrible as its pain, she said, "I'll be fine."

"You should be in bed."

"Nissa, I can take care of myself! I—" She pressed her hands to her chest as more coughs refuted her words.

Nissa went to the stove. She poured a cup of tea from the kettle. Pulling down two boxes from the shelves, she mixed a pinch of the ingredients into the cup, and placed it in front of Gypsy. "Drink it."

Gypsy's hands trembled so, she was afraid she would not be able to lift the cup. She let the oddly fragrant steam wash over her. It eased the tautness of her throat, and she was able to breathe. She took a sip and gagged.

"What is it?"

"Drink it," repeated Nissa. "It's good for you."

Grimacing, she tried again. Her stomach threatened to revolt. "I can't!"

"Peppermint tea and garlic is my granny's sure-enough recipe for getting rid of a cold on the chest."

"Peppermint and garlic?" Before Nissa could answer, more coughs overwhelmed her. "The flavor may kill me."

"Drink it all." Nissa slipped on her coat. "I'm going to bend Farley's ear. He's got to know what's happened. The girls are afraid. They want to leave."

Gypsy stood, keeping a hand on the table to steady her wobbly knees. "Will you go?"

She hesitated. "I like the money I make, but I like being alive more. The season's almost over. The jacks will be able to visit us in Saginaw when the log drive is done.''

''If there's anything we can do to help, let me know.''

Nissa went out the main door. Gypsy forced her rubbery legs to carry her to the window. The madam was ignoring the men who stopped to watch her cross the camp, but having Nissa Jensen here was sure to create all kinds of rumors.

Gypsy leaned her shoulder against the wall and took a deep breath. Keeping the kitchen running smoothly and food on the tables in the dining room would prevent the loggers from overreacting.

She set the soup pot on the stove. Within minutes, she had chicken broth bubbling, and she began to collect the ingredients for pies. She was getting the salt box from the rafters when the door opened and the flunkeys blew in on a puff of cold wind and their laughter.

''Sit down,'' she ordered before they could greet her. Putting salt into the soup pot, she stirred it.

Knocking snow from their boots, the men sat on the benches around the table. She saw the uneasy glances they exchanged.

She continued to stir the soup. ''Nissa Jensen just came here with the news that one of the girls was murdered last night.''

A jumble of questions was shot at her, but Bert's voice was loudest. '' 'Oo was it?''

''Lolly.''

Oscar hid his face in his hands. Pain swelled through her as, too late, she recalled how Bert had accused him of being smitten with the prostitute.

Looking from him to the soup she could not let burn, she faltered. When a strong hand covered hers on the ladle, she stared at Adam in silence. His face was as frigid as the rocks along the river and as roughly sculpted, but she saw no surprise.

Tell me the truth. Tell me the murderer can't be you. Tell me why you're lying to me.

"Help him, Gypsy," he urged. "I'll watch the soup."

She nodded. When she put her hands on Oscar's too skinny shoulders, he threw his arms around her waist and pressed his face against her apron. His sobs burst straight from his gut. Not the soul-wrenching weeping of an adult, not the pitiful keening of a heartbroken child, but a combination of both. She stroked his hair. Bert, Hank, and Per lowered their eyes as if ashamed to show their grief.

Again she glanced at Adam. The compassion for Oscar on his surprisingly candid features shocked her. Wanting to demand why he refused her the same, she bent and gently brought Oscar to his feet.

She hated what she had to say, but a mountain of work awaited them. "Hank, take Oscar to the bunkhouse. We can cope for an hour or two without him."

The obese man nodded and put his arm around the lad. As soon as the door closed behind them, she told the others to unload the sled. She went to the stove where Adam still stirred the soup.

"Adam," she said as she took the spoon, "you should know that Nissa came here expecting to accuse the man who had the stove watch."

"Only expecting to?"

"Yes, only." She let the fragrant steam hide her face in a heated flush. "When she discovered you had the watch, she knew a man with a broken ankle wouldn't be able to go that distance in the amount of time between when I go to sleep and wake up."

"Do I owe you a thank-you for defending me?"

She started to face him, but his rigid hands on her shoulders warned he was as distressed by the tidings of murder as she was. "No, I didn't defend you. There was no need."

"But someone murdered her."

"Yes."

Gently he turned her to him. "Gypsy, be careful."

"Me?" She almost laughed, then realized he was serious. The fervor in his blue eyes could not be feigned. "Why should I be worried?"

"Bert and Oscar were pretty upset about her last week."

"You think one of them killed her?" As cold flooded her, she shook herself out of his hands. "That's ridiculous! I spoke to them here last night."

"Both of them?"

"Yes, both of them. Are you disappointed, Adam, that one of the flunkeys isn't a murderer?"

He swore under his breath. "The sooner you understand how dangerous this could be for you, the sooner you'll realize this isn't a joke."

"I still don't understand why you think I should be worried." She was inured to such fear. She tried to ignore the thought that she might have become too accustomed to it.

"Here's why." He lifted her hand and slapped something on it.

She stared at a small carving knife. Looking at an empty slot on the wall where the knives were kept, she said, "I don't need this."

"Apparently someone else didn't need it, either, judging from where I found it."

"Where?"

He smiled grimly. "Outside the door this morning. Someone took that knife last night. Not only did he take it, but he came back with it. Why?"

With a shiver, she walked to the storage rack and put the knife in its place. "I have no idea."

"None? Last night, you were as skittish as a rabbit with a hound on its tail. What's going on here?"

"I could ask you the same!" she shot back. "You're out wandering around in the middle of the night after some phantom. Now word comes that a woman's been murdered. Are they connected somehow?"

He shook his head. "You're asking the wrong man, Gypsy. I have no idea what's going on." Crossing the room, he grasped her elbows. "All I know is this is just the beginning of trouble."

"I agree," she whispered, afraid to speak the truth aloud.

He brought her eyes to meet his. Her heart faltered on its next beat. Anger, frustration, and curiosity burned in his eyes, but none of them were aimed at her. *Perhaps the curiosity,* she had to admit as his fingers splayed across her cheek.

She closed her eyes. In his arms, she found a sanity that was swiftly disappearing in the rest of her life. As his fingers sifted upward to tangle in her hair, she guided his mouth to hers. Once she had needed his kiss to help her forget past pain. No longer. She ached for that fiery caress.

His tongue outlined her hungry lips, teasing each eager inch, and she tasted the warmth within his mouth. His arms tightened around her as hers curved along his back.

Dancing together and away like two fencing masters, their mouths created a melody that could be heard in her depths. As his mouth glided along her neck, his fingers stroked her side, outlining her with a flush of delight. Her leg rubbed against his as he pressed her to the wall. Each silken hair on his skin was an individual caress, threatening to sweep her mind from her.

She moaned his name when his fingers circled the curve of her breast. His other hand cupped her chin and tilted her head back. Letting his gaze hold her, she quivered before the onslaught of sensations she could no longer govern. His fingertip roved along her, tracing a path until she arched toward him.

When her hands stroked his chest, his heartbeat leaped. In the second before his mouth touched hers again, he whispered, "One other thing I know. I intend to stop this murderer before you can become his next victim."

"Me?" she choked, torn from the pleasure by fear. "Why me?"

"You tell me."

She pushed him away, aching anew that he would use his kisses to entice information from her. *"You* tell me. After all, having a murderer after me is your idea."

His strong hands caught her and spun her back to him. The softness was gone from his face. "Ignore the facts, if you wish, Gypsy, but one woman is dead. Will you be next?"

CHAPTER TEN

Whistling a lighthearted melody did not lessen the pre-dawn cold, but the tune cheered Adam as the icy wind slapped away the last remnants of sleep. It had been hard to rest in the aftermath of the murder at the Porcelain Feather Saloon.

Farley had been very obvious by his absence. Adam's whistling took on a minor key as he wondered if the camp manager had spent the night devising a list of excuses for Glenmark. The company's owner would want answers. The killer had been able to sneak into the brothel and smother a woman without anyone seeing him.

No answers.

No clues.

Nothing out of the ordinary but the knife he had returned to Gypsy. His hope it would frighten her into leaving had been futile. Not that he blamed her, for almost anyone could have swiped the knife. It was chaos at mealtimes. Chance had allowed him to find the knife, but he was not sure it had anything to do with Lolly's murder. If it did not, then there were more questions which had no answers.

The cheerful lilt returned to his whistle in spite of the snow clinging to his boot and moccasin as he hobbled toward the cookhouse, each step a labor. With a wry grin, he looked down at his leg. Soon he could be rid of the cast, but he had to find a way to stay in the cookhouse. He liked the way Gypsy softened like melting butter in his arms, and he was getting close to something . . . and someone.

Ahead of him, Bert and Oscar were walking with an ease he had forgotten. Their light voices drifted to him as they gossiped with Per. He frowned. Hank must have the watch. Hank often let the fire die and failed to mix the flapjack batter. It would be a longer morning than usual.

As he had so often in the past month, he asked himself what he was doing in this isolated camp. His idea that this assignment might be fun had dwindled into disbelief.

"Fun?" he grumbled to himself.

"What's that?" Oscar called back. The lad dropped away from the others to walk with him. Keeping his skinny hands in the pockets of his coat, he shuffled through the snow.

Adam grinned. "I was just trying to decide why anyone would want to start the day at this ridiculous hour."

"I like the quiet."

"You can't be serious."

"I am." He sighed. "Sometimes a man can hear only when nothing else is going on."

Adam draped a companionable arm around the lad's slight shoulders. "Are you all right?"

Biting his lower lip, Oscar nodded. "I went out behind the bunkhouse. Didn't want the others to see me blubber like a baby."

"There's nothing wrong with a man crying when he's got a reason to cry."

"Have you?"

Leaning on his crutch, he faced the younger man. "More times than I like to remember. When I fought in

the War of the Rebellion, I lost many friends. I mourned—
blubbered like a baby, as you put it.'' He stared into
Oscar's face, which was gray in the faint light of the
coming dawn. ''To be honest, if I had a man reporting
to me who didn't cry when one of his buddies died, I got
rid of him. A man with no tears has no heart, and a man
with no heart has no place for courage.''

''I never thought of that.''

The good humor returned to Adam's voice as he clapped
Oscar on the arm. ''It's not something anyone wants to
think about. Let's think about breakfast instead. I could
use a cup of swamp water.''

Oscar held the door while Adam hoisted himself into
the cookhouse. The warmth embraced him as he pulled
off his coat.

Adam limped away from the cold breath of the wind
edging past the hinges. As he snatched a cup from the
shelf, he asked, ''Where's Gypsy? I thought she'd have
the coffee going.''

Hank yawned as he tried to hitch his trousers to his
suspenders, which were inches too short to reach across
his girth. ''She ain't out yet.''

''Not out yet?'' Adam went to the table, where the
makings for flapjacks waited. He began to stir flour into
the batter, but glanced at the closed door. No hint of
lantern light inched under it. In the weeks he had been
working here, he could not recall a single time Gypsy
was not working by the time the flunkeys arrived.

'' 'E's just glad Gypsy didn't find 'im sleeping on the
job again.'' Bert flashed a superior grin at Hank, who
was struggling to button his trouser flap.

''Stop twittering like a blasted British songbird!'' Hank
snapped.

''If Gypsy wants to sleep late one morning,'' Adam
said, ''I don't think you should wake her with childish
quarrels. Hank, get a slab of bacon. Per, you and Bert
can start these flapjacks while I try to brew up the coffee.''

"Gypsy always does the swamp water," whispered Per in awe.

"She can't brew it if she's not here. A hundred tired jacks aren't going to be happy if there's no coffee. Do you want the cookhouse door nailed shut while they look for another crew and you walk?"

The men grumbled, but turned to their tasks. Adam hid his disquiet while, again and again, he gave orders as the gray of dawn inched across the eastern sky. Through the walls, he could hear the rumble of voices as the jacks emerged from the bunkhouse. He frowned. Gypsy might oversleep a few minutes, but he could not imagine her staying abed once the loggers were awake.

Per flipped fluffy pancakes into the bucket on the table. When Adam brought another bowl of batter, the gray-haired man asked, "Why do you think she's not out?"

"I was going to ask you the same."

He looked at the door. "She's never late. Never! First that girlie at the Porcelain Feather. Now Gypsy—"

Hearing panic in the old man's voice, Adam put the bowl on the table. He said nothing as he went to Gypsy's door. Behind him, silence warned the other flunkeys were watching.

He rapped on the door. Time slowed while he waited for an answer. Hearing apprehensive mumbles behind him, he knocked again.

"If she can't answer—"

He snapped, "Don't jump to conclusions, Oscar. She may be exhausted. She's been working hard."

"She always works hard," answered Hank as he came in from the dining room, "but she's never overslept."

Adam turned back to the door to keep the other men from guessing he shared their dismay. The scent of hysteria reeked through the room, obscuring the aromas of muffins and coffee.

The door squeaked as he opened it. He frowned when he saw the room was dark. "Gypsy?"

When he got no answer, he closed the door behind him.

He did not care what the other flunkeys thought. The sparse glow from the small stove did not reach the bed. He banged his toe against a chair, but caught it before it toppled. He cursed his cast as he hobbled toward the bed.

Vibrant, auburn hair was faded to a dull color on Gypsy's pillow. One slender hand rested on her chest, which was covered by a simple flannel nightgown. Its open collar had parted to reveal the lace of her chemise. Her other hand clutched the blankets as if struggling against an invisible demon. Her face was strained and flushed.

Adam listened to the rasping of her labored breaths. Again he cursed as he touched her burning forehead. Gently he lifted her hand from her straining chest and put his fingers over her heart. It raced as if she had run for miles. When she coughed feebly, she moaned, but did not waken.

He growled a curse as he drew the blankets around her. He wanted to throttle Hank for letting the cookhouse grow so cold, but Gypsy was as much to blame. She had refused to rest when the coughs started.

He threw a few sticks in the stove, then went to the door. "Bert!" he called. "Go to Farley's house and tell him we have to have a doctor right away!"

"Gypsy is—"

"Very sick! Go, man!"

Bert backed away, disbelief on his face. " 'Ow sick?"

"I can give you an answer, but you risk her dying because you're dawdling!" Adam clenched his hands against the door, then said more calmly, "Sorry, Bert. Just hurry."

"Sure thing." He ripped his coat off its peg. "Don't want Gypsy to die like this."

"The rest of you serve breakfast," continued Adam. "Don't let any of the jacks learn Gypsy's ill."

"If—"

"Serve breakfast, Oscar!" Seeing the young man's horror, he added, "You know that's what Gypsy would tell you to do."

"Don't make it sound like she's dead!"

As Oscar backed away, then whirled to do as ordered, Adam's fist struck the doorframe. He scanned the room. It seemed so empty without Gypsy. Until now, he never understood that her sharp commands and gentle smiles held the flunkeys together.

He closed the door and sighed when he noticed how her weak thrashing had loosened the blankets. He tucked the covers over her again and kissed her hot forehead. "You're going to get well, Gypsy Elliott. This is one fight we're going to fight together, whether you want my help or not!"

Farley knocked his boots against the log step of the cook shack. Why did everything happen at such an unreasonable hour? He had planned a leisurely breakfast with Rose and perhaps an hour or two back in bed. Instead, that tongue-tied Cockney had come pounding on his door with a message from Adam.

Sick? An ailing kingbee cook was the last thing he needed. First the accident on the hill, then the murder at the brothel—Glenmark was going to have his hide, but his boss could flay his backside only if there was anything left after the jacks discovered there was no breakfast waiting.

He brushed snow from his black wool coat when he stepped into the kitchen and shook melting flakes from his hair in a shower about him. That done, he shoved his cigar back into his mouth and hid his surprise that the room smelled of fragrant coffee and fresh flapjacks.

Pushing past the flunkeys, he walked resolutely to Gypsy's room. He was reaching for the door when it opened. Startled, he backpedaled a pace and swore under his breath. He should have guessed Lassiter would be mixed up in this. No doubt Lassiter saw this as his chance to gain control here.

He ordered, "Step aside, Lassiter. I want to see her."

"Have you sent for the doctor?"

"Mr. Glenmark's policy is that a doctor is necessary only in an emergency. That's something I decide."

Lassiter blocked the door with his crutch. "She doesn't need you bringing in cold air and heaven knows what else."

"Move aside."

"No."

Farley pursed his lips in fury. Aware the rest of Gypsy's crew were listening, he clamped his teeth on his cigar. "Step aside, Lassiter, or you're done here."

"Fire me if you wish, but I'm not moving." He folded his arms on the ragged cloth over the top of the crutch. "I suggest you get a doctor here. If that woman dies because you did nothing, how long will it take Glenmark to send you packing? Camp managers are easier to find than good cooks."

Farley's mouth worked, but no words spilled out. It was true. Mr. Glenmark would be furious if something happened to his prized kingbee cook. Farley would never find another position in the north woods. He had worked too hard to have his career destroyed by a petite dictator who had chosen the worst time to get sick.

"What's wrong with her?" he demanded.

"A doctor could tell you for sure."

"There's no doctor here."

"There would be if you'd send for one!" Lassiter retorted. "Why don't you stop arguing, Farley, and send someone for the doctor before she dies?"

"Dies?" Fear froze his gut. "She's really that sick?"

"Do you think I'd have asked for a doctor otherwise? It might be pneumonia, but only a doctor can tell for sure. She won't wake."

Still unsure, Farley asked, "Have you tried—"

"I've tried everything short of waking her with a kiss like Prince Charming's." Exasperation flared through his voice. "What else do you need to know before you'll send for the doctor? Or do you want to come in and watch her die?''

Hearing uneasy rumbles, Farley strode toward the dining room door. He heard his name called and asked, ''What is it, Lassiter?''

''Next time you come, leave that cheroot outside. No smoking in the cookhouse.''

Hank chuckled as the others turned to hide their grins.

Adam ignored Farley's curse. He told Hank and Bert to begin stew for supper. Cold sandwiches would have to do for lunch. He motioned to Per.

''What is it?'' Per asked, his voice quivering. ''She ain't worse, is she?''

''Yes.'' Denying the truth was useless. ''I swear I don't know where she's getting the strength to breathe.'' Putting his hand on the older man's shoulder, he asked, ''You've been here the longest. How long before Farley can get a doctor up here once he gets off his duff?''

''Day. Maybe two.''

Adam clenched his fist against the door. ''That's ridiculous!''

''Doc Patterson's forty-five miles from here. Doc Ahearn lives even farther away. Last year, it took Doc Patterson a day and a half to get here.''

''She may not have that much time.''

Per rubbed his grizzled chin. ''I know something that may help.''

''Spit it out!''

Per cocked a brow. ''Take it easy. Gypsy's a lot stronger than you would guess by looking at her.'' Chuckling with a cackle that sounded like a contented chicken, he added, ''And I've seen you looking at her a powerful lot of times.''

He ignored the teasing. ''What's this idea?''

''Back in Finland, we used a sauna to draw out a chest thickness.''

He frowned. ''A sauna? What is that?''

When Per started to explain, Adam halted him. "Just get what you need to build this sauna thing."

Adam closed the door to hold the sparse warmth in the bedroom. He pulled the chair closer to the bed and folded Gypsy's limp hand between his. She did not react. Brushing her hair back from her heated forehead, he longed for her green-gray eyes to open and spark at him.

"Fight it, Gypsy," he whispered as he stroked her heated cheek. "If . . ."

A knock interrupted him. His steps were as stiff as the cast as he went to the door.

Per bustled in with the other flunkeys in tow. The men glanced at the bed, and anxious lines deepened in their faces. Scowling at the strange collection of items they carried, Adam did not waste time asking questions. He simply followed the orders Per whispered.

Soon he understood what Per planned. Heavy stones which had been chipped out of the frozen ground were set to heat on the stove. Steam rose as ice seared on the cast iron. The soft hiss was the loudest sound in the room as the men worked in silence.

Per placed a large tub on the floor. When Bert and Oscar came in with buckets of water, the old man pointed that they should be placed next to the tub.

"Put a blanket under that tub," Adam suggested so quietly that Gypsy's rasping breath could be heard over his words. "Otherwise, you'll scorch a hole right through the floor."

Bert stepped aside as the other flunkeys rolled a heated rock into a small pail. When his eyes met Adam's, he looked away hastily and muttered, "Seems like one calamity after another 'ere lately."

"Put your superstitions aside!" Adam snapped. "Gypsy brought this on herself by being as stubborn as a knot."

"That's an awful thing to say."

"It's the truth." Adam watched the men place the rock carefully into the tub.

"Thought you'd 'ave more sympathy for 'er, what with you being so sweet on 'er and all."

Per's warning of "Look out!" saved Adam from answering. Adam held his breath as the old man doused the heated rocks. Water sizzled into steam, obscuring the bed in a white fog. Per continued to pour hot water over the rocks.

Pushing through the water vapor that clung like grotesque jewels to his skin, Adam peered at Gypsy's face, hoping for a change. He pinned her arm to the bed as she began to cough. If she put her hands in front of her face, she might keep the mist from reaching her. His gut cramped at the sound, for the coughs slashed deep within her. Folding her fingers between his, he wished he could find a way to strip the fever away.

The hours Adam sat by Gypsy's bed passed uncounted. He lost track of day and night. When he was brought food, he ate. When the flunkeys peeked in, he gave orders. Farley came to get a report, but Adam ordered the camp manager not to return until he brought a doctor.

White steam clung to the walls, setting the bark to sparkling. The windowpanes froze into sheets of ice. Every attempt he made to get Gypsy to eat was unavailing. He watched the slow rise and fall of her chest and wished he could help her.

Fatigue burned his eyes. Blinking away exhaustion, Adam noticed faint light coming through the window. He tried to determine if it had been one day or two ... or three. Rising, he kneaded the ache in his lower back. Years before, he had huddled behind a redoubt for days. Then he had not noticed the exertion of carrying a heavy rifle and supplies during a forced march or while facing the Confederates.

This was what he got for forgetting his resolve to keep out of everyone else's lives. Hadn't he learned his lesson at that redoubt? He should be doing his job and getting out of here, no connections to anyone or anything. Getting involved was an invitation to heartache.

He looked back at the bed. Somehow Gypsy had invei-
gled her way past all his defenses. He wanted her. He
wanted to discover the flavor of every soft inch of her
skin and to seek rapture deep within her. With her, he
could discover sweet satisfaction—but if he had half a
brain, that would be all.

No connections to anyone or anything. As she coughed
weakly, he knew he must keep his vow. But for the first
time, he wondered if he could.

CHAPTER ELEVEN

She hurt.

Her chest ached, and her throat was raw. Something pounded on her head like the iron burner's hammer on an anvil. Every time she took a breath, another boulder seemed to add to the weight pressing down on her.

Coolness.

Sweet moisture. It trickled down her throat, as luscious as ice cream on a summer afternoon. The trickle became a stream and then a river, washing away the heavy stones.

She took a deep breath. It was as sweet as ambrosia. She savored another. For the love of heaven, she could breathe!

A deep voice rumbled. She could not understand the words. No matter. She could breathe.

Another voice answered, and her heart thumped not with pain, but with happiness. Adam's voice. Adam was here.

"Adam?" she whispered, struggling to push her eyes open.

A shadow slipped over her. She blinked, trying to see his face, but fog drifted through her room.

"Don't talk, honey. Just rest." He smiled and scratched his bewhiskered chin. "You've been mighty sick. When you get feeling better, I'm going to tell you exactly how stupid you were not to rest."

A smile tugged at her weak lips as he bent to kiss her lightly. He would stay here with her, if for no other reason than to be able to say *I told you* so when she was better. She could trust him to help her . . . now. Later was something she did not want to think about.

That thought followed her into a dreamless sleep.

Doc Ahearn inched past the bucket and waved aside the steam. His brows, which were as dark as his unrelieved frock coat and bag, rose along his bald pate. "That's quite an invention, Lassiter."

"I can't take credit for it," Adam said. He had not been able to stifle his smile since Gypsy had reopened her eyes several hours ago. "It was Per's idea."

The doctor smiled at Gypsy, who was unusually quiet. "Now what's this I hear about your being sick? That's not like you."

In a wispy voice, which was all she could manage past her scored throat, she whispered, "I hope this hasn't inconvenienced you, Doc."

"You know I'll take any chance to see you. Might convince you to run off with me yet." He winked broadly at Adam, who was listening and grinning.

"I just might agree. Having a doctor around sounds wonderful."

The doctor's brown eyes narrowed. Picking up her wrist, he put his sausage-thick fingers on her pulse. He opened the pocket watch he wore beneath his coat and counted silently. Looking across the bed, he said, "Excuse us, Lassiter. I'm sure Gypsy doesn't want an audience."

Startled by Doc Ahearn's sudden acerbity, Adam nodded. Gypsy's condition must be even worse than he had guessed. Going to the door, he paused. An astonishingly strong throb of dismay cut through him as he saw the doctor open his bag.

Hank bustled forward. "Sit, Adam. You must be half dead on your feet."

"At least half dead," he agreed with a yawn. Glancing around the kitchen, he asked, "Where's Farley? I thought he'd be here."

"Rose is right put out that he's been worrying about Gypsy." The fat man snickered. "Said he should spend Saturday night with her."

"Saturday? Is it Saturday?"

Bert shoved a glass toward him. " 'Ere. This should 'elp you figure out where you are. Drink up."

Lifting the glass, Adam obeyed. "Whiskey? Farley would have our jobs if he discovered us with this." He grinned wryly. "He'd have our necks."

Hank shrugged. "We deserve a few drinks. It's Saturday night. Just because we want to stay here doesn't mean we have to miss our weekly entertainment."

"No dancing girls?" he jested as he rubbed his left leg. It was definitely time to get rid of the cast.

"The girls were busy when I bought this moonshine from Miss Nissa." Putting the bottle in the middle of the table, the heavy man laughed. "She agreed not to tell Farley as long as we looked after Gypsy. Appears she thinks a great deal of Gypsy."

"It's hard not to think a great deal of Gypsy." Adam held out his cup for a refill. "Tip 'er up, Hank. We'll drink to her health. Even Farley can't begrudge us that."

Hearing laughs from the kitchen, Gypsy rebuttoned her nightgown. She looked expectantly at the doctor. When she saw the number of packets the doctor was placing on the table, she grimaced.

Doc Ahearn chuckled. "You didn't think you'd escape without taking some medicine, did you?"

"I'd hoped to avoid that." When she tried to sigh, her breath caught, and she began to cough. Weak tears oozed from her eyes.

"I don't want you out of that bed until these powders are gone."

"There's enough there for a month!"

"Actually about a week."

"A week!"

"Take it easy, girl, or you'll be here for a lot longer. You've been very ill."

"That's what Adam said."

"Adam is right." He closed his bag with an authoritative click. "He and your boys took good care of you. If they hadn't, you'd be dead."

He strode to the door. Wanting to call him back, for he had left no instructions about what to do with the powders, Gypsy gasped when she heard him call Adam. She sagged into the mattress when the answering clunk of the cast and crutch resonated through her room.

Closing her eyes, she listened to the two deep voices. She delighted in having someone else take a share of the responsibility she had shouldered alone for so long.

A hand lifted hers, and she opened her eyes. She smiled at Adam. The dark whiskers blurring his strong jaw told her how unstinting his care had been. Turning her hand in his, she squeezed his fingers with what strength she had.

"Rest, Gypsy," he whispered.

Every sound reverberated through her aching skull. As she closed her eyes, he tucked the chenille bedspread around her. Exactly when she fell asleep, she was unsure, but she knew Adam would be waiting when she woke. And that was all the comfort she needed right now.

"Good morning!"

Gypsy opened a single eye to discover Adam was coming toward her with a tray. He had rid himself of the cast almost a week ago. *As if his leg had never been broken,* she thought with silent sarcasm.

"How did you sleep?" he continued in the same cheerful voice.

"Fine."

He laughed at her grumble. Placing the tray on the table by her bed, he poured a cup of tea. "Is this how you treat kindness, Gypsy?"

"I'm tired of being cosseted."

His grin vanished as she struggled to plump the pillows. When she began to cough, he grimaced and took them from her. Fluffing them, he stuffed them between her and the headboard. He settled her shoulders against the softness, then offered her the cup.

While she gulped the sweetened tea, he said, "Maybe that'll prove you have no more strength than a newborn kitten. One of these days, you're going to admit how close you came to dying."

"Dying of pneumonia or dying of boredom—which is worse?"

"Nothing's worse than hearing your bellyaching about something only time can cure," he snapped with abrupt heat.

Regret sliced through her. She should be grateful he had tended her. In a subdued voice, she asked, "How are you managing in the kitchen?"

"Me or everyone?"

"Everyone . . . and you."

He smiled as he put jelly on a slice of bread. Handing it to her, he took her cup. "The jacks haven't complained, although they'll be glad when you're back making pies and cakes."

The idea of the same food day after day turned her stomach, but she had to be thankful the flunkeys had kept the cookhouse going. "Why don't you put Oscar in charge of desserts?"

"Me put him in charge?"

She smiled. Leaning back in the comfortable nest of pillows, she balanced the cup on her knee. "If you prefer, tell him *I'm* putting him in charge of desserts.".

When he saluted as he gave her a teasing "Yes, sir," her smile faded. She lowered her eyes.

His finger under her chin tipped her face up to the concern in his expressive eyes. "What is it, honey?"

"Your saluting like that reminds me of the war."

"That's a long time ago."

"Not so long ago." Her eyes grew distant as scenes from the past rushed into her memory. "It seems like only yesterday when Elliott was teasing me as Oscar does."

"Who's Elliott?"

"He was my brother," she answered as she smiled at the recollection she had not savored in so long.

"Your brother's name was Elliott Elliott?"

Gypsy sat straighter. "Of course not! His friends called him Elliott, and the family used that name, too."

"I thought you only had a sister."

"Elliott is dead."

He sat beside her, his hand settling on her drawn-up knee. "In the war?"

"Yes." She spoke the lie easily, for it was almost the truth. A few days did not change the fact that her brother had died while wearing his tattered gray uniform on his way home from the surrender at Appomattox.

"I'm sorry, Gypsy."

"I'm sorry, too." Plucking his hand off her knee, she said, "I've been meaning to ask you. What's happened with Lolly Yerkes's murder?"

"Nothing."

"Nothing's been discovered?"

"Didn't I just say that?"

The bed bounced as he stood, and a splash of hot tea burned through the blanket before she moved her leg hastily.

"You can be sure the murderer's success will encourage him to try again."

When she gasped, a bout of coughing tightened its iron

bands around her chest. He waited for her to stop long enough to say, "Adam, he or she has to be stopped."

"She? What makes you think the murderer was a woman?"

"How could it be a man?" She sipped the tea. "The men were in their bunkhouses, except for you and Farley. Even if one of you had gone there, would you have been able to sneak into the crib without someone seeing you?"

He chuckled as he took her left hand and stroked it, sending pleasure flowing along her arm. "Gypsy, don't be naive. Nissa's girls like to make a few coins during the week. The men are pleased with a little illicit entertainment. Everyone's been happy with the arrangement until now."

"Until now." Raising her eyes to meet the azure glow in his, she nearly gasped again. That fierce heat revealed that longing fluttered within him, too.

His hand curved along her cheek as she leaned against the pillows. Too long ago, he had seared desire into her mouth. Every delectable caress, every exhilarating moment of expectation, every craving to be closer to him, all of it exploded through her.

She closed her eyes as his face lowered toward hers. When his lips grazed her cheek, she moaned a heartbroken denial. Opening her eyes, she put her cup on the tray. Taking his hands, she drew him nearer. Her fingers slid up his arms.

Leaning on his hands set on either side of her legs, he shook his head. "You have a hard enough time breathing without . . ." He grinned. "I want you breathing hard because of my touch, not because you've been sick."

"Adam, I want you to hold me."

"That's not supposed to be part of your convalescence."

"Did Doc Ahearn say that?"

"No," he admitted, smiling, "but you know what that cheapjack Farley would do if he had to send for the doctor again. He'd lose the rest of his temper."

She clasped her fingers behind his nape. "Then kissing me isn't specifically forbidden by the doctor?"

"No."

"And you don't know if it would hurt or help?"

His mustache tilted at a rakish angle. "It sure would help me. Seeing you sitting in this bed day after day with your green eyes spitting like a furious cat makes me forget you should be resting. I'd rather take you on a romp."

He claimed her lips. Sensing his fettered passion, she had no time to react before he lifted his mouth from hers. She steered his mouth back over hers. Again he drew away after the briefest touch.

"As soon as you're feeling better," he whispered, stroking her lips, "I want to kiss you until you beg me never to stop, Gypsy."

She flushed and looked away. The very idea of his beguiling touch and his breath mingling with hers sent a new wave of fire surging through her. Was she a complete fool?

"I should thank you for all you've done," she said, finding sanctuary in platitudes.

"Gratitude?" He sat on the bed again. Refilling her cup, he held it out. His smile vanished when her fingers quivered as she fought to hold the saucer steady.

To cover her disquiet with her frailty, she asked, "Is that so unbelievable?"

"In a way. I thought Gypsy Elliott never wanted to be obligated to anyone."

"Good intentions seldom work out."

"I agree."

Her eyes widened. "What's that supposed to mean?"

"That I need to get to work, honey." Rising, he let his fingers linger on her shoulder. "I promised myself I'd stay only long enough to be sure you could handle eating your breakfast." He smiled. "However, I can't say I mind breaking that promise."

"Will you come back soon?"

Tapping her nose, he said, "You know what a strict

master the kitchen is. Without you, it seems everything takes twice as long.''

''My goodness, Mr. Lassiter! A compliment!''

''You made it look so easy. I'll be glad when you get back to work.''

Her smile faded. ''So will I.''

''Until then . . .'' He scooped up a handful of magazines from the tray. ''Reverend Frisch brought these. He thought you'd be getting anxious for something to do.''

She smiled. ''You're taking such good care of me.''

''A plot to get you well so we can have apple pie.''

Gypsy laughed as he left, but sagged against the pillows when the door closed. She could not laugh or sigh or take a deep breath without care. Walking about the room left her so feeble she had to take a nap. She hated being sick and dependent and useless.

Reaching for a magazine, she smiled when she paged through the used issue of *Harper's Bazar.* Farley owed her a favor for taking Adam into the kitchen. The first thing she would ask him for would be a more recent edition of this magazine.

Looking at the small patterns which could be enlarged, she traced the lines. She had scant need for horsehair crinolines or silk gowns or velvet bonnets, but she longed for such luxuries to brighten the endless drudgery of cooking bread and pies and cakes and biscuits for the loggers.

She dropped the magazine onto her lap and stared across the room to where her extra skirt and blouse hung on a peg. They were almost identical to the outfit flung over the chair. In the box beneath her bed was the gown she had worn when she arrived at camp. The navy blue wool was the only decent dress she owned.

After this winter, she vowed to have a lovely frock made, something fine enough to wear in Saratoga. Wearing a dress with wispy organdy sleeves and layers of petticoats, she could be something other than a kingbee cook.

She smiled as she sipped her tea. She never had time for daydreaming, so she should enjoy this chance. As she closed her eyes, she fell asleep to dream of wearing the elegant gown as she stepped into Adam's arms.

"You needn't stand the stove watch, Adam." Hank was unusually vehement. "You've done too much since Gypsy's been sick."

Adam smiled. "More than she did?"

"He's got you there." Per laughed. "We never thought twice about making Gypsy take her turn."

Hank's jowls lengthened as he glanced at the bedroom door. "Just don't want you to start ailing, too. We need someone to tell us what to do."

"I think you'd do fine if you had to," Adam said.

The round man did not seem convinced. With a grumble, he acknowledged, "Maybe."

Per slapped Hank's pudgy shoulder. "Don't listen to this fool's yapping. He's afraid someone might want to put him in charge. C'mon, Hank, my boy. Let's get a few hours' sleep."

"Wait for me!" called Oscar. He slid the last tray of gingerbread from the oven. "I'll be just a minute."

"Go ahead," Adam ordered. "I'll cut that and put it in the larder."

The lad nodded. "Thanks, Adam. See you in the morning."

The men pulled on their coats and went out into the snowstorm which had settled onto the camp with nightfall. The flakes cleaned the air of the odors from the privies and the stable by the blacksmith's shop.

Adam glanced at Gypsy's door and smiled when he saw no lamplight under it. Although she groused about her convalescence, she had to fight to stay awake.

Easily he sliced the gingerbread. He lifted the heavy tray and carried it into the larder. When the back door opened into him, he glared at Bert. "Look out!"

The Englishman closed the door hastily. "Need 'elp?"

"All set." He put the tray next to the ones Oscar had brought in. Wiping his crumb-covered hands on his trousers, he asked, "Got that barrel secured out there?"

Bert laughed. "You sound like Gypsy. She's always 'arping on us to be sure the lids are on." Digging into his shirt pocket, he pulled out an envelope. "Think she's awake?"

"She's sleeping. Why?"

"Meant to give 'er this earlier. Came with the mail over at the wanigan. Guess it'll 'ave to wait until tomorrow."

"I can give it to her."

"Tonight?" His eyes narrowed as a lecherous grin tipped his mustache.

"Tomorrow."

Bert shook his head. "Chauncey gave it to me. Said to put it directly in Gypsy's 'and."

Adam smiled. "Why don't I slide it under her door?"

For a moment, Bert didn't answer. Then he nodded. "That should work. I can—"

"I'll do it. You're going to miss the poker game over in the bunkhouse if you delay any longer."

"Don't want to miss that." He tossed the envelope to Adam, but did not move toward the door.

Adam knew the flunkey wanted to watch him put the letter under Gypsy's door. Not that he could fault Bert. Chauncey was particular about letters getting to the right person without anyone else reading them.

As he bent to shove the envelope under the door, he frowned. He recognized the handwriting on the envelope and bit back his curse when he saw the blurred postmark. Saginaw! The last time Gypsy had gotten a note with this handwriting and this postmark, she had been distraught.

He pushed the letter partway under the door, then stood, keeping his foot on the small edge still protruding. Folding his arms over his chest, he said, "All set, Bert."

"Thanks."

Take advantage of this offer to enjoy Zebra's newest line of historical romance novels....Splendor Romances (formerly Lovegrams Historical Romances)- Take our introductory shipment of 4 romance novels -Absolutely Free! (a $19.96 value)

Now you'll be able to savor today's best romance novels without ever leaving your home with our convenient and inexpensive home subscription service. Here's what you get for joining:

• 4 BRAND NEW bestselling Splendor Romances delivered to your doorstep every month

• 20% off every title (or almost $4.00 off) with your home subscription

• A FREE monthly newsletter, *Zebra/Pinnacle Romance News* filled with author interviews, member benefits, book previews and more!

• No risks or obligations...you're free to cancel whenever you wish...no questions asked

To get started with your own home subscription, simply complete and return the card provided. You'll receive your FREE introductory shipment of 4 Splendor Romances and then you'll begin to receive monthly shipments of new Zebra Splendor titles. Each shipment will be yours to examine for 10 days. If you decide to keep the books, you'll pay the preferred home subscriber's price of just $4.00 per title plus $1.50 shipping and handling. That's $16 for all 4 books plus $1.50 for home delivery! And if you want us to stop sending books, just say the word...it's that simple.

4 FREE books are waiting for you!
Just mail in the certificate below!

If the certificate is missing below, write to:
Splendor Romances, Zebra Home Subscription Service, Inc.,
P.O. Box 5214, Clifton, New Jersey 07015-5214
or call TOLL-FREE 1-888-345-BOOK
Visit our website at www.kensingtonbooks.com.

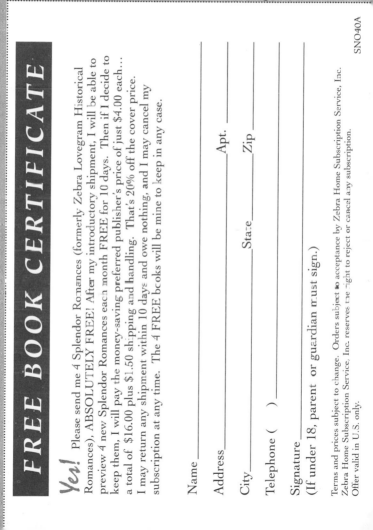

FREE BOOK CERTIFICATE

Yes! Please send me 4 Splendor Romances (formerly Zebra Lovegram Historical Romances), ABSOLUTELY FREE! After my introductory shipment, I will be able to preview 4 new Splendor Romances each month FREE for 10 days. Then if I decide to keep them, I will pay the money-saving preferred publisher's price of just $4.00 each... a total of $16.00 plus $1.50 shipping and handling. That's 20% off the cover price. I may return any shipment within 10 days and owe nothing, and I may cancel my subscription at any time. The 4 FREE books will be mine to keep in any case.

Name _____

Address _____ Apt. _____

City _____ State _____ Zip _____

Telephone ( ) _____

Signature _____
(If under 18, parent or guardian must sign.)

Terms and prices subject to change. Orders subject to acceptance by Zebra Home Subscription Service, Inc. Zebra Home Subscription Service, Inc. reserves the right to reject or cancel any subscription.
Offer valid in U.S. only.

SNO40A

PLACE
STAMP
HERE

llıııluıllllıııılılılıılılıılıılıllıılılıılıılıılllıııl

SPLENDOR ROMANCES
Zebra Home Subscription Service, Inc.
P.O. Box 5214
Clifton NJ 07015-5214

"I'll make sure she's gotten it when I check to see she's taken her medicine."

Bert grinned. "No one would 'ave guessed she'd be this patient. Seems to listen to you as she's never listened to anyone else."

"It's been a struggle, but getting her well is worth every hour of arguing."

"Arguing? I would 'ave thought you two were getting right cozy by this time."

Adam kept his face blank. "And what's that supposed to mean?"

"Exactly what you think." He walked to the main door. "You've worn off 'er rough edges. Thought you were man enough to know when a woman's sweet on you."

"I can't imagine Gypsy being *sweet* on anyone."

"No?"

"No!"

"Don't 'ave much imagination then." He chortled as he tapped his hat onto his head.

Adam gave Bert a wry smile. To think that the other flunkeys were oblivious to his attraction to Gypsy was foolish. When she was in the room, he noticed little else. He enjoyed watching the soft sway of her skirts and the lyrical motions of her hands, even when she was lambasting one of them. Her sparkling eyes enticed him to forget what he was doing and pull her into his arms while he kissed her until she dissolved against him.

His smile became a scowl when the flunkey went out. Bending, he pulled the letter back from under the door. He slipped a finger beneath the loose flap, hoping he was wrong.

He was not.

Glad to hear you are doing better. Didn't want to think you would die of something as quick as pneumonia. Get out of that bed so I can help you into a pine box.

With a curse, he thrust the letter back into the envelope and stuffed it into his pocket.

Someone was threatening Gypsy. Who? Not a single jack had griped about the simple food. Many had offered assistance to get her better more quickly. All their questions had been about how she was faring, not when she was returning to her duties.

Saginaw.

The city was not far, not more than a week's walk. If the threat was related to what he had been sent here to do, he feared Lolly Yerkes's murder was just a prelude to trouble. He had to get answers.

Fast.

Before disaster . . . and death . . . struck again.

CHAPTER TWELVE

"What are you doing up?" Adam ignored the flunkeys' shock at his furious question.

Gypsy pulled her apron over her head. Tying it around her, she disregarded the loose material bunching at her side. If Adam discovered how much weight she had lost, he would be even more mulish. She did not need his misplaced gallantry.

"Bert," she ordered, "get me some flour. The men are going to have apple pie tonight. If—"

"Bert, wait!"

She glared at Adam. "Are you going to countermand my orders? I don't have the strength to waste on arguing with you."

"You don't have the strength to mix pie dough."

"You're wrong." She lifted the bucket for making pie dough down from the shelf. Although her knees almost buckled, she regarded Adam with defiance. "I'm going to make pies. That's all I'm going to do other than keep an eye on you gentlemen to be sure you haven't picked up any bad habits. If you have, get rid of them. Your easy life is over."

Grinning, Oscar turned back to the stove to load more wood. Hank chuckled as he peeled carrots. Only Adam continued to glower at her.

"Do you need something to do, Mr. Lassiter?" she asked.

"I thought you might want me to tote apples out here for you."

Gypsy bit her lower lip. Remembering his tenderness during her recovery, she said quietly, "I'd appreciate that."

He smiled. When he put his hands on her shoulders, she almost gasped. He had been circumspect about touching her in the kitchen. Then she realized pretending was needless. She raised her hands to settle on his.

"Don't change and be pleasant," he answered in a near whisper. "I don't know what I'd do if you didn't snarl at me once in a while. I'd think my Gypsy had vanished."

"*Your* Gypsy?"

"That's better." He grinned and tugged on a loose strand of her hair before swaggering toward the larder.

She shook her head as she reached a scoop to measure out the flour Bert had set by the table. She hummed a light tune and smiled at Adam when he returned with boxes of dried fruit. He winked as she bent to her work. It was grand to be back in her kitchen.

Gypsy rolled over as the door to her room opened. The lamp was off, and the fire was burning low in the stove. A shadow slipped through the door and up the bed to drape her in its ebony warmth.

"Adam?" she whispered, startled.

"Yes."

"What are you doing here?"

He put a tray on the table beside her bed. "I thought you might need something."

"No, I'm fine."

"Or someone."

At the raw yearning in his voice, she stared up at him, but his features were lost in the darkness. Wood crackled in the stove, and light flashed up his face, accenting every strong plane.

"I need you," he whispered. He sealed the soft words into her lips with the fire on his. "I want you in my life and next to me tonight."

Her gasp of protest was muted as he captured her lips.

His arms slipped around her. In her ear, he whispered, "I have the stove watch tonight, thanks to my new schedule."

"I thought Per took you off the stove watch."

"I put myself back on. The other flunkeys agreed when I told them it was your order."

"You lied to them!"

"You've told me more than once I'm no gentleman."

His fingers led her mouth beneath his. He drew her closer as he caressed her, arousing the unsated passions within her. His mouth against her neck sent waves of desire through her as powerful as a tree crashing to earth.

Against her hair, he murmured, "You've driven me mad with desire. For as long as you wish, be mine. I can't imagine becoming tired of having you by my side."

She pushed him away as she realized nothing had changed. "No! I'm not like Nissa's girls."

He shrugged, shocking her. "If making love isn't what you long for—although I know you desire me as much as I do you—then let's eat."

"Eat?"

With a flourish, he pulled the cloth off the tray. He handed her a napkin and served her a generous portion of pie.

"This is sweet potato pie!" she gasped. "Where did you get sweet potatoes?"

"Anything is possible if you want it enough." He put his hand over hers and drew the fork away. "As much as I want you."

"I can't."

"Yes, honey," he murmured before his tongue teased her ear. "You can if you want to."

"But I can't let anyone close to me! When I let someone in my heart, they end up dead." She stared down at the plate on her lap. "I don't want you to die, Adam."

"Right now, the only thing I'm at risk of dying from is this deep craving to savor every inch of you."

Gypsy dampened her lips as his hands covered hers. When he lifted her fingers to his mouth, his tongue toyed with her fingertip. He drew it into his mouth, sucking gently. The plate fell to the floor, splattering pie across the boards, but she paid it no mind when he sat beside her.

"Be mine," he whispered as he framed her face with his hands.

Her breath battered against her chest. She wanted him. She wanted him as she had wanted nothing else in her life. Yet . . .

She drew his hands down and clasped them in hers. Swallowing roughly, she said, "Adam, if I share my bed with you tonight, no one must know of it. And it can be only this one night."

His brow furrowed. "Why?"

"Don't ask. Tonight I'll be yours—if you will never ask me again."

"Gypsy—"

"No. Don't say anything but yes or no."

"How can I?" Sorrow left his face bare to reveal his longing to hold her. "If I say yes, you'll be mine, but only tonight. If I say no, I deny us the rapture we could share."

"You must choose, Adam."

"Do you think I'd tell you I don't want you tonight?"

"No." Asking herself what else she had expected from the man who made no secret of his desire for her, she shivered. She turned away, unable to meet his eyes and the longing they displayed. Slowly she began to unhook the front of her nightgown.

She gasped as he brought her to face him. In the moment before he claimed her mouth, he whispered, "Be mine, honey."

Her hands stroked upward along his flannel sleeves and the brawny muscles beneath them. When she touched his shoulders, his arms swept around her. Held against him, she sensed his escalating desire.

His tongue darted within her mouth, warmed by her sigh of eager passion. As her fingers sifted upward through his thick hair, he explored each succulent surface of her mouth, enticing her to touch him as sweetly. Tremors burst outward from the slick stroke of his tongue against hers.

Loosening her hair to fall about her shoulders, he pressed his mouth against the crook of her neck. When he leaned her back into the bed, she slipped her hands beneath his shirt. His warm, rough skin urged her to explore farther.

Lying next to her, he drew her into his warm embrace. She whispered his name when he tasted the skin at the base of her throat. His hair brushed her skin, stoking the inferno bursting to life within her. With a fervency she did not recognize, she stroked the firm muscles of his back.

His lips sought along the modest neckline of her loosened nightgown as he drew it lower. His heated mouth caressed the curve of her breast, and she moaned with quickening need. Her trembling fingers fumbled on the buttons of his shirt, for she ached for his skin against her.

His laugh swirled through her as he lifted her hand from his shirt and pressed her palm against his mouth. Gazing up at him, she wondered how she could have thought he was interested only in his own pleasures. He was maddening, perhaps. Arrogant, without question. Alluring with his ever-changing eyes, undeniably. But she saw his determination to make this night one that would haunt them forever with memories of ecstasy.

When she began to undo his shirt, a button fell off in her hand. He chuckled and tossed it on the table.

"I'll have to get another spool of thread from Chauncey," she whispered. Her gaze swept along his broad chest as she pushed his shirt along his arms with a whisper of worn material. "Forgive me if I'm clumsy. I don't know what you want . . . I've never . . ."

He rolled her onto her back. Leaning over her, he murmured, "I want rapture, honey, pure rapture."

Greedily he took her mouth with his. As she clasped his naked shoulders, she gave herself to desire. She wanted this, and she wanted him. Not just the sweetly romantic wooing she had seen her sister enjoy with suitors, but the mind-emptying passion he could evoke.

When he grasped the front of her nightgown, he gave a sharp tug. The buttons flew in a dozen directions as it tore. Her half-voiced cry of protest vanished when he traced the top of her chemise with his tongue. As he pulled her nightgown down, his mouth placed sparks along her skin.

He threw the gown onto the floor as he entwined her legs with his. His hands moved along her, entreating her to press against him. The thin fabric of her undergarments sent the heat of his touch all along her.

Steering his mouth over hers, she needed no urging to reach for the buttons at his waist. She slid his denims along his hard legs as her eyes delighted in the virile strength of his male body. Tentatively, then more boldly, she touched him, finding the thrill of giving him pleasure. Each texture of his body was so different. Along his chest, a mat of hair teased her fingers to tangle in it, but she followed its narrowing toward his waist to discover far more silken skin which burned beneath her fingers.

His breath pulsed savagely against her as he loosened the ribbons on her chemise. The brush of his fingers against her inflamed her craving. As he swept her remaining clothes aside, she clung to him, wanting the joy only he could give her.

His fingers skimmed higher along her leg as his lips branded fire into her. She moaned when his tongue circled her breast before drawing its tip into his mouth, taunting it to hardness beneath his gentle assault. Moving against him with the rhythm his hand was creating on her thigh, all thought faded.

She gasped his name when his fingers sought the depths of the flame within her. Each probing stroke accelerated the blazing heat until it threatened to devour her. Hearing his breathless voice against her ear, she could not understand anything but desire.

When he leaned over her again, his rasping breaths filled her mouth as he melded them into one. Everything evaporated in the craving which consumed her. She became the sensation of his body over and within her. As need metamorphosed into ecstasy, she shattered into perfection.

A knock on the door woke Gypsy. She rubbed her eyes as it swung open.

Adam peeked in and asked, "A cup of swamp water to get your day started before the other flunkeys get here, Gypsy?"

"That sounds excellent." She wished he would come closer, so she could let her fingers curve along his unyielding jaw again. "And another piece of that pie before it gets gobbled up."

He shoved the door aside as he carried two cups toward her. "What pie?"

"The sweet potato pie."

He put the cups on the table. "Sweet potato pie? Are you all right?" He put his hand on her forehead. "You're all sweaty. Did your fever return last night? Maybe you should stay in bed today."

When he tucked the blanket more tightly around her, Gypsy stretched past him to look at the floor.

''What do you want?'' he asked. ''Did you lose something?''

She stared up at him. Why didn't he know she wanted him? Didn't he know she had lost her virginity to him?

Or had she?

Her fingers groped at her throat where the high collar of her nightgown was damp, but not torn from his passionate haste. The pillow beside her bore no indentation from his head resting there as they slept cuddled together. Frowning, she reached up to touch the front of his shirt. No buttons were missing.

His hand over hers imprisoned her fingers against the rough flannel. ''Can I hope this is your answer?'' Gentle humor filled his voice. ''Do you want me?''

Shouts came from the kitchen as the other flunkeys arrived for the beginning of the day. Adam bent and kissed her lightly on the cheek. Telling her he would let the others know she was going to rest a while longer, he walked out of the room.

She hid her face in her hands. For the love of heaven, the ecstasy had been only her imagination heightened by a fever that was not as hot as his touch had been—a touch she must never allow herself to savor beyond her fantasies, or this last, most precious dream could be destroyed forever.

CHAPTER THIRTEEN

At the sound of footsteps which were lighter than any male boots, Gypsy paused. The glitter of interest in the flunkeys' eyes warned her who was walking toward them. She wiped her hands on her apron as she turned to greet Rose Quinlan, who looked like an angel in pale pink wool.

"Miss Elliott?" Rose's squeaky voice ruined the perfection of her pose and reminded Gypsy that Rose could not be much more than a girl.

"This is a surprise," Gypsy answered. When the young woman's brows wrinkled in a frown, she added, "A very pleasant surprise. How can I help you, Miss Quinlan?"

Rose turned her back on the men staring at her. Raising her chin in disgust, she pointed toward Gypsy's room. "I would appreciate some privacy."

"Go ahead, Miss Quinlan. I'll be with you as soon as I finish here."

"As soon as—but this is important!"

"So is being sure the jacks are fed." Gypsy smiled coldly. "Farley wouldn't be pleased if his loggers went hungry."

Rose turned on her heel and walked toward Gypsy's room.

When the men started to grumble, Gypsy ordered, "Get to work. You can complain just as well while you're working. As soon as Adam and Oscar get back from delivering lunch, tell them to start tonight's desserts."

She went to her room before someone could see her relief that Adam was not here. If he had an inkling of how her fantasies had come to life in her fevered mind, she did not know what she would do. Or what he would do. Would he laugh? Or would he try to persuade her to make that dream come true in his arms?

Closing the door, she forced a polite smile. She pushed all thoughts of Adam from her head as her smile became a frown.

Rose turned from examining the items on the table. Without apologizing for her curiosity, the blonde sat on the chair as if she were a queen awaiting an audience with her humblest subject.

Gypsy sat on her bed and asked, "What is it you didn't want to discuss out there?"

"I want to leave Calvin."

"What?" This was the last thing she had expected Rose to say. "Why?"

Nervously, she rubbed her gloved hands together. "I have my reasons, Miss Elliott." She touched a bump beneath her glove.

Gypsy guessed it must be a large gem set in a ring. After hearing the adoration in Farley's voice each time he spoke of his mistress, she should have guessed he was beggaring himself to buy Rose grand gifts.

"Why do you want to leave Farley?" Gypsy asked.

Rose moistened her wide, bottom lip. "I would prefer to leave private matters out of this."

Gypsy leaned her elbow on the iron footboard. "Then why did you want to speak to me?"

"I want you to convince Calvin to let me leave."

"Me?" She choked, then laughed. "I don't know what

you think, but it's purely business between Calvin Farley and me.''

Rose put her hand over Gypsy's fingers, which were ingrained with flour. ''I'm not suggesting something ridiculous like your replacing me.''

''I hope not.'' She bit back her retort that she had repulsed Farley's eager proposition the first year she worked at the camp.

''Miss Elliott, he respects you. He'll listen to you.''

''About what?''

Rising, Rose went to the mirror and adjusted her hat with trembling fingers. Gypsy frowned as she noticed gray crescents beneath Rose's eyes. Rice powder could not disguise her fear.

With her hands clasped in a pose of vulnerability, she whispered, ''I'm afraid to stay here.''

''Afraid?'' Gypsy stood. ''Of what? Certainly not of Farley! The man dotes on you.''

''It's not Calvin. It's—it's—'' Her face lost all remaining color. ''It's someone else.''

''One of my men?''

''I don't know, Miss Elliott.'' Tears bubbled from her eyes, and her lip shivered. ''I feel his eyes.''

''You should be accustomed to the stares of the men.''

''Nissa Jensen is leaving. Her girl was killed. Calvin told me, but he said I shouldn't worry.''

''He's right.''

A calculated expression aged her face. ''I know what you're thinking. You consider me a mindless fool who has nothing to be frightened of.''

''How can you expect me to speak to Farley when you won't tell me why you think you're in danger?'' The temptation to laugh taunted her. Rose Quinlan was scared by shadows. Gypsy wondered how Farley's mistress would act if she had received the threatening notes Gypsy had. She let out her breath in a soft sigh. There had been no more letters. Maybe whoever was sending them had gotten tired of the sadistic game.

"All I want you to do is tell him to listen to me," Rose moaned.

"I—"

"Please, Gypsy!"

She blinked at the fervor in the blonde's voice. Rose must be terrified. "All right."

"Today?"

"I can't promise that."

"By tomorrow."

Sighing, Gypsy nodded. When Rose mumbled her thanks and left, Gypsy sank to the bed. She rested her head on the iron rail as the familiar tightness cramped her chest.

Why did I agree?

Rubbing her aching head, she knew if she had not acquiesced, Rose would have created an uproar. This was easier. After a quick conversation with Farley, Rose's fears would be his problem.

Gypsy did not appease the flunkeys' curiosity when she came back into the kitchen. She simply asked how the work was progressing.

While she was talking with Hank about how long to cook the whole wheat bread, she heard a terrified screech. She whirled to see Bert shaking his arm. Flames rose from his right sleeve. Whipping off her apron, she leaped to wrap it around Bert's sleeve. Fire ate the thin muslin.

She pushed him toward the door. "Go!"

"Help me! Help me! For the love of heaven, help me!"

"I am!" She tugged on his left arm as shouts came from the other men, drowning out Bert's cries of pain. "Outside! Come outside."

"Help me!" he screeched again.

She shoved him through the back door. The flames whooshed close to her hair. His feet slid on the ice as he teetered, off balance. She pushed him into the snow. Dropping to her knees, she pressed his right arm into a drift. Smoke rose as the snow hissed and melted. Scooping more snow onto his arm, she ordered him not to move.

His face was the same gray as the dirty snow. She slowly unwound the charred apron and frowned when she saw the wool had seared into his tortured skin.

"Here, Gypsy," came a tight voice from behind her. She took the knife and bandaging Adam handed her. Within a minute, she had Bert's arm bound. She stepped back as Adam assisted Bert to his feet.

"Go over to Chauncey and tell him to give you a bottle of salve," she ordered quietly. "Tell him to charge it to the kitchen. Then go back to the bunkhouse and put some right over the bandage. Get in bed and rest. I'll change the bandages tomorrow. I think we got it out before any permanent damage could be done."

Bert gulped as he stared at his arm. When he started to speak, a peculiar expression crossed his face. She almost gasped as she recalled how he had looked the night he confronted her in the kitchen. He wore the same angry scowl as he stamped away, swaying on every step.

"What's wrong with him?" Adam glared at the injured man. "He looked riled that you saved his arm."

Gypsy shook her head. "I don't know."

Slipping his arm around her waist, Adam guided her toward the kitchen. "Come inside before you get cold." His voice softened. "Have I ever told you how magnificent I think you are?"

"No!"

He laughed. "You needn't sound so flabbergasted by a simple compliment, especially when it's true."

Gypsy wanted to smile, but her lips were too tight. If she spoke to him about the sensuous dream that had left her as sweaty as if the fever had returned, she was not **sure** what he would do. Laugh? She hoped not. Urge her **to make** her fantasy come true? He already did that with every touch, with every glance of his fiery eyes.

Pushing past Adam, she went into the kitchen. She shooed the flunkeys back to their tasks with a warning to be careful. Again she resisted the laugh swirling through her. She was the one who needed to be careful. Adam was assaulting her heart, which must remain barricaded away.

"What else can happen today?" she asked with a sigh, as she began to slice the bread.

"What do you mean?" asked Adam as he took another knife and matched her motions.

"Nothing."

"Come now, Gypsy. Even you, at your most cryptic, don't make statements like that."

She continued to place the slices on the oilcloth. Not looking at him was easier. If she saw her yearnings mirrored in his eyes, she might not be able to fight the temptation any longer. "I wish things would go back to the way they were before."

"Before I arrived?"

"Don't flatter yourself." Her brief smile disappeared. "It's Rose."

He grimaced. "What's wrong with that empty-headed woman now?"

"She's frightened of someone."

"Farley?"

Putting the knife onto her lap, she met Adam's eyes without flinching. If she concentrated on Rose and her silly problems, she could keep her own cravings silent. "Not Farley, but she wouldn't tell me who. She pretends not to know, but I suspect she does."

"You don't sound very sure."

"I'm not."

He leaned across the table and tilted her chin so she could not avoid his gaze, which was filled with curiosity and concern. When his finger grazed her cheek, she rose and carried the bread to the counter. For the love of heaven, even a casual touch threatened to undo her resolve. She walked to the bucket by the stove to rinse crumbs from her hands.

"Gypsy, what are you hiding?"

While she dried her hands on a tattered towel, she said, "Nothing. I have no idea why she came here to talk to me. She's been jealous of every meeting between Farley and me." A short laugh burst from her lips. "As if I wanted to steal her lover from her."

"She knows you could."

"Adam, if you want to play at pretty talk, go find Rose and cozy up with her."

He crossed the room to her. "That wasn't a compliment, Gypsy. That was the truth." His hand slid across her shoulder to curve along her neck. With his thumb tipping her mouth toward his, he whispered, "Any man with a bit of life in him would see you were infinitely more alluring than that child."

She held her breath as she waited for the caress of his lips. Slowly her fingers rose to explore the rough warmth of his cheek. His lips twitched, but she could read the truth in his luminous eyes. He wanted her. And she wanted him.

When he released her without a kiss, she stared in amazement. He sat. Rubbing his left leg, he smiled an apology. She bit back her fury. Why was he still lying to her? Or was he? She was no longer sure of anything.

"No matter what you think of Farley's whore," Adam said, "she's so scared that she's put aside her jealousy to beg you to spend time alone with her lover." Meeting her confused eyes squarely, he asked, "So what are you going to do?"

"I told her I'd talk to Farley."

"And get yourself entangled in this mess?"

"I already am."

"You're a fool."

That she had to agree with, but not for the reason he meant. She was a fool to entangle her life with a man who was not honest with her, but could be put in peril because of her. Others had deemed it a series of unfortunate accidents, as her brother, then her mother, then her father died. She feared it was a curse, that *she* was the curse. Only her sister had escaped the horror. She could not draw Adam into this torment.

She dropped the towel onto the woodbox. "Maybe this is nothing more than Rose's attempt to catch me in a compromising position with Farley."

He laughed with no hint of mirth. "You can't believe that."

"I'd like to." Staring at the red glow in the heart of the stove, she sighed. "It's easier than believing someone is threatening a chit like Rose Quinlan."

She went to the window, where the wind blew past the glass to chill the cook shack. Snow floated in an endless cascade toward the ground.

Once she would have found the number of snowstorms in the north woods inconceivable. Then she had lived in a safe womb filled with simple luxuries and love. She had delighted in traditions that flowed from one year to the next in a pattern as intricate and beautiful as the snowflakes. That had ended with the abruptness of a knife slicing through her heart.

All gone.

Rose's fear resurrected memories of nearly a decade ago, when death came in blue or gray uniforms splattered with blood across unmoving young chests. Brass buttons shone brilliantly in the sun setting across a field of death, a field where she and her siblings once had played, a field which tried to hide its scars beneath a pelt of grass.

She blinked back unexpected tears as she touched the glass. The cold clung to her fingers as the ice melted beneath her touch. All her friendships must be as ephemeral as the frost, gone with the coming of spring thaw.

Broad hands gently massaged her shoulders. She should halt Adam. Yet when he touched her, she was unsure if she could flee again—not when she yearned to stay in his arms.

Slowly she faced him. "We have work to do, Adam."

"That we do." His voice became grave as he added, "And it's about time I got to it."

For once, her curiosity was silent. She rested her cheek against his chest, not wanting to think of what the future might hold. She simply wanted to be held, knowing how fleeting this muted happiness must be.

CHAPTER FOURTEEN

The next morning, Gypsy had no answers for Rose's dilemma or her own. She hurried through breakfast, then left the flunkeys to prepare lunch. Wanting to be done with what she had promised to do, she shuffled through the snow that was melting in the strengthening sunshine. She had heard the road monkeys complaining about having to redo the roads every day. The sleds must not hit a rut, or the load could slide off, injuring someone.

Chauncey waved to her. The inkslinger slogged through the snow. "Howdy, Gypsy. Where are you off to?"

"Farley's office."

His lips became a straight line. "That doxy of his causing trouble for you again?"

Forcing a smile, she wagged her finger. "Don't you know it's impolite to ask a lady her personal business?"

He kicked a rock beneath the snow. It popped out to careen across the snowbanks. "I saw that she-devil bustling to the cookhouse yesterday, looking ready to cause trouble. I hope she didn't cause it for you."

"The only trouble I have is you." She patted his arm as he looked at her with his hound-dog-brown eyes. "Why don't you come over tonight and have a cup of swamp water with us?''

"Maybe." His smile returned. "You're a good woman. Not like some around here."

Waving a farewell to the inkslinger, she continued toward Farley's office. She hesitated at the door. If she went back to the cookhouse, she could pretend she had been too busy. She started to step away, but paused as a detonation of coughs cut through her.

The door opened. Farley, as always, looked dapper enough to be working in Detroit. Chiding her for standing in the cold air, he herded her inside. She paid no attention as she fought to regain her steady breathing.

She perched on the very edge of the bench in front of his desk. He balanced on the corner of his desk and clasped his hands around his knee. That, as much as his brusque greeting, warned he was anxious to be done with whatever complaint she had.

"How are things with you, Gypsy?" He chewed on his cigar and tapped it on an ashtray. He frowned when no ash fell from the unlit end. With a glower, as if she were at fault, he struck a match on his boot and puffed on the cigar.

"I'm fine." She waved the cloud of smoke away and met his scowl with her own.

"And the kitchen?"

"Fine."

"How's Lassiter working out now that he's not hobbling around?"

"Fine."

Fiercely he clamped his teeth on the cigar and growled, "Then why are you bothering me today?"

"Rose asked me to speak to you."

His dark eyes widened in amazement. When he rose and began to pace from his desk to the door, a rapid tic pulsed beside his eye. "What did she tell you? As if I don't know. She wants to leave."

"Yes." Standing, she placed a consoling hand on his arm. "Calvin, you're not the reason she wants to leave."

"Why should it be me?" he demanded. "Haven't I given that little whore everything she's asked for?"

Gypsy ached for him. "She's scared."

"Of the wind brushing the pines against the roof!"

"Calvin, you know it's more than that!" Gripping his wool sleeve, she used the stern voice which worked best in the kitchen. "I swear, if you don't provide her with transportation back to Saginaw, she'll walk."

"She's that stupid."

"She's that scared!" She planted her feet firmly and glared at him. "If you have any affection for her, let her go. Forcing her to stay here is crazy, for a bird will beat itself to death on the bars of its cage."

"I don't have to listen to your platitudes."

"For the love of heaven, let her go. The river drive will be soon, and you can meet her afterward."

Brushing her hand off his sleeve, he sat. The chair's loud squeak underlined his furious expression. He pointed his cigar at her. "I don't know who's more stupid—Rose, for conjuring up these tales to convince me to make a grand settlement on her before I let her go back to Saginaw to find another lover or you, for believing her. Gypsy, I thought you were smarter than this."

"I should have known you'd be stupid," she shot back. "Everything that happens from this point is on your head!"

"Get out of here!"

As she reached for the knob, she was startled to hear Farley call her name in a calmer voice. Without turning, she asked, "What is it?"

He cleared his throat, and she was shocked. He must be standing right behind her. His hand on her elbow turned her to face him. Looking up, she drew away. She found the expression in his eyes disquieting. Calvin Farley should not be staring at her with candid longing. She glanced at his fingers stroking the curve of her elbow, then backed into the door. As it rattled, he stepped toward her. She put her hands up, and he froze.

"Don't do anything you'll be sorry for," she whispered.

"Gypsy, don't leave."

"If you mean leave camp, I don't intend to. I shan't be forced out by your bombastic orders."

He reached for her, then stuffed his hands into his pockets. "Is that how you see me? Bombastic?"

"Aren't you?"

The corner of his mustache tipped up. "It works with everyone but you. Even Rose listens when I bellow."

"Then listen when she cries out for your help. She isn't trying to swindle you."

"Gypsy, you don't understand."

"I recognize fear when I see it!"

He put his fingers over hers and stroked them. "She's using you."

"Why do you want to keep her here against her will? What will that do but make you miserable?" She withdrew her hand from beneath his with a motion she hoped looked natural. The heat of his gaze seared her as she lifted the latch.

"Just stay out of this, Gypsy."

"I'd like to, but she insisted you'd listen to me." With a short laugh, she opened the door. "No one can talk sense to a jackass."

Farley shouted something, but she shut the door behind her. Since he had insisted Adam work in the kitchen, Farley had been distant. Wrongly she had guessed he was worried about Adam. He was upset over losing Rose.

The scents of lunch and early preparations for dinner greeted Gypsy when she climbed the high step into the kitchen, but offered no comfort. She should not let Rose's disquiet infect her. Farley's whore was seeing trouble in shadows.

She snapped terse answers to the flunkeys' questions as she hung up her coat. Their uneasy voices followed when she went into the larder. Taking down a box of walnuts, she returned to the kitchen and collected the ingredients she needed. Setting them to one side of the table, she checked the rising bread. It would be ready for kneading when she finished mixing the cookies.

Each time a flunkey spoke to her, she answered with a single word or just a nod. She was relieved when they took lunch to the crews on the hill. Peabody's men were nearly done on their section, but other crews had been sent farther out. She had meant to remind Farley of his promise to set the men closer to camp, but she had forgotten.

Not that it mattered. Farley would have argued about anything.

Gypsy scooped flour into her mixing bucket. Counting carefully, she was surprised to hear footsteps behind her. Fear iced sweat along her back as her heart hung on a single beat. No one else should be in the cook shack. Her fingers clenched on the galvanized bucket.

When wide hands settled on her shoulders, she shrieked. Familiar laughter brushed the loose strands of hair around her ears.

"Adam!" she cried. Calming herself, she added, "Why didn't you go with the other flunkeys?"

"I thought you might need someone to talk to before you stamp right through the floorboards."

"If you're trying to stay out of the cold, I—"

He twirled her to face him. There was no amusement in his eyes. "What did Farley say?"

"What do you think?"

"He refused to listen." He laughed. Straddling the bench, he added, "Maybe it's because the two of you are so much alike."

"Me and Farley?"

"You both hope if you pretend a problem doesn't exist, it'll go away."

She started to reach past him for the walnuts, but paused when her face was even with his. He glanced from her outstretched fingers to the wooden box. With a smile, he pushed it to her.

She said, "If you aren't going up to feed the crews, you can—"

"You don't understand, do you?"

"No, I don't understand why you find this so blasted amusing."

"It's not Rose's fear you need to be worried about. It's Farley's."

She continued to mix the dough. "What does Farley have to be afraid of?"

"Everyone in camp." He flung out his hands and grimaced when he struck a sticky mound of bread dough. Wiping his hand, he grasped a handful of flour and dribbled it on the dough. "If she leaves him, he's afraid every jack will think he wasn't man enough to keep her happy."

"That's absurd."

"Maybe, but it's the truth."

She opened the box of shelled walnuts. Cracking them into small pieces, she sprinkled them into the bucket. "He'd better be careful. Mr. Glenmark won't want trouble." She smiled coldly. "Maybe you should speak to Farley, Adam. He might listen to a man."

"Not Farley. He's as stubborn as an ox."

"Then the two of you should get along famously."

He grimaced. "I suppose you think that's a compliment."

"Compared to what I called him, it was." Spooning cookies onto a tray, she said, "I thought if I called him a jackass, he might come to his senses. I forgot he doesn't have any."

His broad hands caught hers and pulled them toward him, compressing the bread dough beneath them. The dough oozed between her fingers, but she ignored it as he lowered his voice. "Sometimes a man has to put aside love for other obligations, even though it breaks his heart."

She wanted to demand how he could say such a thing

when Rose was so frightened. As she stared into his eyes, thoughts of the other woman vanished like snow dripping from the pine boughs. Gold flecks floated in his eyes' sea blue depths, burnished by the fire within him. His eyes urged her closer and his fingers continued to hold hers under them as he kneaded the dough. The silken texture softened the strength of his hands, but nothing could lessen the passion searing her.

With a gasp, she drew back. "I have to—"

"Bake those cookies?" he asked, laughter drifting through his words.

She was acting like a fool, but better to be a fool like this than to surrender to yearnings whetted by her dream of him introducing her to ecstasy.

Think about work. That always had worked in the past. She had been able to forget her despair and her wants and everything else in the endless, never-changing tasks.

She lifted the tray of cookies and carried it to the stove. Holding her hand near the heat, she gauged the temperature. Her skin prickled, and she knew it was right for baking the cookies. Sliding the tray into the oven, she closed the door and opened the firebox to add a log.

Silently she stepped aside while Adam pushed the wood onto the fire. When he secured the door, she thanked him quietly. His hand on her arm kept her from walking away.

She whispered, "I should be doing something else."

He took her hands and lifted them to his lips. When she raised her eyes, he bent to brush her mouth. His arms surrounded her as her fingers toyed with the fine hairs above his collar before dropping beneath it to caress his warm skin.

His mouth found the responsive curve of her ear and whispered in it. She did not understand his words as she shivered with the sweet fire of his breath fanning awake her desire. She had no need for words when their hearts were beating with the same frantic rhythm. Bringing his lips back to hers, she gasped against his mouth when his fingers slipped along her side to settle on her breast.

Slowly, excruciatingly slowly, his fingertip inched along her, loosening the buttons on her blouse and sweeping her skin with a storm of sweet sensation. Her fingers splayed along his back. She wanted to relish the seething heat which burned from her to him and back. When his tongue touched hers at the very second his rough fingertip teased the tip of her breast, she was sure she would explode with the rapture.

He pressed her against the cupboards, holding her with each masculine angle of his body. Boldly, her hands swept along him as she outlined his hips and stroked the firm line of his thighs. With her breath straining against his mouth, she ached with the loneliness she had suffered too long.

With a moan, she drew back. She must remain lonely. Until she was sure she was not the curse that stalked her family, she could not let someone else into her life.

"Gypsy?"

She shook her head. "I need to—"

"Talk to me." He spun her back to face him before she could walk away. "Rose and Farley—"

She interrupted as he had. "Talking doesn't seem to help them. I wish I could do something to knock sense into their heads." She did not want to talk about this when her fingers itched to touch him again.

Business, she told herself. *Keep it only business.* That had worked with Farley her first winter here. Maybe it would work with Adam, too.

Ironic laughter burned in her throat. Did she really believe that?

"You can't do anything else," Adam said, and she knew he hadn't guessed what she was thinking. "After all, you risked your job for a woman you despise."

Folding her arms in front of her, she whispered, "I do hate Rose. I hate that she's wasting her life trying to cuddle up with Farley."

He sat and settled his feet on the crosspieces on the table legs. Reaching out, he drew her down on his knees and leaned her head against his shoulder. "I like you cuddling up with me, honey. Maybe Rose and Farley feel the same about each other."

"I think he loves her. I don't think she loves him."

"He's convenient for her."

She sniffed in derision. "She's taking him for everything she can get."

"And that makes you angry?"

Letting her fingers enjoy his firmly muscled chest, she murmured, "Despite what you may think, Calvin Farley is my friend."

"I realized that from the first."

"You did?" She tilted her head back so she could see the smile partially hidden by his mustache. "What else did you guess then?"

"Some things."

"What things?"

"Nothing that matters." His fingers stroked her cheek. "Gypsy, Farley's a big boy. If he wants to pay for Rose's questionable charms, that's his choice. You have to give a man room to explore his foolishness."

"And what are you foolish about?"

"Don't you know?" His husky laugh twisted through her. "You, honey. You fill my day's dreams and my night's fantasies."

His mouth spun her into a vortex of craving as he held her between his hard body and the demand of his lips. Her fingers splayed along his chest, caressing the scratchy wool of his shirt. When his lips sought rapture along her neck, her breath rumbled in her ears with the speed of her pulse.

She opened her eyes to his naked yearning. Desperately she wanted to beg him to kiss her, to probe every inch of her with his fingertips, to satisfy the ache deep within her. She tasted the luscious flavor of his lips and sampled the silken moistness within his mouth, offering him the fervent enticement she could not resist.

Suddenly his hands tightened on her. When she gasped

with astonishment, he set her on her feet. She took a deep breath to ask what was wrong.

As smoke filled her senses, she grabbed the cloth to open the oven door. She backed away from the smoke before pulling out the charred cookies. With a grimace, she tossed the tray onto the table and waved away the thick cloud.

"Looks delicious, Gypsy."

Slapping his fingers aside, she admonished, "Don't burn yourself just to prove you're a blockhead."

He caught her by the shoulders and captured her lips beneath his in a fiery kiss. He released her and grinned as she swayed.

"I've shown you what a blockhead I am," he whispered, "to chance setting my heart on fire when I touch you."

"Go smoulder somewhere else while I try to keep my mind on baking cookies."

"I never thought anything would keep you from noticing smoke coming out of the stove."

The back of her hand stroked his whiskery cheek. "Nothing or no one has before."

Tilting his head so he could tease her palm with the tip of his tongue, he chuckled. "I'll have to remind you of this when you lambast me for not paying attention to my work."

"I'm sure you will." She pulled the spoon from the bucket of cookie dough. "If the jacks are going to have cookies tonight, I need to get these baked."

He picked up the cooled tray. "I'll feed these to the critters."

As he went out into the snowstorm, he was whistling. She smiled as she hummed the same tune. Maybe the worst was over. For the first time, she dared to believe that.

CHAPTER FIFTEEN

Cheers greeted Gypsy and Adam as they drove toward the clearing where the jacks were working. Seeing Adam's bafflement, she motioned toward the river and urged the oxen forward at a slow, steady pace. "Peabody's crew is celebrating clearing this hill."

"They could have knocked down the timber with that roar."

"It's been a long winter."

Adam assisted her down and offered his arm. With a smile, she put her fingers on the crook of his elbow. They walked toward the river as if they were strolling along a city street. Gypsy closed her eyes and imagined them wandering along the elegant streets of Saratoga during the day. At night, they would luxuriate amid velvet and silk while her dreams came to life.

Her steps faltered, and Adam asked, "Something wrong?"

The cold wind slapped her face, a cruel reminder that dreams must stay just dreams. Mumbling something, she hurried to a stack of logs which would be rolled into the river as soon as the ice broke. The jacks greeted them with enthusiasm.

Adam's eyes widened as he looked at the river where the ice had been chipped away. "What are they doing?"

"Birling." She no longer was surprised he did not know the simplest aspects of life in the logging camp. "Log rolling. They're trying to knock each other off the log. It's not easy."

He smiled when one man slipped off with a splash into the icy water. "Not easy? I could do that."

"Don't be ridiculous," she retorted with a laugh as the huge logger pulled the other man out of the water. "You wouldn't have a chance. Swede Kjelson is the best birler in the north woods."

He leaned on one of the logs jutting out of the stack. "I wasn't intending to challenge Swede. I know my limits. What I said is I think I can do that."

"Most greenhorns don't have any idea how difficult it is."

"You sound as if you've tried it."

Laughing, she shifted her feet to keep them from freezing. "Maybe, but I, fortunately, am guided by intelligence rather than male pride. I don't need to prove that I'm better than anyone else in the camp. I'll leave the peacock posturing to you."

"A dare?"

She met his smile with her own. "You'll be upended before you start."

"What do I win if I prove you wrong?"

As pertly, she responded, "What do you want?"

His eyes narrowed, but he could not hide their sapphire fire. Slipping his arm around her waist, he pulled her tight to him. She had to fight herself to keep her eager arms from embracing him. The jacks' eyes were on her, for every man would be amused to see the camp's kingbee cook in the arms of a flunkey. The story would be exaggerated all over camp by sunset.

"Don't you know, honey? I want you." The naked

hunger in his voice flayed her heart open, teasing her to speak of her longings.

Putting her hands on his arm, she eased herself away. "I'd enjoy watching you make a fool of yourself again."

"So you agree to the terms?"

"Why not?" She laughed to cover the trembling within her as she imagined him claiming his prize. "You aren't going to be able to stay on that log."

He unbuttoned his heavy coat and slid it past the suspenders over his plaid shirt. "How can any posturing peacock resist such a challenge?"

"Are you sure your ankle is up to this?"

Adam glanced over his shoulder to see her uneasy expression. Only years of experience kept him from showing his astonishment. Although he smiled roguishly, deepening disquiet panged through him. He told himself not to overreact. If Gypsy had suspected he was lying, she would have denounced him. In her kitchen, rights and wrongs were sharply defined.

Once he had been that innocent. At least, he supposed he had been, although he could not recall. His work might be lucrative and exciting, but it demanded more than he had realized. Being alone as he went from one job to the next and doing the best job he could had lost its enticement. He preferred to think of staying in this isolated camp with Gypsy and tasting sweet passion with her.

"I'll never know how my ankle will do until I try, will I?" Not giving her a chance to answer, he walked to where Peabody sat on a stump and smoked his pipe.

"Lunch time?" the bull of the woods asked.

"The food's back there." Adam hooked a thumb toward the sled as another man fell into the river. When Peabody laughed, slapping his knee, Adam asked, "How about me birling?"

"You?"

"Why not?"

Tapping his pipe against his hand, Peabody chuckled. "Ever done it?"

"Not yet." Adam rested his foot on the stump. "Figure it's about time I got my baptism under fire."

"You'll get wet—that much is for sure." Peabody stuck his still smoking pipe in his pocket and motioned toward the water. "C'mon, Adam, m'boy. I've been itching to give a greenhorn a dunking."

"You?"

"Changed your mind?"

Adam grinned. He had a better chance against the bull of the woods than Swede. "Naw," he drawled in a copy of Gypsy's Southern accent. "I'd just as soon dunk you as any of your men."

"You dunk me?" He clapped Adam on the shoulder. "It's time you learn some humility, greenhorn."

As the two men walked toward the ice-coated shore, Gypsy's hands tensed on the bark. It crumbled beneath her fingers as Adam stepped on the log. Even from where she stood, she could see his surprise at how buoyant a log became in the water.

Peabody gave Adam quick instructions as well as the few rules. When Adam nodded while he edged along the log, the crew chief raised his hand to signal the start. Before he could lower it, Adam wobbled.

Gypsy laughed when he dropped with a geyser into the river. Quickly she poured a cup of coffee. Hurrying down to the shore, she watched Peabody offer Adam a hand. The crew chief laughed at something she could not hear, but drew Adam to his feet.

Shaking his soaked hair, Adam waded out. The men laughed as he brushed freezing water from his flannel shirt. Someone dropped a blanket over his shoulders.

"Don't say I told you so, Gypsy," he said.

"Why not? Now you know falling off a log is as easy as falling off a log." She handed him the cup of steaming coffee. When he put his hands over hers on it and drew the tin mug to his lips, she was forced to take a step toward him.

Aware of the sudden quiet around them, she was sure

every jack was staring at them. She started to pull away, but coffee sloshed in the cup, threatening to burn through her glove. As he took a slow, appreciative sip, his fingers stroked hers.

Peabody leaped to shore, and someone brought him a cup of coffee. Raising it in a salute, he chuckled. "Got your baptism, Lassiter. If you want lessons, come back out here. You couldn't beat Gypsy at this point."

When Gypsy joined the laughter, Adam frowned. His damp finger under her chin brought her face up to his and another silence among the loggers. No doubt the jacks would be agog with gossip tonight.

Quietly he asked, "So you think you could do better?"

"I couldn't do worse."

He snorted as he pulled on his heavy coat. "You can say that only because you won't try it."

"No?"

Peabody gave her a gold-toothed grin. "Want me to dump him again, Gypsy?"

"How about giving me a chance?"

"Why not? You're part of the Glenmark Timber Company crew. I always said I'd take on anyone who's eager to be dumped into the river."

"I'll have to do it in stocking feet." She lifted her skirts to reveal her ankle-high shoes.

"You need calked boots for birling."

"Whose?" She pointed to his boots with the long spikes. "Yours? Or maybe you want me to borrow Swede's?"

He grimaced. "Gypsy, I can't believe we've never made you a pair. Even Farley has a pair." With a wry grin, he added, "Maybe Rose likes to see him in them."

"Peabody, are you going to keep jawing, or are you going to give me a chance to dunk you?"

Pulling off his coat, he motioned toward the log. "Now?"

"Just a minute." She squatted to unbutton her shoes. Glancing at the mud frosted with ice, she shrugged aside her qualms. Her feet were already soaked, so she could not get them much wetter by walking to the water's edge.

She kicked off her shoes and smiled at Adam. Her expression wavered when she saw his fury. She turned away, knowing silence was best. He twisted her to face him.

Ignoring the loggers' astonishment, he demanded, "What do you think you're doing?"

"I'm going to show you I can birl better than you did."

"Don't be an idiot, Gypsy! That water is cold."

She wiped away a drop from his soaked hair. "As I don't intend to go swimming like you did, it's not something I have to worry about."

"You're not going!"

His fingers tightened on her upper arm and he drew her toward him. His wet clothes clung to him like a layer of oil on a skillet. Each ridge, each powerful angle of his body lured her to put aside thoughts of everything else.

She found refuge in anger. "Mr. Lassiter, I can make my own decisions."

"Not when you're acting as bullheaded and short-sighted as Farley." Hoots of laughter met his words. His straight mouth was so rigid, white puckered at the corners. "Aren't you the same woman who called men posturing peacocks? Are you going to be a posturing *peahen?*"

She hesitated. He was right, she had to admit.

A jack laughed. "Looks like Lassiter has tamed our Gypsy!"

She jerked her arm out of Adam's grip. When he reached for her, she slapped his hand away.

He snapped, "Don't let their goading convince you to do something stupid!"

"Stupid?" Turning her back on him, she strode to where Peabody stood near the edge of the water.

Adam glared at the man who had laughed. Clenching his fists, he considered choking the man, but it was too late. That would not stop Gypsy now. He refused to chase her like a lovesick idiot, especially when she would snarl some snide comment and then do what she wanted.

He watched her balance on the log next to Peabody. His gaze swept along her to settle on her slender legs beneath her kilted skirt, and longing tore through him. When she was in his arms, her soft curves pressed eagerly against him. If she saw him staring like a lad suffering his first crush, she would laugh.

Falling in love under any circumstances was wrong. He should evict her from the dreams which tortured him night after night. There would be other women in other places when the time was more convenient. But he wanted Gypsy Elliott.

Gypsy tried to ignore Adam's worried gaze. Grasping Peabody's hand, she let him help her along the log.

"Ouch!" she gasped when water splattered on her feet. "That's colder than I thought."

Peabody continued to hold on to her as she adjusted her feet on the log. An oddly gentle tone filled his voice. "Nobody would think less of you, Gypsy, if you decided to quit."

"Afraid I'll dump you in front of your crew?"

"Not at all."

She gripped the log with her toes. As he released her wrist, she heard cheers. Peabody slid to the far end of the log. That he was careful not to bounce it as he had with Adam told her the bull of the woods would treat her differently.

Just as she was about to chide him for the unwanted gallantry, the familiar tightness filled her chest. Wanting to hold her hand against her breastbone, she nodded to Peabody. She could not back down now.

He grinned as his calked boots rotated the log. She matched him step for step. Shouts of encouragement came from shore. She thought only of Peabody and the log. Watching his eyes, she was prepared when he sped the log until she was running to maintain the pace set by his longer legs.

She was sure the length of wood had gained life beneath her feet as her breath rasped in her ears. She fought to maintain her footing and breathe.

With one arm out to balance herself, she pressed her hand to her mouth as coughs ripped out of her. The log slowed. Voices made no sense through the cacophony of her coughing. An abrupt motion toppled her backward. Her scream clogged in her ravaged throat.

Hard arms caught her before the icy river could. Gasping, she leaned her head against a muscular shoulder. She closed her eyes as she realized Adam held her. He would not drop her. Her thoughts coiled in a dozen different directions as she kept her hand against her chest. The pain resurrected the dark hours when she had feared she would not live. Then, as now, Adam had saved her.

When anxious voices surrounded her, she opened her eyes to a tapestry of arms in brightly colored shirtsleeves reaching out toward her. The arms around her tensed, and she heard Adam's taut voice ordering, "Get back so I can get out of this ice water."

She seized his shirt with feeble fingers when he lurched up the steep bank. A heavy blanket was thrown over Adam's shoulders, nearly smothering her before someone tucked the scratchy wool around her. She saw Peabody's concern on his wind-etched face. She wanted to assure him she was fine, that she had had fun, but her throat burned as if scoured by a saw blade.

"You'd make a great jack, Gypsy, if you were yourself," the crew chief said with a wobbly smile. "Next time, a rematch with no quarter allowed."

"Peabody," growled Adam, his voice echoing beneath her ear, "she doesn't need you to egg her on."

Gypsy did not argue that she could speak for herself. Remaining quiet was the only way to quell the coughs caught like frozen fire beneath her breastbone. Huddling in the blanket, she sat in the sled as the jacks took their lunch off the back. Even on the way back to the camp, she said nothing.

When Adam stopped the sled before the cookhouse, she started to slide along the seat. His arm around her shoulders halted her. He scooped her off the seat, ignoring the curious glances as he carried her into the kitchen past the other flunkeys.

He kicked open her bedroom door and set her on her feet.

"Go to bed, Gypsy."

"I can . . ." Her raspy retort ended in more coughs.

"Get in bed, or I'll put you in your nightdress myself."

Heat raced along her face as the flunkeys chuckled. If she protested, Adam would do exactly as he vowed. She shivered as she imagined his fingers on her, resurrecting the ecstasy she had found in her dreams.

Whirling away, she tripped on the blanket. Her dignity was as tattered as the wool. When she heard more laughter, she was tempted to snarl an answer. She halted herself, knowing Adam would remind her that she had enjoyed his mortification earlier. She took satisfaction in slamming the door.

She threw the blanket on the chair and undressed. She was interrupted by another spasm of coughs. With her hand on the footboard, she leaned her head against the cool iron. She slipped to the mattress when her knees refused to hold her.

At a knock, she struggled to pull her nightgown over her head and button its high collar under her chin. She rested back against her pillows just as the door opened. When she saw Adam was wearing dry clothes, she was astounded he could change so quickly. He carried a tray. Except for his missing cast, it could have been the horrible days when she had been confined to bed. She took a serrated breath and tried to hide how weak she was.

"Here." He shoved a cup of steaming tea directly beneath her nose. When her fingers quivered, he grumbled another curse before pouring some of the tea back into the pot. "I don't need you spilling this. We've had enough of your stupidity today."

She argued in a hoarse whisper, "*I,* at least, knew what I was doing instead of making an ass of myself by diving into the water before the log took its first roll."

He grinned. "You have me there, Gypsy. Where did you learn to birl?"

"Old Vic gave me lessons last winter." When he regarded her with confusion, she explained, "You've met Old Vic. He works in the carpenter shop."

"That old coot is a log birler?"

She started to laugh, but the cough halted her. Sipping on the tea he had sweetened with honey, she whispered, "He was a champion in his time, or so he tells me. With all the tall tales in the north woods, I never quite believe anything anyone tells me."

"Even when someone tells you to be sensible?"

Taking the piece of cake he offered her, she smiled. "I didn't plan on going in the water."

"You didn't."

"I guess I have you to thank for that."

"I—" Adam turned at another knock. "I told them you weren't to be disturbed."

"Don't be so hard on the flunkeys, Adam."

"Why not? They're hard on you. Why can't they let you rest for five minutes before they bother you?" He stormed to the door.

Gypsy smiled as she hugged her drawn-up knees. She never expected her dashing knight would be dressed in a flannel shirt and denims which clung to his lean body. When he reached for the door's latch, she admired his hands, which could steal her mind from her with a fevered caress. She sat straighter when she saw who stood in the doorway.

Farley pushed into the room. His anger became shock when Adam grasped his arm. "Get out of my way, Lassiter!"

"Let him in, Adam," Gypsy said as she brushed crumbs off the blanket.

"Just a few minutes," Adam said grudgingly. "She's pushed herself too much, Farley."

The camp manager crossed the floor, his boots resounding hollowly. He tossed her forgotten shoes on her lap. "What did you think you were doing? Do you think the jacks will put up with swill so you can play games in the river?"

"It would be very difficult to get another kingbee cook now, wouldn't it?" Folding her arms over her chest, she laughed. "Your compassion is overwhelming, Farley."

"Why should I care if you want to break your neck? You don't listen to a thing anyone else says."

"I listened carefully when I learned to birl."

"Who taught you that?"

"You can't believe I'd tell you." When he started to protest, she added, "If you don't know, Farley, you can't write to Mr. Glenmark to explain why you sacked one of his loggers."

His lips tilted in a smile. "Aren't you ever going to let me win an argument?"

"You won when you sent Adam to work here."

"So I did."

Gypsy saw Farley's troubled expression before it was masked. The camp manager wished he had lost that battle. Was he suspicious of Adam for the same reason she was? Did Farley know of Adam's late-night wanderings? That was ridiculous. Farley had been busy with Rose the night of the murder. He had not seen Adam.

There had to be another reason, and that scared her.

CHAPTER SIXTEEN

"Coming to the 'urrah, Gypsy?" Bert asked as he hammered the top on an empty molasses barrel.

"Make sure that's tight. I don't want hungry critters camping behind the cookhouse." When he grimaced at the warning she repeated every time a flunkey carried out an empty barrel, she laughed. "I haven't decided. It's been quite a while since the jacks have had to entertain themselves on a Saturday night."

He chuckled. "I 'ope it'll be a party instead of a dirge. The lads miss Nissa's gals. Sure to be moaning aplenty tonight."

"Is Stretch Helsen's hand well enough to play the fiddle?"

Bert nodded, his beard bouncing with enthusiasm. "Frostbite's nearly gone. Didn't lose a joint, either. Says 'e's going to play tonight, if Old Vic will bring 'is mouth organ."

"If there's any liquor at the hurrah, Old Vic won't stay sober long enough to toot more than a few notes."

"Liquor? You know Farley's rules, Gypsy."

She laughed. "I know how easily those rules will be forgotten if the jacks want to drown their loneliness."

He hefted the barrel effortlessly. "So I'll see you there."

"Maybe." Gypsy closed the door and shivered. Leaving her cozy cookhouse on such a blustery night would be silly. After the berating Farley had given her—rightly, she had to admit—she should make it an early night and a late breakfast.

She pulled out the recipe book, which was splotched with stains. With less food in the larder at the end of each day, she must be more imaginative. She paged through the book and smiled as each page resurrected memories until she could smell her family's fragrant kitchen. That stove had been smaller than the monster here, but it had been just as black and had gleamed with the same chrome accents.

Closing her eyes, she leaned her head against her folded arms. She wanted to forget the past, but the memories refused to be forgotten.

"All alone?" Adam's voice broke into her thoughts.

"It would appear so, Adam," she said, straightening.

"Busy?"

"Why?"

"I thought you'd like an escort to the hurrah, Gypsy."

As she looked up, her answer died unspoken. From the first time she had seen Adam Lassiter, she had been unable to ignore the rugged planes of his face. Brawny men were hardly the exception in the Glenmark Timber Company camp, but something about Adam always drew her eyes.

When he walked to where she was sitting, his boots struck each board resoundingly. It was a noise she was accustomed to, but the sound usually came in a storm of hungry loggers. He smiled as he rested his elbow on the table so his eyes were even with hers.

"I didn't expect to see you tonight," she murmured.

"Did you think Farley would tell me to walk?"

"Not really, but he was mighty peeved after he stormed out of here."

"I'd say he's pleased with me at the moment."

"Pleased?" His cheerful words and the twitch of his lips warned he was about to send her life spinning out of control again. "What makes you say that?"

"Farley's appointed me your cookee."

Gypsy stood and glared at him. "How dare he? I don't need an assistant." Pulling off her apron, she slammed it onto the table. Adam leaped back to avoid the whipping apron strings. "If that's how he wants it, I'm walking."

"You quit? Don't be ridiculous, Gypsy."

"Do you think Farley's going to hire *you* as kingbee cook? It's time he learns the truth—that you can't break an egg without spending an hour hunting for the shells."

"Gypsy, be reasonable."

"Now you sound like Farley! He always has a soft spot for those who fawn over him." Fiercely, she stated, "I've had enough of this."

When he stepped in front of her, she tried to push past him. He caught her arms and halted her with the ease of muscles strong enough to wrestle logs. Anew, she wondered why he stayed in the kitchen when he could be earning higher wages on the hill. The answer always came back the same.

Adam Lassiter was not a lumberjack.

As he stroked her stiff arms, yearning threatened to swallow her anger. Her gaze rose along his wool shirt. No beard hid the strength carved into his face's rigid lines. His blue eyes were as heated as a hazy summer sky.

His slightest tug drew her to him. The tips of his boots brushed her shoes, and his sturdy chest was only inches from the lace on the front of her blouse. She should say something, anything. She could not.

His arm encircled her waist and brought her against him. She sighed with delight. Although he was not a man of the woods, he possessed its wild ferocity. She could imagine his fierce eyes in a beast amid the trees.

A shiver cut through her. She must not let passion blind her. "Adam," she whispered. Her voice betrayed her, trembling with the need surging within her.

"Hush, honey." He bent to tease the whorls of her ear with his tongue. Each flick burned like a brand as her fingers clenched on his shirt.

Unable to fight the melded power of their desire, she clung to him while his lips traced a path along her throat. Even that was not close enough, for the fabric separating them offered a hint of the luscious sensation of skin against skin.

With a moan, she pulled away. His hands tightened on her for a half second, then released her. She backed away, gasping, "You can't convince me to accept Farley's dictates this way!"

"Do you really think that's why I want to kiss you?"

Gypsy refused to be beguiled out of her anger. It was all that kept her from being tantalized by his kisses. "I don't know how you coerced him into giving you the cookee job when he thinks you're trouble."

He laughed, the cold sound penetrating her more sharply than the winter wind. "Don't you understand? He didn't promote me because he likes my baby blues. He made me cookee to repay you for risking yourself on a log."

"That proves how stupid he is!"

"It does."

Gypsy choked back her retort at his startling agreement. When his finger stroked her cheek, she closed her eyes. She could not fight the craving to be in his arms.

"Honey," he whispered, "you still haven't answered my question."

"Question?" Her eyes opened to find his face only a shadow's distance from hers.

"Why don't we go over to the hurrah? Why don't you let me take you out in style?"

She blinked, startled because she had expected—had

hoped—he would say something very different. He would have in her dream.

For the love of heaven, she must remember that was only a fantasy brought on by her fever. Or had it been the craving of her heart to belong to someone? Groping for her coat, she sought to silence her own doubt.

He smiled as he plucked her coat off the hook. Holding it so she could slip her arms into it, he laughed. "You have to grow a bit more, honey."

"I'm afraid I've reached the size I'm meant to be."

"Exactly perfect to be in my arms." He teased her nape with gentle nibbles until she moaned with the craving for his lips on hers.

Turning, she led his mouth to hers. Everything she wanted was in that kiss, but it was not enough. Each touch made her ache for more.

As her fingertips touched the warm skin beneath his upturned collar, he whispered, "We need to get going, or we'll be late for the hurrah."

"It's so cold out." She should not be saying this, but he had honed her longings to obsession. She wanted to discover if her dream could come true.

"I think we should get going before it starts snowing again." His words were slow, as if they were distasteful.

"But, Adam—"

"Let's go." He dropped her bonnet on her head and laughed. The sound was as strained as his voice.

She fumbled as she tried to tie the ribbons. Was she mad to throw herself at Adam? It would be better this way. A few kisses and nothing more except good-bye. It *would* be better. Wouldn't it?

'All right," she said. Taking a deep breath, she struggled to smile. "It's about time you kept your promise to give me a night out, Mr. Lassiter. A gentleman never goes back on his word."

"I'll have to remember that." He lifted her down from the door as if she were dismounting a horse. Pulling the door shut, he held out his hand. "It's been a long time since I've been in the company of a fine lady, Miss Elliott. I trust you'll correct my manners if necessary.''

''I'm sure I will.''

She was not sure if his laugh or hers sounded more hypocritical.

Gypsy clapped her hands as the fiddler started a square dance. The sparse space between the bunks was filled with jacks. Others crowded onto the bunks. Near the stove at the far end, a piece of twine was draped with drying socks.

The man with the fiddle-box had earned his name Stretch. His head brushed the rafters when he stood to call, ''Bucks, find yourself a gal and swing her out into a square.''

When Adam held out his hand, Gypsy smiled. She was the only woman in the bunkhouse, but the men wearing a handkerchief on their right arms were the ''gals.''

Old Vic picked up his mouth organ in his gnarled fingers. With no hair on his head and his body bent from too many winters, he refused to retire. He would not leave the north woods until Reverend Frisch came to speak a few words over his body in a box made from the pines around them.

Gypsy laughed as the music began, and she sashayed from one man to the next around the square. When she came back to Adam, he whirled her about and put his arm around her waist as he promenaded her to the beat of clapping hands, which nearly obliterated the cheerful melody. She took Edvard's broad hands and spun with him in the center of the lopsided square, then stepped back as Adam linked arms with Edvard's bulky partner, who wore a garish green handkerchief around his arm. She laughed as the men's boots struck the floor like thunder.

Her breath exploded out as Adam twirled her into his arms. When he paused, the other dancers in the square bumped into them, but he ignored the grumbles. Concern darkened his eyes to nearly purple as he asked, "Gypsy, are you all right?"

"I'm fine." She slipped her arm through his and urged him to follow Edvard and his partner. "Don't worry so much."

As they watched the others spin in the center of the square, he smiled. "I like to worry about you, Gypsy," he whispered against her hair.

She had no time to reply as Stretch urged everyone to promenade with the person to their left. Swinging along with Peabody's enthusiastic dancing, she found her gaze returning to Adam. The warmth of his smile surrounded her as he took her hands and turned her into his arms as the dance brought them back together.

The room exploded into applause when the dance ended. Before she could speak, Stretch began the next tune. Adam grinned as he bowed to her.

More than an hour later, the musicians took a breather. Gypsy leaned her head against Adam's shoulder while she wiped sweat from her forehead. In the packed bunk-house, it was warm for the first time all winter. Someone pressed a cup into her hand, and she sipped gratefully. She was not surprised it was whiskey.

Peabody's men bragged about the scale of lumber that would come from the hillside they had cleared. The other crews announced their own figures. Under the laughter came a steady ping as the men chewing tobacco spit into metal spittoons.

When Stretch plied the bow across his fiddle, Adam asked, "Do you want to dance again?"

"I've had enough dancing for a while."

"Me, too." His hand curved around her elbow as he bent to whisper in her ear. "Would you like to hear what I'd really like to do? I'd like to lay you back on one of these bunks and make love with you until you burn all around me."

"Adam, not here!" She glanced at the men, but they

were intent on Peabody, who was clearing the middle of the bunkhouse.

His fingers inched along her arm to brush the soft upsweep of her breast. When she gasped, he smiled. "I want you, Gypsy, so bad I've forgotten what it's like to sleep all night. It's not the lice that keep me awake. It's the thought of holding you and being part of you."

"Don't!"

"Why not?" He framed her face with his wide hands. "I want you, Gypsy. Do you want me?"

She quivered as she pulled away. Lying was impossible, for he knew how she responded when he tempted her into madness with his touch.

When she gathered up her coat, Stretch's fiddle let out a mournful groan. She paused as Peabody called, "Dancing's over for now. How about some louse races?"

"There's enough of the critters in the beds," shouted back a jack. "I don't want to watch the bloodsucking creatures."

Peabody surveyed the room as he crossed his broad arms over his broader chest. "We've been remiss in not welcoming the new men to Glenmark Timber Company's camp. It's time to find out who's the best among the greenhorns."

When Adam swore under his breath, Gypsy could not help laughing. Even a man as unaware of logging camp life as he was could not miss the amused anticipation in the bull of the woods' voice.

"Let's let the newest greenhorns prove themselves." He pointed to Bert. "You first, Sayre."

Bert shuffled forward, grinning. Whiskey splashed from his cup, and she guessed from his weaving steps he had drunk more than his share. Peabody had him standing against the wall by the door. The flunkey held the cigar he was not allowed to smoke in the cookhouse.

"Jump forward as far as you can," Peabody ordered.

The flunkey grinned, waving his arms. "Back away, boys. I'll be 'alfway across the room."

His long legs did not take him halfway to the door, but he put several feet of floor between him and the wall. When he was about to look back, Peabody shook his head.

"You're only half done, lad. Now jump back."

"Jump back?"

Laughing at Bert's astonishment, the crew chief urged, "That's right. My boys must be able to jump in any direction, fast and far, when the cry of 'timber' goes up. Maybe you boys in the cook shack aren't as nimble."

Yells of encouragement filled the room as Bert bent his knees. Edvard slid a pail behind him. Raucous cries hid the sound. When an arm settled around her shoulders, Gypsy glanced at Adam and quickly away. How could she resist him when he wanted what she wanted?

Bert started to jump, but his feet caught in the bucket. He toppled to the floor. The pail crashed against the bunks to appreciative laughter.

"Kicked the bucket!" crowed Hank. "Now you're a jack, Bert!"

Adam offered the Englishman a hand. With a fierce curse, Bert knocked it away. He scrambled to his feet. His glower was met with more good-natured chuckles.

Adam shrugged and asked no one in particular, "What's wrong with him?"

"Some men don't like being made a fool of," Gypsy answered. "Others seem to have a skill for it."

He arched a brow. "Let's get out of here before it's my turn."

"You got your hazing when you fell off that log."

"Don't remind me."

As they walked out into the wintry night, she twined her fingers with his. He led her through the fragrant pines, and her feet slid through the snow in front of the cook shack. The glitter of the moonlight on the drifts made them a collection of gems waiting for some titan to wear.

"How beautiful it is tonight!" she breathed. "Wild and free."

"That's why I wanted to bring you to the hurrah, Gypsy. So you could enhance this loveliness with your own."

She gazed into his eyes, which were shadowed by the dark. When his arms went around her, her fingers clasped behind his neck. "You're a charmer, Adam Lassiter."

"Part of the service, my fine lady, to lure you out of the cookhouse and charm you with sweet phrases to bring you into my arms."

"Which is where I am."

"So I noticed."

"It seems you've succeeded admirably with your plan, Mr. Lassiter."

His arms tightened as he whispered with sudden seriousness, "Only with the first part, my dear Gypsy."

Her answer was swept away by his lips capturing hers. Knowing no one would intrude, she welcomed his mouth against hers. Her breath was ragged as he tasted her cheek before bending to tease the skin along her neck.

When she shivered, he laughed and offered his arm. She put her gloved hand on it as she held her skirt out of the mud, which was frozen into oddly sculptured shapes. Snow drifted lazily toward the ground.

When she yawned, he chuckled. "I didn't mean to keep you out so late, Gypsy."

"Usually I'd be getting up in just a few hours." She edged around a slushy puddle.

"What made you come north?"

At the abrupt question, she glanced at him. What little she could see of his face in the light from the kerosene lamps on the bunkhouse revealed only genuine interest. "After the war, there wasn't much left for a decent woman in Mississippi."

"Mississippi?" He chuckled. "I would have guessed you were from Virginia or maybe North Carolina by the way you barely drawl your words. Not like those folks down on the gulf."

She hoped her face was as shadowed as his. "Maybe all this Yankee jargon has rubbed off on me. If I ever go home, they'll be more offended than they were when I left.''

"Why did you leave?''

"After the war there was nothing for a woman who didn't want to cozy up with a carpetbagger. I saw an advertisement for a cook, and here I am. I'm sorry my reason isn't more dramatic. Certainly not like yours.''

Adam stopped. When she walked past him, he called, "What's that supposed to mean?''

"If you want to continue this conversation, it'll have to be by the stove.'' She turned to face him and grinned. "I'm smarter than a Yankee who doesn't know enough to come in out of the cold.''

"I want to continue this conversation, Gypsy. There're some things which need to be said between us.'' He held out his hand, his voice abruptly serious. "Now.''

CHAPTER SEVENTEEN

The quiet of the kitchen was shattered by the snap of embers in the stove. When Gypsy lit the lantern by the door, light spread through the molasses darkness. Adam lifted the lamp and hung it on a rafter.

"Thank you." She drew off her gloves and stuffed them into the pockets of her coat.

"My pleasure." Shrugging off his jacket, he tossed it onto a bench. "Reaching the ceiling is one of the few things I can do in this kitchen better than you."

"True." She hung her coat on its peg between the door and the window. Everything was just as it should be, except his gaze stroked her with frank longing.

As she poured two cups of coffee, he sat at the table. "I've told you dozens of times that I'm astounded how well you handle everything in this kitchen. Why can't you accept a compliment?"

She collected a slab of cake from the counter. Putting it and a cup in front of him, she said quietly, "If I accept anything from anyone, I'll be beholden."

"I've noticed you like to be independent."

"You have?" She stirred sugar into her coffee before pushing the bowl toward him.

"It would be hard to miss." He glanced around the kitchen. "Who has the stove watch tonight?"

She sipped the coffee. "Me."

"You had the stove watch just two nights ago."

"I know, but Oscar was supposed to be on the stove watch tonight. He should stay and have a good time."

Lifting his cup, he said, "You're going to have to be careful, Gypsy."

"Careful?" She almost laughed. Didn't he realize his touch was what she found the most dangerous?

"Doing something nice like letting the poor boy smile for the first time since Lolly's death is going to ruin your fierce reputation." Lowering his cup to the table, he smiled. "I have to admit that when you're right about something, Gypsy, you're right. There was no sense in arguing out there in the cold."

"If arguing is what you want to do, you're welcome to do it alone. Just turn down the lights before you leave." She stood and brushed crumbs from her skirt. "I'm going to check the firebox."

"Without getting answers to the questions I see in your lustrous eyes?" he asked as she reached for the quilted cloths to open the stove's door.

"I didn't think I'd get any honest answers, so why bother?"

"How can you be sure unless you try?" He pulled the stool next to where he was sitting and patted it. "C'mon, Gypsy. You're frothing with curiosity. Why don't you admit it?"

She hesitated. If he was so eager to cooperate, he did not intend to speak the truth.

"I don't think I'm the one who has anything to admit," she said as she perched on the stool.

Resting one elbow on the table, he put his hand on her knee. He grinned as if daring her to order him to move it. "Perhaps you're right, Gypsy. I have something to admit. Why don't you tell me what you think it is?"

"Me? Why should I waste time on such a ridiculous exercise?"

"Ridiculous exercise?" His fingers strayed along her leg, spiraling pleasure from where he touched her until she ached to lean forward and steal the smile from his lips with her kiss. A soft huskiness filled his voice. "I can think of exercises with you that I'd enjoy more, but there's a lot to be said between us now."

Gypsy batted his questing fingers away. "All right. You want the truth?"

"Always?"

"You aren't a jack. At first, I thought maybe you'd bamboozled Farley into hiring you and then keeping you on when you hurt your ankle."

"So what do you think now?"

"I think you're working directly for Mr. Glenmark. Why? To find out something, I'd guess."

"That's a good guess."

"Who are you investigating, Adam? Me?"

"Not you." His grin vanished. Rising, he put his cup on the counter. "I should have known I couldn't fool you long."

"It might have helped if you'd had someone really break your ankle."

He faced her. Blue sparks burned in his eyes, but they were not anger. She could not guess what he was thinking as he asked with studied calm, "So you know about that, too?"

She scraped her tongue along her arid lips. "I saw you wandering about without the cast the night Lolly was murdered."

"You didn't say anything. Not that night or later."

"No."

"You didn't accuse me of lying when I told you I was chasing someone else."

She gasped at the confessions she had not expected. "No, I didn't accuse you then."

"Why not?"

"To be honest, I didn't think, at least not for very long, that you killed Lolly."

"I guess I should say thanks for that backhanded compliment."

"It's not a compliment. Just the truth."

He chuckled mirthlessly. "The truth doesn't explain one fact. Why was she killed?"

"Jealousy?"

"Maybe, but it might be something else. If the murderer's goal were to cause trouble, for example, he succeeded. Lolly's death created chaos here."

"Are you trying to convince me to tell Farley you're involved with that murder?"

"Along with the so-called accident on the hill?"

She shook her head vehemently. "Bobby Worth was killed by a falling tree. Accidents happen."

"Exactly what a murderer might wish you to think." With a sigh, he said, "I hope you're right. There's no question that Lolly Yerkes was executed by some madman." His grin struggled to lift one corner of his mustache. "But that madman isn't me."

"Then why are you here?" She sipped on her coffee, but its sweet flavor could not ease the bitter bile in her mouth.

"You act awfully guilty for someone who has no reason to be."

"I'm just curious why Farley insisted on your being in my kitchen."

Taking a deep breath, he stroked his chin reflectively. "What I'm telling you, Gypsy, can't be repeated."

"I don't gossip like an empty-headed jack."

He put his boot on a rung of the stool. "The truth is Farley doesn't know why I'm here. He was told by Glenmark to hire me, put me to work, and not order me to hit the hay trail in spite of anything I might do."

"I saw the letter Mr. Glenmark sent to him. I don't understand why he wrote that letter when all you had to do was walk in and ask for a job."

Regret dimmed his eyes. "That I can't tell you, but I promise you you're in no danger."

She rubbed her palms together, wishing she could lessen the cold cramping them. Moving closer to the stove would not help, for this iciness came from within her. She wondered how he could speak the words which had rung through her head too many years.

No danger, she had been told before her world vanished into horror. Then it had been summer, and she had wanted to believe the words. She wanted to believe Adam even more.

"I think you're being honest," she whispered, "but I want you to leave."

"Just like that?"

She stood. "Just like that. This is my kitchen."

"You don't have any choice."

"No choice? *I* work directly for Mr. Glenmark also. He'll listen to me."

He grasped her arm. His wide shoulders seemed to eclipse everything in the kitchen. Before she could force her frozen feet to move, he drew her into his embrace. His fingers swept up to tangle in her hair as he whispered, "You have no choice at all."

Wanting to push him away and remind him she was the boss in the cook shack, she knew she could not govern her desire. She ached for his touch when she was alone in the middle of the night.

For so long she had not thought of the future. She had refused to think about happiness. Now she wanted both— wanted both with Adam. As her fingers inched along his shoulders, she gave herself to the boundless yearning.

She whispered a denial when he eased out of her arms. When she looked from his smile to his hand held out to her, she saw his other hand on the latch of her door. His dreams matched hers, and tonight they would make those dreams come true in the one place they could be alone.

Her hand did not quiver as she placed it on his palm. His fingers closed around it, not imprisoning, but welcoming and warm. When she followed him into her bedroom, her skirts sang her heart's song across the boards. She closed the door and leaned against it. With a smile, he put his hand behind her head and looked down into her eyes.

His finger traced her eyebrows and along her cheek before easing across her mouth, which hungered for his kisses. When it reached her chin, he tilted her face so her lips were beneath his. He bent and tasted the soft downiness of her right cheek, then her left.

With a low chuckle, he teased the corners of her mouth with his tongue. Longing flowed out on her sigh. He captured her lips and pressed her to the door until she felt his heartbeat through his shirt.

She clutched his shoulders when his mouth left hers to move along her face. While his fingers loosened the pearl buttons along the back of her blouse, he teased awake pleasure on the skin revealed by her gaping collar. She moaned as moist heat burned from deep within her when his tongue delved beneath the lace of her chemise. Whispering his name, she held tightly to him to keep her knees from sagging beneath the sensuous assault.

Slowly he drew her sleeves down her arms, his fingers lingering on her bare skin. His avaricious gaze swept across her, setting her ablaze. He traced an invisible path of delight along the lacy strap of her chemise. When she quivered at his touch across her breast beneath the whispering silk, he smiled.

"It's your choice, honey," he murmured.

"I thought you said . . ." Her words became a sigh as he slipped his hands around her to settle on the buttons holding her skirt in place. When he did not undo them, she gazed up into his face, unable to ask the question preying on her muddled mind.

Close to her ear, he whispered, "I want you to want this as much as I do. I want you to burn with the fire searing my soul and think only of touching me while I discover every inch of your body. Say yes, honey. Say you've shared my nights of longing and you want to share this night and these desires with me."

Her fingers sifted through his raven hair. As the coarse strands wove along her hands, she drew his mouth to hers. The answer he wanted she could not give him with words, for there were none to express her need for him.

With eager fingers, she slid his suspenders along his sleeves. The breadth of his shoulders lured her hands to touch them, to explore them, to tease the skin beneath the plaid wool. Her fingers clenched on his shirt's topmost button when he pulled the pins from her hair to send it tumbling along her in a russet stream. Greedily, he buried his face in its silken softness as his tongue caressed her ear.

When she faltered on each button, he whispered, "Are you sure you can do this?"

"I think I can handle it."

"You think?" His ragged laughter flowed along her skin, heating it with gentle warmth. "I never thought I'd hear Gypsy Elliott be unsure about anything."

"I've never been as sure of anything as I am about wanting you tonight," she murmured as his shirt fell to the floor.

The expanse of his bare chest tantalized her fingers as she explored his skin. His eager moan urged her to take his hands and lead him to her bed. As she sat, he knelt and unbuttoned her high-topped shoes. When she laughed, he winked and tossed her shoes aside.

His hands roved up her legs to find the garters holding her stockings in place. Slowly he drew off the lace and threw them atop her shoes. She slipped her hands along his bare shoulders as he rolled her stockings down her legs, each touch an exquisite agony.

Standing, he slanted toward her. As she leaned back

into the mattress, his hands slid up her legs, pushing her petticoat higher. He pressed her deeper into the mattress as his fingers enticed her bare legs to wrap around his denims. His lips over hers silenced her breathy gasps. Probing deep in her mouth, his tongue sought every pleasure as her hands curved along his shoulders.

When he stretched out beside her on the narrow bed, he ran his hands down her back to hold her hips tight to him. With a soft laugh, she kicked away her bulky petticoat.

He rolled her onto her back, and she brought his lips back over hers. Nothing was as wondrous without his mouth on hers. When he wove a web of delight along her neck, she writhed. His fingers caressed her breast as he undid the ribbons holding her chemise together. The silk dropped away to bare her to his eager eyes.

His fingertip meandered along the upsweep of her breast to tease the very tip. She opened her eyes to discover his smile close to her. When he clamped his lips over hers, she tugged him against her.

Not content with her mouth, he left a fiery path of kisses along her throat and across her naked skin. She shivered as he tasted the sensitive surface of her breast. Each brush of his tongue, teasing and demanding, loving and alluring, freeing and controlling, sent wildfire through her. When he pushed the last of her underclothes away, she touched the buttons at the waist of his denims.

His light kisses across her face begged her to free her desire to savor his strong body against her. Each button loosened reluctantly as his lips bewitched her. He laughed huskily when he tossed aside the trousers, but his eyes burned with the craving throbbing through her.

She gasped at the touch of his skin as he pinned her to the mattress. Giving her no time to delight in the unbridled pleasure, he commanded her senses to surrender to rapture. She touched his enticingly male body, reveling in his sharp intake of breath when she stroked him intimately. She wanted to ensure his mind was as intoxicated with joy as hers. Not even her most sensual dreams had been this glorious.

Such thoughts evaporated when his fingers explored upward along her naked legs to discover the maelstrom within her. She clutched his shoulders, afraid of being flung away from him. His touch exacerbated the fire, consuming her.

When he brought them together, her gasp echoed within his mouth. The quivering ache coalesced into ravenous need as the rhythm of their passion magnified into an ecstasy, an enchantment, an anguish. She lost herself in the flawless melody of their bodies. The song soared around her, becoming her, becoming him, becoming everything in a potent crescendo when every beat of their hearts was in the perfect unison of love.

Hours later, centuries later, seconds later, when time regained its meaning, Gypsy opened her eyes to see Adam's smile. How naive she had been to believe she could imagine anything as wondrous as Adam being a part of her in passion!

"You are a sweet temptress," he said with the breath-lessness that careened through her. "I don't know why I waited so long for you to open your arms to me."

"Did you ever stop to think that a lady likes to be courted?"

He ran his hand along her side, delighting in every curve as she leaned her head on his shoulder. "A trip to a two-bit whorehouse and dancing with a bunch of burly jacks are hardly the ways I would have chosen to woo you, honey."

"The fate of anyone who wants a kingbee cook."

He scooped up a handful of her hair and rubbed the soft strands between his fingers. "I want to love you until you quiver beneath me. I want to taste your breath pulsing through you and share the flame blazing within you."

"I want you holding me and being a part of me." Her arms encircled his shoulders.

"All night, honey."

She started to agree, then hesitated. "I have to check the stove. If I let it burn too low—"

With a laugh, he pushed her back into the pillow. "Let it burn low. Our fires will heat this cook shack. I can guarantee you'll be awake to tend to breakfast." A roguish smile tipped his mustache as his lips descended toward hers. "I don't plan on letting you sleep tonight."

Her agreement was unheard as she welcomed his kiss and the ecstasy which surged through her. She grasped the love he offered, knowing it would be as fleeting as the night. In the morning, she must face the consequences.

For now, she ceded herself to the magic once more.

CHAPTER EIGHTEEN

If the flunkeys noticed a difference in how Gypsy smiled at Adam when he came into the cook shack each morning, none of them made any comment. Often she found Adam watching her with an invitation in his blue eyes. She wanted to ask him so many things, for their conversation had been interrupted by passion, but she could not when the other flunkeys were about.

When Adam cornered her in the kitchen after the other flunkeys had finished their work the following Sunday afternoon, she smiled. Folding her hands behind her, she looked up into his eyes, which sparkled with the heat that could bring forth a firestorm of pleasure.

"I have the stove watch tonight, honey," he said quietly.

"I know, and I have it tomorrow night."

He brushed her hair back from her face as he whispered, "Two nights in a row, honey?"

She wrapped her arms around his shoulders. "I changed the schedule."

"I noticed."

"I thought you might have." She closed her eyes as

he pressed his lips against her throat. Quiescent no longer, desire exploded within her, swaying her against him.

Footsteps sounded in the dining room. Gypsy drew out of his arms. When she opened the dining room door, she forced a smile as she saw Bert, Per, and Hank sitting at a table. In their hands were playing cards.

"Want to play some poker?" called Hank. His wide belly pressed against the table as he stretched to place chips on the ante pile.

"No—no, thank you. Some other time."

Bert glanced over his shoulder. "If you change your mind, we 'ave a seat for you."

"I'm sure you do." With a laugh which sounded fake to her, she closed the door. As her gaze met the question in Adam's, she sighed. "They're playing cards."

He held out his hand. "Let's take a walk, honey. By the time we get back, they'll be gone, and I'll be even more eager to let you warm me."

"What a charming invitation!"

"I thought so," he returned with a chuckle.

The sunlight was muted by thickening clouds. The distant sound of a bird heralded a false spring. Spring was coming, albeit slowly, for winter refused to surrender its hold on the forest.

The snow had softened to slush. Walking was a chore, but Gypsy did not mind. She smiled as Adam took her hand. They fit together so perfectly, in so many special ways. When her gaze rose to his, the winter cold no longer bit into her.

"It's wonderful to have a few minutes with you," she said.

"I think that's as close as you've ever come to complimenting me."

"I didn't compliment *you*. I complimented the fact we can be together." She laughed and looked around the camp, which bore the scars of more than two years of lumbering.

"You really love it here, don't you, Gypsy?"

She nodded, smiling.

"Not the place I'd have chosen for a Virginian."

"I'm from Mississippi, Adam." She tried to keep her voice even. "Haven't I told you that?"

He chuckled. "Probably. I can't say I've heeded much of what you said when I can think only of stealing a few minutes away from that crimson-eyed stove." His gloved hand stroked her cheek, which was reddened by the wind. "Little did I suspect once I convinced you to let me join you for a night of love I'd have to wait a week before I could return."

"Adam, it's not my choice, but—"

"I know," he interrupted with gentle regret. "You can't ignore the appetites of a hundred jacks simply to satisfy mine. Maybe I should convince the other flunkeys to let me watch the stove every night. Then I could make love with you until we had our fill of each other."

As her arms swept up along his wool coat, she whispered, "Is that possible?"

"For me to have my fill of you?" He shook his head and smiled. "I can't imagine a time when you aren't in my mind and in my dreams, even if you can't be in my arms."

"But tonight you have the stove watch." She teased the warm skin beneath his collar. "It would be such a shame for you to watch that stove all alone."

He drew her bonnet ribbons aside. Each moist flick of his tongue sparked through her soul to settle in the heated depths of her body. As his mouth glided along her chin, she fought the yearning to beg him to love her in the nearest snowdrift.

He smiled. "Let's make this a short walk, honey, flunkeys or no."

"I think you're right." She tugged on the brim of his hat and laughed when he grimaced. "What an amazing thing! Adam Lassiter is correct about something."

"It's not so unusual. I was right about—" His face became rigid.

"What's wrong?"

"Wait here, honey."

Gypsy followed his gaze. Something darkened the road ahead of them. She squinted, but could not discern what the jumble of bright blue fabric might be. "Adam, what—"

"Just wait here." He strode down the road.

At his startled curse, she cried, "What is it, Adam?"

"Just a minute." His voice sounded as if he had swallowed wrong.

"Adam?"

"I said just a minute. Can't you have patience for once?"

When he knelt, she clasped her gloved hands in front of her face. Another low curse struck her ears. The pain in the single word sliced through her with the force of a blizzard wind. She stepped forward.

"Stay back, Gypsy." Before she could take another step, Adam surged to his feet. He seized her arms and pushed her back, all the time staying between her and what lay on the ground. She opened her mouth to protest, but he interrupted her. "You don't want to see her, Gypsy."

"Her? What—"

He whipped off his coat. When he turned away, she knew he was covering what remained of Rose Quinlan. It must be Rose. She was the only other woman here.

Gypsy's stomach wrenched when she saw the stain on her sleeves where Adam had touched her. Slowly she lifted her arms in the faint light of the setting sun.

The blood on the dark wool shattered dams of memory, spilling forth scenes of mangled corpses rotting in the sunshine. Week after week, death had exulted amid smoke from vomiting cannon and the numbing crash of artillery. They had feared the world was coming to an end. As the days passed with the same suffering, they feared it never would.

That had been only the beginning of the horror.

The never-ending horror.

"Gypsy?"

"No," she groaned.

"Gypsy!"

She shook her head. So many dead. She could not escape.

Adam gripped her shoulders and jolted her out of her terror. She closed her eyes and clung to him. "Gypsy?" Gray tainted his features.

She whispered, "Is it Rose?"

"Yes, but you guessed that."

"Yes," she answered as quietly. "Is she dead?"

"Yes."

"I can go back and—"

"No!" He grabbed her arm, not noticing how she winced as his bloody hands touched her. "I'll take you back to camp. She can wait. Curse Farley and his asinine pride!"

"But who could have done this?"

He smiled coldly. "That's the question, isn't it? I can give you one guess."

"The same man who killed Lolly Yerkes?"

Herding her ahead of him, he said with a grim tone which ate into her heart, "You'd better hope it is. Otherwise, we're dealing with two murderers. One we might be able to uncover. With two, we're at their mercy."

"Don't even suggest that, Adam."

"It's time someone did. Before you end up as dead as Lolly and Rose."

Adam's words rang through Gypsy's head. She stayed in the kitchen, agreeing not to leave it without one of the flunkeys. When he went to take the terrible tidings to Farley, she sat at the table and cradled her forehead in her hands.

A cup was shoved in front of her. Steam struck her face, but could not warm the frozen emptiness inside her.

Slowly she looked at Oscar, who was lowering his lanky form onto the bench across from her.

"I don't know where you keep the key for the liquor cupboard, Gypsy, but . . ."

She waved him to silence. "Whiskey won't help."

"Forgetting will."

"Then I'll have a headache and a heartache." A smile strained her tight lips.

He clasped his hands on the table, tightening them until his knuckles were as colorless as his face. "Gypsy, could it be the same man who killed Lolly?"

"I asked Adam about that. For the love of heaven, who would want to kill those two women? They have—had— nothing in common."

"They both slept with a man for a price." A flush climbed his cheeks. Leaning his head against his fists, he whispered a prayer.

She patted his soft hair. Anything she said to comfort him would be a lie. His shoulders quivered, and she knew he was sobbing.

"Come on, Oscar," she whispered. "Someone will have to go for Reverend Frisch, so we'd better have food packed."

"Gypsy, how can you act normal when things are so crazy?" he choked.

"Farley is my friend, and I must be strong for him."

"That's not fair!" He bounced to his feet.

"It's not meant to be." She sighed. "Let's get to work. It's the only way to deal with the pain."

Gypsy took her own words to heart as she busied herself fixing a grand meal for the jacks. As she had expected, the men drifted into the cook shack. She served sandwiches and bowls of thick soup. Listening to their questions, she told what little she knew. She was surprised in retrospect that Adam had not told her how Rose had died.

When she came back into the kitchen, Adam was talking to the flunkeys. She flung her arms around him. He rubbed her back gently and asked, "How are you doing, Gypsy?"

"I'm all right. How about you?"

"Not all right. Not by a long shot." He sighed as he glanced past her.

Her fingers clenched his arm. One slot of the knife rack was empty.

"Lor'!" gasped Bert.

"Do you think *he* stole it?" Per's voice was less than a whisper.

Lurching to the stove, Gypsy poured coffee for her crew. She put the cups on the table and fixed sandwiches. She had to keep busy. Otherwise, she would see . . . she swallowed her moan.

She froze when Bert asked, "Do you think 'e'll come back 'ere with the knife? We should set a watch for 'im." He glanced back at Gypsy. "Not 'er. 'E might be after 'er next."

"Gypsy's off the stove watch for good," Adam answered with an authority no one questioned.

If she protested, he would convince Farley to send her to Saginaw. But she could not go there. The person who had written those horrible notes had sent them from Saginaw. Maybe he was gone, because no more letters had come. But maybe he was still there, waiting for her.

"Good," mumbled the Englishman around a mouthful of sandwich. "She must be watched before 'e gets the idea 'e can slit 'er throat, too."

With a soft cry, she whirled away. She grabbed her coat and raced out the back door.

Glaring at Bert, Adam demanded, "Why are you blabbing all the gory details?"

"I thought she knew. She was with you when you found 'er."

Per interjected, "Adam would have kept her from seeing what was done to Rose." His aged gaze settled on Adam. "Gypsy should leave."

"She won't."

"If you spoke to her—"

Adam chuckled coldly. "No one can convince Gypsy Elliott to do what she should."

"Farley?" suggested Oscar.

"No one." He pushed away from the table. "I'll talk to her, but we all have to keep her from bumbling into that madman's hands."

Bert nodded as he lifted his cup. "We'll not let 'im near 'er. You can be sure of that! Gypsy won't die like Rose did."

Gypsy battled the sickness aching through her. Her fingers inched along the logs as she walked around the back of the cook shack. She seldom used the missing knife, because it was unwieldy. Holding her hands over her middle, she ordered her stomach to stop tumbling like a snowball down a hill.

A man strode toward her. The silhouette wore a frock coat. Farley! She had thought he would remain with Rose's body at his house.

"Calvin, I'm so sorry," she said when he drew even with her.

"I don't want to hear it!"

"Hear what?" She had not expected her sympathy to be thrown back into her face.

"I don't want to hear you say I told you so!"

"You did what you thought was best."

Tears glistened in his dark eyes, burning like liquid fire. He grabbed her arms. Shaking her viciously, he cried, "What I thought was best? Rose is dead! Dead! Because I didn't listen to her!"

"Calvin," she moaned as she tried to escape his fury and grief, "hurting me won't change anything."

"Do you know what it's like to have your beating heart ripped out of your chest and know everyone blames you for what has happened?" His laugh had a hysterical tint as he shook her on each word. His fingers cut like steel blades into her arms.

She groaned, "No one blames you."

"No?" He jarred her teeth with another sharp jolt. "You do! Why couldn't it have been you instead of her?"

"Farley, let her go!" came a shout. Adam rushed out of the cookhouse.

"Get out of here, Lassiter, or you'll be walking. I'm not finished with Gypsy yet."

With what sounded like a laugh, Adam said, "Oh, yes, you are."

Fabric tore with a scream. Gypsy stumbled backward and stared from her torn sleeve to where Adam had spun Farley away. Her hands pressed to her mouth as Adam's fist crashed into the camp manager's chin. The older man dropped to the snow. Blood coursed from his lip, but he didn't move.

Adam called to the kitchen crew. Bert rushed forward to heave Farley's arm over his shoulder. Taking the other side, Adam grinned when they lifted the senseless man to his feet.

"Can we put him in your room, honey?"

She nodded, not caring what Adam called her in front of the flunkeys. Everything was falling apart. How could Calvin Farley say he wanted her dead? She had thought he was her friend. She had thought . . . for the love of heaven! Had Farley sent the threatening notes? No, she could not believe that.

Stumbling after the others, she whispered her thanks to Per as he helped her inside. She pulled off her coat. Staring at the torn sleeve for a breathless second, she tossed the wrap on the table. Her legs were numb as she staggered toward her bedroom. When she bumped into a hard form, she pushed past Bert and went into her room.

Adam did not smile as he stared at Farley, who was sprawled across the bed. "I hit him a little harder than I should have, I guess. He's still out." Rubbing his sore knuckles, he added, "Are you all right?"

She pulled a washcloth from the pile on the table and dipped it in the tepid water. Putting the cloth on Farley's head, she whispered, "Not really. It's not easy to hear a man wish you were dead."

"He may not have meant that."

Tossing another rag into the water, she laughed coldly. "He was pretty clear."

"I heard him. Better than you, I'm sure." He lifted a strand of her loosened hair from her shoulder. "I think he was lamenting the fact he couldn't win your heart. He knows you wouldn't have been frightened into doing something as stupid as leaving camp alone."

"I'm not so sure of that." She walked toward the door.

He followed, halting her with his hand on her elbow, wanting to draw her into his arms and soothe her pain. "I am, Gypsy. He may have joked about your taking Rose's place, but he was serious."

"It doesn't matter," she answered with a sigh. "Rose is dead."

"And you're in danger."

"You're making something out of nothing. I'm not in danger."

"You are. I know—" A groan interrupted him.

He cursed under his breath as she bent over Farley. Why hadn't he seen this before? The answers to the puzzle he was trying to solve might be hidden in Gypsy's soft green eyes, which could not conceal her fear.

CHAPTER NINETEEN

Oscar brushed fresh snow from his shoulders. Like everyone in the camp, his steps were heavy and his smile fleeting. Instead of offering Gypsy a joke, he placed a folded newspaper on the table near where she was pouring a cup of tea for her lunch.

"Chauncey told me this came in the mail for you," he said as she regarded it with surprise.

"For me?" She picked the newspaper up and slit the brown paper around it. The Saginaw newspaper! The cold quaking of premonition clawed her stiff shoulders. Turning the brown paper over, she did not recognize the handwriting.

"I can take it back to him, if you want."

She dropped the newspaper's wrapping on the table. "No. I guess it's meant for me."

"All right." He appeared dubious, but left.

She heard the other flunkeys telling Oscar to climb aboard the sled. In the two weeks since Rose's savage murder, the men gladly traveled together. She was sure the camaraderie would fade along with the horror, but she wondered when that would be.

She opened the newspaper. Spreading the wide pages on the oilcloth, she scanned the headlines. The paper was more than a week old.

She turned the pages. When she read down a narrow column set in tiny type, one name leaped off the paper as if a lamp burned through it. She stared at Rose Quinlan's name, but could not read the obituary. Once she read it, she could no longer pretend Rose Quinlan's death had never happened.

Closing her eyes, she leaned her forehead against the heels of her palms as she wondered if the newspaper was another warning.

She was looking for trouble. That someone sent the newspaper with Rose Quinlan's obituary to her meant only that the sender knew she would share it with the jacks. Perhaps it was from Reverend Frisch, for the sky pilot would not be back at the camp for another week.

Gypsy bent to read the obituary.

Warm lips teased the back of her neck, and she cried out in shock. Hearing a laugh, she whirled to see Adam. She could not decide whether to throw her arms around him or berate him for frightening her.

He kissed her lightly. Her arms rose to his shoulders as she leaned against his strength. Twining her fingers behind his neck, she sought escape in the pleasure of his touch. She could not keep from smiling as his tongue teased her lips and his wet hair, which glistened with melting snow, brushed her cheek.

"It's been a thousand eternities since I've held you," he whispered.

"You were the one who stole half our nights together when you set the rule I shouldn't have the stove watch."

"Why not steal a few minutes with me now while the flunkeys are gone?"

"Now?" She laughed without mirth. "You know my work must come first."

His lazy smile suggested ecstasies she had only begun to sample in his arms. "Tell me you don't think of me while you supervise this kitchen. Tell me you don't remember our bodies merged in rapture. Tell me you don't long to share it again.''

"Don't, Adam," she breathed.

"Don't? Why not? Why shouldn't we want to recall every glory of the few nights we can have together?''

She was about to reply when her arm brushed the newspaper. As she caught it before the pages could scatter to the floor, renewed horror swept through her.

Her reaction must have flashed in her eyes, for his voice became studiously emotionless. ''What's wrong?''

"This."

He picked up the sheet. With a low whistle, he shook his head in disbelief. "So our Rose wasn't honest with Farley. Instead of Miss Quinlan, it should have been Mrs. Quinlan. I wonder if Farley knew, or if she simply convinced him to bring her here so she could take him for every penny she had.''

"Do you think her husband came out here to kill her because she left him and their children?" She smoothed out the page and stared at the unbelievable words. "Four children! Who would have guessed she was more than seventeen or eighteen years old? According to this, she's older than I am.''

He tipped up her chin with his finger. "You could look as young if you used the rice powder and belladonna she did. Actually, you're prettier without the cosmetics.''

"Wonderful! Not only do I usually look like an old hag, but now I'm prettier than a dead woman.'' She pushed him aside. Folding the newspaper, she pointed at the larder. "Get some apples out and put them to soak. It's time to begin the pies.''

"Gypsy?''

Reluctantly she turned to look at him. As she had so often, she wished he was not so tall. Tilting her head back at such an odd angle left her at a disadvantage. "Adam, I don't have time for idle chatter.''

"This isn't idle by any stretch of the imagination.'' He

crossed the room. When he did not touch her, she hid her shock. "The idea of her husband chasing her all the way from Saginaw is ludicrous."

"Murder is ludicrous."

"Murder is rational to those with a predilection to it. Sane people, like you and me, can't comprehend anyone tormenting and slaying someone, but—" He interrupted himself as she turned away. "Gypsy, I didn't mean to frighten you."

"Yes, you did."

"All right, I did." Adam resisted the temptation to draw her into his arms. When he had started working for her, he was misled by her calm control of her cookhouse. He had learned Gypsy cloaked her vulnerability with sarcasm.

"There's no need," she whispered. "I'm frightened enough already. I thought the greatest danger here was the stove blowing up or an accident on the hill."

"We've had an accident on the hill."

"Do you want to spook the whole camp worse than it already is? Every man is looking over his shoulder. They watch me as if they expect someone to swoop down and murder me right before their eyes. Do you know what it's like to have silence follow you everywhere?"

He hooked his thumbs around his suspenders. "No one with any sense expects you'll be murdered."

"Jacks have no sense!" Flinging out her hands, she said, "The floorboards must be set just so. Not a splinter of poplar can be used in camp. For the love of heaven, if I were foolish enough to pick up poplar branches for the firebox, I'd be locked out of my own cookhouse and sent on the hay trail."

"Spare me your charming colloquialisms, Gypsy. You can't hide from what you can't see."

"This murderer *is* invisible."

He snarled a curse, but his arms enfolded her to him as he sought in her mouth for pleasure. His embrace gentled as he delighted in her softness against him. The familiar longing could not be satisfied for another two nights.

At the thought, he throbbed with the desire festering in him. He yearned to pull aside her lacy blouse and the silk beneath it. Then he would kiss her until her breath burned against him.

Groaning, he released her. Seeing surprise in her volatile eyes, he smiled sadly. "Honey, it's not easy to hold you like this when I long to hold you in your bed." His grin became rakish. "Of course, I could invite you to join me in mine, but I don't think you're interested in sharing my bunk with me and fifty jacks."

"Adam, I wish you could stay here, but . . . ."

"But?"

Gypsy's happiness disappeared in a thunderclap of pain. She cared too much for him. She loved him too much to endanger him. Staring at the wall, she could deny that no longer. She loved Adam Lassiter. The joy washing over her when he looked in her direction, when he touched her, when he made love with her had to be love.

"There's no but," she answered quietly. "I'm not thinking clearly."

"I would say you're not. You have to leave camp."

"Leave? Are you mad?"

"Allowing you to stay would be mad. You can't risk your life for the last few weeks of the season."

"You're panicking like a superstitious jack."

"Superstitions don't worry me. Facts do."

"Facts?" She laughed as she went into the larder. Carrying a bag of flour to the table, she dropped it, raising a cloud of white dust. "Just because every logger here thinks I'll be the next victim doesn't make it so. Perhaps Bobby Worth's death wasn't an accident. Then it could be any of us who might be killed next. Nobody else is leaving. The jacks are willing to work until payday comes."

"If it's money, Glenmark will take care of you. He doesn't want his kingbee cook murdered. Even Farley should be able to see it'd be better to pension you off so you can come back next year when things are settled.''

She ladled flour into her mixing bucket. ''It's not a matter of money. I appreciate your concern, but I won't leave.''

He grasped her elbows and drew her toward him again. ''Won't? Or do you mean you can't leave?'' When she flinched, he demanded, ''What is it, Gypsy? What's frightening you so much that you're hiding here? Is it those notes?''

In a strangled voice, she gasped, ''Notes? How do you know about—I mean—''

''I want to know what's scared you so.''

Only inwardly did Gypsy cringe away. She kept her face serene. It would be deliciously sweet to share the burden with someone who wished to help her, but that was impossible.

The latch on the dining room door rattled, and Adam swore as Oscar and Hank entered, blowing on their hands and knocking mud and snow from their feet.

Hank announced, ''Farley's posted a reward for any information about Rose's murderer.''

''How much?'' Adam's tone suggested he was neither pleased nor surprised.

''A thousand dollars.'' The fat man's eyes twinkled with greed. ''That would buy any information I had—if I had any.''

Oscar clapped him on the shoulder. ''Can't you come up with something? You must have talked to Rose a time or two.''

He peeled his coat off and hung it by Gypsy's. ''Too good for the rest of us, she was. I wouldn't be surprised if someone took offense to her uppity ways and decided to take her down a notch or two.''

''Hank!'' gasped Gypsy.

A sheepish expression stole the humor from his wide jowls. Glancing at Oscar, who was pretending to be busy, he mumbled, "Sorry, Gypsy. It's just that none of us liked how she treated you."

"She treated me fine."

"When she wanted something from you," interjected Oscar with uncharacteristic fury. "She knew what she was, and she knew what you are."

As she cut lard into the flour, Gypsy said, "I don't care what she thought. I will hear no laughing at the dead."

As the men went into the larder, Adam said, "Gypsy, you're going to have to let them deal with the horror."

"By making fun of a dead woman?" She glanced at the newspaper. Wiping her hands on her apron, she wadded the pages into a thick ball then opened the firebox and threw the paper on the fire. "Rest in peace, Rose Quinlan," she whispered.

When Adam put his arms around her, she could not halt her tears. She clung to him, afraid as she never had been before. Not for herself, but for him.

She vowed not to let the threat sweep her away from the man she loved. He would survive, no matter what she must do to protect him.

CHAPTER TWENTY

"Hank, you've got to be mistaken." Gypsy wiped her hands to loosen the flour clinging to her fingers. Sunday afternoons were a good time for making cookies.

"No, Gypsy." His broad belly rocked with vehemence. "Farley wants to see you lickety-split up at his house."

Sighing, she pulled off her apron and reached for her coat. "Why can't this wait until tomorrow? Today's supposed to be our day off!"

"Do you want me to go with you?"

"I can walk across camp by myself." She smiled to lessen her brusqueness. "Or do you want to get out of baking the rest of the cookies, Hank?"

He grinned, his wide cheeks stretching as easily as pine pitch. "Give a man credit for trying."

"Per and Bert should be along shortly. Oscar is taking out the last of the trash."

"How about Adam?"

She frowned. "He went over to the wanigan. Maybe he got caught up in a game of cards with Chauncey. I'll stop by on my way back and send him over if he's still slacking."

"Gypsy?"

She shoved her arms into her coat. Shrugging it into place, she reached for her bonnet. "What?"

Hank met her gaze steadily. "Don't think me out of line, but Adam's good for you. You've been happier since he's arrived. You've been singing around the cook shack."

"You're not out of line," she said in a low voice. "I'd better go see what's irritating Farley."

"Maybe you should think about leaving with Adam when the spring drive comes," continued the fat man.

"I'm needed on the drive."

"I meant after."

She smiled as she settled her bonnet on her hair and tied the ribbons under her chin. "I haven't thought about what I'll be doing after the drive. All I know is that it'll be somewhere there's no snow."

Hurrying out the door, she rushed toward the house hidden in the trees beyond the camp. To stay would force her to admit Adam had said nothing of a future together.

Not that they could have one, she reminded herself. She knew so little about Adam Lassiter.

And he knows nothing about you.

With a sigh, she wondered how she could love Adam but find it impossible to trust him with the deepest terrors of her soul. She wanted to share the truth. She must not. That could suck him into the horror.

Coincidence, she could hear her sister saying. Was it? Had she banished herself here for no reason? No, it could not be just a string of misfortunes that had stalked her family. The notes proved that, but they had stopped. She wished she knew what that meant.

Stuffing her hands into her pockets, Gypsy hurried through the snow. The cold wind chewed on her bones as the weak winter sun dropped toward the tops of the trees. When she reached the house, the first thing she would do was remind Farley exactly how precious her free time was.

Her irritation withered when she recalled how distraught and disorganized the camp manager had been since Rose's murder. Farley had not spoken to her more than once during the past two weeks. She guessed he was embarrassed. Maybe he wanted to apologize privately.

Footsteps intruded on her thoughts. Before she could call a greeting, she heard a low, guttural laugh. She looked in both directions, but saw nothing except trees and snow. As she hunched into her coat, she started as one branch struck another. When she saw a rabbit hop from the underbrush, she laughed shakily.

She would not panic like poor Rose, who had spent her last days in a hysteria which might have led to her death. She hurried along the road, jumping over the ruts where sleds had cut into the ice. The sound of a jack's laughter must not spook her.

Alarm sped through her when a man jumped out from the brush in front of her. The sparkle of steel at his side could be a knife or a gun. He walked toward her, and her eyes widened when she heard his odd laugh again.

"Who are you?" she called. "What do you want?"

He laughed and lunged at her. She fled. Boots pounded the frozen turf behind her. Closer, closer—ever closer, and so loud her rough panting could not cover the sound.

The man caught her arm and whirled her against a tree. She tried to tug away. The flash of a knife froze her.

His massive shoulders could have belonged to any man in camp. In horror, she stared at a hat which was pulled down to conceal the upper half of his face. Eyeholes had been cut through the tattered wool. His brown eyes were filled with malevolent anticipation. A dark beard hid the rest of his face, except for his satisfied smile.

He twisted the blade so the metal caught the day's last light. Laughing, he held the knife in front of her face. She pressed back against the trunk. For the love of heaven, let someone come along the path.

That would not happen. The woods were empty on Sundays.

"You don't scream like they did," he mused as he shoved the knife up against her throat. "Maybe you're not scared enough yet."

If she told him her heart was beating so thunderously she had trouble hearing him, he might kill her. To lie could bring the same death. Had he written those horrible notes? Was he the man who had murdered Rose? The one who had smothered Lolly? Was he all three?

She tried to edge around the tree. The dagger against her vulnerable throat paralyzed her. When he laughed, she almost choked on whiskey fumes.

She moaned when he pinned her between himself and the trunk. The rough bark jabbed her spine. The gleam in his eyes warned he was delighting in her despair. Keeping his knife at the base of her throat where her pulse rattled unevenly, he loosened the buttons along her coat.

"Please," she whispered, "don't do this."

"I won't hurt you . . . yet."

Fear roiled through her. Which one of the jacks wanted her dead?

When he had undone the buttons along the front of her coat, he ordered, with another laugh, "Take it off, Gypsy."

"For the love of heaven, it's barely above freezing."

He chuckled as he scraped the knife up her neck. "You won't have to worry about being cold. I'll keep you warm before you spend the rest of eternity in Hell."

At the deranged sound of his laughter, she slowly lowered her coat down her arms. She kept her eyes locked with his. When the time came to fight, she would, but she refused to die arguing over her coat. It fell with a thump to the ground behind her. The frigid wind bit through her thin blouse. When she started to wrap her arms around herself, he crushed her against the tree. Her breath exploded in a pained gasp.

"I told you, you needn't worry about being cold, Gypsy."

Something about his rich voice teased her with familiarity. But who? She could not guess. Her mind was crippled with terror.

Spreading her hands along the snow-pitted bark of the tree, she whispered, "Why don't you stop before this goes too far?"

"Too far? Gypsy, my girl, I wouldn't send you to your grave a maiden. Or am I too late? Lassiter has been slobbering over you. Has he bedded you?"

"My private life is none of your business!"

"It is now." He laughed again. When she turned her face away from his putrid breath, he used the flat side of the blade to force her lips beneath his.

As his mouth ground into hers, demanding an intimacy she had offered only to Adam, his fingers slipped around her waist. He pulled her away from the tree. When she raised her hands, he tipped the knife beneath her jaw again.

"Stop!" Her words became a shriek as he shoved her backward. Falling into the snow, she rolled to jump up.

He seized her arm and pushed her into the icy embrace of a drift. Flakes sifted into her face, blinding her. He groped for the high collar of her blouse. Her heel struck his knee. Tottering back, he cursed viciously. She leaped to her feet.

His broad arm encircled her waist. She was flung to the ground, her skirt tearing. Gasping for breath, she stared up at him. He stood over her with one foot on either side of her skirt. With a laugh, he kneeled. She cringed as his legs brushed hers.

Again the knife appeared, only inches from her face. "Don't make me angry, Gypsy. Then I'd have to kill you now."

"I'm not going to let you rape me!"

"No?" He gripped her collar. When the material refused to rip, he swore.

She flinched as he slit the front of her blouse away

from the stubborn collar. Knowing what she risked, she raised her hand to block his.

His smile vanished. "I told you to cooperate, Gypsy!"

He curled his fingers into a fist.

It was caught in a wide hand and jerked back. "Let her go!"

"Adam!" Gypsy screamed. "Look out!"

Adam jumped aside when the knife slashed toward him. He lifted his clenched hands and brought them down on the man's wrist. The man's howl sliced through the silent woods, and the knife skidded through the snow.

The attacker hit Adam.

Adam rocked back a few steps. He shook his head groggily and hefted his fists. Gypsy shrieked. When the man turned, Adam grabbed him by the arm. Gypsy's warning was too late. The man laughed as he clubbed Adam over the head with a branch. Adam collapsed into the snow.

She scrambled on all fours through the drift, her tattered clothes tripping her. Even as she heard maniacal laughter behind her, she found the knife. She gripped its hilt. She whirled as the man lifted the branch to strike Adam a death blow.

"No!" She struggled to her feet. "Get away from him!"

The man swung the branch at her. She tried to evade it, but the end caught her elbow. The knife flipped end over end to disappear into the shadows. Pain thundered through her. Had he broken her arm?

She backed away, not daring to glance at Adam. The man grasped her arm. When she sobbed in agony, he released her to fold up at his feet. He gripped her hair and yanked her head backward at a painful angle.

"Next time, Gypsy, we won't be interrupted."

His laughter remained behind as he vanished. Ignoring the tears that ran along her face, she crawled through the snow's smothering softness to where Adam still lay. He must be alive. She dropped next to him. He was face down. Turning him over onto his back would take more strength than she had.

"Adam," she whispered. "Please wake up, Adam."

She shook him with the strength she had remaining. They must get back to camp. To stay in the snow would mean freezing to death. "Adam, you must wake up! Please!"

Slowly his head rose. He shook it and moaned.

"Adam?"

He turned toward her. Even in the twilight, she could see astonishment in his eyes. His arm swept out and pulled her to him. A smile pulled at his lips in the moment before he captured hers.

A strangled scream erupted from her throat as she pulled away. Confusion returned to his eyes as he sat up. "What happened to you, Gypsy?"

"Just help me back to camp," she whispered. She swallowed her pain as she stretched to grab her coat. Swinging it over her shredded blouse, she fought her way to her feet. She swayed and leaned against a tree.

In a motion as wobbly, he rose. With his hand against the back of his head, he mumbled, "If this is a hangover, I hope the rotgut was worth it. Who was it, Gypsy?"

Startled by his sharp, suddenly lucid question, she whispered, "I don't know. Someone in camp. No one else would have come all the way up here just to . . ."

"To murder you?" He laughed, then grimaced. "I must be getting soft to be taken down so quickly." Lurching to her, he gasped when she cowered away. "What's wrong?"

Her hands trembled when she tried to button her coat. "Adam, just take me home."

"After you explain why you act as if you've never been in my arms before."

"But he—he—"

Adam's jaw tightened, and he pulled her coat closed, securing the top button. "He didn't, honey. You're safe."

"Am I?"

"You are! He's gone."

When he wiped frozen tears from her cheek, she buried her face against his ripped coat. He stroked her messed hair as she shivered.

He found Gypsy's bonnet and placed it on her head. His eyes would not focus, but he managed to tie a lopsided bow under her chin. When she winced, he knew he was not the only one hurt.

Fury cut through him. He had let the fool knock him senseless. His skull still rang. Then that cur had hurt Gypsy. She could have been raped or killed or both while he slept in a snowbank.

"Adam," she whispered, "he said he's coming back."

"He'd have to be crazy to try this again."

Her voice splintered. "He's mad. He vowed to finish what you interrupted."

"Don't worry, honey. We'll be prepared." Rubbing his head, he smiled grimly. "He won't escape next time."

"I don't want to talk about next time. Just take me back to the cookhouse, Adam."

He put his arm around her shoulders and staggered as they walked slowly along the path. "You sure you can walk?" he asked.

"Are you sure you can?" Gypsy returned when he swayed against her.

He might have smiled if his jaw would stop throbbing. "Not much of a hero, am I?"

"We're both alive."

"And we're getting out of here."

She shook her head and winced. "No, I can't leave."

Pausing, he said, "Why not?" When she hesitated, he said, "I think it's time for honesty."

"From both of us."

Reluctantly he nodded. "I just hope it's not too late."

CHAPTER
TWENTY-ONE

The kitchen was deserted when Adam opened the door and helped Gypsy in. She looked at the knife rack. The empty slot was an accusation, but the knife her attacker had used was not the missing one. It had been one of the hunting knives the jacks wore on their belts.

Awkwardly she undid her coat. Adam lifted it off her shoulders, and she moaned. The pain centered around her right elbow. With every motion of her arm, she ached from her wrist to her shoulder.

As she held her ripped blouse closed, Adam cursed. "I'm sorry I didn't teach that son of—"

"Adam, don't."

He frowned. "You've heard me say worse."

"You can call him whatever you want, but I don't want to hear it. I don't want to think about it. I just want to forget."

"You can't." His voice became more gentle as he brushed a shred of her sleeve back over her shoulder. "Why don't you change? If the others saw you like this, I'm not sure I could keep them from getting together a lynching mob."

"And lynch who?" she whispered as she hurried to her door.

"I'll load the stove," he called after her.

Wobbling across her bedroom, Gypsy pulled off her ragged blouse. Tears clung to her eyelashes. She pushed them away and tossed the ruined blouse onto the floor. She wanted to throw it into the cast-iron stove. She had burned the notes there, but she had not succeeded in fleeing from the truth. Now she had dragged Adam into the horror.

Her fingers were clumsy with fear as she tried to button the high collar of her nightgown. Slipping her arms into her bulky wrapper, she grimaced as the collar slapped her face. She looked into her small mirror and saw a bruise on her left cheek. Her elbow pulsed with pain.

Footsteps sounded beyond the door. She whirled at a knock. "Who is it?"

"Adam."

"Go away!" Somehow she had to keep him safe. She had no idea how, other than forcing him out of her life.

The door burst open and slammed against the wall. His face could have been carved from stone.

"Adam!"

"No more games, Gypsy." He closed the door. In the dim light from the lantern, the bandage he had put over the bloody spot on his forehead glistened obscenely. "At least you showed sense in getting your nightgown on. Why aren't you in bed?"

He scooped her up into his arms before she could protest. Gently, he placed her on her bed. He drew the blankets over her thick wrapper and placed her pillow against the headboard.

"You sit here." He leaned on the footboard. "I'll sit here, and we can talk without everyone hearing."

Gypsy entwined her fingers and fought to keep her tears from falling. Here, where she should think only of the ecstasy she found in Adam's touch, evil had invaded. She yearned for Adam to put his arms around her and tease the fear from her, but that could not be.

She must convince him to leave. If the only way she could do that was by being honest, she must reveal the truth. She prayed it would not destroy him.

"Tell me what happened," he ordered when she remained silent.

"When?"

His brows rose, but he said only, "Start with today."

"I got a message to meet Farley at his house." She drew her knees up to her chest and wrapped her arms around them. "Farley has never been interested in work after he closes the office for the day. I thought it might be different . . . now."

He laughed shortly. "Exactly what your charming friend wanted you to think. You walked right into his trap."

"How was I supposed to know?" she countered with sudden heat. "Who here would want to harm me? After all, the men depend on me to feed them. That inspires a certain loyalty."

"In all but one man." He put his hand on hers. "Forgive this question, but it must be asked. Is there a jack who believed you'd be interested in an assignation? I've seen how they look at you, Gypsy."

"Do you think I'd arrange a tryst when—" It was the wrong time to speak of how she had fallen in love with him. Pointing to her bruised cheek, she asked, "Do you think I'd arrange a tryst with a man who'd treat me like this?"

"Perhaps he was disappointed when I interrupted. I would have been."

"Adam!"

He smiled an apology. "I'm only asking the questions others will. A woman alone on a deserted road just before dark meets a man. When the rendezvous is intruded upon, the scene becomes ugly, for her would-be lover assumes she's invited this other man, as well."

"Except that he planned to kill me. Lust for sex is different than lust for murder."

Adam released her hand and rested his shoulder against the footboard. Amusement sparkled in his eyes, but his voice was somber. "I won't ask how you know that." He sighed. "You must be extra cautious of anything unusual—like those notes you've been getting from Saginaw." He added, without contrition, "I read one while you were sick."

"What did it say?"

"Does it matter? It tipped me off to the fact that you're in more trouble than you want anyone to know." He tipped her face up so she had to meet the apprehension in his eyes. "Don't run off by yourself again. Take someone with you."

"Who? That man could have been anyone."

He took her hands in his and lifted them to his lips. "You can trust me, honey. I'm going to have the scars to prove it."

"Thank you," she whispered. "I should have said that before."

When he offered her a gallant bow, he clenched his head and swore. "He would have killed me if my head weren't so hard." He sat next to her and sandwiched her hands between his. "Gypsy, when I think about him touching you, I want to castrate him."

"Touching me would have been the least of his crimes."

"Perhaps, but it's the most heinous one to me."

Gypsy found it easier to smile than she had expected when she ran her fingers along Adam's whisker-roughened cheek. "I never guessed you'd be a jealous lover."

His arm swept around her waist and pulled her to him. "I'm jealous of any man who looks at you. I want to hoard away all your smiles for myself. I want every glow in your green eyes to be just for me."

She curved her fingers along his nape and steered his lips over hers. Hungrily he pushed her back into the mattress as his mouth brought her delight. She forgot the twinge of pain along her jaw as he warmed her face with kisses while his fingers caressed her. When he bent to sample the length of her throat, he pulled back. She opened her eyes to see his frown before he tilted her head away to look at the red marks there.

"You're lucky he didn't slit your throat," he snarled.

She shivered. "Don't say that, Adam. Please, for the love of heaven, don't say that."

"Gypsy, what's wrong?"

"What's wrong?" she gasped. "What do you think is wrong? That man nearly kills me, and you make it into a joke!"

He caught her face between his thumb and forefinger. "I find nothing amusing about this."

She brushed her aching elbow against the mattress and moaned.

Adam pushed up her sleeve to discover the swelling along her upper forearm. Cautiously he probed the colorful bruise to make sure no bones were broken. Looking into her eyes, which were jeweled with unshed tears, he swore. "He plays rough. I'll have to give him some lessons on how to treat a lady the next time we meet."

"I was ready to play rough, too."

"You?"

"He used the stick he hit you with to knock his knife out of my hand." She held her pillow to her chest like a shield. "I would have stabbed him if he hadn't. He was going to kill you."

Adam wiped away a tear sliding down her cold cheek. That she had defended him with the fervor of a she-bear protecting her cub did not astound him. That she would attempt to kill a man to save him did. The man would come back for her, and Adam could not wait to repay him for destroying her gentle spirit.

''It's time for the truth, Gypsy, about what you're afraid of.''

''You haven't figured out what I'm frightened of?''

He put his arm around her quivering shoulders and looked into her hooded eyes. ''Gypsy, the truth. Not about the attack today, but what happened before. What's frightening you so much that you're hiding here?''

''How—'' Swallowing roughly, she whispered, ''Is it that obvious?''

He smiled swiftly, but his dark brows lowered. ''It is to me. After this, it's going to be obvious to everyone.''

''They told me I was overreacting, that it was just sad coincidence.''

''They? Who?''

''My family.'' She bit her lip, then whispered, ''Before they died.''

''How?''

Gypsy flexed her right hand to be sure she would be able to use it when she started preparing breakfast. ''It all started after the siege—''

''Which one?''

Pain coursed up her arm as she adjusted it to rest on her lap. ''Petersburg.''

''In Virginia?''

''Yes.'' She put her hand on his arm. ''Forgive me for not trusting you, Adam, but I've been fleeing for so long I don't dare to trust anyone. Until you came here, no one questioned that I wasn't from Mississippi. Most of the men here are from New England or Canada. To them, one Southern accent sounds like any other.''

He waved aside her apology. ''The siege was over in '65.''

She closed her eyes. ''At first, I wanted to believe it was coincidence. That's what everyone told me it was. My brother was slain after being mustered out of his unit. He was killed only a few miles from Petersburg. Of course, none of the authorities cared about the fate of a Johnny Reb. My mother died before winter that year.''

"How?"

Her hand went to the red line on her neck. "Her throat was slit."

"And they called *that* a coincidence?"

She shuddered and sagged against the pillows. Opening her mouth, she whispered, "You have to understand what it was like in the months after the war. No one knew who was in charge of anything. The carpetbaggers came to steal everything. They didn't want the law around. It was easier for them to ignore it. I don't know how they could. I don't understand . . ."

Adam swore silently. From the horror in her voice, he guessed she had been the one to find her mother's corpse. That explained the incapacitating terror in her jade eyes. Quietly, he asked, "Was that the end of it?"

"It was just the beginning."

"Who else?"

"Everyone who was left."

In disbelief, he choked, "Everyone in your family?"

Tears flooded her cheeks. Years of trying to hide her mourning made the agony even more intense. "All of them. My brother, my parents, my grandmother, one uncle. Only my sister and I survive."

"Do you know why?"

"No, but does it matter? My parents didn't deserve to be killed! None of my family did!" She clenched her unhurt hand by her side. "I couldn't stay and be murdered, too! Without telling anyone, I slipped out in the middle of the night. I walked north until I could get to a train. I rode it until I reached the end of that line. Then I got on another and another until I reached Lansing. Finally I came here."

"So you never knew if the murderer had been caught?"

Gypsy shook her head. The pain in her arm was climbing through her body to dull every nerve. "To try to find that out might reveal where I was. But it's all been for naught, because he's found me. I think I'm beginning to understand what his scheme is."

"He wanted you to see the others die horribly before you."

"He's succeeded."

He stood. "Staying here would be insane."

"Wherever I go, he'll find me."

"But—"

"Nothing!" She edged off the mattress and went to where he was standing before the stove. She smiled sadly. "Adam, I didn't want to involve you in this mess."

"That's why you kept pushing me away?" He smiled as his arm encircled her waist. "Gypsy, we're in this together now."

She whispered, "I'm sorry."

"Don't be. While I'm here, I might as well help you at the same time I'm helping Glenmark."

"And what are you doing for him?"

He kissed her lightly and grinned. "I think we could use a cup of swamp water. How about it?"

"Adam!"

As he held out his hand to her, he said, "We can talk over that cup."

Her hand rose to her bruised cheek when she saw the flunkeys gathered in the kitchen. Glancing at Adam, she realized he was not surprised. Renewed tears stung in her eyes. He must have heard the men and knew inviting her out into the kitchen was the best way to dodge her questions.

Gypsy sighed. Adam was her ally, but she was not his. He still refused to reveal what he was doing here. Slipping her fingers into his, she wondered what would happen when his work was finished. There might be no place in his life for her, and that frightened her more than the madman stalking her.

Bert called, "Gypsy, what 'appened to you?" He dropped a partially peeled onion and glared at Adam. "If 'e 'it you, Gypsy, say the word, and me and the boys'll make 'im pay."

"That's right!" Oscar wiped his hands on his stained apron. "We'll take him apart."

She tried not to smile at the unexpected chivalry. "This isn't Adam's fault." She pointed to the bandage on his hair. "He saved me."

The men swarmed over them, demanding to know what had happened. None of them noticed Adam answered all the questions. When she heard him deflect some with ease, she feared he had been lying to her from the beginning.

Slowly she sank to the bench. As her gaze met his across the room, her breath caught. The desire burning in his eyes could not be faked. Could it?

" 'Ere, Gypsy."

"Thank you, Bert," she whispered without looking up. His accent was instantly recognizable, along with the reek of the onions he had been cutting. More slowly than usual, she noted, as he opened and closed his fingers that must be cramped from the work. She could not scold him when all the flunkeys were more interested in talking than in finishing their chores. She took the cup of cocoa.

" 'Ow are you doing?"

"Honestly?"

Sitting across from her, Bert frowned when she winced as she opened her mouth to sip the cocoa. "You don't know 'oo did this?"

"No." She sighed, meeting the compassion in his dark eyes. "But I fear it's the same person who attacked Lolly Yerkes and Rose Quinlan."

"Murdered 'em, you mean." When a shiver sliced across her shoulders, he added, " 'Scuse me, Gypsy. I shouldn't 'ave said that."

"Why not? It's the truth. I'm lucky Adam happened along to save me."

" 'Appened along? 'Ow is it that 'e was there?"

She glanced toward Adam, who was speaking with the other flunkeys. That was a question she should have asked. She had been so grateful for his arrival that she had not been curious about what brought him there exactly when she needed him.

Folding her hands on the table, she said, "I don't know, and, to be honest, I didn't care. Just having him there to save me was enough."

But it's not enough now, she added silently.

CHAPTER
TWENTY-TWO

"You've got to fire her." Adam leaned his fists on Farley's desk.

Daniel Glenmark sat behind the cluttered desk. Smiling, he folded his hands, which emerged from the perfectly pressed sleeves of his gray suit. They were as rough and broad as the hands of any man in the woods. Glenmark had made his money on his own labor as well as what he hired to cut the trees on the lands he leased and bought, but he had never lost the authority he had gained while fighting in the last war.

"Fire Gypsy?" He shook his head. "That's the most ludicrous thing I've ever heard."

"Not as ludicrous as having her dead."

Glenmark stood, frowning. "What's wrong? If I were talking to any other man, I'd say he was panicking, but you don't panic. At least, you didn't used to."

"I'm not panicking, just looking at the facts."

"I've seen the facts." He glanced at the bandage on Adam's head. "I don't like this, not after what happened to Farley's harlot."

"So you will fire her?"

''No.''

Adam pounded one hand on the desk and swore. ''How can you be so shortsighted, sir?'' His eyes narrowed as Glenmark toyed with a piece of paper on Farley's desk. ''You sent me up here to do a job and—''

''Do it.''

''And let Gypsy be the next to get murdered?''

''Don't worry about her.'' Glenmark tugged on his vest. ''I'll deal with her.''

''What do you mean?''

Glenmark did not meet his eyes. ''I mean I will deal with her.''

''And fire her?''

''No.'' He laughed shortly. ''I can't fire the best kingbee cook in the north woods. The jacks would follow her.''

Adam scowled. ''I guess I don't understand.''

''You don't.'' Glenmark sat back behind the desk. ''I'll deal with her, and I suspect the outcome will be what you want.'' Clasping his hands on the desk, he leaned forward. ''She's not like other women. This has to be handled the right way, or this whole camp will self-destruct.'' He arched a silver brow. ''And that may be exactly what our faceless friend wants.''

''Or you may be playing right into his hands, Colonel. Leaving Gypsy here could mean her death.''

''Don't you think I've thought of that? I can't—''

The door swung open, and Adam stepped behind it. He put his hand beneath his coat, his fingers curling around the butt of his pistol. If he had carried it before, he might have put an end to this on the path to Farley's house.

A light voice came around the door. ''Farley, what did you want to talk to me about? I—Daniel, I didn't—'' Gypsy's face lost all color as Glenmark frowned. ''Mr. Glenmark, this is a pleasant surprise. I had no idea you were coming up here.''

When Glenmark motioned for her to sit in front of the desk, Adam saw Gypsy sneak a glance behind her. Her

eyes widened as they met his. Leaning against the wall,
he crossed his arms over his chest.

"When I received word of the trouble up here," Glenmark said, "I thought I'd see for myself."

Adam scowled. Glenmark's answer gave no hint of
anything unusual. His words were the trite ones he would
have shared with any loyal employee.

"I'd planned on speaking with you in the kitchen later,
Gypsy," Glenmark continued. "If this would be more
convenient, I'm sure Adam will excuse us."

"That's not necessary." Gypsy jumped to her feet and
backed toward the door. "I'm here only because I got a
message Farley wanted to see me."

"He's up at his house. If you wish—"

"No!" She did not want to go along that empty road
even in the middle of the day. "I'll talk to Farley later."

Adam said in a voice as bereft of emotion as his face,
"Mr. Glenmark, I can come back."

"That's not necessary," Gypsy repeated. "I'm busy
baking cakes. Later will be much more convenient for
me." Trying to maintain her serenity, she added, "Adam,
I expect you back to oversee the cooking of the biscuits—
if that's possible."

He looked at her, then away swiftly. She almost
laughed. Perhaps he regretted admitting that he was working directly for the owner of the lumber company, but it
was too late. She intended to get answers. Somehow.

She called a greeting to Chauncey as the inkslinger
waved from the wanigan, but did not stop to chat. She
was unsure if she could keep from blurting the truth. In
the cookhouse, she could control her rebellious emotions.

The familiar task of kneading bread dough while the
cakes baked with the delicious aroma of chocolate soothed
her uneasiness. Silken flour swirled over her fingers as
she rolled the dough. She was careful not to push too
hard, for her elbow still ached.

A different sort of pain pounded through her. She could
not keep from recalling the strength of Adam's hands

as he had kneaded the bread with her. He had become enmeshed in every part of her life, making it impossible to flee from the truth. She loved him.

When the door opened and cold air gushed through the kitchen, Gypsy quietly ordered, "Per, keep everyone working. We're already behind schedule." She wiped her hands and turned to smile at the man in the doorway. "Mr. Glenmark, welcome to the cook shack. Can we get you a cup of swamp water? There are some cookies in the larder."

"I'd like to talk to you." He motioned toward her room. "Alone."

"All right." She ignored the twisting in her stomach. Never had Daniel asked to speak to her privately. Avoiding her crew's shocked expressions, she led the way into her room. When Daniel shut the door, she asked in a whisper, "Do you think this is wise?"

He shrugged, but the motion was sluggish, as if he carried huge logs on his shoulders. "Let them think what they wish. We need to talk alone. Even Farley's office isn't private."

"Daniel, I'm sorry I burst in there like that."

"Don't apologize, Gypsy." He sat on the chair next to her bed. His graying mustache drooped over his mouth. "Even after all this time, it seems odd to call you Gypsy."

"It's my name. Papa always said I'd end up wandering the world like a gypsy."

"Because he never expected you to, I'm sure."

"Maybe not, but I've seen more than I ever thought I would."

He smiled weakly. "At last I can tell you I didn't think you'd last a season in the north woods. Now you're finishing your third winter up here."

"This snow came as an eye-opener. Sometimes I think I'll never get warm again." Her studiously cheerful expression faded. "How are you doing, Daniel?"

"Fine. Fine."

"Daniel?" She had not expected the tension to remain in his voice. "What's wrong?"

"Nothing."

"Sylvia—"

"Is fine."

Gypsy closed her eyes. His terse answers could not hide the truth. Putting her hand on his arm, she whispered, "I know I should have written, but—"

"You're always busy." He laughed. "Blame that on your boss."

"I usually do." She took his hand and squeezed it. "Are you here because of Rose Quinlan's death?"

"That disturbed me, but what I've heard since bothers me more." He folded her hand between his. "Why did you try to keep Farley from sending word about the attack on you?"

"I knew how you'd react. You'd come up here and insist I leave."

"Justifiably."

"I can't leave here, Daniel."

"Of course you can." His lip twisted as he looked around the room. "You could come back to Lansing with me."

Laughing, she sat on the bed and rested her elbow on the iron footboard. "When my feet are half frozen and the stove refuses to stay warm at four in the morning, I'd jump at such an offer. However, my life is here."

"But for how long? This arrangement was never meant to be permanent. Why don't you come back to the life you should have?"

"Honestly, Daniel, I like it here. Every day is different from the one before it."

"Especially the day you were attacked in the woods?"

"Adam Lassiter is an efficient spy."

He smiled sadly. "That's exactly why I hired him. Farley was supposed to use him in the office, but apparently his being here in the kitchen has worked out well."

"Yes." Looking past his broad shoulder, she could

keep from meeting his steady gaze. She did not want to risk revealing how wondrous Adam's tenure in the kitchen had been. "Does this mean you've come to let him know his work here is done?"

Rubbing his hands together, he shook his head. "You don't know how much I wish I could tell you yes. His work isn't done. Farley is still in danger."

"Farley?"

"I thought you knew I'd sent Lassiter to keep an eye on Farley. I'm surprised Lassiter didn't tell you." He sighed. "You might as well know the truth. Farley is the target of the trouble here. Unfortunately for Mrs. Quinlan, her death was just a warning to him."

She stared at the floor. In retrospect, all the facts fit together. By killing Lolly Yerkes, the murderer convinced Nissa to leave behind a camp of angry, bored men. Rose's death had increased fear among the superstitious loggers. If the camp's cook had been slain as well, Calvin Farley could have been ruined.

"But why?"

Daniel raised his hands in a frustrated shrug. "If I had that answer, I'd know the murderer's identity. I have no answers. Lassiter has none. Do you?"

"To be honest, I never thought of anyone wanting to kill Farley. Beat sense into his head? Yes, because I've wanted to do that myself. But kill him? No."

Rising, he said, "That, however, is the truth."

"Does Farley know?"

"I think he suspects. Haven't you noticed how oddly he's been acting?"

Laughter was easy. "He always acts odd."

"That's true. Now tell me, how's your staff this year?"

"Excellent. I have them well-seasoned by this time."

"I have no doubt." Putting his hands on her shoulders, he smiled more sincerely when she placed her hands over his. "This has worked well for both of us. When you asked for this job, I never guessed one of the most famous kingbee cooks in the north woods would be a queen bee named Gypsy.''

"I like surprising you."

"You never fail to." He bent to kiss her cheek, but froze at a sharp knock on the door.

It opened before they could move. The expression of amazement on Adam's face became anger. The rest of the flunkeys stared at what looked like an interrupted tryst between their boss and the owner of Glenmark Timber Company.

Gypsy stood as Daniel pulled his hands back. While he made a production of straightening his vest, she went to the door.

"I wasn't under the impression you had free access to my private quarters, gentlemen." Her voice remained even, but the flunkeys crept away.

Except Adam. He smiled coldly. "You told me to get the biscuits ready, but I need to know how many you want."

"The usual amount." She pushed past him. When she did not hear him follow, she turned. Her words died unspoken as she saw the quick glance exchanged by Adam and Daniel. "The bread is ready for baking, Adam. See to it, please." Without a pause, she added, "Mr. Glenmark, will you be joining us for supper tonight? I know the jacks would enjoy your company."

"I'll be dining with Farley."

Again her calm wavered. "Perhaps you can convince him to move back into camp. The camp manager should be here with his men and not out there alone with his grief."

He started to put his hand on her shoulder, but pulled it back hastily. Clasping his hands behind his back like a naughty boy, he said, "I'll be here for breakfast."

"I'll be sure to make the coffee extra strong."

He grinned. "You think I can't stay awake without a powerful jolt of swamp water?"

"When was the last time you got up before the sun did?"

"You're right, Gypsy. Have it strong." He walked out of the kitchen, silence in his wake.

The flunkeys flinched when Gypsy clapped her hands sharply. "Gentlemen, this isn't a museum. If you want to pretend to be statues, do it elsewhere. The jacks will be here in two hours."

As she reached for a clean apron, a hand grasped her uninjured elbow.

Adam asked in a low voice, "What did Glenmark tell you?"

"What did he tell *you?*"

"You know I must be circumspect about my work." He frowned. "I can tell you he's distressed about what's been going on here."

"And that's news?"

"Honey, I can't say more at this point."

"You can. You don't trust me."

"You didn't trust me, either."

"*Didn't!* But I told you—" She glanced at the other men.

"So when are you leaving?"

"When the spring thaw comes."

He put his arm around her shoulders, herding her toward the larder. "Gypsy, didn't Glenmark order you to leave?"

"No." She shrugged off his arm. "He asked me if I wanted to go."

"Gypsy, you need to get out of here. If that guy comes back—"

"He can't come back when he's already here in camp."

"All the more reason for you to leave."

She shook her head. "Here I have a hundred men who are watching over me. If I leave, who would look after me? You?"

"I can't."

"I know. You're here to watch over Farley."

"He told you that?"

"Yes." She folded her arms in front of her. "He trusts me."

Although she thought he would retort angrily, he said, "Gypsy, getting involved with Glenmark could be dangerous for you. Think about what you're doing."

She smiled icily as she raised her chin in defiance. "I am, Adam. I can assure you that, for the first time in longer than I want to admit, I'm thinking clearly. Getting involved with Mr. Glenmark might be dangerous, but becoming involved with you was just plain stupid."

When she walked away, he called after her, "Gypsy, wait!"

Whipping her coat around her shoulders, she ordered, "You get to those biscuits. I need some fresh air. I'm tired of the stench of lies." She slammed the door to cut off his retort.

She had hoped when she offered Adam an ultimatum, he would relent and be honest. Instead, he had shut her out again.

She wondered how many times a heart could be broken.

CHAPTER
TWENTY-THREE

Farley looked peaked as he lurched across the dining room to grab an unused coffee mug off a table. Holding it out, he commanded, "Fill it up! Now!"

Glancing at Gypsy, Oscar obeyed. He filled it only halfway because Farley's hands trembled as if with palsy. When the camp manager started to argue, Gypsy motioned the younger man away.

"Sit down." She pointed to a table which had been cleaned of dirty dishes.

Farley dropped heavily to the bench. Coffee splashed on the table, but he ignored it. "Why didn't you tell me, Gypsy? I thought you were my friend. Why did you keep this a secret?"

"Keep what a secret?"

"Why Lassiter is here."

She wiped up the dark stream of coffee. "I didn't know until Mr. Glenmark told me yesterday."

"He wants me to move into the bunkhouse. He already arranged for a sled to take my furniture into Saginaw, where I can get it at the end of the season. Generously, he's allowing me to stay on until the drive down the river.''

"Then?'' she prompted.

He gulped his coffee. "He offered me a position at the sawmill. I have my choice of taking it or finding another job. He's determined I won't be out here next winter.''

Gypsy sighed. Like her, Farley loved life in the north woods. The sawmill would bore him.

When she opened her mouth, he held up his hands. ''No false consolation, Gypsy.''

"If you want honesty, I'll give it to you. After all, it's a refreshing change.''

"What do you mean?''

Realizing she had said too much, she answered, "Nothing, except that I think you should be honored Mr. Glenmark thinks so highly of you that he wants to protect you and keep you at Glenmark Timber Company. No, listen to me,'' she ordered when he began to interrupt. Rising, she put her hands on his shoulders. "He could have told you to walk. That would have been the easiest for him. He could have ignored whatever convinced him to send Adam here. For the love of heaven, Calvin, he's spent money to keep you alive!''

"I should have known you'd defend Glenmark! After all, you've enjoyed having Lassiter here. With him drooling over you, he's let two women be slain.''

"Adam's been trying to help.''

He stood and sneered, "Lassiter will leave you as soon as Glenmark crooks his finger. You've just been convenient for him.''

Gypsy's hand struck his cheek before she could halt it. Hearing a startled gasp behind her, she stared, wide-eyed, at Chauncey. The inkslinger's face was as colorless as Farley's. She said nothing to either of them as she rushed into the kitchen.

Oscar asked, "Gypsy, are you all right?''

"Farley's just in one of his snits.'' When she saw his disbelief, she continued, "Let's get going on lunch.''

"Are you sure?"

She smiled. "I'm fine. Thanks, Oscar. You're a good friend."

"Just want to make sure you don't get hurt again."

"Get to work!" She slapped his arm playfully as he turned back to the table. Glancing about the room, she noticed Adam was not there. She was not surprised he was gone while Daniel was here.

She wondered what the two men were discussing. Then she wondered why she cared. A sorrowful chuckle cramped in her throat. She did care. That was the problem. As much as she might despise Adam for failing to trust her, she could not halt her heart from yearning to belong with him.

Somehow she must change that.

She simply had no idea how.

The oxen led the sled along the rutted road. Gypsy kept one hand on the seat and the other on her bonnet as the runners bounced into a pothole. Beside her, Adam swore. The sled hurdled a deep chuckhole. He put out his arm, but she gripped the seat.

"Thank you," she said quietly.

"I guess a thank you is a start."

"A start?"

His grin lightened his voice. "I wasn't sure you'd even speak to me after I barged in on you and what Oscar generously calls your gentleman."

She looked at the swaying haunches of the oxen, her gloved hands clenched in her lap. "Mr. Glenmark isn't my gentleman, as both you and Oscar put it. He's my boss."

"Uh-huh."

"He is!" She clamped her lips closed when he regarded her from beneath his hat, which was drawn low over his ears. Defending herself was useless. In his jealousy, Adam refused to listen. A fresh pang slashed through her. She had given him the very excuse he needed to end their uneven relationship.

"Your protests show me you'd rather I didn't probe," he said dryly.

"You can think what you want, but Mr. Glenmark and I have a business relationship. Nothing else."

He chuckled as he held the reins lightly. "All right, Gypsy. You're right. I should have waited before I opened the door."

"You should have."

"You could tell me to pack my turkey sack and leave. Glenmark wouldn't force you to keep me in the cookhouse."

"I could," she agreed quietly. "Perhaps I should."

"But you intend to make my life miserable."

Gypsy smiled coldly. "How perceptive of you, Adam! You've been slacking."

"Slacking? Woman, if you had any idea what—" He glowered at the oxen.

"You've learned why my cookhouse has the best reputation in the north woods. It comes from hard work. I won't have slackers and troublemakers in my kitchen."

"I've never seen anyone who works as hard as you do and makes it look so easy. The first time you were halfway across the kitchen and told someone to stir a pot because it was burning, I thought you were showing off."

"I was serious."

He smiled. "I'm simply in awe of your skills."

Sharply, she retorted, "Mr. Glenmark is in awe of exactly the same skills."

"All right," he said as he held up his hands in surrender. "You'd just better be careful. Others could get the same idea I did and not be so easily talked out of it."

"If I wanted to have an affair with him, it's no one's business."

Adam watched the side of the road to be sure a log was not sliding toward the river. "I would hope I had a voice in the matter, but if you want Glenmark, you certainly wouldn't be doing anything wrong. With his wife's accident several months ago—''

"Accident! What are you talking about?"

He drew back on the reins and stopped the sled. "You and Glenmark seem to be good friends, so I thought you'd know."

She gripped his sleeve and gasped, "Tell me! What happened to Sylvia?"

Adam's eyes narrowed as she stared up at him, fear blanching her face. Her dismay proved what he had suspected. Colonel Glenmark and Gypsy were not just employer and employee. Until his inadvertent intrusion, there had been no gossip among the lumberjacks about any indiscretions between the kingbee cook and the owner of the company. With all the chatter about Farley and Rose, he knew the jacks would discuss Gypsy's romance with Glenmark eagerly. It must be something else that linked them. All the answers were in front of him, but he could not put them together.

Quietly he asked, "You know Sylvia Glenmark?"

"I've been working for Mr. Glenmark for several years," she answered in a tranquil voice he was sure was fake. "It's been convenient for me to meet him in his office in Lansing before the camp opens. As his office is in his home, I've had the pleasure of meeting his wife then."

"I heard Sylvia Wilkins Glenmark was a remarkable woman."

"Was?" she gasped as she gripped his sleeve again. "Adam, what happened to her?"

"A carriage accident. An axle broke, and the carriage tumbled into a stand of trees."

"How is she?"

"She's confined to bed, unable to walk."

"Oh, my!"

"She's lucky to be alive, Gypsy." He plucked her hand off his sleeve and curled it between his. "I guess that's good news."

Her brows lowered. "Trite phrases don't ease the sorrow of friends."

"Friends? I wasn't under the impression you were that friendly with the Glenmarks."

Gypsy reprimanded herself. She must never forget how important it was to guard every word. "If you prefer the term 'acquaintance,' I can use that."

"That's not necessary." He shifted on the hard seat. "I didn't plan on starting an argument just because I commented on the fact Glenmark clearly appreciates your talents."

As he drove the sled along the road again, she said, "Mr. Glenmark knows good cooking keeps jacks in a camp."

"You can call him Daniel like you did when you thought no one else was listening."

"He's my employer and deserves respect."

Slipping his arm around her, he brought her to face him. "Leave off, Gypsy! Who are you trying to fool?"

"Adam, please don't pry into things which are better left alone."

"Why?"

"Because I asked you to. Isn't that good enough?"

He drew back on the reins to slow them in front of the stable just as snow began falling again. With a nod to the man by the door, he tossed the reins onto the uncomfortable seat. He jumped down and held his hands up to Gypsy.

Wanting to refuse his help, she could not keep her fingers from reaching for his. She wanted to touch him. She wanted to be touched. Even so, as soon as her feet settled into the crunching snow, she pulled away, grabbed an empty food box, and walked toward the cook shack.

Adam took her hand and placed it on his arm. He waited until they were out of earshot from the stable before he whispered, "Maybe being asked to leave well enough alone would be reasonable from other people, but not from the woman I love. How can I protect you when you won't be honest with me?''

"You love me?''

The irony returned to his laugh. ''Haven't I told you in a hundred ways?''

The cold wind swirling the snow around them disappeared as she was warmed by the fire glowing in his eyes. ''You've told me with your kisses, but you've never spoken of love.''

''I shouldn't now.''

His arms swept her against him as he captured her lips. The box fell into the snow, forgotten. Refusing to be denied any pleasure, he explored her mouth. Slowly, savoring each stroke of his lips, she let him prove how true his words were. So many nights had passed while she yearned for him to hold her exactly like this. As her fingers relearned his burly back, she shivered at the sensual dance of his tongue against hers.

''When I saw Glenmark with you, Gypsy, I knew I couldn't remain silent any longer.'' His fingers brushed wisps of hair back from her face. ''You'd be smart to get involved with Glenmark. The life he could give you would be luxurious.''

''Are you trying to convince me to have an affair with a man I could never love as I love you?'' With a soft laugh, she said, ''I *would* love an elegant home with floors that are warm in the morning and servants bringing me breakfast long after sunrise. Yet I love the freshness of these forest dawns and the enthusiasm of the jacks.''

''I can't stay here forever.''

Her happiness faded. Once she discovered he was working for Daniel, she had known when Adam got what he'd been sent to find he would leave. In a strangled voice, she whispered, ''I understand.''

''You could come with me.''

''No.''

''If you'd let me help you . . .''

She smiled ruefully. ''If I thought you could, I wouldn't

hesitate to ask, even if you are a pigheaded, jealous, lovesick fool.''

"Thanks . . . I guess.'' He stroked her shoulder as he put his arm around her. When she leaned her head against him, he mused, ''It's a step in the right direction. If you trust me, trust me to keep you safe.''

"Safe? How?''

"Leave with Glenmark. Don't say anything to anyone else. Just go.''

"But the jacks—''

"Will have to get by with the flunkeys' cooking.'' He tilted her lips beneath his. ''Trust me, honey. I'm going to do anything I must to keep you alive, even if it means I have to cart you out of the north woods over my shoulder.''

"You wouldn't dare!''

His eyes twinkled as he whispered, ''Trust me, honey, I will.''

CHAPTER
TWENTY-FOUR

The wind howled against the glass. Snow blew beneath the door in the dining room, gathering like small mounds of salt in the corners of the room. Cracking branches struck the logs, and the snow scratched to get inside.

Gypsy stepped back as another gust shook the whole building. Spring should be here. Instead, the worst blizzard of the winter imprisoned her in her cookhouse. Only a few of the jacks had come for supper. The rest had not wanted to risk getting lost in the storm.

Picking up a sugar bowl that had been overlooked, she went into the kitchen. She gripped the door as the cook shack shuddered again.

"Did you order this?" Adam asked from by the stove. He shoved another log into the fire.

"I ordered spring."

He chuckled. "I thought you might have wanted to put off leaving for a few more days."

The long sleeves of her wrapper dropped back on her arms as she put the sugar bowl on the shelf next to the others. "Spring's arriving would solve a lot of problems."

Going to her room, she added more wood to the smaller

stove. She looked up anxiously as the wind screeched under the eaves. If this kept up, the whole roof might be stripped off.

"The stove's set for a few hours, Gypsy."

She turned to see Adam standing in the doorway. Her wrapper rustled behind her as she walked toward him. She laughed as she noticed his shirttails were hanging out of his denims and his bootlaces were slapping the floor. "I didn't think you had the stove watch tonight."

"I didn't." He smiled. Shutting the door, he took her hands. "Per hinted it would be a good idea if we switched nights. The funny thing was I intended to suggest exactly the same thing to him."

Drawing his hands around her waist, she whispered, "He's a dear friend. From the day I started working here, he's been determined to make sure I'm all right."

"He's given me that task for what should have been your last night here." His gaze moved along her face in a gentle caress. "I think Per wants you to be happy again."

"He knows you make me happy."

"He knows I love you." His fingers combed through her hair, letting it fall around her shoulders in a rust shadow.

Closing her eyes to relish his touch, she swept her hands up his sturdy arms. He pulled her to him. Through her nightclothes, she sensed every hard angle of his body. His mouth found hers with the memory of the few nights of sweet love they had shared. She laughed when he lifted her into his arms as if she were as light as an empty barrel.

"What's so funny?" he asked, laving her neck with fire.

She loosened the buttons on his shirt. "It's amazing that we can be arguing one minute and loving the next."

"And undoubtedly arguing the minute after that." Placing her on the bed, he leaned over her as he kicked off his boots. He nuzzled her neck until she giggled. The bed squeaked softly when he rested next to her and slipped

his arm under her shoulders. "In a few weeks, we'll both
be out of here. I think you and I should pay a call on the
nicest hotel in Saratoga."

Chuckling, she stroked the strength of his chest. She
fought to keep the teasing sound in her voice, because
she could not let him know the truth. Once she left this
camp, she must never see him again. That might be the
only way to protect him from the curse surrounding her.

"Saratoga?" she asked. "If I knew you'd choose the
place I joked about, I would have said I summer in Paris."

"Paris is beyond this cookee's budget, but how would
you like to show some snooty folks how to have a good
time? Saratoga or Newport or anywhere you'd like." He
tapped her nose. "Within reason. You and me and a
private hotel room where we can sleep until noon and
make love all afternoon."

"With our meals cooked by someone else? Or do you
want me to cook your favorite beef stew?"

He loosened her sash. As his fingers flowed along her
nightgown, his eyes burned with yearning. "The only
thing I want is you."

As he tasted the longing on her lips, her legs stroked
his. She ran her fingers beneath his loosened shirt and
explored his back. The open shirt gaped to tease her skin
with the caress of his while he undid the buttons along
her high collar.

Breathless, she matched his fiery kisses. When he bent
to place gentle nibbles along her neck, she circled his ear
with the tip of her tongue. She smiled as his hands tightened on her while his breath scorched her with its swift
fire. She pressed on his shoulders to lean him back into
the pillows, but he shook his head and eased off the
mattress.

"The bed is too cramped, honey." He held out his
hand as he knelt on the rag rug. "Come here."

When she sat beside him, he leaned her across his lap.
The keening of the storm vanished as his hand swept
along her side, settling on her hip.

Meeting him mouth to mouth, she sighed with a longing that refused to be silenced.

As he sprinkled kisses across her face, she slid his shirt down his arms. The motion of his body against hers as he slipped off the sleeves sent fierce shivers of yearning to the very tips of her toes. Wanting to touch all of him, she pushed him back onto the rug. He grinned rakishly as he pulled her atop him.

His fingers twisted through her hair to hold her lips over his. As his tongue probed deep into her mouth, he drew off her wrapper and tossed it on the bed. With a laugh, he twisted out from beneath her and rolled her onto her back.

He bent to press his mouth against her breast. Gasping out his name in desperate need, she clenched her hands on his back as his tongue made a blistering exploration. Taunting and tempting, it fired a tempest within her. Even as he lured the tip of her breast into his mouth to surround her with rapture, he pushed her nightclothes aside. Her fingers inched to the waistband of his denims.

Caught up in the turbulence of passion, she was lost in quivering heat. It pulsed with each breath, growing stronger as she pushed his trousers along his sturdy legs. His frayed breath seared her skin.

When she leaned over him, she teased the rough skin along his neck. His moans swirled through her with the power of a twister. She enticed him to the very pinnacle of pleasure with the touch of her lips and her fingers' light caress.

Clamping his arms around her, he captured her lips, not letting her escape even when his breath burned swiftly into her mouth. Powerful passion erupted through her as their bodies merged into one. She was consumed by the sensations cascading from her through him and back to entwine them. Whirled out of herself, she fell into an eddy of ecstasy where the only sound was his gasp of rapture in the moment before she was lost in the very essence of their love.

* * *

Gypsy woke to the grotesque shadows sprayed on the wall. The room was all wrong. When she heard rumbling snores next to her ear, she smiled and rose to look down into Adam's face, which was smoothed with sleep. She rubbed her elbow. It was uncomfortable sleeping on the floor, although she had not noticed the discomfort of the pine boards while they were making love here.

"I love you," she whispered and kissed him softly.

He murmured something in his sleep and shifted to reach for her. Smiling when she discovered that she remained in his dreams as he was a part of hers every night, she stood and pulled on her wrapper. As long as she was awake, she would stoke the firebox. Later he could wake and spend the time he would have used for that job to delight her again. She wanted to savor every moment, storing away each precious sensation for the time when she had only memories for company.

The floor was frigid beneath her bare feet as she tiptoed across the room. She was cautious not to slide her feet, because she did not want to get a splinter. She ran her fingers along the kitchen wall to guide her to where the stove glowed.

A man-sized shadow moved behind the stove. Was it real or a trick of the dim light? Someone was lurking there in the darkness. The intruder seemed to know his way about her kitchen. She hoped he would take whatever he wanted and leave right away.

She edged backward. The silhouette exploded toward her. A hand clamped over her mouth. A flannel-covered arm pulled her against a wide body. The sound of his fear was loud in his rapid breathing. Something cold and sharp pressed against her throat. A knife! She moaned against his palm, which was covered with icy sweat.

"No! Not you!"

Her eyes widened in horror. This was not the same

man who had attacked her in the woods. This man's voice was deeper.

The knife quaked.

"Please let me go," she whispered, although her words were muffled by his hand.

He mumbled something. As the knife lowered from her throat, she dared to take a deeper breath.

"Stay right here," he whispered.

She nodded. To save her life and Adam's, she would do almost anything.

"Don't turn around."

"I won't," she murmured as he drew his hand away.

"Count to twenty. Then go back to bed."

"I will."

"Slowly. Count slowly." Fear quivered in his aged voice.

"I understand. I—" She gasped when a sound came from the bedroom.

No, Adam! Stay away! Please!

Light spilled into the kitchen as her bedroom lantern was lit. A curse was spat in her ear, but the sound vanished as she shrieked in pain.

She stared at the bloody incision across her left arm. The knife clattered to the floor. The door crashed against the wall, and the man fled.

Her knees buckled as agony seared up her arm. Nothing had ever hurt like this. Her arm was on fire even as her fingers became numb beneath the black river of blood flowing over them. She heard a moan and an oath. Had she spoken? Or was it someone else? She could not guess.

Arms appeared out of the darkness and caught her. She collapsed against Adam, leaning her face against his bare chest.

"Gypsy, what is it?"

Slowly she raised her left hand. Blood glistened on her lacerated arm and surged across her arched fingers. She wanted to tell him what had happened, but could not.

His arm around her moved, flapping his unbuttoned

shirt against her injured arm. Pain swept her at the inadvertent touch.

"Sit, honey."

"Adam . . ."

"Sit."

She folded up onto the hard plank, struggling not to faint. She moaned when he stepped away from her. She needed him. Without him . . .

When he caught her face between his hands, she watched his mouth move and struggled to concentrate on what he was saying. Somehow she managed to understand, "Where are your medical supplies, Gypsy?"

"I . . . I . . ."

"Gypsy, tell me!"

Light and dark merged and disappeared. She swayed on the bench. A new wave of agony stung her. She gasped as she saw Adam pressing a cloth over her sliced arm.

When she moaned, he whispered, "I'm sorry, honey, but I have to stop the bleeding."

"I . . . know." She gulped each word past the lump in her throat.

"Where do you keep your medical supplies?"

"Over the counter."

"Wait here."

Whether he was gone a minute or an hour, she could not tell. She battled not to drown in the anguish from the blazing river inching along her hand.

"Gypsy?"

Adam's face wavered before her as if he stood beyond a shimmering curtain. She put her right hand on his arm.

"I'm going to bandage this, honey." Regret filled his voice. "It's going to hurt really bad when I do."

"I know."

"Scream if it helps."

She closed her eyes as he lifted her left arm and wrapped soft cotton around it. When she had ordered the medical supplies, she never guessed she would be the one needing them.

As he twisted the material around her wrist, Adam asked, "Did he say anything this time? Or did he simply try to kill you?"

She started to nod, but her head threatened to fly off her shoulders. Wanting to wiggle her fingers to be sure they worked, she kept her hand still. "He said he didn't want to hurt me."

"If this isn't hurting you, I don't know what is."

"I think he meant it. I know Chauncey wouldn't—"

His hand gripped her wrist tightly. "What did you say?"

Wanting to deny her words, she could not. The truth had been in her head from the moment she heard him speak, but, in the midst of her terror, she had not recognized the truth. "It was Chauncey Lewis. But he wouldn't hurt me on purpose!"

"No?"

Without giving her a chance to answer, he strode to where his coat hung by the door. He reached into a pocket and pulled out something that gleamed malevolently in the meager light.

When he tilted the pistol to check its steel cylinder, she gasped, "Adam, you can't shoot him!"

"I'm not planning on shooting him." He buttoned his shirt and tucked it into his denims, then shoved the gun into his belt and reached for his coat. "This will make sure Chauncey cooperates when I ask him to explain some things to Glenmark."

"Be careful."

He smiled grimly and walked to her. Ignoring the flaps of his boots, which slapped against his insteps on every step, he whispered, "Stay here. I'll send one of the flunkeys over to sit with you as soon as I have a chance."

"All right." Her head ached with the steady pulse in her arm.

"He won't be back, but . . ."

The uneasy timbre of his voice brought her gaze up to his taut face. "But what?"

"That has to wait until later. Now I have to catch up with Lewis before he hits the hay trail." He caressed her shoulder before he hurried toward the door. Snow exploded into the room as he rushed out.

She stared at the table, unable to move. Wanting to deny the truth, she wondered where the madness would end. When it did, there might be nothing left of Glenmark Timber Company's logging camp—or any of them.

Morning light was glowing through the snow-coated window before Adam returned. Hanging his coat on its peg, he looked at Gypsy, who was standing at the stove. He sat at the table, and she put an empty cup in front of him. Picking up a quilted cloth, she reached for the heavy coffee pot.

"I'll do that, Gypsy." He poured a cup for himself and another for her. "I'm not going to say you should be resting. I know it's a waste of breath."

She went to the window and looked out to discover a crowd of jacks in the center of the camp.

Adam drew her back from the window firmly, but gently. "Gypsy, don't think about going out into that mob."

"Mob?" Pain scorched the single word.

"The jacks aren't happy to find out one of their own killed two women and hurt you." Adam checked the bandage on her arm. Shadows of blood seeped through the material. "You need to keep this on for a few more hours before we change it."

"I thought Chauncey was my friend."

"Maybe Lolly and Rose did, too." When she flinched, he turned her against him and stroked her back.

The door opened, and Gypsy raised her head to see Per and Hank's tense expressions. They stared at her, clearly wanting to determine the extent of damage done to her.

Adam broke the strained silence to say, "Gypsy made some coffee and biscuits, so we might as well eat."

"You made biscuits?" Per's voice was as close to

anger as Gypsy had ever heard. "I don't care if you are the kingbee cook, girl! If you'd let Adam tend to the stove as he—"

"I made the biscuits," she interrupted with a hint of her customary authority. "If you want them, eat them. If not, don't."

The old man rubbed his hands in distress. "Sorry, Gypsy."

"You heard the lady, gentlemen," Adam said. "Help yourselves while I persuade her to rest." When the men shuffled toward the table, he lowered his voice. "Do you want to sit here, honey, or do you want to lie down for a while?"

A shiver of distaste wrenched her away from him. "I'll be fine. Don't mollycoddle me."

"Gypsy, it would make *me* feel a lot better to pamper you for a while."

"It wasn't your fault," she whispered, understanding his underlying pain.

"If I hadn't been sleeping instead of tending to the fire, you wouldn't have been hurt."

Her fingers eased along the hard line of his clenched jaw. "My love, if you hadn't been sleeping by my side, we wouldn't know this joy." Standing on tiptoe, she tilted his mouth over hers. She did not care if the flunkeys were watching. She wanted to be in his arms and know they were safe from the terror.

He kept his arm around her waist to steer her to the table. She leaned her head against his shoulder until he urged her to sit. In silence, she did.

"I'm fine," she whispered. "Or, to be honest, I will be fine."

The door opened again, letting in more cold. Bert wiped mud off his feet as he came into the kitchen. "Gypsy, you and Adam are wanted over at Farley's office. 'E said 'e wants to see you right away."

A shiver ached across Gypsy's shoulder blades, and she was sure her face was whey-colored with fear. She let Adam assist her in putting on her coat. Saying nothing, she walked out of the cook shack.

"Honey, I can speak to Farley if you don't feel up to this," Adam said quietly.

"If I can supervise my kitchen, I can listen to Farley's complaints." Despite her boasting, she sighed with relief when he put his arm around her shoulders and helped guide her past the widening puddles. The sunshine was nature's warm apology for the late season blizzard. "We'll be leaving for the river drive in a few days if this weather continues."

"Then we'll head for Saratoga."

She smiled. "That sounds wonderful."

"I've had enough of the north woods to last me a lifetime."

"Me, too."

He paused to stare at her. "Do you mean that?"

"Now. Come autumn, I may be itching to return." Tapping the brim of his hat, she laughed. "Maybe not."

"I think we should talk about this later."

"Later?"

He entwined his fingers with hers as they continued toward the camp manager's office. "I'm going to have the stove watch tonight again."

"You're going to exhaust yourself doing that every night."

"You're going to exhaust me with your luscious loving, honey." When she flushed, he chuckled. "Don't worry. We'll have plenty of time for sleeping and other things when we leave here."

"Maybe. Maybe not."

He laughed. "I like the way you think, honey."

Gypsy's reply was halted when they stepped up onto the porch of the camp office. Glad that Adam did not release her hand, she let him open the door and usher her into the small room.

When Farley rose from his desk, she was astonished to see the camp manager wearing denims and a wool shirt like the jacks. Gray circled his eyes, and deep lines were ground into his face, which must not have endured the scrape of a straight-edged razor since the attack on her two days before. Whiskers could not shadow the strain along his lips.

"How are you doing, Gypsy?" he asked.

"I'll be fine," she answered, as she had so many times. Glancing at Adam before looking back at Farley, she continued uneasily, "How are you?"

"How do you expect?" He leaned his hands on his desk. "What have you learned, Lassiter? Has he confessed?"

"He's admitted to smothering Lolly and killing Rose." Dampening her arid lips, she asked, "Did he say why?"

"Yes."

"What was it?"

He stared at the floor. "He said they had flirted with him, made him want them, then jilted him."

Farley cried, "Rose wouldn't have—"

Gypsy put her hand on Farley's arm. "Don't let him hurt you more. He must have imagined it all." Glancing at Adam, she looked hurriedly away, but not before she saw he believed, as she did, that Rose had enticed Chauncey. Perhaps Rose had hoped to use that flirtation to get something more out of Farley.

Gypsy was surprised when Farley demanded, "And did he admit to attacking Gypsy in the woods?"

"No," Adam said quietly.

"Then—"

"Then nothing." Adam scowled. "We have enough to send him to hang."

The camp manager hesitated before saying, "Gypsy, I suppose I should ask if you want your thousand dollars now, or if you want to wait until after the drive."

She frowned. "Thousand dollars? Are you telling me to walk?"

A smile struggled to tilt his tight lips, but failed. "The reward for uncovering Rose's murderer. It's yours. Of course, you can share it with Lassiter. I'm sure the two of you can spend it in style.''

"I don't want your money, Calvin."

As if she had not spoken, Farley demanded, "Your gun, Lassiter." He held out his hand.

Adam withdrew the pistol from under his coat and offered it to the camp manager. "Be careful. It's loaded."

"I expected it would be." His haunted eyes looked from the gun to Adam. "You should have told me you'd brought this to camp."

"It would have been impossible to explain why I had it."

"That's true. Glenmark felt obligated to keep me in the dark. Maybe if he had . . ."

"Where is Daniel?" Gypsy asked.

"Busy." He scowled at Adam. "I assume you'll be leaving soon."

"I'm here until Glenmark tells me otherwise."

Gypsy glanced at Adam in surprise as she heard his disquiet. He wanted everyone to believe the danger had ended with Chauncey Lewis's capture, but he did not believe it himself.

"Maybe that's not a bad idea," Farley answered in the same tight tone. "We may need you around after . . ." He rocked the gun in his hand, admiring the gleaming steel and the mother of pearl grip. "This is a fine weapon, Lassiter. Have you used it often?"

"I prefer other methods of settling problems."

Farley rounded the desk. "Ah, yes, as you did with Lewis. You could have shot him, but instead you convinced him to surrender while we wait for the constable."

"Who should be here soon."

"I haven't sent for him."

Gypsy gasped, "You haven't sent for the authorities? What are you waiting for?"

As if on cue, the door opened. Adam pulled Gypsy behind him as the inkslinger was pushed through the door by Peabody and Benson. The crew chief scowled at being kept from the hill to guard a prisoner.

Chauncey Lewis stood silently between his two guards, his arms tied behind his back. He stared at the floor, but his gaze rose to meet Gypsy's. "I'm sorry, Gypsy. I never meant to hurt you. You're—" He looked past her and shouted, "No!"

Adam leaped forward. The gun detonated with an ear-shattering shriek. The jacks shouted and jumped aside. Gypsy screamed as Chauncey rocked back into the door. Blood spurted from the front of his mackinaw shirt. Amazement rippled across his face before he crumpled to the floor to lie in a crimson pool.

Farley shoved Adam aside. Turning to Gypsy, he lifted the gun again. Adam grasped his wrist, but Farley shook him off as he held the gun out to her.

In an emotionless voice, Farley ordered, "Take it, Gypsy."

Her fingers trembled as she took the weapon, which still belched smoke. Balancing the heavy pistol in her hand, she watched as Farley walked to where the corpse sprawled in front of the door.

"Curse you, Lewis!" Farley's voice was raw with agony. "You made Rose's life torture. I hope you burn for all eternity."

Gypsy shivered. His words echoed the ones her attacker had spoken. *No, Farley could not be that man.*

"Take it away and put it in a pine box." Farley's mouth twisted out each word. "Even a beast deserves a few words from Reverend Frisch."

Peabody nodded, glancing at Benson. He grasped one arm of the corpse as Peabody took the other. Neither spoke as they pulled the body out of the office.

Gypsy fought sickness as she stared at the bloodstain left in their wake. When Adam stepped over the scarlet line to close the door, Farley walked back to face her.

"Gypsy," he said, "with Glenmark gone, I surrender to you."

"Daniel is gone? Where is he?" she cried.

"On his way back to Lansing."

"Lansing?" Adam frowned. "Why?"

Farley hunched into himself. "He got news his wife has taken a turn for the better. Apparently she's even taken a step or two. He couldn't wait to see for himself."

Gypsy whispered, "For the better? Really?"

Adam did not give Farley a chance to answer. "Glenmark left without Gypsy?"

"Why not? She didn't want to go." Farley regarded him with tear-filled eyes. "And why should she now? Lewis is dead." He dropped to the bench. "Send for the constable, Gypsy, and I'll give him my full cooperation." He bowed his head. "Is this what love means? Being willing to do anything for the one you loved?" His voice broke as he whispered, "Even when it's too late?"

She bit her lip. Looking past the shattered man to where Adam stood, she held out the pistol to him. He took it without speaking, but the brush of his fingers against hers teased her to find solace in his arms. Instead, she went to Farley. Kneeling by him, she ignored the pain racing along her arm as she put her hand over his clenched knuckles.

"I wish I could tell her how sorry I am," he said.

"You have." She put her fingertips in the middle of his chest. "Calvin, she knew what you felt in your heart. Surely she can hear that even now."

He straightened. "Strange as it may seem, you're in charge of the camp, Gypsy. Just tell me where you want me to wait for the authorities. Then, when I pay for murdering Lewis, I can tell Rose myself what I feel."

"I'm not sending for the constable."

"Gypsy, if you don't, you can be considered an accessory to my crime." He stood, gesturing to Adam. "Tell her she's being foolish to throw away her life, too."

Rising, she cradled her aching arm. "There's no crime in defending yourself against a man set on killing you."

"He didn't—"

"She's right," interrupted Adam. "We'll all testify that you saved our lives today."

Farley choked, "That's a lie!"

"That's our opinion," Gypsy said. "That's what we saw." Relenting slightly, her voice softened as she put her hand on his arm again. "Calvin, this camp needs you. No one else can oversee the river drive. If you aren't here, someone is sure to be hurt."

He blinked. "You'd do this for me?"

"You'd do it for me, wouldn't you?"

Slowly he nodded. "Anything for those you love, right?"

She smiled. "Anything, but please not too often, Calvin. I don't think we can withstand your heroics again."

He went to his desk. Taking a key out of his pocket, he unlocked a drawer. "Gypsy, I owe you—"

"I can't take your money. I didn't find Rose's murderer. He found me." Her smile wobbled.

"Lassiter?" he asked, looking past her again.

"Glenmark is paying me." Slipping his arm around Gypsy's shoulders, he grinned. "If I had the money, I'd just spend it on something I probably don't need."

"Thank you," the camp manager whispered.

Adam nodded. "I'd like to say we know you'd help us, but I hope it never comes to this again."

Gypsy tried to recall the camp manager's grateful smile the rest of the day. Her conscience taunted her. Over and over, she reminded herself if Chauncey Lewis had come to trial, the result would have been the same.

When Adam returned to the kitchen, whistling, she knew his discussion with Peabody and Benson had gone well. Neither of them would reveal the truth. Farley was already a hero. She heard the flunkeys talking about a party in his honor.

When the work was done for the day and the stove

was filled with wood, Adam came into the bedroom. His smile was as icy as his eyes.

"Go ahead, and say what you've been itching to say all day," he urged.

She did not pretend not to understand. "Why are you lying to everyone about Chauncey Lewis being the man on the road? You don't believe it!"

"Are you daring him to finish what he's started?"

Incredulity widened her eyes. "So you *do* believe the man who attacked us wasn't Chauncey?"

"Of course." He sat on the bed and unlaced his boots. With the flaps hanging like peeled bark on a downed tree, he leaned his elbow on the footboard. His compelling gaze held hers. "Honey, I'm not the tallest man in this camp, but Lewis is—was several inches shorter than I am. The man who ambushed you stood eye to eye with me."

"Then why did you argue with me?"

A slight tug brought her closer, and he settled her on his knees. Slowly he reclined her back onto the mattress. She wanted to enjoy his loving touch, but she could not.

"He's still here," she whispered.

"Yes."

"And he'll be as eager for revenge against you as to murder me."

"Yes," he said again in the same unemotional voice. "That's why I want you to pretend I've convinced you Lewis was your attacker."

Her eyes widened. "Are you trying to convince him we're growing reckless? Do you think that will draw him out again?"

He lifted her bandaged arm before her face. "If you hadn't gone to check the stove, we wouldn't have known about Lewis. Luck's on our side. Let's take advantage of it."

She looked out the window to where the moonlight glistened on the snow still clinging to the trees. The perfect, sugar-coated world of winter and the logging camp was evaporating to reveal the rot.

"Do you know who?"

He chuckled coldly as he massaged her tense shoulder. "Honey, I know who he *isn't.*"

"Is he why you're here? Is he the same man you think is after Farley?"

Adam hesitated. So many times he had been tempted to explain why Colonel Glenmark had sent him to the logging camp. The truth might endanger her more. Bending close to her ear, he whispered, "I've told you why I'm here."

"No, you haven't told me. Daniel told me, not you!"

"What did he tell you?"

"Something you've never told me. The truth."

"I'm surprised."

"Why?"

He sighed. The bed creaked as he rested next to her. Leaning her head on his shoulder where it often rested in the afterglow of their passion, he said softly, "I didn't think he'd tell you about how we met."

"Why?"

"If you know him well, you know he hated his time in the army."

"I know."

"Especially his time in Virginia."

She flinched. "Did you serve there with him? Was it Captain Lassiter?"

"Major Lassiter, actually." With a short laugh, he arched a brow. "I thought he told you everything."

"He told me that he fears for Farley's life. Why?"

"Honestly, Gypsy, I don't know why Glenmark is so concerned about Farley."

"You don't know?" Gypsy sat and regarded him with bafflement.

"I know why I'm here, but I don't know if what I'm looking for is here. Some letters were stolen from Glenmark's office. They had Farley's address. That convinced

Glenmark to send me here to find out why Farley may be in trouble. That's not much to go on.''

Folding her arms across her knees, she said, ''Answer one thing for me.''

''If I can.''

''Is the man who attacked me the one you're seeking?''

With a sigh, he nodded. ''I suspect so.''

''So I'm the bait?''

He looked away. ''I'd rather you phrased that another way.''

''But it's the truth?''

''Yes.''

She gasped and stared at him in disbelief.

''Honey, I'm doing everything to make sure you're in no danger. That's why I've arranged to stay here with you every night.''

Shaking her head, she stood. ''So now I'm the bait to catch your murderer so you can get what I'm sure is a generous reward from Daniel. I thought you loved me!''

He surged to his feet. When he reached for her, she whirled toward the head of the bed. Gripping the footboard, he growled, ''Gypsy, be reasonable!''

She threw the pillow at him. When he ducked, it hit the door with a soft plop. ''Get out! I don't have to be reasonable when everything is totally unreasonable. Woo yourself some other victim for your prey.''

Storming toward her, he seized her shoulders. ''Do you think he won't kill you if I leave?''

''We won't know until you go, will we?''

He released her. When she sank to the bed and cradled her wounded arm, he snapped, ''All right! Have it your way, Gypsy Elliott. Be the luscious victim he hopes you'll be.''

Pain burst within her as he scooped up his boots and walked to the door. ''Did you ever really love me, Adam?''

''Does it matter what I say? You wouldn't believe me,''

he answered fiercely. ''What did Farley say? He'd do anything for love. Maybe it's time you did something for ours. Maybe it's time you believed your heart. But I guess that's impossible. You've gotten so used to distrusting everyone, you can't even trust yourself.''

CHAPTER
TWENTY-FIVE

As soon as Farley announced enough ice had melted on the river, the logs were released from their towering piles to be sent downstream. The jacks packed their turkey sacks. What was left in the wanigan was brought to the cook shack.

Planks were nailed over Gypsy's bedroom door and over the doors leading to the larder and dining room. The kitchen was separated from the other rooms and logs hammered beneath it. Water was frozen in a wide swath to the river. The river hogs worked to send the kitchen, now called the wanigan, down to the river.

Listening to the distant shouts of excitement as the men moved the wanigan, Gypsy stared at the lonely, broken walls of what had been her home. During three long winters, she had lived here. In the past weeks, she had discovered love here.

Now her bedroom was a shattered shell, already tipping awkwardly to its left. Once the ground beneath it softened into mud, the walls would collapse into a pile of jumbled logs.

She would have to cook in the kitchen, which was

cramped with barrels of molasses and cartons of lard. The tobacco and kerosene from the old wanigan were also stored in there, as well as an extra table and the mattress from her bed. The rest of her furniture would be shipped to Saginaw on a sled with Farley's goods.

As she turned to watch the wanigan set to float on its raft, her gaze was caught by something near what had been the root cellar. Sliding down the steep, slimy embankment, she picked her way across the muddy hole.

Her brow furrowed as she bent to gather up a battered piece of material. The wool was half frozen to the ground. She pried it loose, curious about what could have been dropped beneath the kitchen.

With a horrified gasp, she sat on her heels as she looked at the hat. Two holes had been cut into it at eye level— the hat worn by the man who had attacked her and Adam.

Sickness ate at her. The attacker could not be one of her flunkeys. Hank was too fat to be her assaulter, nor could she imagine grandfatherly Per or gentle Oscar or kindly Bert as that man. But only she and her crew had access to the root cellar, because the door was always closed before the jacks arrived to eat.

Gypsy stuffed the hat into her pocket and climbed out. Wiping her gloves on the filthy snow to clean off the mud, she hurried toward the river. The loggers were crowding the shore. The start of the log drive meant payday at the end.

"What's wrong, Gypsy?"

She looked up to see Adam beside her. Torn between wanting to reveal the truth and begging him to leave her out of his games, she said, "I didn't expect to be so upset to see my home being skidded down to the river."

His frown did not alter. "Is it bothering you so much that you look like you've been kicked in the gut?"

"How charming! Do you speak this way to all the women in your life?"

Grasping her arms, he kept her from walking away. "You know you're the only woman in my life."

"I'm the only woman in the life of any jack here!" she retorted to hide her aching need to be held, to be comforted by his strength.

"Are you going to continue to be bullheaded?"

"I'm not using the one I said I love as a lure."

"I told you my work has nothing to do with what's between us."

Swallowing her tears, which had come too readily in the past days, she demanded, "What's between us? Distrust?"

"You trusted me enough to tell me the truth about what happened in Virginia."

With a gasp, she whispered, "Don't!"

"Gypsy, we're alone, or we might as well be. Everyone is watching the wanigan being lashed to the raft." He put his arm around her waist and drew her into his embrace. "No one's paying attention to us."

"Then tell *me* the truth you're hiding. Why did Daniel send you here?"

"I've told you."

"You've told me you're trying to stop Farley from getting killed."

"Yes." He sighed. "It's that simple, honey."

She shook her head. "It's nowhere near that simple. Daniel didn't send you here because someone stole a couple of letters. He must have had cause to believe that Farley was in real danger. What was it?"

"Glenmark couldn't or wouldn't tell me. He just told me to come up here and snoop around. I was to get a job in Farley's office because it was the center of activity."

Frustration at his evasiveness became fury. "And that's it?"

"Gypsy, when are you going to trust me?"

"When you're honest with me."

"I am!" He pulled her tight to him. His hand under her chin brought her face up toward him. "I'm honest when I say I love you. And you know *this* is honest."

Her breath was swept away by the intensity of his lips

over hers. Even as she battled the desire swarming through her, she softened against him. She wanted this gentle madness. She wanted to believe him, but . . . with a sob, she pulled out of his arms and rushed across the snow to where the jacks were spinning tall tales about previous drives.

Adam started to follow her, but paused when he saw her stop to talk with Peabody. His eyes narrowed. She was keeping her hand in her right pocket. Was she hiding something in it? Something she was concealing from him? He had thought she was being honest with him, but she was lying.

Not lies, for she hated falsehoods. She was not telling him everything. Again he wondered why, because he could not doubt her love. He longed to go to where she stood with the crew chief and whirl her into his arms. Then he would spill out the truth which burned in his gut like the need for her warm body.

He should just let her go. She was making it clear she wanted to be left alone, and he should do as she wished. He slapped his hand against a tree. What had he told himself at the beginning of this job? Go in, do what he must to get the man Glenmark had sent him after, and leave. No complications, no connections, no one getting hurt.

His fingers curled into a fist against the tree. For almost a decade, he had been able to keep the vow he had made on that blood-soaked battlefield when he watched his two best friends die. *Don't get your life mixed up with anyone else's. Then you can't get hurt like this again.*

That had been such a simple credo to live by until Gypsy's sparkling eyes looked in his direction and he found himself wanting to be an intimate part of her life.

He almost laughed. Now she was giving him a bitter spoonful of his own medicine. She was right. He was using her to find his prey, but why didn't she trust him? He did not want her hurt.

A sardonic laugh bubbled past his lips. He did not want

her hurt? He had not allowed himself to worry about anyone else since that horrible day during the war. He had just done his job and gotten out with his skin—and his heart—intact.

Folding his arms over his chest, he nodded absently when Bert asked him if he were riding aboard the wanigan. He didn't add he intended to keep a close eye on Gypsy. He had made a mess of everything else, but one thing had not changed. He always found whomever needed to be found. He could not fail now when Gypsy's life depended on him.

The wanigan floated in the sunlight sparkling on the water. Beyond the cove, the river shrieked its spring song. Gypsy inched past the heavy casks and stacks of supplies. The floor rocked gently under her feet. Sunshine inched past the boxes set in front of the window, but did not reach the stove.

Her ears still rang with the clamor of the logs being released from their props on shore. The river hogs had chopped away the wood pegs to release the piles to crash into the river. Spinning like jackstraws, the logs surged along the river, with the wanigan following.

Now all she heard were curses as the men worked on a huge logjam. This was the fourth jam in as many days, but Gypsy had heard this one was major. No one spoke of two years ago when six river hogs had been killed in a jam a few miles downriver. The men had been crushed, their peavey poles, which had guided the logs along the river, floating away untouched. The superstitious jacks would not use a dead river hog's pole.

From the shore, Peabody yelled instructions. He ran along the raft holding the wanigan and crossed the logs as easily as he would a city street.

Ropes anchored the wanigan to a thick tree. The jacks wanted to be sure it was not caught in the rush when the logs erupted into the current again. With a sigh, she realized there was no worry about that happening soon. The logs were packed so tightly in the jam that even Adam should be able to walk along them now.

Adam!

Gypsy looked out at the shore. She had not seen him in three days. The flunkeys had stopped asking where he was but they had made sure she was never alone . . . until today.

How could she have been so selfish? He might be dead because of her. She could not share that fear with anyone, because she had no idea whom she could trust. Going to where her mattress was hidden behind the stove, she wondered if Adam would still be here with her if she had shown him the tattered wool hat.

She walked back around the stack of flour bags propped against barrels of salt pork and molasses. Flapjacks, coffee, salt pork, pies—an unending repetition of the same meals during three winters.

It was over. She must leave Glenmark Timber Company and not return. Mailing her resignation from Saginaw would allow her to disappear into the Rocky Mountains, where she should be able to find work.

"Look at you, Gypsy Elliott," she mused as she ran her hands along her waist. "You could become a whore. Nissa would give you a recommendation." Pain sharpened her laugh into a sob. "If he ever comes back, maybe I should ask Adam for one. After all, I kept him satisfied for as long as love can last for someone like me." Her shoulders sagged as she gripped the bag. "If he ever comes back."

"What's that?"

Hope died in her heart as she recognized Bert's strong accent. "Where have you been?" she asked. "I've been waiting for you to load the wagon for almost an hour."

"Peabody wanted us to 'elp 'im steady some of the logs for the river 'ogs." He grimaced at his wet trousers. "Our 'elp wasn't worth much. The logs are still stuck. We got back as quickly as we could."

"I don't mean to be short with you," she said as the rest of her crew came in to carry the boxes of sandwiches to the wagon. "I don't like to be late serving supper when they've been working so hard all day."

Bert put pies into a box and handed it to Oscar. "If you want, I'll go with you."

Pointing to the stove, she urged, "Stay and dry off before you catch your death of cold."

He hefted the box and followed as she carried the last box of sandwiches. Carefully she stepped off the raft. Her feet sank into the mud. She walked up the hill to where the ground was more solid and thanked Bert as he assisted her onto the driver's seat.

Gypsy picked up the reins and sent the horse along the narrow path worn by the jacks' feet. As the wagon wove among the trees, she heard shouts from where the water was stained blood red by the setting sun. She caught glimpses of water where the trees thinned, but could not see the logjam.

The path turned away from the steep bank. Behind her, the boxes bumped together as the road became even rougher. She wondered if her pies would survive the trip.

If any of them would.

She shivered at the thought. For the love of heaven, why had Adam vanished without saying good-bye? Maybe he was waiting downriver and would meet them when the jam was broken.

"Giddap," she called to the horse. The sooner the jacks finished their supper, the sooner they could get back to work on breaking up the jam. Then the drive would be under way again.

A crack shattered the air. She shrieked as the wagon rocked. Boxes crashed and tumbled out as the wagon tilted. The horse whinnied in fear.

Clutching the wood plank under her, she pulled back on the reins. Her teeth jarred and pain seared up her arm.

She moaned as she was thrown to the ground. Jumping to her feet, she ran out of the way of the wagon as it fell into the mud. The path was littered with pies and sandwiches—an afternoon's work ruined.

Calming the horse, she squatted to look under the wagon. One wheel was on its side, several spokes cracked. The whole axle was broken.

Leaning her arms on the side of the wagon, she stared at the boxes of food still inside. She could not carry all of them, even if she had a way to get them on the horse. With a curse, she kicked at the wheel. She leaped aside when the wagon collapsed flat onto the road. Mud splattered over her.

She nearly sank to the ground as her unsteady knees folded. If she had been peering under the wagon just then, she would have been killed. Holding her hand over her furiously beating heart, she stood.

A bullet twanged off a tree behind her.

Terror pushed her to run. She had gone only two steps before an arm encircled her waist.

"Let me go!" she screamed, pounding her fists against the broad arm. "Let me go!"

"Gypsy!"

She shoved her panic aside to gasp, "Adam, what are you doing here? Where have you been? I thought—"

Pushing her into the mud behind the wagon, he ordered, "Stay down!" He hefted a rifle. When she tried to scramble to her feet, he grasped her arm. "You still don't trust me, do you?"

"Would you trust me if I pointed that rifle at you?"

The fury tightening his bewhiskered face softened. "Gypsy, did you think *I* was shooting at you?"

"Someone was."

"But not me."

She stared up into his eyes, which were shadowed by the deepening twilight. So often she had seen them narrowed in rage, laughing, glittering with desire. Adam loved her and wanted to protect her from her headstrong idiocy.

"Where have you been?" she whispered.

"On a wild goose chase. I intercepted another of the notes. Idiot that I am, I couldn't resist checking it out." He scanned the woods. "Thank goodness, I'm back in time to save you." He scowled at the wagon. "You're luckier than Mrs. Glenmark was."

Gypsy's heart froze in mid beat. How could she have forgotten Sylvia's carriage had crashed with a broken axle? Just like the wagon here. She wanted it to be a coincidence, but she knew it was not.

"Let's go," Adam said. "Whoever was shooting at you is gone."

"But who was it?"

"That we need to figure out right away." Gripping her hand, he stood. A few quick slices with a knife freed the horse from the traces. He scowled at the wagon. "This was no accident."

She wrapped her arms around her muddy coat. "I don't like to believe someone in the camp would want to hurt me."

"No?"

When he shoved something into her hands, terror choked her. The wool hat.

"I found this peeking from beneath your pillow when I was going to leave you a message to stay put," he said as he settled his rifle under his arm. "Who are you trying to protect?"

"You."

"Me?"

"If I'd given it to you, the murderer might have seen. Then he would be more determined to kill you." She stepped closer to him. "For the love of heaven, Adam, I love you too much to risk you like that."

"And I love you, honey. Fool that I am, I've let you convince me to break the most important vow I've ever made."

"What vow?"

"To keep from getting caught up in anyone's life again,

so I'd never have to risk getting hurt by seeing someone I love get hurt."

"You're a fool."

His smile was grim. "Maybe so, but I've made another vow."

"Will you break this one?"

"Never." He ran his fingers along her cheek. "I was heartsick when my friends were killed in the war. I couldn't save them, but I'm going to save you."

"Adam," she whispered, all jesting gone from her voice, "you should go and not come back. He's after me and those I love. If you go now . . ."

"Too late. Everyone in camp knows I love you." He took her hand and stepped over the ruined food. "Let's get back to the wanigan. I want you to stay there until we unmask this coward."

She shivered. "The hat was under the kitchen."

"I know, but I'm not sure where else you'll be safe now. This logjam has to break soon! Come on."

Gypsy did not ask what had been in the note, and he did not tell her. They hurried in silence through the woods. When the wanigan came into view, he helped her down the steep hillside and onto the raft.

"Wait here while I check inside," he said. He shoved the rifle into her hands. "Do you know how to use this?"

"Yes."

"Use it if you have to. Don't trust anyone."

"Even you?"

His grin could not warm his cold eyes. "Trust *me*, Gypsy, but if anyone else pops out of the woods, fire over his head. That should scare him."

"Anyone? If one of the flunkeys—"

He gripped her arms. "They're gone."

"Gone?"

"No one was here when I came to leave you a message. I saw Oscar and Per wandering along the shore to watch the river hogs working."

She frowned. "They were supposed to be—"

"Forget about feeding the jacks for a minute, Gypsy! I'm trying to keep you alive."

Another shudder arched across her tense shoulders. "I know."

"Fire the gun if you see anyone other than me." He put his hands over hers. "Can you do that?"

"Yes," she whispered.

"Good. I'll be quick."

Gypsy held her breath as he vanished into the kitchen. Looking at the woods, she started at every shout echoing up the river. Someone must have been smoking nearby, because the heavy odor of a cigar surprised her. Her flunkeys knew better than to smoke in her kitchen. She pressed her back against the wanigan wall and tightened her grip on the rifle.

"Gypsy?"

She whirled, raising the gun. She lowered it as she stared, wide-eyed, at Adam.

Gently he took the rifle and put his arm around her shoulders. "It's all right, honey."

"I'm so scared."

"I know, but don't worry. There's no one inside."

When he bent by the rope holding them to shore, she asked, "What are you doing?"

"Taking you for another spin, honey. Not to Nissa's Porcelain Feather Saloon this time." He sawed through the thick rope. Shoving against the shore, he pushed them out into the river. "This way no one can sneak aboard tonight."

"But the flunkeys—"

"Can sleep on the shore with the other jacks." He opened the wanigan door as the slow current drew the raft into deeper water. "This gives us a chance to share what information we have without other ears around. There must be some clue to tell us who's chasing you."

"And who you're chasing."

His lips grazed hers before he steered her through the door. "One and the same, honey. Now, let's find a way through this mess. I could use a cup of very strong swamp water.''

She edged past the barrels. Tossing her bonnet on the table, she turned to Adam. Another man stood behind him in a cloud of cigar smoke. As she started to greet Bert, the words clogged in her throat.

He raised a pistol just as Adam asked, ''What's wrong, Gypsy?''

''She doesn't want your head aired in front of her, Lassiter.''

Bafflement widened Adam's eyes. ''Bert?''

''Don't recognize me without the accent?'' He laughed. ''You fools!'' His voice lost any hint of humor. ''Put the rifle down, Lassiter. This is between Gypsy and me.''

When Adam hesitated, Gypsy whispered, ''Do as he says, Adam.''

''That's right,'' Bert mocked. ''Do what your boss says.''

Adam's fingers clenched on the rifle as hers fisted at her sides. She wanted to plead with him, but did not dare to speak. If he tried to save her, he might die.

She released the painful breath burning in her chest when Adam set the rifle on the floor. Calmly, he said, ''The gun is loaded, Bert. Be careful with it.''

''I'll be careful.'' He chuckled. ''You should have checked behind the wanigan as well as in it. I figured if Gypsy didn't do everyone a favor by dying out on the road, she'd be back. You were a fool to come with her, but you made it easier by cutting the wanigan loose.''

Gypsy whispered, ''Let Adam go. You don't want him.''

''No, but you do.'' He jabbed the gun against Adam's nape. When she gasped as Adam winced, Bert laughed. ''You'd do anything for your lover, wouldn't you?''

''Let him go. Then you can—''

''Shut up, Gypsy!'' snapped Adam. ''Don't make promises he'll make sure you keep.''

Bert pushed Adam forward a step and closed the door

so no one on the shore could see what was happening in the wanigan. Bert's shirt bulged. Another weapon? She prayed not.

He gave her no time to ask. "I should thank you, Lassiter."

"Thank me? For what? Not killing you before this?"

"You kill me?" He laughed sharply. "I could have killed both of you out by Farley's house if I hadn't been so worried someone would hear Gypsy's screams." Jabbing the pistol against Adam's neck again, he chuckled. "Of course, then I wouldn't have had all this fun."

"Then why—" Gypsy choked on the rest of her question as Bert pulled back the hammer on the pistol.

"Shut up!" he snarled. When she nodded, he slowly put the hammer back without firing the gun. His grin returned. "Until you tipped me off, Lassiter, I wasn't really sure Gypsy was the woman I was searching for." Looking at her, he smiled around the cheroot he held in his teeth. "At first, I was pretty sure. She was as white as a ghost after I made sure she got one of my notes."

"You sent them?" she cried. "But how? They were postmarked from Saginaw, and you were here."

"I got a friend to postmark the envelopes before I came out here." He frowned. "But you stopped being afraid, Gypsy."

Adam laughed, shocking her. "That's because I was making sure she didn't get your sadistic notes, Sayre. And maybe she isn't the woman you're looking for. Those notes would have scared anyone."

"Oh, she's the woman I'm looking for. I knew after I heard you two cozying up the other day and talking about Virginy. Then I knew my guess wasn't so far off the mark."

"Why are you doing this?" she whispered.

With a growl, he snapped, "Because of Joby."

"Joby? Who's Joby?"

"He *was* my older brother, but you killed him!" His lips twisted.

Horror teased Gypsy when Bert poked Adam again with the gun. He wanted her to beg for their lives. She would. She'd do anything to save Adam. "I don't know what you're talking about."

"You don't?" he shrieked. Raising the pistol, he put its tip against Adam's ear. "Do you want to see me kill this no-good sneak now, or do you want to tell him first about how you killed my brother?"

"Joby? Joby Sayre?"

"Corporal Jonas Sayre of the New Jersey Light Artillery." He laughed when she gasped. "So you do remember that name, Gypsy Elliott! Or do you prefer to be called by your real name? You were a fool to take your brother's name."

"Elliott?" asked Adam in a taut voice.

Bert chortled. "Your brother's name wasn't Gypsy, was it, Elizabeth Wilkins?"

"Wilkins?" Adam repeated fiercely.

"Mean something to you, Lassiter?" He emphasized his question with another nudge of the sharp barrel.

"Colonel Glenmark's wife's maiden name is Wilkins." Adam saw the silent apology in Gypsy's eyes. Not that he could blame her, for he had been as secretive. If one of them had revealed the complete truth, they would not be about to die.

"Fooled you, too, Lassiter? Don't blame your boss. He just did what his wife asked. Sylvia Wilkins Glenmark helped her sister hide in the north woods by telling her husband lies. He doesn't have any idea why Gypsy wanted to come here, does he?"

She must choose her words carefully. She did not want Daniel to become his next victim. "Sylvia told him I was trying to get away from a broken heart. He believed it was a lover I was fleeing, not just the grief of seeing my family die one by one. It wasn't coincidence, was it? It was you!"

"I thought Sylvia had paid for helping you, but she's still alive." He chuckled. "I'll take care of that after I take care of you.'' His lips tightened in distaste as his thumb played on the hammer of the gun. "At first, I hadn't planned to kill her, because she was married to Glenmark when you murdered my brother.''

"I didn't—"

"You did!" Tapping the ashes from his cigar onto the floor, he said, "I searched Glenmark's home for an address for you. The fool thought Farley was the target. That must be why he sent this sneak to find me.''

Adam interjected quietly, "You said you weren't sure who Gypsy was until—"

"Trying to squirm out of being so caught up seducing her that you let the truth slip out, Lassiter?'' He laughed. "I wasn't sure she was stupid enough to come *here*. I knew Glenmark's wife had helped her hide somewhere, but I thought it would be at Glenmark's mill or office. I went there first, but she wasn't there. The last place connected with Glenmark was this damn logging camp. But which woman was she? Farley's mistress or one of Nissa's harlots or the camp cook? I began to suspect Gypsy was the woman I've been looking for. You confirmed it for me, Lassiter, with your talk about Virginy.''

Gypsy put her hand against the molasses barrel in front of her. Too many lies had played them into Sayre's hands. If only she had been honest with Daniel and Sylvia. If only Daniel had urged Adam to tell her the truth. If only she had told Adam her real name. Those ifs meant nothing now.

"If you've stalked and murdered my family in retribution for your brother's death,'' she said, "then you've committed your crimes for no reason.''

"You lured Joby into your home. When you discovered he was a Yankee, you killed him!''

"Corporal Sayre was dying when he stumbled into our yard. He'd been caught by a Confederate patrol in the city. The bullet was in his chest! How he lived to reach us, I don't know.''

"You're lying.''

"I'm not." Renewed despair filled her as she let the memory flow out. "Mother and I helped him into the house. He had lost consciousness before we could get him to the settee in the parlor." She swallowed past the thickness in her throat. "Within minutes, he was dead."

She raised her gaze to Bert's. He must believe her.

"Bert, we were so scared. If we had contacted the Confederate garrison, we could have been shot for trying to help a Yankee." Her hand clenched on the barrel. "The only choice was going to the Yankees, but, with my brother having fought for the South, I knew they might not listen. I went anyhow. If I had not been able to say Colonel Daniel Glenmark was my brother-in-law, they would have . . ."

"Shot you?" sneered Bert. "That would have been too bad."

"I don't know what they told you in the official report," she whispered as she straightened her shoulders. "We did nothing to harm him and could do nothing to help him."

"You're lying! I read the letter my mother received from Joby's commander. He died by a Confederate ball fired by Elizabeth Wilkins at her parents' home. Right then and there, I promised to see all of you dead. I took care of them. Now it's your turn."

She shook her head. Sickness cut through her at the thought of so much death caused by a miswritten report. "I'm telling you the truth, Bert. If we could have helped him, we would have."

"You're lying! You—"

Adam interrupted, "Sayre, she saved your life! Don't you owe her something for that?"

"Saved my life?" Incredulity widened Bert's eyes.

"You would have burned to death if she hadn't been so quick when you caught your sleeve on fire."

Gypsy watched Bert's face. Emotions sped past his eyes, contorting his lips. Slowly he lowered the gun. She shivered with relief. She took a step forward, raising her hand to Adam. A fierce curse froze her in place.

"Don't move, Gypsy!" Bert shouted.

"Bert—"

"Shut up, woman!" The deranged glitter returned to his eyes. "If you think I'm grateful to you, you're mad. I wouldn't have been burned if it weren't for you."

"Be sensible," urged Adam. "She's been honest. She didn't kill your brother."

"Whether she did or not, one of her Johnny Rebs did. I loved my brother. He's dead. Soon she will be. Get over there, Lassiter."

The gun in Adam's back seconded the order. Walking around the cask in the middle of the floor, he fisted his hands at his side as Bert kicked his rifle out of the way. It clattered against the door.

Gypsy backed away from Bert's satisfied smile. The cruelty which haunted her gleamed in his eyes. Eight years of pain and betrayal might end before she drew her next breath. She wanted to apologize to Adam for drawing him into this lunacy. She had let love entrap her and the one she loved yet again.

"Sit on the floor, woman!" Bert laughed. "Sit like a good girl if you don't want me to kill Lassiter now, Gypsy. Gypsy or Elizabeth? Which name do you want on your grave?"

She refused to answer. The horrible memory of her family's faces, frozen in the torment they had suffered before this man murdered them, flashed through her mind.

His smile vanished. "Sit on the floor!"

"All right. Just—"

"Do as I tell you, or I'll let you see the color of Lassiter's blood."

"Bert—"

"Sit!"

Carefully she lowered herself to the floor. She leaned back against the table as he ordered.

"Lassiter, on your knees."

As Adam obeyed silently, she held out her hand to him. She wanted to touch him once more before they died.

Bert slapped her hand away and whirled to hold the gun inches from Adam's face. "Tie her hands behind the table leg, Lassiter."

"Listen, you stinking—"

Bert reaimed the pistol at Gypsy. "Tie her up tight, Lassiter, or she's dead now."

Adam jumped to his feet. Bert raised the gun to Adam's chest.

Gypsy cried, "No, Adam! Don't!"

Grinning when Adam hesitated, Sayre said, "Listen to her. She has more sense than you."

With no choice but to obey or watch Gypsy be murdered, Adam knelt on the floor. Sayre shoved a ball of thick twine into his hands.

When Gypsy obeyed Sayre's order to put her hands behind the table leg, Adam leaned forward. "I won't leave you here," he whispered as he secured the rope around her wrists. "I love you."

"Save yourself," she begged, her luminous eyes glowing with tears. "You can't save me."

"Up!" ordered Sayre before Adam could answer. Keeping the gun aimed at her, he checked the ropes. "Good job, Lassiter. Or do you prefer *Major* Lassiter?"

"The war is over, Sayre. Let the past go."

Bert ignored him and continued, "Too bad you got mixed up with Gypsy here. You're not a bad guy for a sneaky cop."

He stood. "I'm not a police officer. I'm a private detective."

"Not much difference in my book. Either way, you're going to be a dead one. If you'd just hit the hay trail and kept going, you'd have been left alive to mourn Miss Wilkins and her sister along with Glenmark. Now . . ." He motioned with the gun toward the door.

Adam hesitated, glancing at Gypsy. She was making no effort to escape. She would sacrifice herself for him.

Too late, he understood why she had tried to keep him distant from her heart. She had been afraid *he* would get hurt.

His hands fisted at his sides. He had been an ass for trying to keep her out of his heart because he feared being hurt again. She had brought feeling back into his life. Feelings like irritation and exasperation. Feelings like happiness and love.

They both had been fools. They should have taken the chance and savored the love that might now be doomed.

The prick of the gun's barrel in his side pushed him toward the door. He stopped at Sayre's order.

"What is it?" he asked. "Do you want me to hold the door for you?"

"Very funny." Bert did not laugh as he picked up the rifle. Flinging it out the door, he smiled when it splashed into the river. "Don't you have any final words for Gypsy?" When Adam did not answer, Bert chuckled. "If you don't, I do. But first . . ."

Sayre shoved a barrel over. The top fell off and careened across the floor. Molasses poured out heavily. He laughed when Gypsy pulled her feet back as the thick river coursed over her.

"Out, Lassiter!" he ordered.

"If you think I'm going to leave her here—"

He pressed the gun to the back of Adam's neck. "If you want, you can leave her here dead."

He pulled a bottle from beneath his shirt. He tilted the whiskey to his lips, then, laughing, tossed it at her.

Gypsy screamed as the bottle smashed against the floor and across her skirt. Pungent whiskey sprayed over her. A shard of glass sliced through her blouse and into her arm.

"Gypsy!" Adam shouted.

Sayre laughed and pulled out a second bottle.

Adam pushed past him. He took only a single step before something struck the back of his head. He dropped

to his knees, his head ringing with pain. As he struggled
to get back to his feet, the pistol crashed into his cheek.

He fought to hold onto his senses. He could not let
Sayre kill Gypsy. Hearing Sayre's laugh, he flinched when
the second whiskey bottle struck the floor. He raised his
head to see Sayre pull the cigar out of his mouth.

Sayre blew smoke in Gypsy's face. As she coughed,
he chortled. "Molasses burns slowly, Gypsy, but whiskey
will take this place up fast. I figure you won't suffer
anywhere near as long as you should."

"No!" she cried when he tossed the lighted cigar into
the pile of trash by the woodbox. Fire erupted to lap at
the wood.

Adam strained to get to his feet. Blood ran down his
face. As Sayre jerked him up and shoved him toward the
door, Gypsy struggled against the ropes which held her
to the table. A spark fell into a pool of whiskey and
exploded into flames.

"Sayre, let her go!"

"You should be begging for your life, sneak!" He
raised the gun.

Adam swung at Sayre. He missed the flunkey as the
wanigan hit something. The floor bucked, throwing Sayre
off his feet in the doorway. Adam knocked the gun from
his hand. It flew out into the river.

The wanigan rammed the logjam again and rocked
back. Sayre's feet smacked Adam in the gut. Adam teetered back several steps as he fought to keep his footing
on the uneven logs.

Sayre ran out and jumped onto a log beside the raft.
When Adam chased him, he shouted, "Come and get me,
sneak!" Sayre raced from log to log.

Adam swore. After his one shot at birling, he knew he
would never catch Sayre now unless . . . he pushed aside
the thought. Forget his perfect record of apprehending
every man he had been ordered to find! He ran back into
the kitchen.

Smoke blinded him and clogged his throat. Throwing

his coat over the woodbox, he waved aside the smoke and plucked a knife from the rack on the wall.

"Adam!"

He leaped over the cracked barrel and the line of fire inching across the floor. It flared wildly when it reached a puddle of whiskey. He stamped out the flame. Quickly he cut through the rope on Gypsy's wrists. He laughed when her sticky skirts clung to his legs.

"Where is he?" she whispered.

"By this time, he's halfway to the other shore." He ground out another fire licking the floor near his feet. "Let's get out of here."

Gypsy reached for his hand.

A flash, brighter than lightning severing a hot summer sky, seared her eyes. She flung her arms around Adam as noise tore through her ears. The floorboards came alive beneath her. Struggling to reach the door, she tugged on Adam's hand. They had to get out of here.

"No!" he shouted. He pressed her to the floor.

Debris shot through the door. Bits of wood struck her. Water sprayed everywhere. The noise grew louder and louder, until she was sure her ears would burst.

His arms tightened around her as the wanigan swirled out of control in a mad whirlpool. Logs crashed against the walls, sending glass showering over them. Boxes pelted them.

Adam pulled her beneath the table. The firebox door crashed open. Coals bounced across the floor, sizzling as water washed through the door.

Gypsy was not sure when the noise stopped, for it continued to toll through her skull, endless and painful. Watching Adam crawl from beneath the table, she took his hand and let him help her to her feet. She bumped into him as the wanigan continued to pitch wildly.

"What happened?" she whispered. Or maybe she shouted. With the din in her head, she could not tell.

"Peabody must have decided to dynamite the jam." He gripped the windowsill. "This is some ride, Gypsy."

Putting his arm around her, he drew her next to him to watch the riverbank race past. "Will the river hogs catch up with us?"

"Eventually. We've got quite a head start on them. Adam, if Bert went—"

Facing her, he wiped blood from his cheek. "He's probably dead. If not, I'll hunt him down. Now that I know his identity, he's as good as caught by me or one of the others in my agency. He'll pay for his murders, if he hasn't already."

"I'm sorry." She clasped her hands behind his neck.

"For what?"

"For not telling you everything."

He shook his head. "You had to protect your sister. I could have been the one who was terrorizing you."

"You think I thought *you* were the one threatening me?" she asked with feigned shock.

Grinning, he said, "At least be honest with me now, Gypsy." He caught her as the floor listed wildly when the wanigan collided with something and spun like a leaf in the current. "You *did* suspect me one or two times through this."

"More than one or two times." She leaned her head against his shoulder. "You were right. I'd forgotten how to trust anyone."

"Gypsy, my love, it's over. We're going to get out of this runaway shack, and then we're going to find Reverend Frisch. It's time we got married and went for that fine honeymoon in Saratoga."

She pulled away to stare at him. "Honeymoon?"

"Why not?" He tapped her nose. "I know you're a good cook. I'll never go hungry, even though I'll hunger for you more every day."

She answered him in the sweetest way she knew. As she tasted the passion on his lips, the sound of someone jumping onto the raft came from beyond the door. She ignored the excited voices of the river hogs as she savored the love which dared her to do anything to keep it.

"C'mon," he whispered against her ear, sending renewed shivers of delight along her. "Let's go let the river hogs play hero."

She laughed and took his hand as they walked to the door and the life that waited for them beyond the north woods. With Adam, it would be unlike anything she had ever imagined, but everything she wanted.

AUTHOR'S NOTE

Thanks for reading *Anything for You*. The idea of a woman cook in a logging camp was inspired by a friend's mother, who worked at a logging camp in the Adirondacks.

My next Kensington historical will be a Zebra Ballad, *Shadows of the Bastille #1: A Daughter's Destiny*. It is the first book of a trilogy. Brienne LeClerc's life is tipped topsy-turvy when a handsome stranger, Evan Somerset, comes to her salon in London and offers to buy a vase decorated with a lightning bolt. It is one of the few things she and her family brought from France as they fled the revolution. Is Evan using his fiery kisses to persuade her that he is her ally when he is really her enemy? Brienne is unsure as a tapestry of secrets begins to unravel, and she learns that nothing is as it seemed. It will be available in August 2000.

My next Regency will be a short story "Not His Bread-and-Butter" in *Sweet Temptations,* available in July 2000. This fun collection includes recipes that are used in the stories.

I enjoy hearing from my readers. You can contact me by E-mail at:

jaferg@erols.com

Or by mail at:

> Jo Ann Ferguson
> PO Box 843
> Attleboro, MA 02703

Happy Reading!

BOOK YOUR PLACE ON OUR WEBSITE AND MAKE THE READING CONNECTION!

We've created a customized website just for our very special readers, where you can get the inside scoop on everything that's going on with Zebra, Pinnacle and Kensington books.

When you come online, you'll have the exciting opportunity to:

- View covers of upcoming books
- Read sample chapters
- Learn about our future publishing schedule (listed by publication month *and author*)
- Find out when your favorite authors will be visiting a city near you
- Search for and order backlist books from our online catalog
- Check out author bios and background information
- Send e-mail to your favorite authors
- Meet the Kensington staff online
- Join us in weekly chats with authors, readers and other guests
- Get writing guidelines
- AND MUCH MORE!

**Visit our website at
http://www.zebrabooks.com**